Brothers

Also by Da Chen

MEMOIRS

Colors of the Mountain
Sounds of the River

YOUNG ADULT

China's Son
Wandering Warrior

兄弟

Brothers

a novel

DA CHEN

THREE RIVERS PRESS • NEW YORK

Published in the United States by Three Rivers Press, an imprint of the Crown Publishing Group, a division of Random House, Inc., New York.
www.crownpublishing.com

THREE RIVERS PRESS and the Tugboat design are registered trademarks of Random House, Inc.

Originally published in hardcover in slightly different form in the United States by Shaye Areheart Books, an imprint of the Crown Publishing Group, a division of Random House, Inc., New York, in 2006.

Library of Congress Cataloging-in-Publication Data
Chen, Da, 1962–
Brothers : a novel / Da Chen.—1st ed.
1. Stepbrothers—Fiction. 2. China—History—Cultural Revolution, 1966–1976—Fiction. I. Title.

PS3603.H4474B76 2006

813'.6—dc22 2005036267

ISBN 978-1-4000-9729-6

Printed in the United States of America

Design by Lynne Amft

10 9 8 7 6 5 4 3 2

First Paperback Edition

To my baba and my uncle, Wen Yuan Chen.
Two brothers separated for forty years by one Cold War.

Acknowledgments

I wish to thank the following people for their contributions to the making of this novel:

Sunny, my beautiful wife, a brilliant author herself. You have been essential in my writing career, from planting the seed and encouraging me to write, to the deft editing that you performed to shape this book, and surely many more to come, into its final form. The Chinese word *An*—peace—consists of two parts: the upper portion, meaning "roof," and the lower portion, meaning "female." Sunny, you are the one who makes me feel peace.

Our daughter, Victoria, and son, Michael. You have grown to become my best buds and ferocious badminton opponents. You rule! When I first started writing this book, I wrote a line in brackets—*My son is born on this day*. And now, Michael, you are eight. The book has grown as you have grown.

My mother, who came to live with us after Father passed away. I feel loved every day. All should have a mother like you.

My in-laws, William and Alice Liu. You are two of the most noble-minded and generous human beings I know, and enormously special grandparents to our kids. William, with my own father gone, you fill that void for me. May you and Alice, together with my mother, live forever.

Acknowledgments

My agents, sagely Robert Gottlieb and young but prodigious Alex Glass of Trident Media Group. Thank you for providing guidance in all my creative endeavors.

Deborah Artman, an author and playwright of distinction. You offered deep insight into the art of fiction, and valuable lessons in the creative process.

Sibylle Kazeroid, many thanks for your artistry.

My writers group, small but highly talented. John Bowers, Laura Shaine Cunningham, Nina Shengold, Ron Nyswaner, Mary Louise Wilson, and Zach Sklar—you guys provided me with wonderful support. My dear friends. I cherish the time we share together.

Jenny Frost, the president and publisher of Crown Publishing Group. You are a visionary, a true builder of things to last and shine. Your leadership will take Crown to its zenith. It is my good fortune that our paths cross.

Shaye Areheart, publisher and editor in chief of Shaye Areheart Books. It's an honor to be one of your select group of authors, nurtured under your tutelage. You are a transcendent being envied by us ordinaries. Your brilliance as an editor, wisdom as a publisher, and noble spirit as a friend overwhelm me each time I am in your presence. And as my father, a very wise man, would say, the pair—Jenny and Shaye—are the jewels to keep and treasures to relish.

Shento 山头

CHAPTER I

1960
BALAN, SOUTHWEST CHINA

To tell the tale of my birth, I must start not from the beginning, but from the end to my beginning. I was born twice, really. First when I tore through my mother's dark passage. The second time when the old medicine man saved me.

The young woman who gave birth to me meant to end it all, not just her life, but also mine, right at the moment of my sunrise. She was in a hurry to leap off the cliff atop Mount Balan, but I outraced her swollen legs and slipped out of her womb just as she struggled toward the edge of that fateful precipice. One was left to wonder why she did it, making herself a myth, leaping off the zenith of the mountain with me still attached to her by the rope of life, the entangled umbilical cord.

I burst through before she burst off, born in the air, hovering over it all. I imagine her flying off that rugged cliff like an eagle gliding downward, free from her nest, her moorings, her sins, or her final lament, to be forgotten by the wind that fluttered her youthful hair up as she rushed down. We, the twinned and wingless angels, free-fell. But the unthinkable happened. The hand of destiny intervened. I, the wailing newborn, falling in the wake of my mother along the face of the vine-crawling cliff, was suddenly caught in the branches of a tea tree growing out of a cave's mouth.

In one slowed second that could have lasted a lifetime, the umbilical cord snapped. Arrested by the two springy branches, I let out a frightful scream—my ode to the strenuous tea tree. My mother—the angel of my birth, my death—and I parted in the air, blood aspill, splattering the tea leaves. I bounced, suspended aloft by the branches of the blessed tree. She plunged farther, a diminishing dot of herself, then vanished into the secrecy of the valley below, never to be seen again. Why she chose to sing her death song this early in her life, I would only come to know later. For now, I was left dangling, as dangling as one could be.

But fate intervened once more. Grace descended upon me in the shape of a scrawny village medicine man, old and faithful. When he heard me crying and saw me caught on the wind-blasted cliff, he climbed down to fetch me as a monkey would. Fortunately, he was as nimble as one, for his vocation dictated that he roam the mountain ranges from peak to peak, from valley to valley, and from cave to cave in search of the rare ginseng and scarce swallows' spit only to be found in the capricious spots reached by birds.

He flung himself down, breaking through tree branches, missing a few footholds, nearly dashing himself to death. But on that given day heaven allowed only one death. Breathlessly, he got hold of me. That was the moment I call my second birth, one given me by the grace of Buddha through the hand of one who had done his virtuous deeds day and night, caring for a village full of sick and poor. I say Buddha's grace and it was rightly so, for had another man heard me and, Buddha willing, found his heart wanting to save the little bundle, whether he was a virtuous man or not, he might never have done what the medicine man did, for in the old man's heart rang a lonesome bell of childlessness. The cry I made, the cry he heard, as he would later recount, was that cry deep in the recesses of his soul. It was not just a cry of any boy, but that of his own blood.

He was inches away when a blast of wind nearly took me away from it all again. But, one arm holding to a tree root, he reached for me, catching my tiny leg just in time to swing me into the crook of his arm. To save time, to save me, he did what no one dared do before, sliding hundreds of feet down the steep cliff, scraping his knees, his heels, nearly breaking his bones, then running home to his wife of forty years before the nocturnal mountain cats could smell our bloody trail.

The goat was chased and the milk milked. His wife fed me the milk as if it came from her own breasts. Then and there they named me Shento, the mountaintop, the zenith.

"He will soar for the sky like our sacred Mount Balan," Baba said.

"And he will rise toward the heaven like the spirit of our ancient soul," Mama said. "Can we really keep him as our own?"

"Of course. He is a gift from our beloved mountain, a reward for the deeds we have rendered."

"And he looks like he belongs in my arms," Mama crooned, stroking my cheek.

So ends the tale of my birth and begins the story of my life.

THE SUN WANED and the moon waxed and I gradually grew to be a sturdy village boy with an appetite of a child three years older. Mama fed me with an adult-sized bamboo spoon. No birdie song needed to be sung to get me to eat. I would chow down one spoonful after another until I gave out little burps. My favorite food was sweet sticky rice cake. In our poor village where the staple diet was yams, sweet rice was rare and precious. Baba walked miles to visit patients in remote villages to earn extra money for those precious rice cakes. He went to the ancient forest, chopped down the finest bamboo poles, and made a sturdy playpen big enough for me to crawl and sleep in. Baba put the pen near his desk in the infirmary. With Mama's assistance, he saw his patients, dispensed advice, and performed acupuncture with me nearby.

Against one wall in the infirmary leaned a massive medicine cabinet containing drawers of herbal medicine that Baba sold to his patients by the ounce, and some by the pinch. The drawers were labeled with arcane Chinese inscriptions that only doctors versed in the classics would recognize. I startled Baba one day at two-and-a-half years by naming and locating ten of the most common herbs. By three I could name more than half of them. When I was four I pointed out one day that Baba had pinched the wrong herb for a particular prescription. The correction, Baba said, saved the pregnant woman from having a miscarriage. Baba and Mama were convinced that I was no ordinary boy. From then on,

Baba read me classic medicinal texts and schooled me to memorize acupuncture points.

One night, lying in bed before falling asleep, I overheard Baba whisper to Mama, "Our son is destined to be the most gifted doctor these mountains will ever know. Imagine how many cures he might find for diseases with his extraordinary mind."

"No!" Mama retorted.

"No? Why would you disagree with that?"

"His destiny is beyond your narrow wish," Mama said. "One day he will lead thousands and rule millions."

"Aren't you a bit too ambitious, my dear wife?" I heard Baba say.

"Not at all. Don't you see? He suffered tragedy at birth, not unlike many emperors who rose from nothing to the golden throne."

Baba was quiet for a moment. "I did read somewhere that tragedy breeds extraordinary men."

"Yes. Unfortunately those great men were never entitled to much happiness."

"Oh, I much rather he be ordinary and live happily and long enough to see us die," said Baba.

"It is too late. His destiny began when he took his first breath off that cliff. It is already great fortune for us to have him for as long as our good Buddha allows."

That night, I broke the rule and snuggled into their bed, sleeping between them till the sun rose. But no matter how often they talked about me, they never came near the subject of my birth parents. It was as if once that taboo were broken, the ghost from my past would come to haunt our nearly perfect though simple life.

Tan

唐

CHAPTER 2

1960
BEIJING

I was born the son of General Ding Long and the only grandchild of two influential families in China: the Longs, a banking dynasty, and the Xias, a military powerhouse. The two prominent families were as different as night and day.

Grandfather Xia had no education. But he walked with Chairman Mao in the Long March, a pedigree that won him the lifelong post of commander in chief of China's navy, air force, and army.

Grandfather Long, an Oxford-trained Communist economist, an oxymoron in itself, was the governor of the Bank of China. His brothers had long prospered in the capitalist colony of Hong Kong as bankers. A sophisticated financier who spoke Parisian French, perfect formal Japanese, and flawless English with an Oxford accent, Grandfather Long preferred Savile Row–tailored suits, Cuban cigars, fine wines, Beethoven, and Shakespeare—some minor sins picked up in his university days at Oxford back in the thirties. He was the only Chinese national during the Cold War years to receive, on a daily basis, the *Wall Street Journal,* the *New York Times,* and, his favorite, the brownish-looking *Financial Times* of the United Kingdom.

In keeping with his image as China's top banker, he was given a classic model Mercedes-Benz, a liveried chauffeur, and China's only chef trained in Western cuisine from the kitchen of Beijing Hotel. Grandfather

Long was, after all, head of one of the biggest banks in the world, second only to the almighty Federal Reserve of the United States. The balance sheet said it all. The Bank of China owned the country with all its mountains, rivers, air rights in the sky, mineral rights under the ocean floor, and everything else in between.

Grandfather Xia may have been a five-star general, but he was still grubby and rough, preferring to sleep on hard solid wood and a carved wooden pillow. Soft, spongy mattresses with springs made his back ache and shoulders sore. He often wore a pair of straw sandals, his feet's best friends during his youthful days as a messenger when he had walked rocky mountains and waded rivers for the great Chairman Mao during the infancy of China's Communist Party in Yenan, of the Shaanxi Province. He had a confessed northern peasant mentality and didn't trust flushing toilets, preferring to use night pots instead. He said that fine cigarettes were an insult to real smokers such as he, whose lung cells could only be awakened by a special type of foul-smelling tobacco from a little village near the mountains of the Himalayas; all other smoke only put his lungs to sleep.

His favorite daily wear, if he had a choice, were hand-stitched baggy linen shorts. For entertainment, nothing was better than the *yee-yee-yaa-yaaing* Peking Opera that he hummed along with in a guttural, off-tune voice that easily scared children. But the most shocking was his daily diet of roasted bull testicles, raw oysters, pork knuckles, and fish heads—the greasy handiwork of his private chef, a distant cousin who was originally a country butcher from his village. Everything was served in big pots and plates, in great quantities and variety, country-style home cooking, each meal a little feast that could have fed a village. He would sample each dish, burp, and give the rest to his staff, guards, and their families, the way emperors did a dynasty back. He was a king in his own court, leading the biggest army in the history of the world—10 million soldiers at peacetime, which could easily double or triple from the reserve with the hint of any war. His favorite joke was that if anyone were to cause any trouble, all China needed to do was have all their men pee and their enemy would be flooded in a nasty deluge.

As different as they were, Grandfather Long and Grandfather Xia formed the north and south poles of Chairman Mao's feudal-like reign over the most populated nation on earth. Grandfather Long kept Mao from going bankrupt, at least on the books. The bank reserves were higher than ever with loans aplenty. He supported every ideological movement initiated by Mao, and gave him all his financial might. Grandfather Xia kept the chairman from going out of power. And if there were any attempts on his life, Mao never heard about it because Grandfather took care of them the old-fashioned way: He made them disappear.

My two grandfathers never saw eye to eye, even at the most intimate meetings with the aging chairman. They quarreled constantly like schoolchildren. The fights were legendary and sometimes even came close to fists. Mao's only comment on their bickering was that they reminded him of his younger third wife, the notorious Madame Mao.

Like all the emperor's trusted men, my grandfathers were loved by their ultimate leader and rewarded lavishly. They had mansions in Zhong Nan Hai, the elegant prime location in the capital city of Beijing, surrounded by scenic mountains and lakes. Their residences were walled, protected from the eyes of ordinary people and the din of the congested streets. Fashionably furnished vacation homes were also built and given to them on the long, deserted sandy beaches of Beidaihe, a government resort near the China Sea. A private train with sleeping compartments and mah-jongg rooms, staffed by a culinary chef, scurried them back and forth from the city and country as they wished.

By virtue of their ranks, they were both given the same government rations, the same number of servants, the same color TV, and an equal number of phone lines. Naturally, their properties were located on the same strip of land, constructed in the same style, and decorated in like manner, down to identical furnishings. Chairman Mao's nonpreferential treatment meant the two men were always in each other's shadow, at work or in leisure, neighbors in the city and at their beach retreats. Their relationship was so uncompromising that one refused to let the other enjoy himself and followed him around to the different locations just to irritate the other with his presence.

All things nonetheless went well except for one tiny consequence that took root, grew, and blossomed in their backyard like a willow seed dropped off by a passing swan. Hua, which meant "flower," was Grandfather Xia's only daughter. A concert pianist, she was beautiful, shy, and artistic. Grandfather Long, the banker, used to call her a pretty flower growing out of a pile of manure.

Grandfather Long's only son, Ding Long, was a young general in the army. Every chance they had, ever since they were young, Hua Xia and Ding Long had snuck into the garden separating the two homes and played together. In the summer, when the families vacationed by the sea, the two kids raked clams and caught crabs together whenever their fathers weren't around. They left secret codes on the beach by writing on the sand with their bare toes, signaling meetings at night under the moonlight and stars, hidden behind the dunes and sea drifts. Friendship grew into love. While my grandfathers snored away, only the gentle darkness was witness to the budding romance. The innocent kids thought their love and eventual marriage would end the hatred between the two men.

One rainy summer day along the windswept beach of Beidaihe, Ding Long and Hua Xia appeared hand in hand before the two old men, who were at the moment kicking sand at each other, squabbling over the nonexistent border between their properties. The lovebirds ordered the men to stop fighting and told them they were going to be in-laws soon. The general and financier almost had simultaneous heart attacks. Each had to be taken to his living room by his nurse.

Mother and Father wed under a red flag. In a ceremonial toast to each other as in-laws, my two grandfathers shook hands for the first time.

To no one's surprise, on the day of my birth, both were in great spirits and in an even greater hurry to outrun the other to catch the first glimpse of their first grandchild. The banker moved his daily meetings with his lieutenants from the bank's ornate conference room into the parking lot of the hospital where my mother was. Grandfather Long huddled with his men in their Red Flag stretch limousines while his secretary ran back and forth as messenger from car to hospital ward. He was feeling so lucky and charitable that within one hour after my birth he put his personal seal on the biggest disaster relief loan in China's history, a whopping 200 million Chinese yuan to some southern province. Historians later recorded that the loan saved a million lives.

The general, on the other hand, woke up from his mahogany bed on the day of my birth only to be greeted with the frustrating news of another uprising. Thousands of Miao monks were imprisoned for throwing stones and knives at the Red Army. The general, usually of the mindset of a ruthless conqueror, had a change of heart that day. "Free them," he said. He then departed in his helicopter for the hospital. Told in advance by his intelligence that his banker in-law was already in the parking lot, he issued an emergency military order to the general manager of the hospital to have the parking lot closed to any outside use. Grandfather Long could only grit his teeth as dust flew when the air force helicopter landed noisily on the lot from which he had just been vacated for bogus military reasons. "Remind me to suggest a severe military budget cut tomorrow," he told one of his lieutenants.

But when both grandfathers finally saw me and held me in their arms, all they could do was laugh and smile like two silly old men and compare who had the bigger wet spot made by my sudden bursts of urination.

AS EXPECTED, my grandfathers competed for my affection and each determined to shape my future by exerting as much personal influence in my daily life as possible.

Grandfather Xia taught me how to crawl military style when I was six months old. We squirmed along on the carpeted floor of the mansion every day, pulling ourselves by our elbows. When I was ten months old, the general taught me to walk like a soldier with feet lifted high. No dragging or shuffling. Left, right. Twice a week, he kidnapped me and my nanny and drove us around the city in his armored jeep, followed by his entourage, to review the military base off the city proper. I never said hello or good-bye to the general. I saluted him, solemnly.

Realizing that there were too many toy soldiers and nearly no toy bankers in the market, Grandfather Long allocated a large sum of money to a government toy factory in Beijing and had some made, complete with Mao's suits. He composed lullabies out of multiplication charts and drew interest rate fluctuation diagrams with colorful crayons hand in hand with me. On Saturdays, when the world stock markets were closed, Grandfather Long sat me in his large mahogany leather chair while he paced the room, listening to his lieutenants' weekly economic briefings on the rest of the world.

He was pleased when he noticed that I was particularly quiet during the weekly report of the US interest rate, the Dow Jones Index, and the Federal Reserve offering of the government Treasury bond, which was delivered in the sweet, soothing voice of his staff economist, a Harvard-trained PhD, the only female.

My room bore evidence of my grandfathers' contest of wills. Against one wall were the toys from the general: rifles, tanks, jeeps, and soldiers. On the other wall hung a drawing of colorful world interest rates and the valuation fluctuation of the world's major currencies.

But the real competition came on my first birthday. As was the tradition, I, well scrubbed and dressed in a brand-new navy suit, was placed on the floor surrounded by different objects. The object I chose would signify what I would be when I grew up. To everyone's surprise, I didn't pick up the abacus or the tank, which were strategically placed right under my eyes and within easy reach as both grandfathers begged and coaxed on their knees. Instead, I picked up a miniature globe and sunk my teeth into it, cracking it into a few pieces. Then, with my right hand, I picked up the abacus, almost immediately discarded it, and picked up the tank. The banker declared victory, but the general claimed that he would have the last laugh. It was decided that by grabbing the globe, I was destined to be a world leader. But I would be ambivalent as to which tool to use to achieve this.

Shento

山头

CHAPTER 3

1967

BALAN

The year of my birth coincided with the outbreak of border skirmishes between Vietnam and China. My village of Balan, nestling along China's mountainous border, became a busy outpost overnight, with thousands of People's Liberation Army men and women stationed for combat. An elaborate army compound was built in the center of the village, and we locals saw our first truck to ever tread the muddy trails. We marveled at the magic of electricity. The noisy generator that provided enough power for the compound only deepened the prehistoric darkness in the rest of the village after sunset.

While the armies waited for orders from above, the military men and women threw parties and consumed an abundance of good food every day—beef, pork, eggs, barrels of lard. Cigarettes were plentiful, fabrics fashionable, and movies played in the courtyard every Saturday night. Only a couple of village leaders got invited to the talking pictures. The rest of the villagers climbed the treetops for a glimpse of the modern-day wonder. Dances were also organized and a few lucky village girls were invited.

Ding Long, the young general in charge, had a school built for both the army and the village children. The local people feared and worshipped him like a living god for the virtuous act.

On the first day of school, I got up before sunrise and donned the new white linen shirt made from cloth that Mama wove on the loom and then stitched by hand. I clunked around the hut on a pair of new wooden sandals that Baba scrimped for months to afford from the outrageously expensive army store. As soon as I was out of my doting parents' sight, I took off my cherished little sandals and put them in my school satchel lest they be ruined in the mud.

At seven years old, though I was the youngest in a class crowded with more worldly and much better dressed army children, I was determined not to pedal behind the others. I was well versed in the Chinese classics from Baba's tutoring, and I composed elegant essays. But my favorite subject was math. I knew the importance of counting money from being Baba's cashier and I had no need for the abacus. My mind proved faster than the ancient clicking and clacking tool.

The teacher taught me extra material from higher classes; I digested it easily and begged her for more. The teacher soon spread word about me around the army depot.

At our dinner table, Baba and Mama listened to me recite texts learned in school as the soft glow of the setting sun warmed our porch. I discussed complicated math with Baba, who usually stayed up late into the night resolving the problems we discussed on his clicking abacus.

At the end of the year, I surprised everyone by winning the biggest prize in school—a bag of candy and a red silk flag with five stars. Additionally, I received an unexpected invitation to dine with the general and to watch a war movie inside the compound. This invitation caused much excitement in my heart. The dinner was to happen on New Year's Eve and the wait seemed endless.

Finally, on New Year's Eve, Mama put the red flag on the wall above our hidden shrine and I shared my precious candy with them. The sweets were heavenly and the wrappings so colorful and beautiful that I saved the paper in a bamboo box. For dinner, Mama cooked a large bowl of steaming pork knuckles, which Baba bought on credit from the local butcher, who in turn would soon buy herbs for his rheumatism from Baba. I was happy, but my parents were quiet. Too quiet.

I could not understand the mood. "Did I do anything wrong?"

"No, son. We are very proud of you," Mama said in a small voice.

"But you don't seem happy for me." I grabbed Baba's arm and shook it.

"Son, you make me the proudest old man in the whole world. We only worry that this powerful general is taking too much interest in you. We do not know his intention," Baba said.

"It is an honor. He is the youngest general in Chinese military history and he is the commander for our defense against Vietnam. You are not going to keep me from going, are you?"

"No, of course not. But why do you want to go so much?" Mama asked.

"Someday I want to be a general just like him," I said.

Mama and Baba shook their heads and smiled for the first time that evening.

GENERAL DING LONG was a tall man with a full shock of black hair and deep sparkling eyes. His handsome uniform fit him well, outlining his broad shoulders and narrow waist. At six sharp, the general graciously welcomed me, his guest of honor, when I was led to his office by a uniformed soldier.

I wore my only linen shirt, the best I had, and the still-new wooden sandals, which I soon regretted wearing as they clanked loudly against the hardwood floor in the general's office. I thought about taking them off, but the elegant surroundings stopped me.

I felt dwarfed by the tall general as he bent over to shake my hand with a firm grip. Our eyes met and the general examined my face carefully.

"You look a lot like my son, only a little darker."

"I am sorry, General." My heart raced like a wild horse. Why was I sorry? I was not sorry.

"No reason to be sorry. Sit down," the general said with a smile.

"Thank you, General."

I sat on a tall chair facing the general, who eased into a huge seat covered with a tiger's hide.

"Who named you?" he asked.

"My baba. It means the summit of the mountain."

"Yes," the general said. "Ambitious."

"Not ambitious enough. They want me to be a village doctor and cure sick people. But I want to be a general like you. I want to lead thousands of men, guns and all, to attack our enemies and be victorious, battle after battle."

The general looked amused.

"What are these plaques on the wall?" I asked, pointing to the framed papers.

"Come, let me show you." The general rose and led me around his office. "That plaque is my college diploma from Beijing University, where I read history. Next to it is my diploma from East Military Academy. And you know who that is in the photo with me."

"Our great leader, Chairman Mao. Who is the other gentleman?"

"My father-in-law, the commander in chief of China's army, air force, and navy."

"You have met a lot of important leaders."

General Long nodded. "Yes I have, and that includes you. You are also an important young man."

"Maybe not now, General, but I will be one when I grow up. You watch."

"I will." The general pinched my cheeks, and ruffled my hair with affection.

"Is he your son?" I asked, pointing to a picture of a boy standing between General Long and his beautiful wife.

The general nodded, "His name is Tan. The same age as you."

I stared at the boy for a long while. "Do you miss your son?"

"Yes, I do, Shento."

"Is that why you wanted to see me?"

He didn't answer me. For the rest of the evening, I basked in the gentle glow of the general, who treated me to a five-course dinner with chicken, beef, goat, and even tiger paws. I chowed down each course, though with good manners, which were met approvingly by the general's eyes. The war movie was exciting, full of battle scenes, but I must have fallen asleep midway. All I remembered was waking up in the general's arms and being passed to Baba at the front gate of the army compound.

That night I found my hero.

The following day I begged Mama to make me an army jacket just like the general's with patches of stars. Baba made long trips again into the mountain to harvest herbs for the green army fabric sold in the army store. In the evenings, I urged Baba to carve me a toy rifle out of bamboo. I marched about our backyard every day with my new outfit and weapon, stabbing straw men as if they were Vietnamese enemies.

After school I would linger in the schoolyard, only an iron gate away from the army compound, climb up the iron bars, and peep at the life on the other side. Everything in there was a world away from my humble home surroundings. The radio played music while the soldiers played soccer. Children sat on benches with their mothers or nannies, snacking on candies and cheering along. Female soldiers in skirts and white blouses laughed and shouted, tossing canned drinks to the running men.

When the sun fell behind the courtyard's coconut trees, a voice announced through the speakers that dinner was ready. From the kitchen chimney a delicious gut-wrenching fragrance would rise up, permeating the air, tantalizing my nostrils and stirring my hunger. One need not stretch his imagination to see what was laid on their tables in great abundance: big barrels of steaming white rice, delicious soup, baskets of fresh fruits, and dishes of sea delicacies that I could only dream of. If someone had asked me what heaven was like, I would have said that it was only inches away from me, beyond that iron gate. And the general inside that compound was my god.

IN LATE SPRING of that year, the Buddha of my fate would open a crack of his heaven and drop onto my lap another divine favor, this time in the form of a certain hidden knowledge. Such knowledge, cursed or blessed, would shape the course of my life, and mold the path of my destiny.

Buddha was wise and opportune. Ar-Q, the village beggar, was his earthly tool on that given day. The beggar had been starving for three days, with not a rotten fruit to chew on, or a petty bowl of soupy rice congee to slurp in. That year the monsoon was wetter than ever, flooding the region. Crops were ruined, and the harvest was minimal.

I bumped into the beggar that fateful rainy afternoon on a narrow path while I was returning home from school. He stood there tall and shaggy, staring at me. Then he bent down and sniffed around my satchel, within which I carried my afternoon snack, two goose eggs boiled with jasmine tea and spices. In a singsongy, fawning tone, he begged me for food, quoting the same verse customarily used by itinerant monks on pilgrimage: "Grace be given. Grace be given." Then he uttered the following words of bargain: "Gift your eggs to me, and I will share a hidden secret about you."

"What secret?" I asked.

"About the man who is your real father, and how he abandoned you to the care of the old couple that you call Baba and Mama."

"You are lying. They are my real Baba and Mama—"

"But they are old enough to be your grandparents," he interrupted slyly.

The ding of truth rang loud and hurtful. I'd always wondered about their advanced age, lamenting when they couldn't play with me in the backyard or swim with me in the robust rivers. "Who, then," I asked, "is my real father?"

"A powerful man from inside the army depot" was his answer as I surrendered my first egg to him. Hurriedly, he stuffed the egg into his mouth, and then he was all eggs and teeth. Without breaking the rhythm of his tale, he continued in mumbled tones. "Yes, yes, a powerful man from inside the depot, that he was. On the night of the Water Spraying Festival, years back, he invited your birth mother, Malayi, an orphan, to his banquet. She was a beautiful village bloom that every man itched to pluck and sniff its scent, if you know what I mean.

"On that festive night, that man of power from the inside the depot fed her potent brew and spoke sweet words of favor, making her cheeks red and rosy." He paused to wipe his mouth, swallowed drily, as if tasting the liquor of his own description. "Afterward, the man of power took her to this very grove. Moonlight was shining. The man lifted her colorful dress and had her up against that mango tree. He dipped his gingerroot into her, making a woman out of her. How do I know all this, you may ask. I know because I was up in my tree, minding my own business, trying to sleep, but the moaning and giggling woke me up."

"What happened then?" I asked.

"What happened then was what happens to any ripe girl with round hips and swollen breasts. Soon her belly grew big with you. The village leaders urged her to marry a half-wit cripple from another village, but she refused. Then they tried to force your baba to pluck the baby out of her womb, so the seed of evil would not be born to shame and suffering. But your baba would hear none of it. What was a poor girl to do with a melon belly like that, shaming herself every day that she lived? On the day of your birth, she climbed the tallest peak of Mount Balan, wanting you to die inside with her. But it was not to be. The medicine man was there, hot on her trail. He saved you, sure enough, though he would have saved your mother as well had he been tipped to her whereabouts earlier."

I trembled like a leaf, hearing this for the first time.

"You're not going to faint, are you?" Ar-Q asked with concern.

I shook my head and stuttered, "Wh-wh-who is that man of power?"

"The evil general, Ding Long." His words struck me like midday thunder, clapping my ears numb and sending my young heart racing. My face flushed; my vision blurred. I felt joy and sadness all mixed together, and could not tell where one began and the other ended. I didn't remember much afterward, except passing the second egg to his eager hand and hearing him warn me never to repeat the tale to another soul. "It is a secret for us all to bear, a truth forever to be hidden," he said.

"Why?"

"Because the villagers love your baba, and fear the general."

Tan

唐

CHAPTER 4

1967
BEIJING

St. John's School, perched on the green hills near the Forbidden City in Beijing, was originally an elegant Catholic school opened by American nuns in the 1920s to accommodate the increasing needs of US expatriates. It was known then for its dull uniforms, boring food, strict curfew, and bighearted sisters, who sang boisterous choruses every morning in the ornate chapel. But now, in the Communist new China, it stood as the pinnacle of China's privilege. The attendees were no longer Catholics but the children of the nation's political and cultural elite. For that purpose, this vestige of imperialism was kept intact with all the trappings of American opulence and luxury, contrasting sharply with the bareness of other public schools in the sprawling city.

On the stage of its spacious auditorium stood an old grand piano, handmade by the brothers of Steinway & Sons, New York. St. John's housed one of the few indoor gymnasiums complete with basketball and volleyball courts and gymnastic equipment. In cold winter, the school was fully heated by a steamy furnace. The scorching summer heat was overcome by numerous General Electric fans that were driven by the school's own power generator. While other school children used stinking outhouses at the edge of the school playgrounds, the children at St. John's flushed their crap away in rushing toilet bowls.

One summer day, the dean of this elite academy, a white-haired

Columbia-trained educator, arrived at our residence. My mother served the old dean tea and little finger foods brought by a maid as we sat in the garden under an old oak tree, amid colorful peonies. Father, who had flown back from his army depot in Balan especially for this occasion, came out and greeted the dean. I, now seven, was asked to sit with them at the meeting. The old gentleman smiled, revealing his mouth, which had been hidden under a bushy mustache, and stated the purpose of his visit. According to his records, which were kept in the big leather-bound book that the dean held carefully in his hands, I, the first son of the Long and Xia family union, would be ready for first grade in the fall. He glanced down at me and continued. I was one of thirty first-graders whom he would personally visit and evaluate, and was the second on his list. The first happened to be the grandson of Chairman Mao. My parents nodded in unison and smiled understandingly. The dean humbly presented them with a red envelope containing the invitation, which Father immediately stood up to receive with a bow. Then Father offered a toast with a cup of precious green tea, which the dean accepted with both hands. After a period of silent respect, the meeting ended and we saw him off all the way to the foremost entrance.

On the first day of school, I picked out my own clothes, a blue navy outfit with white stripes over the shoulders. Since September in Beijing was still warm with high blue skies and white clouds, I wore no hat and parted my hair in the middle after deciding it to be the neatest way of ordering my unruly hair. Father and Mother were at hand to help me. So were the two nannies and my driver. I refused their offers to straighten my shirt and tie my shoelaces and solemnly told them that I wanted to do everything by myself from that day on. But I would be needing the car, I added, winking at the driver, who readily winked back.

I looked at the little watch on my wrist, given to me the previous night by my parents. I was hoping to see my grandfathers before I went off to school for the first time. Delayed by an early meeting with Chairman Mao that morning, the two arrived just as I was being helped into the jeep. Ordering the driver to wait, I jumped down to hug both of them. In return, my banker grandfather gave me a little abacus made of silver and said that money could be my friend if I had it, and my enemy if I did not. My general grandfather offered me a little toy rifle made of chocolate, adding that might was right; guns ruled the world, not money. I just smiled. There were times when even a seven-year-old knew when adults were being insane. I dropped the abacus into my empty satchel and ate my chocolate rifle on the way to school.

School proved easy for me. On the first day, I told my math teacher about the existence of a decimal point and numerous smaller numbers behind it when the teacher asked the class what was the smallest number they knew. No one in my class knew or cared what I was talking about. My language teacher was no less surprised when I recited a short poem from the Tang dynasty in 840 BC and volunteered to write it out on the black board to show that I truly understood it. I excelled in all sports except the high jump, where I found that my height wasn't really an advantage. All this brought me instant popularity among my classmates, except for a small clique sitting at one of the dining tables, headed by Hito Ling, a lobster-headed grandson of China's minister of foreign trade. That little gang rarely spoke to me, quieting when I approached and resuming their whispering after I left, much like a noisy bunch of flies. The ill will was not only annoying to me, but I realized it hindered my prospects of being elected class president.

One day I took the initiative of greeting Hito when we passed each other in a narrow hallway on campus. Hito not only kept silent but turned away and spat on the ground. Angry, I went home that night and asked Grandfather Long, who had joined us for dinner, what he thought of the minister of foreign trade.

"He's a corrupt idiot who is campaigning to get my job!" Grandfather said, puffing on his pipe. "Not only did he steal from the trade, he is running the ministry to the ground. He doesn't understand the rule of commerce: buy low and sell high." Grandfather was furious because the ministry was sucking the blood out of his bank by losing millions in foreign trade every year. Grandfather would have gone on and on if I hadn't distracted him with some other question.

Taking a page from Grandfather Xia, I organized my campaign. I began with a background check on everyone in my class. The result was quite to my satisfaction. Out of the thirty people in this exclusive class, about 90 percent of their fathers or grandfathers occupied ministerial positions that were in worse financial shape every year in the face of a deteriorating Communist economy and the unproductive Cultural Revolution. They would be begging for loans from the central bank where my grandfather was the governor. I then took the time to sit down with each of them to let them know who I was and why it was important that they make friends with me. I explained that if no more money was to come from the bank to support their father's or grandfather's work, their families would all be out of business soon. The children of political families were unusually sensitive about the political and practical implications of such a friendly threat. Soon Hito was effectively isolated. All it took, after that, was a small rumor whispered from one ear to another that Hito's father would soon be thrown out of Beijing into some remote reform camp in Xinjiang, China's Siberia. Hito was a convert in less than a week. I won my first campaign against unwanted adversity, as well as the class presidency, through wit, not through fists or blood. My report card at the end of the first year was framable material for any proud parent—straight A's for all subjects.

As spring came, Mother decided to have me take piano lessons while Father was still at the Balan Army Outpost near the Vietnamese border. Being sensitive by nature and a pianist by training, Mother was worried that I was being wrongly influenced by the poison of the military and the seduction of finance. Both were things for which she had little interest and felt enormous distaste, even though she had chosen to marry a general who had a banker father. She hoped I might become the finest artist in my generation or choose another career that did not include the stain of blood or the dirt of money. She had higher hopes for me, though I demonstrated an unwanted degree of Grandfather Xia's aggressiveness and Grandfather Long's calculation. One night, before putting me to bed, she said that my strong will matched that of my father's and frightened her.

Knowing that a mother made the worst teacher in the world, she hired the best piano professor from China's top music conservatory,

Professor Woo, through the recommendations of the wife of the minister of culture. I received lessons every spare moment I had while Father was away.

Summer came with its long days and humid nights. Father returned home shortly before our traditional family retreat to the seaside resort in Beidaihe. To his astonishment, I had become a pianist during the months of his absence. All Mother could talk about was my progress and how deeply I appreciated the meaning of difficult pieces by Western masters. Father inspected my hands and was alarmed to find my calluses gone and the fire that used to burn in my eyes replaced with a soft gaze, the simmering look of a softy.

A compromise was ironed out. I would spend half of every weekend learning music and literature, the other half wrestling in mud, taking fencing lessons, and riding horseback. When Father mentioned that night at dinner that I was to meet my kung fu teacher the following day, Mother burst into tears. I used one hand to console my teary mother and the other to clasp my father's hand in thanks.

Shento

山头

CHAPTER 5

1972

BALAN

For the next five years, I won every coveted annual invitation awarded to the best student by the office of General Ding Long. Winning that invitation became my secret purpose for excelling in school. The year I turned twelve, on New Year's Eve, like a ritual, I ate with the general in his private dining room attended by the same two manservants who had served me ever since I first set foot there. As usual, General Ding Long and I had great fun chatting with each other. Only this time after dinner, the general surprised me by showing me a wooden model of the local terrain used for planning attacks on the Vietnamese. There were even glistening lights marking each mountaintop and roadblock. I studied it with enormous interest.

"When are we going to attack Vietnam?" I asked.

"Tomorrow," the general replied. He took off the silver medallion necklace that he wore and hung it around my neck. "I am giving you this," he said.

"Why?" I rubbed the shiny metal with my thumb.

"Wear it. It will mean the world to me."

I studied the character engraved on the back. "I know this word. It means 'dragon,' doesn't it?"

"Yes, it does. Long, my family name, means 'dragon.' This necklace was a gift from my grandmother and has brought me good luck. I hope it will bring you some as well."

"Thank you. I will always cherish it," I said.

The general took me into his arms for a moment, and then together we walked out into the courtyard, where an audience of soldiers awaited. Ding Long sat me next to him, then jumped up to stand at the podium. As he made a brief but powerful speech to his men, fire burned in his eyes. The soldiers rose to their feet and responded with great shouts. They saluted their leader and sang the national anthem. I felt proud of him and secretly of myself. That sweet feeling lingered long after the lights dimmed and the moving picture jumped onto the wide screen.

The following morning before sunrise, everyone in the village heard the soldiers march off toward the border. Before daylight thousands of soldiers stormed into a Vietnamese camp after shelling it with cannons. Dark smoke rose high into the sky and the air was filled with the smell of acrid gunpowder. News came back that the surprise attack was a victory; no casualties on our side were reported. The troops under General Long's command spearheaded farther into enemy territory. All seemed well as planned, but by noon, panic gripped our village. There was a resurgence of thick, heavy gunfire near the border. The sly Vietnamese, who had hidden themselves in underground tunnels, attacked from the rear in surprise, after the Chinese forces had passed.

Stretchers poured back with dozens of dead and dying soldiers. Screams of pain and the smell of death permeated our village. The army compound, once a fountain of pleasure, was now a sight of mournful morbidity. Baba tended the screaming, wounded soldiers under a tent with two army doctors. Mama, one of the nurses, washed and dressed the wounds of the injured men.

A young female soldier gathered all the children into the school, guarding us there.

"If you let me out I can help those soldiers because I am a doctor's son and know how to care for them," I begged her.

"It is too dangerous out there. The Vietnamese could attack anytime. Bother me no more. I have a hundred kids to take care of."

The Viets were coming! My chest tightened. Where was the general? Was he all right? Was he injured? Was he dead? I couldn't bear that thought.

The young soldier led us in singing popular school songs, trying to distract us from the chaos afoot. Most of the kids were happy there was no school. But I was not to be swayed. I needed to find my general. As the singing went on, I ducked low and snuck to the back of the schoolroom, pried open a window, and climbed out noiselessly. Soon I was peeping through a little hole in the medical tent. I saw Baba bending over a young soldier with a bleeding leg stump. There was no foot. The soldier was screaming and begging, "Let me die! Let me die!" Baba gave him an injection and the man's cries weakened. Soon he was asleep. I saw Mama kneeling on the ground, tending to a young man with a bloody face. One of his arms was missing. Mama was a strong woman but her back was jerking; she was clearly fighting tears.

Three more stretchers were carried in by sweaty, breathless villagers. When the nurses pulled themselves away from the work at hand to attend to the newcomers, I saw my chance and slipped quietly into the tent, carefully searching row by row. To my relief, there was no sight of the general. I went on to check more than twenty bodies covered by sheets stained with crimson blood. I clenched my teeth, squatted down, and lifted the first sheet. The man's eyes were wooden like those of a dead fish and there was a gaping hole in his chest. I quickly dropped the sheet. The second man had his left shoulder blown away. It was not the general. The last man I checked had no head, rendering him extremely short. I had to run out of the tent as vomit rose up my throat. The headless man couldn't be the general. General Long was much taller and much bigger, I was convinced.

Night was falling and the casualties kept coming. One by one I checked their faces. Still there was no general. I went to the edge of the village, picked the tallest coconut tree, and climbed up, hoping to gain a glimpse of the battle far away. A southern breeze swayed the thin branch upon which I perched. The air, thirty feet above the village, was the first fresh breath I had taken all day without the stench of blood and decay. I closed my eyes and let the breeze rock me gently back and forth.

The southern climate was as changeable as a young girl's heart. The breeze suddenly stopped and mosquitoes buzzed around me. I strained my neck to gaze across the Vietnamese border but saw nothing except for a distant village still smoldering and heard only occasional gunshots fired sporadically. The battle seemed to have quieted down. I was about to slide down the tree when I heard voices coming from the thick bush surrounding our village. The soldiers were returning. I glided down a few notches. There were more noises. This time I heard Vietnamese spoken.

The Viets were here to kill us! What should I do? I must warn Baba and Mama. I screamed at the top of my lungs, "The Vietnamese are here! Run! The Vietnamese enemies are here!" and kept screaming and screaming. There was hurried movement beneath me in the bushes. A shot was fired, hitting me in the chest and nearly knocking me out of the tree. I held on to the branch. Another shot hit my thigh, but that didn't stop me either. I continued to shout "Vietnamese! Run!" until pain weakened my voice to a tremble. Finally, a light was switched on, sweeping the entire compound.

Faint with pain, my hands gave in, and I fell twenty feet headfirst into the arms of a Vietnamese soldier, who dumped me on the ground and shoved his gun to my temple.

"You troublemaker," the soldier said through clenched teeth.

"Gunfire will give our position away. We can finish him later. Let's go," his officer commanded.

The soldier kicked me in the stomach and they rushed off. As I lay panting with pain, I heard gunfire near the compound and saw the spray of heavy machine guns sparkling in the darkness. I could almost hear my baba and mama screaming in fear. I had long heard of the Vietnamese cutting off their enemy's heads as trophies. Baba! Mama! I tried to get up, but pain drilled me like a burning needle in my thigh and all my strength seemed to have escaped me, leaving me limp with weakness. How I wished I could charge at my enemy with a machine gun and spray them to a bloody death. But I did not even have a wooden gun at hand, and the few soldiers inside the compound would not have a chance against the Vietnamese.

In a lull of gunfire, I heard desperate screams. Soon flames engulfed the entire compound and spread along the veins of my village, inflaming the nearby woods and huts. The whirling sizzle of fire gained power as the bamboo-thatched roofs, dried from months of drought, collapsed, igniting one after another. The last to fall was the schoolhouse. Children's cries were muffled and snuffed by the flames. Then came an explosion. The tent where my parents were working blew into the air, pieces falling in the night sky like the remnants of fireworks. Within a matter of minutes all was silent. Not a sound of a child. Not a sound of an adult. Only the yakking of that ugly enemy language echoed in the quiet night, accompanied by occasional gunshots.

Baba! Mama! I bit my lips to keep from crying out. As I crawled toward the compound, footsteps rushed my way. They were coming for me! Bullets sprayed the area around me, missing my head by a few inches. I picked myself up, dragging my bad leg, but I could not run far nor fast. How I wished there was a hole in the ground that I could vanish into like a mountain rat. A hole in the ground! Suddenly, the hope of survival loomed big. I remembered an old well nearby, half-covered by wild weeds. I crouched amid the waist-high thorny growth and crawled as noiselessly as I could manage until I came to the edge of the well. Sweeping away the rampant weeds shielding its mouth, I found the rope of life, a rope fastened to the handle of a bucket used to fetch water down below.

There were many frightful tales about the old well and it being the nest and breeding ground for an ancient serpent, but none was as frightful or deadly as those whizzing bullets that continued to trail me.

I grabbed hold of the bucket and dropped myself into it. The rope attached to the bucket spun. After what seemed an interminable fall, I hit the bottom with a splash. The bucket tipped over and I was dumped into ice-cold water that was up to my neck. Moments later a flashlight swept over and past the mouth of the well as I remained still. Then the noise dimmed and the quiet buried me in the night.

I grabbed the mossy rope and tried to haul myself into the bucket, but I kept tipping over back into the water. The water grew colder as the night aged. I shivered, my only company in the darkness the occasional frog jumping off its perch hidden along the mossy shaft. One fat frog slapped its meaty belly into my forehead, making my skin crawl with disgust.

At midnight, a full moon slowly traveled to the center of the sky and shone straight into the bottom of the well. What a glorious sight it was. I felt warmer just from the gentle touch of the gracious rays. How I wished that the moon would stay there forever. The fear of returning to darkness stirred me to risk shouting again. "Help! Somebody help." My voice echoed back tiny and thin like an arrow at the end of its arc. I repeated my cry ten, twenty times, until I lost count, my vocal cords strained to their limit. Sadly, the only reply from above was the monotonous lullaby sung by cicadas and insects beyond the well.

Were they all dead up there? Was I the only one left to suffer this lonely death? I felt my strength fading and the pain in my thigh deepening. I groped for the necklace gifted to me by the general, my only hope and comfort now. It was still there, hanging tight around my neck with a new dent at its heart. My medallion of life. Thank you, General. It brought me luck as you promised. But what is protecting you now, my general? Am I ever to see you again? I pressed the cold silver against my lips.

The moon slipped away from the dome of the sky. Darkness prevailed. If I closed my eyes, I would collapse instantly and fall asleep forever. All pain, hurt, hunger, and cold would cease to be. I clutched my precious necklace tighter and in the darkness began to see the general's face smiling. If the general had been in this well, what would he have done? I wondered. He would fight and live rather than die, because he was a brave man. I dipped my head into the cold water, waking myself up, and shouted some more. Still no answer. Finally, I rested my head in the hanging bucket and dozed off.

When I woke again, it was daylight and a dog was barking into the well. I looked up painfully to see it sniffing eagerly, yanking the rope attached to my bucket.

"There's someone in the well," a man shouted. "Get the rope ladder immediately."

The army rescue team found me as cold as ice, my skin bluish gray. My only sign of life was a weak pulse and slight breathing as I was carefully laid on a padded stretcher. I half-closed my eyes, resting, too weak to speak, my thoughts shimmering far away in a dream. I saw figures moving around me. A nurse stripped off my wet clothing, noticed the engraving on the silver necklace hanging around my neck, and reported the discovery to a white-haired old general, who came immediately to my side and examined the necklace with intense interest.

"This belongs to my son-in-law," he said. "What is this boy doing with it?"

"He must have stolen it," one of his men said.

I wanted to protest but couldn't find strength to move my lips.

"There may be hope that this boy knows where the general is. Send him to the army hospital immediately," the general ordered.

BIRDS SANG NOISILY beyond the window. A cool breeze blew in, making the curtains dance. Outside, a garden blossomed with a host of flowers—pink peonies, red roses, white lilies, and yellow sunflowers bending to face the sun.

Where are the coconut trees that reached for the sky? Where are the bananas that swayed in the mountain breeze? Where am I?

I found myself lying on the softest of pillows and the whitest, silkiest sheets that had ever touched my skin. There was a thick bandage over my thigh, but I seemed to be alive, for I was staring at a pretty young woman dressed in an army green skirt and a white blouse. The skin on her legs was fair and tender, unlike that of the village women. An inland city woman? Her hands held mine and her big eyes smiled sweetly at me. I wondered if this was a dream. I must have died and this was what lay beyond earth.

"Little friend!" said the young woman. "You are safe. Don't be afraid."

"Who are you and where am I?"

"You are in the city of Qunming, and this is the Army Special Hospital for Officers."

"Qunming?" I repeated. I remembered the name. It was the capital city of our province. Baba had once pointed it out to me on an old map.

"Yes, you are in a big city now. Do you remember what happened in your village?"

"Why am I here?"

"Something terrible happened to your village," came a man's voice. It belonged to the old general. "The Vietnamese enemy killed everyone there. We fetched you up from a well."

"What about my baba and mama?" I asked, tears rolling down my cheeks. "They burned down everything, didn't they? They burned my parents, didn't they?"

"Most of the villagers died in the fire. Those few remaining have fled to other villages. I am deeply sorry," the old man said.

"Baba . . . Mama . . ." Heaven caved in upon me. The well-lit room darkened as my head throbbed with aches. I sobbed and sobbed. When I woke up again, my pillow was soaked and the nurse and general were still by my side, looking sad and concerned.

"Are you feeling better?" the old man asked.

I shook my head. "Where are my parents buried?"

"With the villagers, in a mountain cave where a sweet spring runs."

I started to choke up again but composed myself. I was the only one left of my family. I must be strong, for Baba and Mama, I told myself.

"You must tell me everything you know about that night," the general said.

Slowly, I recounted in a shaken voice, "General Ding Long led a surprise attack on the border. They were gone a whole day. The village was only guarded by a few soldiers. The Vietnamese had hidden and attacked from behind."

"The general attacked the Vietnamese first? He was gone before the Vietnamese came?"

"I am sure of it."

"So he could be alive," the old man said.

"He has to be alive. He's the bravest man and ablest general in our army. But why do you ask? Don't you know where he is?"

"We don't. We are afraid he might be dead."

"No, he can't be. He told me he would take Ho Chi Minh City with his army."

"You know him well?"

I nodded, reaching for the necklace. But it was not there anymore. "Someone took my necklace!"

"It is the property of the hospital now, if it really is yours," the old general said.

"But General Ding Long gave it to me as a gift right before he left for the battle. I swear it upon my ancestors."

"Why would he give this to you? It is a family heirloom."

"Because . . . because . . . I can't tell you."

The general waved to the nurse and she left the room instantly. "I am the commander in chief of China's army, air force, and navy. Keeping secrets is a very important part of my job. You can tell me anything."

"He is my father," I whispered.

He was taken aback and asked, frowning, "How do you know that?"

"The village beggar told me the whole story for two boiled eggs. He said I looked like the general because I was his son. He had seen the general and my mother together in a mango grove one night during the Water Spraying Festival."

"And who is your mother?"

"She was a beautiful girl, the village bloom. But she died, jumping off a cliff after giving birth to me."

When the old man spoke again, his bushy silver mustache quivered. "Young man, he is not your father. You have been fooled. From now on, tell no one of this lie."

"But it is not a lie. Everyone in the village knew it."

"They all died in the fire, and the lie should die with them."

"But it's not a lie. The general loves me! That's why he gave me his necklace, you see . . ."

Unexpectedly, the old general slapped me across the face and screamed, "You will stop telling this lie or you will die!" and stormed out. I was left holding my stinging face, confused and scared.

The nurse returned with a tray of steaming meat, green vegetables, and a bowl of rice. My hunger gnawed at the lining of my stomach, tickled by the assault of such culinary wonder. I declined her offer to feed me. She watched with big eyes as I wolfed down half of everything in three big mouthfuls, then scooped the rest into the plastic wrap that had covered the food. I licked the bowl until it was clean and hid the food under my pillow. I told her I wanted to save it for the road, wherever I was to be banished to, and begged the nurse to give me some more food. She was soon back with another tray. This time the rice was piled up like a hill. I grabbed the nurse's hand and kissed it in gratitude. I downed another half in three gulps and wrapped the rest again. Then I thanked the nurse profusely. She brought me my old clothes and helped me dress.

"But where is my necklace, Miss Nurse?" I asked after searching the pockets.

"I can't give it to you," she said.

"Why? It is very dear to me."

"I have a specific order from the general to turn it in to my head nurse."

"I am begging you, it is an heirloom from my father. There is nothing else left for me to remember him by."

"Stop. I can't help you. You will get me punished." She frowned.

"You are such a kind lady. I wish you could have been my own mother. Please let me have it."

The pleading seemed to soften the nurse and she said, "I will show you where it is. You will have to figure out the rest."

"Thank you," I bowed.

The nurse guided me along the hallway to an office. She showed me a box and unlocked it.

I hid under the counter while the nurse gave the key back to the head nurse and left for home. When a call from a patient in another room required the head nurse's attention, I quickly found my necklace in the box and ran back to my bed.

Jan

唐

CHAPTER 6

1972

BEIJING

Every day I had to run the gauntlet of demands and expectations from my two grandfathers. I called my banker grandfather every morning to discuss financial matters, while in the evening I would consult my general grandfather about war affairs and other world events that I read about in the newspaper.

By the age of twelve, I had amassed my own library. My collection of books ranged from stimulating to deeper, philosophical readings. *The Art of War* was a book that I thumbed through again and again. Another was the translated version of *David Copperfield* by the British writer Charles Dickens. In the first book I found the wisdom of Sun-tzu to be highly useful in real life. In the latter I sympathized with David's lonely existence. There was something beautiful about a tragedy. I yearned for my own Emily. I began to look at girls in a different way, but I found them all to be spoiled brats except for one—a thin, almost pretty girl named Lili. She was the daughter of the agricultural minister who had just been promoted from a remote province of Fujian, which explained her southern accent and the simple handmade clothing that she wore. When she was questioned by the teacher, her answers were simple, too, and clear like her big eyes. She was a perfect outcast and attracted me madly.

When bored by my teacher's lectures, I would cover my eyes with both hands and peep at Lili through the gaps between my fingers. She had a tall and elegant nose, and a regal chin that was long and pointed. Her eyes were beautiful when she smiled, resembling a pair of shy flowers in half bloom, dreamy and sweet. Her hair fell to her waist, braided in one long tail that was tied with a dull rubber band rather than the usual colorful ribbon. Her neck was long and swanlike, like a queen that I once saw in a picture book. Her silence spoke loudly and eloquently. The more I looked at her, the prettier she became.

I found myself nervously passing her in the hallway, my knees weakening. The worst and the best moment came when, at the tender age of twelve, I dreamed about Lili one night, a dream that ended in a scary, sweaty orgasm that left me troubled for the rest of the long, dark hours before sunrise.

The year of 1972 was a tough one for the people of Southeast China near Fujian Province. A four-month flood broke dams, devoured houses, and rotted the harvest. Hundreds of thousands had died from cholera and famine; millions more would follow if no help arrived. Rumors of men eating men occurred daily. Chairman Mao became paranoid. A hungry mob was a dangerous mob. His order to his trusted men was simple: "Feed them or they will eat us."

Long, my Oxford-trained grandfather—the almighty governor of the central bank—immediately drew up a plan to issue 1 billion yuan of bonds to help the flood-stricken provinces. In this country that had limited or no discretional income, Grandfather issued an executive order to the entire nation. A percentage of income was automatically deducted from government employees, 80 percent of the total population, for this Patriotism Bond, as it was called. Thus 1 billion yuan was easily raised.

One night not long after the nationwide bond issue, I asked Grandfather Long, "What is the government's guarantee for the Patriotism Bond?"

Grandfather frowned at me and answered proudly, "The seal of the Bank of China with my name on it. So long as I live, they are as good as gold."

I nodded silently and said no more about the subject. I had asked Grandfather about the bonds because nobody seemed to take the bond certificates seriously. They didn't believe in the government's promise that the money would be paid in full after the long maturity date. Kids in my school played with original bond certificates, pretending that they were poker cards and trading them for cheap, silly toys.

The next day, I emptied my pocket money from my little bank that I kept on the top of my piano, bought a sack of the most popular toys with the money, and brought it to the school locker room. I put a small notice on the announcement board that said that I was collecting bond certificates in exchange for good toys. The response was nothing short of a deluge. Boys and girls cleaned out their parents' certificates and traded them to me. The response was so good that I began to ride my bike outside the school, conducting trades with kids on the street. I even hired my friends in school, compensating them with toys, and sent them out into the far-flung neighborhoods. I became so caught up in this venture for the next three months that my piano lessons suffered, but every day my large school bag filled up with bond certificates, which I deposited neatly into a mahogany trunk safely tucked away under my bed.

I spent the last moments of each night posting a ledger in the most careful writing. Then I would fall asleep with a smile and dream about how I would use the money when the bonds matured. I made travel plans in my mind. My favorite was to the blue Caribbean—magical islands in the sun with pirates that Grandfather Xia often talked about. Then there was North America—the Rockies, Yellowstone Park, grand Alaska. Close to my heart was my ambition to go to one of the Ivy League universities in America. Oxford was out of fashion now—America was the place to be. Harvard, Yale, or Columbia. I had looked up the term "Ivy League" in the dictionary and was fully convinced that if I wanted to be anyone in the eyes of the world, not just China, I needed to be affiliated with one of those great universities.

All these dreams were framed by the money that was inching toward maturity with every second ticking away. What a beautiful concept, to make money while you slept or played. According to the terms printed on the back of the certificates that I had by now memorized, the bonds would mature in seven years. I collected them at the price of one cent for each dollar. This would yield a phenomenal one hundred times gain of value. Looking through historical bond books, which my grandfather kept in his library, my return would be the greatest of all the bonds ever issued in history. I carefully marked the date on my small calendar book: May 1, 1979—the day I would officially become a millionaire on paper. Glowing with that thought, I played Chopin especially well for Mother, surprising her and moving her to tears.

At twelve, Lili, the Fujian girl, blossomed into a vivacious young lady who led the class chorus and dance team, and was head-to-head with me in all subjects except math, in which I was the undefeated champion. My attempts to gain the attention of the leggy girl so far were not successful. She wouldn't even look in my direction and was constantly surrounded by her girlfriends. She was the moon beyond reach, cool as an autumn pond. I was more in love than ever.

Then one day I caught her sneaking looks at me. It sent shock waves through my body. That afternoon for physical education, the class went rowing in a nearby lake. I was randomly matched with Lili. We had to share one little boat and compete with the others.

The lake, in a beautiful suburb of Beijing, had tall willows and geese and was surrounded by endless wheat fields. As we sat in the boat, Lili smiled an awkward little smile. My heart was at my throat. I could barely breathe. I had never felt so warm, had never been so close to her before. With her budding breasts, tiny waist, long flowing hair, and big moody eyes, she was even more beautiful up close. I could smell her clean scent.

We sat next to each other quietly, waiting for the others to get ready. Then the PE teacher blew his whistle and everyone rowed blindly, splashing the water in the lake and chasing the geese away. Trying to impress Lili with my prowess, I rowed madly. But Lili pushed her oar lazily, almost deliberately out of rhythm. Our boat lagged behind the others, trailing even the weakest team on the water.

"What is the matter? Come on, hurry!" I shouted.

"I can't," she said, smiling.

Despite how hard I tried to propel us, we were twenty yards behind. "Are you feeling all right?" I asked her.

Lili just shook her head, her hair blowing in the wind. All the boats turned around a bend, disappearing from sight. Suddenly Lili turned around and faced me. "I have wanted to do this for a long time, Tan," she said, twirling a strand of hair. "Please let me." She leaned over and kissed me, right on the mouth.

Her lips tasted like a rose with the scent of summer. I dropped my oar into the water and held her in my arms. She was supple and yielded for a second before she pushed me away, giggling with her long arms over her chest. My eyes were still closed, lingering over the heavenly moment, when Lili deliberately rocked the boat, sending me flying into the cool water. She screamed with laughter, so happy and lively. I tipped the boat so that it was Lili's turn to fall in. We embraced in the water closer than ever until the teacher rowed breathlessly back to fetch us.

For the rest of the semester, my heart was with Lili. I did everything for her, writing her songs and love letters, which she answered with simple, terse words that had more bite than sweetness. In public, she pretended not to know me. Only when we were alone would she let me hold her hand. Her conversation was always critical, never praising or flattering, least of all loving. At times, I was so puzzled by the mysterious Lili and felt so lonely and painful about not being able to reach out to her that I sometimes wept in the late night, unable to fall asleep. I speculated that she might be having an affair with an older boy, someone more to her liking, or maybe she simply didn't think much of me after that first embrace.

I sent my friends to follow her after school. The reports were consistent. Lili lived in the agricultural minister's household and had a private dance instructor teaching her ballet after school. In the morning, her voice teacher accompanied her in the garden and her sweet songs filled the morning tranquillity in that part of Zhong Nan Hai.

While my bittersweet puppy love left me frustrated, my popularity among my peers in school remained high. I was the soccer team captain and the only one to have a soccer superstar's picture in his room—Pelé of Brazil. I was also the debate team captain and defeated the son of China's Supreme Court chief justice. The topic of that particular debate was China's financial future. The other side argued that law should rule the land, but my winning argument came from Darwin's famous survival-of-the-fittest theory. On National Day—October 1—I performed *The Ode to the Yellow River* for the entire school on the aged Steinway piano in the school auditorium, receiving a standing ovation. At the close of the concert, Lili was waiting for me backstage.

"Can we go for a walk?" I asked.

Lili was silent, then nodded slightly. Relieved, I held her hand and we ran into a wooded area near the school. The night was young and the moon was a perfect fireball that hung low on the horizon.

"You know, I've been hoping for this moment. Isn't this wonderful? I could compose a song just for this walk," I said. "Look, we are disturbing the birds." I stretched my ears to listen to the lonesome chirping of a gu-gu bird.

Lili turned to me and smiled. "You look handsome, especially in this light."

"You mean the moonlight?"

"Yes, my favorite time of day."

"Mine, too. Let's stay longer then."

"I can't." Lili stopped and narrowed her eyes, studying the round moon thoughtfully. "My mother won't allow me. I agreed to walk with you because I need to find out something before our friendship goes any further."

"You sound serious."

"I am. We live in a snobbish world."

"Enough about the world. Now what about us?"

"I'm not the daughter of the agricultural minister," Lili declared.

"You mean your father has resigned?"

"No, he is not my father. I live in that household because my mother is their housemaid. We moved with them to the capital because the family trusts us."

"But it can't be. You have the same family name as his."

"It is a coincidence. One-quarter of Fujian people have Chen as their last name."

"Well."

"Well, what? Why don't you run back to your rich family now and leave me alone?"

"No. I am not going to do that."

"And what do you plan to do?"

"I shall marry you when we grow of age."

"I'm not sure I want to marry you."

"What do you mean?"

"People like you and I don't even sit at the same table in the minister's household. We don't belong together. Your mother the pianist and your father the general will tell you so."

"That's rubbish. My grandfather—my mother's father—grew up very poor, much worse than you. At least you live in a warm house with good food on the table."

"Your grandfather may have been poor once, but now you are rich and powerful. You don't want to be with the poor anymore. That is the whole point of striving in life."

"Do you hate me then?"

"Yes, I do, very much." Her eyes filled with a mischievous light. She pinched my arm and leaned against my shoulder.

"You love me then?" I asked.

"I dare not. I only see a tragedy ahead of us."

"I love tragedy. It is the only thing that moves me."

"You are too idealistic. You should be matched with a girl who can help your career as a future leader of this country. Someone either with a lot of money or a lot of influence. Let's see, your family has the finance and the military. You should marry the old spinster daughter of the navy commander and have as a concubine the youngest daughter of the air force commander. Then you will be the president of the country in no time." Lili was cruel.

"No, Lili, I shall marry you, I promise. I am talented and ambitious enough that I will not need all those influences to succeed in life. I shall marry whomever I fall in love with, not someone my parents fall in love with. In fact, I am, at this point, the first and youngest millionaire in this land."

"That's a given since your grandfather runs the Bank of China."

"No, I am a millionaire in my own right. At a staggering discount, I have bought up Patriotism Bonds to the total value of one million and change. I am confident that the Bank of China will honor the issue at maturity."

Lili laughed. "In the streets of Fujian, kids wipe their butts with them and the potholes are full of them."

"Don't laugh, Lili. Finance is a serious matter. Our nation now lives in the age where there are no stock exchanges, no bonds, and no contractual obligations. One day we will be like the rest of the world, like America. Bonds and stocks will be like bread and butter to our people."

"That day will never come. But let's assume that you are a millionaire. What do you intend to do with your money?"

"I will buy a bank."

"And be like your grandfather who counts money at the end of the day every day for the rest of your life?"

"No, it's only a means to an end."

"And what is the end?"

"I will create a financial empire in China like J. P. Morgan."

"Again, you are concerned about money only."

"Yes, money will change this country, not Marxism. And then when we all have more money, life will be better and misery and hunger will be gone."

She sighed. "Well, you do think like a leader."

"Is that a compliment?"

Lili bit her lips and leaned into my arms. "I wish time would stop and we could stay the same way forever."

"I wish so, too."

Lili put a slender finger over my mouth to quiet me. I held her tightly in my arms, never wanting to let go.

At dinner the following night, Mother was silent, hardly moving her chopsticks. When Mother was quiet, it meant one of two things: either she was having a migraine or she was very, very upset. When Mother was upset with Father or anyone else in the household, she stayed in her rooms, not coming out for days as she banged away at some sad European piece on the piano next to her bedroom. When the subject of her anger was me, she left her hair undone and wore no makeup. Unfortunately, today her face was plain and her hair hung down her back.

"Mother, eat. Your food is getting cold," I urged.

"Mother can't eat. There is something choking my heart," she said darkly. It was not good. From her pocket, she fished out a handwritten note and slammed it on the table. "Love letters at twelve? I have never heard of such a disgrace. Tan, how do you explain this?" She had intercepted a love letter from Lili.

"She wrote me a love letter?" I exclaimed, reaching for the paper.

Mother slapped my hand away. "She's not suitable to be your friend. She's the adopted daughter of a servant in the minister's household. On your shoulders ride the hope and glory of the two most prominent families in this nation. You're being groomed to be a leader. Do you know what that means?"

"I do," I said, slumping back in my seat.

"No, you don't. Your two grandfathers will be very disappointed in you and your father will never forgive you if you fail. In his youth, he was always the best in everything he did. You will be going to the same high school where his plaques of honor are hung all over the walls. Many of the teachers who taught him are still there. You have to outshine him or you will dishonor him. This affair with the girl must stop at once."

"I have freedom to choose what to do with my life and who my friends are."

"No, you don't! Not in this household."

I ran upstairs without finishing dinner. Father came to my room later and told me that if I wanted to be considered a serious man in China, I should not flirt or meet with girls at such a young age. Men built things and ruled the world. Women were but a decoration to men. I should not make too much fuss over a mere girl. Love was only a fallacy. He agreed with Mother that when I was a grown man, I should be matched with the most suitable candidate—beauty, wealth, power . . . someone who embodied all of these. I told him angrily that I did not need that. Father said that I would know better when I grew older and wiser. He left, and I spent the whole night thinking of Lili.

When I dragged my feet across the classroom the following day, I didn't see Lili's red skirt. In drama class, which I enjoyed the most, working and rehearsing in Lili's company, the bespectacled teacher read the roll call, but one name was noticeably missing. I raised my hand. "Teacher, you forget to call Lili's name."

"No, I did not. She has been transferred as of today."

A buzz started among the class.

"Where was she transferred to?"

The teacher shook his head. "Let us continue with act three of the play."

Normally at this time, my eyes would meet Lili's and we would smile. But now she was gone. I knew very well that it was Mother's octopus arms, reaching into my territory. I knew my mother. At this point, Lili could be on any train waiting to leave the Beijing station. Her mother must have been fired from the minister's household. In her place another would be found, and Lili would be wiped off the face of the earth as far as Mother was concerned.

That weekend was my twelfth birthday. With the help of her society friends, Mother transformed the mansion into a festive dreamland. The chauffeur drove me to a tailor early in the morning to be fitted for a new Mao suit made with the finest wool from Xinjiang Province. Then I was driven to Grandfather Long's personal barber, trained in the great salon of old Shanghai. I came in with a rumpled mop and came out with neat hair evenly parted on one side. The ladies who washed my hair massaged my head and shoulders so comfortably that I understood why it always took Grandfather a full Saturday afternoon to have his hair done every week.

When the limousine arrived back home at noon, according to Mother's schedule, I found a dozen limousines parked in our front yard. The house was filled with music. Mother was at the grand Steinway with a handsome tenor at her side. There must have been more than a hundred guests, all Mother's friends and their daughters. Most of the girls were my age, shy and giggling. A dozen were older, smiling and studying me. All were dressed in attractive skirts with big butterflies in their curled hair.

Upon my arrival, Mother started playing and singing the birthday song, with the guests joining in. Father, dressed casually, smoked his cigar and lingered around Mother's piano. Then a dance teacher put a cassette in Father's tape recorder and taught us the waltz. The teacher first taught everyone the steps in groups, then she grabbed me and matched me with an older tall girl with a sweet smile and a prominent bosom that made my breath shorten with every step I took. We were forced to twirl around the waxed floor under the decorative lighting and colorful paper. At first I felt awkward, then gradually the tall girl, who happened to be a stylish dancer, guided me, and smiled even when I stepped on her feet a few times. She made me feel confident, comfortable, and eventually fluent. At the end of the first dance, she introduced herself as Sha-Sha. Her father was the leading conductor of China's Central Philharmonic and she was currently studying ballet at the prestigious Music Conservatory. Her waist was tiny and her legs were long, and a pair of round, bulging breasts were constrained under a transparent brassiere. I could not help fixing my eyes on them.

Mother smiled and Father sipped from a wineglass. Grandfather Long dropped by to join the dancing. He was magnificent. The girls all wanted to dance with him. He wished me a happy birthday and gave me a large package as a gift. The party, Mother's handiwork, was a success, and she was happy. She made me dance with a dozen waiting girls. My touch on their mature bodies and the memory of their scent made me stare at the ceiling of my bedroom late into the night. I was a little confused and very excited. I was allowed, I had been told by Mother at the end of the party, to make friends with any of the chosen few that were invited. She had made a list of their names with pictures attached for easy reference, along with their addresses, telephone numbers, and, of course, the names of their prominent parents. I did feel better after meeting the girls at the party and had enjoyed their encounters more than I would admit to my parents. But in the end, all I could think about was Lili. One day I would see her and make her my woman forever and no one would take her away from me.

THAT WINTER, when Father flew south and returned to his post in Balan, was marked with an indelible darkness. Soon after the New Year, we received a telegram about a sudden turn of events at the Vietnam-China border. There had been a raid into Vietnam, but something had gone wrong and Father was missing. Mother tried to keep the news from me, but her anguish and haunted look betrayed her worry. I begged to know the truth, sensing something was greatly amiss—I had not received my usual New Year's phone call from Father—but Mother shut me out. Only through a young guard did I learn the severity of the situation. Father was missing in action. He could possibly be dead, killed by the Vietcong. Grandpa Xia had flown down to the Southwest Command to search for him.

For days, Mother and I, together with Grandfather Long, waited for news—any news—from the south. Mother was mad with worry when the phone finally rang in the early morning of the ninth of January. It was Father himself. He'd been ambushed near Ho Chi Minh City and had survived by hiding in a cave. Though most of his men had perished, they still managed to inflict a major blow to our enemy's blockade.

The government hailed my father as a hero, a true soldier who put his life on the line for his country and Chairman Mao. In flowery calligraphy, the chairman himself wrote a plaque in Father's honor that said, "Heroic spirit pales the sky," which Mother spat on after the soldier who delivered it had left.

I had long detested that place called Balan. To me, it was a vague and ominous territory shrouded by its proximity to the enemy. The south, mosquitoes, unknown evil, Mother's headaches, and Father's absences—Balan was the place we rarely spoke of, the duty that kept my father away, as if he had another family, a more important one. I often wished that I could be there with him and his brave soldiers, fighting battles and drinking the southern brew that he brought home to Grandpa Xia. I felt envy, too, seeing Father's eyes light up as he told tales of dancing in the Water Spraying Festival—it sounded so free, romantic even.

Now Balan was no more. The border post would be run by another brave general, for Father had been promoted by Chairman Mao to the position of first deputy of the Central Military Command in Beijing.

All Mother could say at that was that it was about time.

Shento 山头

CHAPTER 7

1972

FUJIAN, SOUTH CHINA

A young soldier drove me in a jeep to the Qunming train station and put me on a freight train. He told me that I was going to an army school in Fujian, the coast province to the east, and threw my petty belongings in the compartment after me.

The train gave off a long shriek that seemed to tear the sky to pieces. Tears blinded my eyes as the train pulled out of the station. Towns and villages swept by, mountains ran backward, and the old Balan shimmered in a foggy distance as if it were a mirage floating on a cloud among palm trees, papaya groves, and mango forests. And then I finally saw them, the wrinkled faces of Baba and Mama. They were smiling, saying goodbye to me with their knowing eyes. They knew where I was going. They were happy for me. Their faces raced after the train, traveling in the air with me until light faded and day darkened into night.

I rode on the train for five days before arriving at the remote province of Fujian. When I peeped through the cracks of the train door, the earth was no more. A vast ocean faced me. It was my first glimpse of the sea. For my young heart, the ocean held the grand promise of all possibilities, like mountains near Balan. Now I was going to another school. Maybe one day I would be a soldier, and maybe, just maybe, even a general. And what was a general without thousands of warships that cruised the ocean to attack and conquer faraway continents? Women would stand at the shores welcoming me and cannons would salute me. I searched my memory of geography. This must be the Pacific Ocean, the bottom of the world. How fortunate for me, who had come from the foot of the Himalayas, to witness both that extraordinary mountain range and this fathomless sea in only one lifetime. I was mystified by what lay beneath the shimmering face of the water. How I wished I knew this dark Pacific as well as I knew the big mountains back home and the many secrets within them. How I wished I knew the life-forms down below as well as I knew the song of the mountain birds and the words of a jungle monkey.

The journey ended. Before me lay a lonesome strip of land jutting into the sea. A few gray buildings were scattered at the tip of the peninsula, surrounded by a high, forbidding wall. A surly driver in a rusty truck picked me up and dropped me at the principal's office, hidden on the west corner of the leafy campus. The principal was a four-foot-tall man with thick glasses. He looked small behind his big mahogany desk, but was lent a sense of authority by the ornately carved monstrosity.

"Another overachiever. Too young to die and too old to change." The principal shook his head and sighed.

I chose a chair and sat down.

"I did not ask you to sit, did I?" the little principal barked. "Do what you are told to do, no more and no less. You have to live by that rule from now on. Did you know just ten years ago, men only came in—they never left this place alive?" he said without much expression.

I shot up from my chair and declared, "I don't intend to die here. I want to be a general."

"Did I ask you to speak, young man? Second rule: Never speak until spoken to. Do you understand?"

I nodded, gritting my teeth.

The principal shouted out and a big guard appeared. "Take him to room 1234." He turned to me. "You will enjoy your roommate. I make sure you all are coupled like a perfect marriage. You will see why."

My room was a ten-by-ten cube at the end of a hallway on the second floor of a rectangular building. There was a squeaky bunk bed. Two little desks leaned against the eastern wall with matching wooden chairs. In the dim light, it reminded me of gloomy graveyards and ancient caves deep in the mountains. The guard told me to listen for the whistle that blew at dinnertime. He added that if I was a minute late, I would be locked outside and made to starve until breakfast. He left with a wicked smile.

I lay down on the lower bunk, stretching out for the first time in days on a real bed. No matter how squeaky, narrow, and hard, it felt heavenly. Within minutes, I dropped into a deep sleep. Hours went by. I was suddenly awoken by the thumping rhythm of a pair of heavy feet.

"Who the hell are you?" a six-footer announced, looming over me.

"Who are you?" I asked in return.

"I am the boss here. Get out of here!"

"The principal assigned me here to be your roommate."

"That monkey! How many times do I have to show him I don't need one? Get out, get out!" The thickly built boy started kicking me with his clunky old boots. I slid off the bed only to be met by the boy's fists. The boy kept pounding me till I curled into a small ball in the corner next to a chair. How could the principal have put me here with this monster? But more urgently, I needed to fend off this crazy attacker, who was pulling out a dagger. The blade shone brightly even in the dim light.

"I come in peace. Name your price, my friend," I said.

"My price is your death. Anyone who dares venture into my room doesn't live to regret it."

"But I just came. I did not know."

"Asking for sympathy? You coward. I hate cowards." The boy put the blade under his nose and sniffed it as if it were something delicious. He closed in on me, inch by inch, with menace on a face that was pitted with more than one scar.

What do I do now? What do I do? What would Baba do? Forget prayers. This dog wouldn't buy it in a million years. What, then, would the general do? The answer came as I glanced quickly to my right. But the boy was quicker. He grabbed my neck with one hand and pointed his dagger at my nose with the other. Shaking and gasping, I grabbed a chair and smashed it right into the pitted face. Fortunately, a blunt leg caught the boy's right eye socket and blood spurted out, reddening his right cheek. The little giant cursed loudly, but the pain drilled into his soul and he collapsed in front of me. I took a long breath and congratulated myself on my first victory in this new territory. Calmly, I went to the door and met the crowd that had been drawn by the commotion. A guard walked in unhurriedly and poked his choke stick at my roommate's head. "You still alive?"

"The little punk hurt my eye," he said, crying.

"Is that true, you hurt his eye?"

"He tried to kill me. It was self-defense. He is a foot taller and ten times stronger than I am, sir. Please give me mercy. I am sorry, I was really scared." I knelt down at the man's feet and grabbed them and shook them. "Please don't punish me."

"There will be no dinner tonight," he told me. "And you, useless little rats," he said, gesturing to the onlookers at the door, "come in and carry your boss to the school clinic. What's there to see? The fight is over."

My roommate was carried out of the room by four equally big boys. He was crying and cursing. "You little shit. You'll die soon. My boys will cut your balls off. Just you wait."

"Get him out of here before I club his teeth off," the guard said before locking the door and sauntering off as if nothing had happened. At midnight, a knock came on my door. I turned on the weak bulb of my light. A little window at my door was pushed open. Two small hands held a bowl of rice with a chunk of meat.

"Take it," a boy's voice whispered. "Here, the chopsticks."

I quickly took the bowl and whispered back, "I don't know how to thank you. Who are you?"

"Shhh. It's not important. We thank you for beating that big dog up. But you have to be careful; revenge will be coming soon. Watch out for yourself."

"Thank you," I said. He was gone.

The food was cold but delicious. Holding the empty bowl, I felt deeply touched by the warmth of that little boy. If there was one out there who called himself my friend without even meeting me, then there must be another and perhaps many more. But first I had to survive my roommate, who would come back and surely kill me.

"Morning exercise. Get up! Morning exercise, you lazybones," a rough voice roared from the soccer field, echoing in the quiet of the morning hour. The sea beyond the walled compound was calm. Only a little breeze dusted the wild weeds that grew along the edge of the ground and the tops of the pine trees. The guard unlocked my door and announced sarcastically, "My young friend, I will let you out, but you should commit to your memory what I am about to say. There are two things you do not do in this paradise." He paused to suck his cigarette. "One, you don't fight Hei Gou, which you did. That was too bad."

"Hei Gou? Who is that?" I asked.

"Black Dog, your roommate." A knowing smile creased his face. "Because it's a guarantee that he will kill you when he returns. If he doesn't, his buddies will." He chuckled. "Now that you know what is in store for you in this great school and might be entertaining the idea of running away, I feel it is necessary to tell you the second no-no."

My heart was pumping with anger over the guard's petty delight at the expense of my fear. "What is that?"

"What's the hurry, young man? Ha-ha." He paused to smoke again. "Listen carefully. You don't try to escape. I'm sure you have heard our principal mention his favorite phrase, 'They never leave alive.' Let me say that it's true and he means it. Don't even try unless you're a kung fu master who could jump the twenty-foot-high walls or can swim among deadly sharks if you prefer a bloody escape by the sea."

I was quiet, hating every word being uttered. I felt as if I were living among animals, not humans. Revenge is near, I kept repeating to myself. "Watch out for yourself," my young friend's voice rang in my ears.

In the foggy morning light, I saw at least a thousand boys standing in columns. Farther to the north stood one lonely row of girls in slacks, no dresses. I was told by the guard to stand at the end of the third column. Exercise consisted of haphazard stretching of arms and legs. Guards stood along the sideline to rein in any unruly limbs. As soon as the exercise was over, another whistle was blown, this time causing a cheer of excited shouts and laughter from the hungry youngsters. "It's breakfast time."

The columns broke and the crowd knotted into a mess, rushing into a windowless warehouse. Boys took the lead and the girls trailed behind. I was in no hurry to get in that madness and deliberately tried not to draw any more attention to myself. I looked around and stayed away from the bushes and tree trunks in case one of Black Dog's boys was hiding there to jump me.

Inside the dining hall, I was given my portion, a bowl of porridge with some pickles floating on top. My stomach rumbled with delight at the sight of the meager meal. I found an empty table in the corner and, with my back to the wall, ate and observed the crowd, attentive to any sign of trouble. There was a food fight two tables away. I saw a guard smack the kids with his weapon of choice, the stick. The ruckus soon ended with the instigator being led away with the stick choked around his throat.

The children all had cropped hair and suspicious looks in their eyes that did not match their age. Some were wilder, running around and chasing each other, fearless of the constant hitting by the guards with their sticks. Others were subdued and seemed resigned to the rules and regulations, whatever they might be. They had a dead look in their eyes, like prisoners whom the world had long forgotten. There was no gleam of hope, only the burden of daily chores and fear. Their faces were green and gaunt. One boy had a pair of trousers that had been mended over many times but still did not cover the holes at his knees.

I looked to the far end where the girls were cluttered around five tables. Their looks were timid, their manners ghostly. They wore dark blue blouses and baggy pants of coarse fabric. Their hair was chopped short above the ears to be free of fleas and lice. The only feature distinguishing them from boys were their flimsy frames and undeveloped feminine voices. How I wished there were some wildflowers adorning their hair. And what a difference it would make if they wore floral dresses, wrapped tight around their slender girlish bodies like the budding young girls of my village. A guard came over and tapped his stick on my table. "Hurry up. What do you think this is, a banquet?"

I stared back at him and quickly chewed my rice. My face froze when I bit into some nasty grains of sand at the bottom of the bowl. I had to cover my mouth to keep from gagging. The rice tasted stale and pickled, reminding me of things rotten. But I did feel better. Only the mouth tasted things; beyond that point taste and flavor did not matter. I ate to fill myself up and survive. To enjoy food was the least of all considerations.

The amplifier in the dining hall crackled and a voice came on, precise and calculating, one that could only belong to the little weasel of a principal.

"Students! Due to an urgent demand from our government for the product that we produce, canned tuna fish, from today on all students will be working in the fish factory all morning and will attend school in the afternoon. Remember, reform is your only redemption in this world, and reform costs money. It is your duty to work for the food you just ate and the many more meals you will consume. Nothing is free, and bad deeds will be punished. Now, will the guards please get the crowd moving. That will be all for now. Good day."

There was an uproar of curses and obscenities from the students. Clubs landed on heads again and the crowd flowed out of the dining hall slowly and reluctantly, shuffling their feet toward the gray building clearly marked with red paint on the entrance—CANNED FOOD FACTORY.

The smell in the factory was unbearable and the temperature dizzying. I was sent by a guard dressed in overalls and gloves to start at the easiest job, scaling and boning live tuna. Boys and girls lined along a long sink full of jumping fish. We were given knives and simple instructions. The guard barked among the din, "Chop the head off first, scrape the scales, then slice open the belly and gut it."

"Can I have some gloves?"

"No."

I shivered at the brutal execution order, then squeezed into the line between two boys and grabbed a foot-long tuna in my hands. The fish was slippery and strong. It flapped its tail and flipped out of my shaky hands. Someone laughed; another called me stupid. I chased the devil all over the floor for a good minute to no avail before I finally stabbed the fish in the head. It was the first living thing I had ever killed in my life. As the head was smashed, blood splashed on the pants of two boys who appeared suddenly next to me. I instantly recognized them as Black Dog's buddies. I apologized sincerely, "Sorry, it's my first day here."

"Lick the blood off my pants, you little punk," the tall boy demanded.

"I promise to wash it for you when the work is over," I begged. The tall one with a big Adam's apple grabbed a huge fish head and threw it into my face. It exploded between my eyes. I stumbled backward until my head hit the dirty bloodstained wall. My feet slipped on the wet floor covered with fish scales and bones and I landed hard on the floor. The crowd cheered. As I leaned back to stabilize myself, I saw the shorter boy flip the fish knife in his callused hand then aim briefly at me before throwing it carelessly. It landed miraculously with its tip stuck in the wall, half an inch away from my ear. Revenge had arrived.

"Chop, chop, chop." The pair circled around me, taking turns kicking my chest, back, and head. "You're going to be headless like the fish, boned and canned," the taller one shouted among the cheers from the boys who had stopped their work to watch the circus.

In pain, I wiped my eyes quickly and stayed low and small like a mountain rat, searching for a hole in the earth where I could hide and survive. But the kicks landed like pelting raindrops. I was defenseless and had little chance to fight back with my feet slipping out from under me. In a frenzied blur, I glimpsed the knife still stuck in the wall. I pushed myself up and then threw myself all the way to the wall to catch the handle of the knife. "Chop, chop, chop!" This time it was my wild cry. I swung the knife, left and right, feeling the impact as I plunged and stabbed at the two big boys. The crowd was now very quiet. The circus had turned deadly. The boys were crawling away, leaving a bloody trail behind them. I didn't let them go that easily. I chased after them as I had with the half dead tuna and kept swinging the knife as they howled like hurt dogs.

Then the guards arrived, swinging their sticks, which landed like drumsticks on our backs. We were finally separated. I was picked up by my collar and dragged into a smelly toilet, where my head was dunked into a bucket of dirty water. I held my breath until I was ready to burst, but the guard kept his powerful hand on my head until the bubbling stopped. The guard dropped me on the floor and left.

When I opened my eyes again, a slanting sun cut through the tiny window in the toilet. My broken skin, soaked with blood and sweat, stung like little needles. It was late in the afternoon. No one had come to help me. Had it not been for the stench that attacked my nostrils, I would have been out a lot longer—I might never even have woken up. I pushed myself up with my hands. My body ached all over. I was covered with dark bruises, bloodstains, and open cuts, some of which were still oozing reddish liquid.

"Clean yourself up before the principal sees you." I heard a voice coming from outside. "Move, do you hear me?"

I climbed up with much effort and stretched my neck long and high enough to catch a peek of myself in the broken mirror hanging on the wall. I couldn't believe what I saw. My swollen and puffy face looked like a corpse's. My eyes were slits of light and my forehead was a mound of bloody flesh. My chin was split open and my cheeks resembled two rotten peaches. Flies were buzzing all over me, finding my head more appetizing than the fish heads, which were lying at the bottom of the toilets. I turned away from the morbid picture and leaned against the sink to wash my face carefully.

"When the hell are you going to be ready? Here, let me help you with your cleanup." The guard came in and picked up a bucket of dirty water and dumped it over my head. "Now you look ready, pretty boy. Follow me."

The principal was smiling as I dragged myself into the office. "Looks like you are surviving fine, my friend."

"I want to report to you that they want to kill me out there, Principal. You've got to help me, sir," I said, weak on my feet but determined to stay upright until I was told to sit down. "Black Dog and his friends have to be punished. They ganged up against me from the very beginning."

"Well, let me tell you something about this place if you haven't figured it out yet. There is no punishment here from me or anyone. We have a perfectly natural system of survival within the walls of our proud school. Survival of the fittest. See, on the day of your arrival, you ruined one of Black Dog's precious eyeballs, for which he is still receiving medical attention at the army base nearby. Did you get punished?" The principal swiveled in his oversized chair. "No, not a word from me. Strange? Perhaps. But it is good for you. You will see what I mean when you graduate from this place in six years. I can assure you that you will be a changed man. For better or worse no one knows, but changed, yes. If you turn out well, the country might find you useful. If you make it, that is."

"You're not going to do anything?"

"No. In fact, the only reason I even wanted to see you is not to give you any hope or comfort you, but to clear from your mind any illusions about getting help from me or anyone here. You only have yourself to fend for. Nobody else. Of course, if there is a broken bone or a bloody cut, we have the duty and responsibility to treat you with the best care so that you can go back to your battlefield and fight on. Now go."

For two days, all I could do was lie in bed and moan in pain. Even the short walk to the bathroom was an excruciating journey that seemed to last forever. I slept in a stupor of fever that wrapped around me, and I found myself talking deliriously at times. My mouth tasted bitter like poison. My breathing was labored. I thought I was seeing death; in some dreams, I even met my mama and baba again. In others I was sitting on the lap of the general. The only thing that reminded me that I was still alive was the sound of the nasty whistles that punctuated the routine of this hellhole. Farther away, the occasional horn from arriving ships drifted toward me from the docks.

On the third day, I found enough strength to walk down the stairs and head for the dining hall at midday. I was lightheaded but felt refreshed by the sea breeze and enlivened by the sunlight. It seemed like ages since I last saw the faces of my schoolmates clustered around their squeaky tables fighting noisily over the soupy meal. But something strange happened. The hall became silent and the boys looked at me with fear in their eyes. Their stares trailed me until I got to the long line for lunch. What was even more surprising was that a few taller, older boys wordlessly gave up their places in line to make way for me. They smiled as they bowed their heads to let me pass. I bowed back, overwhelmed with the unexpected reception. People were beginning to notice and pay respect to me, I thought happily. What happened next amused me even more. The girls in line next to me all giggled as I came near them. I waved to them and smiled, but my eyes stopped and fixed on a beautiful girl. She was smiling like the others, but her smile had a special sweetness to it that drew me to stop and linger. Her eyes were intelligent and big, her nose narrow and straight, and her face long and thin with high cheekbones. For a moment that seemed like eternity, our eyes met and locked until I blushed and forced myself to look away. But when I turned back to steal another look at the angel, our eyes met again. My heart throbbed like a little fist right above my empty stomach. My hunger was replaced by a thirst to know that girl who stood tall and elegant among the others. I saw not the dull color of the uniform but a beautiful budding rose smiling haughtily, defiantly burning with bright colors among the dead leaves in cold winter. The warmth of spring filled the recesses of my empty, lonely soul.

Soon routine set in. Black Dog's cronies quieted with their boss still away. We kept our distance, occasionally exchanging a glance here and there, nothing more. In the mornings, it was tuna canning for all. I had quick hands and learned fast. In a week's time, I was scaling and boning two hundred pounds each morning, one-third faster than the most skilled in the school. My hands grew callused from handling the blunt knife and my fingernails were roughened from having to scratch out the last bit of guts from the flesh. My back ached from bending over the sink and wrestling with fish that did not face death submissively.

I was soon promoted to the less-tedious job of hauling the day's catch from the dock to the plant. I was given a squeaky barrow with two wheels. Each morning, I made at least twenty runs, five more than the quickest man on the job. All the boys fought for the outside job as it gave them fresh air by the sea. On rare moments when I was able to rest by the dock, I wondered about the sea as I once had about the mountains of my village. Soon the sailors and fishermen began to call me Mountain Cat, because of my nimble long strides. Though I was skinny, I showed great strength.

In the afternoons, it was schooltime. Most of the children didn't know which to hate more, the dirty heavy smelly work or the tedious mind-bending academics. But they could sit down and with the help of the breeze take a nap until they were rudely awakened by their teacher's bamboo cane. I, however, loved the classes. The teachers were adequate and, best of all, there was a library. I sat in the first row and took the cleanest notes, sitting straight until the end of every class. My favorite subjects were math, language, and music. While others were caned for not doing their assignments, I would ask the teacher for more homework. It was soon obvious that I was the top student in math and was second only to one in language, which upset me a great deal. Since I was a young child I had always taken pride in my ability to express myself in the most accurate and simplest way. My teacher never told me who was ahead of me, but that secret was not kept for long.

At midterm there was a composition competition. The best student would be given some clothing and allowed out of the compound for an outside trip. I stayed up late for a week to work on my composition. After many visits to the library, I presented in neatly written copy what I considered the best work of my life to the teacher. The winner's original composition would be posted on the school's display board where other students could admire it. When the results were posted, I waited nervously and was the last one to check the board. I made sure that the yard was completely empty, with no one to witness my loss if again my competitor had come out on top of me.

To my surprise, two compositions were posted side by side; there was a tie for first place. My pulse quickened as I searched for the name of the other winner. There in dark bold letters was the name Miss Sumi Wo, who must be my unknown nemesis. A girl! In my wildest imagination, I would never have guessed. But which girl? How bright she must be to be head-to-head with me! As I walked away in shame, I heard my name being called by a sweet voice. "Shento, wait."

I turned and saw the girl whose beauty had caught my attention in the dining hall. "Are you calling me?" I asked.

"My name is Sumi Wo. I have always wanted to know you." Her

face was as beautiful as I remembered and her voice made my heart flutter. I should have introduced myself like a gentleman, but something about her, the beautiful angel, made my feet shake and teeth rattle. There is no worse defeat than one dealt by the girl to whom one is so attracted. The attraction was working in reverse, for some reason; it seemed to have walled me up. I couldn't even open my mouth to converse in my usual confident manner. All I wanted to do was run away from her, the farther, the better, even though my heart wished otherwise.

"I have to go," I muttered, bowing and backing away from her.

"Wait. All I wanted to tell you is that I enjoy your composition more than my own and think you deserve first place. I don't." She smiled and flushed red, looking like a budding flower waiting to ripen into something dangerous.

I ran like a headless ghost back to the dormitory.

Sumi. What a lovely name. I lay on my bed that night, not a thread of sleepiness in my mind, but with a heart full of songs, the most beautiful songs that I knew. The moon was as secretive as my mood, hiding behind the chasing clouds, maybe even dreaming itself. I lived and relived the moments of my encounter, and wished I could compose a piece of music to accompany the moving picture in my mind. I held my pillow in my arms and only drifted into sleep when the moon had set in the Western Hemisphere and the first light of day painted the universe silver.

The following morning, I wheeled my barrow of tuna faster than usual so that I could take a break to see Sumi, who was in a separate building where army clothes were made. I wiped the sweat off my forehead and leaned over a window in the building where she worked and peered in. To my joy, Sumi was sitting right there! She had her head buried in the fabric, all army green. Her feet pedaled fast to make the sewing machine run. The hall was filled with girls engaged in the different chores of embroidering, cutting, packing, and buttoning. It was steaming hot and noisy with dozens of machines humming and clanking away. When I tickled her with a blade of a white flower, Sumi looked up, surprised to see me. "Hello," she said. "What brought you here?"

"I just wanted to let you know that you deserved to win first place and that I enjoyed reading your composition even more than all of mine put together."

"Is that a lie or the truth?" She smiled without opening her mouth. Her face, covered with beads of sweat, was red, and her soaked blouse was stuck to her skin. Her flat chest was vaguely defined by two budding mounds.

"I swear on my mama's tomb."

"You know, I have always wanted to thank you for taking an eye out of Black Dog and crippling two of his cronies."

"Why?"

"He bothered all the girls here, and we were praying for his demise when you came along. Quick, leave now before our guard clubs your head."

"Can I see you again?"

"The library tonight."

From that day on, I met Sumi every night in the back row of the shabby library, hidden behind bookshelves. Over the weeks, I learned that Sumi was an orphan from the south. Her parents had been executed for writing plays and dramas criticizing the Communist Party. The gift of writing was in her blood. She wanted to be the best writer or actress in the country one day. She was only thirteen but seemed to be ripening right before my eyes. Everybody, especially the guards and the cooks in the dining hall, openly admired her growing beauty. She held her head high like a lady, even in the face of lewd insults and crude remarks.

She had read every book they had in the library twice and was reading them through for the third time. Her favorite book was the dog-eared copy of Charles Dickens's *David Copperfield,* which she had found buried under a pile of rubbish. Sumi worshipped Dickens, reciting the dialogue and soulful passages and crying easily over poor little David. Before I came, she had always been lonely at the top of the school, proudly holding herself above the others, whom she considered sad orphans with drunken fathers and prostitute mothers and destined to repeat their parents' fate. But that belief changed after my arrival.

Sumi saw me in the light of a rainbow, full of promises. I loved to stare at her big bright eyes, tall straight nose, and full lips as I talked about my ambitions. She said I had the perseverance and endurance to match my goals. I told her she had the heart of a writer and the soul of a poet. Many times I just wanted to merge myself into her and be with her forever.

Tan

CHAPTER 8

September 1976

BEIJING

Grandfather Xia and Grandfather Long were the only ones present by Chairman Mao's bed deep in the ancient palace of the Forbidden City when he died. They decided to hold off informing the congress of the leader's passing till a successor was chosen. The nation was at that very moment in danger of having a coup right at its door. My grandfathers had to consolidate their position in the military and finance and choose a leader as soon as possible to ensure the succession of power. But their enemy, who was also Mao's enemy for the last few years of his life, was the very woman whom Mao had married, his third wife, the former actress Madame Mao. To get rid of her was to fight the Garrison Force, China's finest soldiers guarding the capital, under her control. These soldiers could take over the government organs before Grandfather Xia could mobilize the armies outside Beijing. The whole country could be paralyzed from the waist down.

That night my grandfathers arrived not by their usual limousines, but by a simple jeep, to our residence. I waited anxiously and rushed to them as they entered our living room. "Are you all right, Grandfathers?" I embraced them in a bear hug.

The two just nodded, patted my disheveled hair, and entered Father's office, leaving the door ajar. I was surprised to see Father dressed in combat uniform and arms, studying a detailed map of Beijing.

"What happens now?" I asked.

"Son, come here." I stepped into his office, which smelled of leather and cigars. Father held my head with his two hands. "Mao has just died. Your grandfathers and I need to work now because there might be a coup that we have to put to rest."

"Can I stay?"

"No, son. One day we'll need your help, but not today." Father kissed me on the forehead and sent me out.

In the music room, Mother softly played Debussy's "Clair de lune."

"Mother, would there be war?" I asked.

"That's what they are trying to avoid," she replied, keeping her eyes on the music.

"What is China going to be tomorrow?"

"Whatever the next president wants it to be."

"Who will be the next president?"

"You, one day," Mother said.

It only took the three men half an hour to arrive at a unanimous conclusion. My grandfathers agreed on something for the first time in their lives without any fistfights or quarrels. They made two phone calls. The first was to Father's secret agents; it was in these men's blood to live and die for the Longs. They moved like dark shadows into the night. The other call was put through to a fallen angel of the Communist cause, Mr. Heng Tu, who at that moment was sleeping in a chilly cell of a maximum security prison in Hubei Province, dreaming about the next day of heavy labor ahead of him.

Before sunrise, six masked and heavily armed men raided both the chamber of Madame Mao, who was found sleeping without her wig under the same quilt as a handsome married ballet dancer, and the residence of the commander in chief of China's Garrison Force, Major General Wan Dong Xing. There was no gunfire heard, no bloodshed. Even though it was the turning point in a major chapter in my country's history, no footnote would ever be found about the incidents. Here one moment, gone the next, much like a meteor that swept the sky once in a long while.

In Hubei Province, at the mountainous temple converted into a prison for political prisoners, a navy jet penetrated the dark sky and landed at the airstrip. A bonfire of burning dried lumber on the dark ground marked the landing spot for the plane. As soon as the jet taxied to a stop, a door slid open and a fully armed soldier climbed down the ladder. He carried a letter signed by the head of the Joint Chiefs of Staff ordering the release of Heng Tu. The brief order was read to the prisoner, who fell silent at the heavy words being rewarded him. This man, clad in rough prison garb and one of the earliest founders of the revolution, was to take over Mao's position as the next president of China. By sunrise, a well-tailored and clean-shaven Heng Tu was introduced to the world.

The next day, Father became the first man appointed commander in chief of Beijing's Garrison Force, the most important segment of China's military, before the age of forty-five. My two grandfathers, the kingmakers, had put aside their animosities so as not to give up their power. Their common and mutual goal, never outwardly spoken or confirmed, was to have Father next in line for the presidency. They could have named him president that very night instead of Mr. Tu, but he wasn't ready; the country wasn't ready. Therefore, it was not to be. A young leader was an inexperienced leader in the eyes of the Chinese. Father needed to grow some silver hair and gain more recognition as the new garrison chief. He would be the top military adviser to President Heng Tu, stand behind him at all public appearances, and accompany him on state visits to major foreign countries to expose Father to foreign affairs.

My grandfathers knew that Heng Tu was their man. His presidency was only a temporary leasehold in his possession until Father was ready. Then Heng Tu would turn over the presidency without a fuss. They had done Heng Tu a favor, which he was to return when the time came. He need not be reminded. That was the game of China's politics. A soft form of tai chi, subtle and quiet.

AT SIXTEEN, I had sharp luminous eyes that shone in the sunlight and a pair of sword-shaped eyebrows. My nose was unusually tall and thin and ended with a determined tip. My mouth was that of Grandfather Long, with full lips that gave one an impression of trustworthiness, an asset that a fortune-teller once said was crucial to my future as a leader. I had my father's chiseled determined chin, hooked at the end, which caused the same fortune-teller to predict I would live to be a hundred. My shoulders were broad and my waist narrow like a swimmer. I preferred sweatshirts printed with the Garrison Force insignia, but Mother, now the queen of Beijing's society, insisted that I wear slacks cut and tailored by a Hong Kong shop and jackets from America. How she managed to acquire these was a mystery to all. China in 1977 was still a closed and isolated empire. Only the most privileged were given access to the colorful world outside. Such was the picture when I entered the classroom of my new school, Dong Shan Senior High School, another exclusive club for youngsters of the most important families in the land.

The first class of the day was English, taught by an attractive young teacher, Miss Yu, a volunteer from Hong Kong who had been educated in America. As a six-footer, I was placed in the last row. My eyes were on her the entire hour. Something about her made me forget the world around me. Everything about her possessed a rhythm, a melody, heightening my interest in the subject of English. I harbored the ambition of being able to read the *New York Times* and the *Wall Street Journal* within one or two years. I considered it a handicap, not being able to read the most important dailies in the world like my grandfather. My hand shot up at least five times during the forty-five-minute period, and I was lavishly praised by my teacher, who found my pronunciation of the alphabet to be better than that of the rest of the class. At the end of the hour, as the other students filed out as if they had been holding their breath under water for too long, I walked up to my teacher, who stood only to my ear and blushed prettily in my presence.

"Miss Yu, I want to be able to read the *New York Times* in two years. What should I do?"

"Work hard like your father," she said with a smile.

"My father? How do you know my father?"

"Well, his name is all over the school record books. I am sure you will do as well as your father if you try."

"Do you think I need private lessons to go beyond the crawling pace of this class?"

"I'm afraid I don't have the time."

I was quite upset. There were few things in the world that I could not just get by wishing for them. Mother offered to hire the best English professor from the prestigious Beijing University, but his British accent seemed too stilted. I wanted to speak with an American accent. Only Miss Yu could do the job for me. Mother promised to speak with her.

"No, Mother, I will deal with her myself. The last time you were involved, I never saw that person again."

Mother took that as a compliment. "Just let me know if you need help, son."

The next day after school, I found Miss Yu playing badminton with another faculty member on the lawn. She was dressed in a tight red sweater and white faded pants that fit like a second skin. Her long legs were athletic and her full bosom bounced with each stroke of her racket. Upon a closer look, I could see that there were holes in her pants at both her knees. Noticing me, Miss Yu stopped the game and invited me to join in. My face reddened, but I grabbed a racket. I would do anything to be near this gorgeous creature who glowed with health, beauty, and youth. The other teacher, considerably winded, took the opportunity to leave.

"Your pants need mending at the knees, Miss Yu," I said, weighing the racket in my hand.

"Well, thank you, but this is the fashion in New York, where I went to college."

"That's interesting. New York, huh?" I dropped my racket on the ground and cut a hole in my pants at each knee with my pocketknife. "Look, I have holes in my pants also."

"That's so cute of you." She couldn't stop laughing, her chest jerking with motion.

"You like it?" I asked.

"They look awful."

"Why?"

"Because they're not jeans."

"You mean your white pants that are made of coarse rough fabric?"

"Yes, another American fashion. The cowboy pants."

Embarrassed, I bent over and rolled up my pants to cover the holes. It was a tough game but I let her win, still bearing the illusion that she might give me private lessons. Walking toward the entrance to the school, I asked, "Where do you live?"

"Why do you want to know?"

"I would like to offer you a lift." I pointed to the limousine parked under a willow tree. It was an antiquated Red Flag model that was bulletproof and weighed a hefty three tons.

"Great! I wish I had a car here like I did in Hong Kong. I hate the bus."

When we came to the car, the uniformed chauffeur grabbed me aside and whispered into my ear, "Young Mr. Long, who is this?"

"My teacher. We'll be giving her a ride home."

"I am afraid I do not have the permission to accommodate her, young master."

"You do now."

"No, I don't, because she is a foreigner and cannot ride in a military vehicle."

"Yes, she can, and you might have to drive her around the city a great deal, maybe even daily from now on." I turned to Miss Yu and said politely in English, "Females first."

"That's ladies first, thank you."

The driver unwillingly but obediently drove us to Miss Yu's apartment in central Beijing, and she was happy when we parted. Everything had a price in this world, my banker grandfather often said. For the beautiful English teacher, it was a chauffeur and a companion, something I didn't think a woman like her would need. My request for another chauffeur to drive Miss Yu around at her disposal was easily granted. And my offer to her, as expected, was accepted with gratitude. We then agreed that she would come and visit every other day after school to tutor me. Helped by Miss Yu's Hong Kong efficiency, I made fast progress. As a teacher she was strict, but when my lessons were over, we often ended up talking or playing games.

One Saturday afternoon, Father asked to be introduced to Miss Yu, as he wanted to show his respect to someone who contributed to the intellectual growth of his son. Chinese people believed that teachers were as important as parents, if not more; they molded young minds and shaped young souls. But I knew he also wanted to make sure this exotic Hong Kong princess wasn't a bad influence on me.

I noticed the blush on Miss Yu's face when she almost curtsied upon meeting Father. Father guided her to his spacious office and asked for tea to be served to them while they chatted for an hour. I heard laughter through the doors. I waited outside, anxious to know what Father thought of her. Fortunately, he emerged from the meeting with a smile on his face. Father encouraged me to continue on with my study. Miss Yu was approved.

Mother also had her concerns. At first, she spied on Miss Yu through the window of the piano room, pretending to play leisurely on her piano but really watching my teacher's every move. Any female younger than she was automatically looked upon with great suspicion. Mother knew Father's taste for young impressionable creatures. But Miss Yu showed only innocence and diligence in teaching me. After giving up afternoon tea with her friends for a two-week period, Mother was convinced that Miss Yu was up to no evil. She was tickled one afternoon when Miss Yu knocked on her door and asked if the women's club headed by Mother would accept a donation of some Hong Kong fashion magazines. "Your music is simply breathtaking," Miss Yu added. With that, Mother was finally convinced that Miss Yu could be a friend rather than a foe. Nonetheless, Mother commissioned a watch on my teacher. The task fell, inevitably, on Miss Yu's driver.

Shento

山头

CHAPTER 9

1976
FUJIAN

In a week-old newspaper dated September 10, 1976, that I found in the library, I read about the death of the much-feared Chairman Mao. What incredible news—what else had I been missing in the world beyond the thick walls of my school? With Mao's demise, the Cultural Revolution that he had initiated would now end.

"It means only one thing," I whispered urgently to Sumi. "The country is going to be thrust into chaos and unrest. Anyone with the power of the army wins. The country is up for grabs."

"What should we do?"

"I need to be in the army now or I will never catch the boat to my dream, Sumi! Can't you see? A dynasty has just ended. The country, the biggest in the world, is awaiting the coming of a new leader. And I see none among those sitting in the cabinet. The country is at its weakest moment now. Chaos frightens the weak, begets the brave. Oh, how I wish I could join the army."

"Join the army? What about me?"

"You write! Isn't that what you want to do? And what is a better time to write than in a time of turmoil?"

"Yes, you're right," Sumi said, thinking of her heroes. "Charles Dickens wrote during England's Industrial Revolution. Cao Xueqin's *A Dream of Red Mansions* was born when feudalism died. Oh, thank you for that inspiration." She touched her lips to mine for the first time, then we were kissing with the craziness and drunkenness of youth. Sumi pulled away from my embrace reluctantly. She had to wait; so did I. I had armies to lead, battles to win, and she had epics to write. But she belonged to me only, no matter where we were and where we chose to go.

In a most painful tone, I whispered, "I do love you."

"I love you even more."

"It can't be. Nothing can match the depth of my feelings for you."

"Oh, yes, mine certainly can."

"I will wed you when I become a general."

"And I you when the country kneels at my feet."

The promise for life and love only brought another long round of kisses that made me feel weak and yet strong. Fortunately, the library was empty, as was usually the case.

With the changing politics, I was hungry for news about the leaders. I began reading all the newspapers in the library, even though papers were delivered weeks late to this remote Fujian seaport town. I read every word and tried to interpret the meanings behind them. The leading newspapers such as the *People's Daily* and *Guangming Daily* maintained a calm tone about the sudden end of the tumultuous Cultural Revolution. I kept wondering who was in charge. And if no one, then when was the coup going to happen? It would only be a matter of time before a new leader appeared—that, or bloodshed. In the smattering of history I had studied through my nightly readings beyond my course work, I knew that rarely did a dynasty survive its creator and power never changed hands without the stain of blood.

I slept little. All I thought about was joining the army now that I was sixteen. I was wasting time here. In reality, though, there were many obstacles to my goal. Even if I could leave the school, would the army even accept me at my age or with my reform school background? I knew there was a naval base about ten miles away. And I had heard rumors of hidden nuclear plants in the deep mountains. I grew more and more anxious, and my agitation worried Sumi.

"You're not doing your homework. What's the matter with you?" Sumi asked me one day after school.

"I wish I could fly like a bird up in the sky," I said, leaning against the windowsill and looking out at the patchy clouds.

"You're not eating enough, and you look terrible."

"I need to fly or I shall perish."

Sumi came up behind me and drew wings on my shoulder blades with her finger. "Then fly, my bird. I shall bid my farewell from earth to sky."

"Only you understand me." I tucked her under my arm and pulled her close.

"When you float on the wind, remember, I gave you your wings," she said, smiling.

As always, we ended in each other's arms with lingering kisses, only this time I hungrily reached for her budding breasts. She sighed lightly but pushed me away and showed me a copy she'd found of the *Military Journal,* a monthly magazine about life in the military. "There is a report about a young general who was a war hero in Balan and is now promoted to commander in chief of the Garrison Force."

"Just another privileged boy promoted by nepotism." I passed my opinion casually. "What is his name?"

"General Ding Long."

I froze. "What did you say his name is?"

"Ding Long. What is the matter? Do you know him?"

"No, no, of course not. I just heard the name before," I said.

"Then why did you suddenly turn pale?" Nothing escaped the sensitive Sumi. "Are you all right?"

"I am. Is there a picture of the general?"

"Handsome, isn't he?" she said, passing me the journal.

"Quite so." My eyes darted hungrily at the page.

"Something about him reminds me of you," Sumi whispered and bit her lip.

I stilled a moment before mumbling, "Don't tell me you're attracted to older men?"

"You silly, I'm going to beat you." Sumi drummed my chest with her fists and ended up in my embrace again. "You know, I can imagine you in ten years in that uniform. You'll have a dark beard and your eyes will be sharp with insight and depths. You will be General Shento one day," Sumi said dreamily.

I read the article intently. There was a picture of the general, his beautiful and sophisticated wife, and a teenage son with the same perfect features as his dad. The article said that he was a devoted father to his only son and a virtuous husband to his lovely wife.

I hoarded the old military journal, hiding it under my pillow, and read it over and over again. I floated for days in a heightened mood, fluctuating from euphoria to sadness. *He lived,* I kept saying to myself. *He lived!* Should I contact the great general and seek his aid in releasing me from this hellhole? Ding Long had ascended to the highest rank of supremacy. All he had to do was send the order and my life would be forever changed. I dared not dream on. There were so many shades and colors to the dream; I feared that one day they would all pop like soap bubbles and be gone. I reminisced on the past the great general and I had shared. Those cozy little moments of my previous life on many occasions sustained me in my current bleak existence. Ding Long was a generous man, a man of the heart, a man of dreams, a man's man and a woman's man as well, otherwise my mother would not have fallen for him, and I would not have been born. In his generosity, after hearing from me, the general would surely fling open his arms and take me into his loving family in the warmth of Beijing. How I longed for the moment, that divine moment all bastards on earth dream about, when the general would purse his lips and utter lovingly the precious word, "Son."

How sweet it would be. What heavenly joy that would bring. I shivered, imagining an exhilarating drive along a paved road in an army jeep, wind blasting my face as I sat next to my father, with me maybe dressed in the same color as he, if not the same uniform. What a comfort it would be to finally step inside the compound, a world far beyond this world.

If the family, for some unknown reason, found me undesirable—which was possible, infidelity and betrayal, so on and so forth—in the worst case, it would be a temporary thing, for the general being the general, in or out of his family compound, his words were words of iron, never to be disobeyed. I could live—temporarily, that is—somewhere away from the family but still in the convenient vicinity, so that father and newly found son could meet frequently, maybe to play chess or just sit and chat. By this time, the general would, of course, after seeing me grown so strong and determined, send me to a genuine army school, maybe the same one the general had attended in his youth—East Military Academy, located in the seaside city of Da Lian.

If the general—touted by the papers, magazines, and other governmental documents as a family man—saw this new son as something that might tarnish his military career (virtue, after all, was a requirement of the Communist canon), then he did not even have to call me son. He could be a silent father—be there for me, love me, offer help when I stumbled, pick me up when I fell, like any father would do. No need for me to *call* him father—such formality.

I was so confident of Ding Long's generosity and kindness toward me as a young boy that a fortnight after reading that article I decided to write a letter to him at the Central Committee of the Garrison Force in Beijing. I chose the center's address rather the general's home in the commonly known Zhong Nan Hai, to avoid having to deal with the general's wife, who might receive the letter at home before it reached the general.

In the dim light of my room, after much pencil biting, I wrote the following letter:

> *Dear General,*
>
> *I am writing on the occasion of having read about your ascendance into the most powerful officialdom of our national military post, to offer my humble congratulations on that promotion, which I had little doubt even a half decade ago that you would obtain. Here and now you might wonder who I am and why I am writing this letter. Well, I am Shento, the doctor's son from the village of Balan, which, in a stroke of historical misfortune, was burned down to the ground, rendering me the sole survivor of that tragedy, which, in turn, for good or bad, led me to where I am.*

If the name does not strike you as anything but another well-sounding and well-meaning name among many, then I must tell you that I was that bright little boy who, for six years on end, won the most coveted prize and most-yearned-for opportunity to dine with you in your glorious office within the compound where your army resided. The moving pictures I saw, the food, and most important, you, your firm handshakes and the encouragement and honor that you, the general, bestowed upon the little boy that I was, were the sole reasons for my urge to excel in school and in life. I do not feel ashamed to tell you that our brief encounters formed the most precious moments in my little life. More than once, I contemplated leaving my humble hut and climbing into the compound so that I could be there every day to receive your acknowledgment.

You shaped the course of my life by giving me the ultimate treasure of your necklace. Ever since that day of darkness when my village was destroyed, life has changed its course as a river would, from mountain to the sea. We have both reached another plateau in life. You, to the top of your career, as you so deserved, and I, shamefully, to the sordid south of fate, dumped in an orphanage in the name of a school, which is, at best, a sweatshop, condemning all here, girls and boys, to a life, in the prime of youth, of toil, torture, shame, triviality, and hopelessness. In this sunless isolation, tomorrow is always a darker day. We do receive three meals a day, if one were forced to call them such. I would not name them so. We work, though work I mind not, for I was made sturdy as a mountain man, and toiling only makes firmer the body and more resolute the will. But work for what? There is no future here, no tomorrow. We are here only to labor and be tortured or, worse, torture another in the name of survival. We are chained to this school, slaves for life, ghosts for eternity. Condemned, though young and innocent. Punished, though unworthy of such. Please exonerate me or I shall perish in this drabness of waste.

The reason I am compelled to compose this letter is to beg you to release me from this inferno. You might have a thousand reasons not to honor my request, for you are a busy and important man, but write this I must because my young heart retains a message from the innocence of my youth—that you care for me and would liberate me from this slavery if you could. If you do not pity my station in life, then think of the promise you made me, that silent and tacit promise accompanying the gift of your engraved necklace, which, by the way, has already saved me once by stopping a bullet from entering my chest. Though it might be unseemly, what I am about to ask you, ask you I must, for I am left without anyone in this world (my adoptive parents burned to death that terrible day). Do you remember Malayi, the village bloom, whom you loved one Water Spraying Festival? She was my true mother. I am your flesh and blood.

Oh, my dearest father, please do what you can to save me and make something out of me. I pledge that I won't be a black mark to you. I am bright, as you have witnessed and determined. With a little of your nurturing and Buddha-given fatherly love, I shall be what you desire me to be, and more, much more.

It is not my intention to sound pitiful, but life does leave marks without one's realizing it. I am a strong man. I write to you not just to seek help but to offer my hand, for I believe in the days to come, with appropriate accommodation and tutoring, I might rise up to be a force behind you, as you no doubt expect your other son to be. I will do so instinctively, to aid you in your ambitions to soar even higher in the tower of life.

Please, dear father, set me free—if not for me, then for my dead mother, who died so young and whom you once must have loved.

Signed with blood,
Shento

Barely a week went by when a letter was rudely thrust into the little hole in my door at night. What joy! My head buzzed with such excitement that I felt faint. The return address was that of the Central Command office, with its insignia of a red flag, a sickle, and a hammer. There was no mistaking it. I blinked back tears as I ripped the envelope apart, then shut my eyes to calm myself. When I opened my eyes again, the icy words leaped into my vision:

> *Comrade Shento,*
>
> *You are hereby ordered to cease any further false accusations again me, concerning your being my illegitimate son. What you have committed by writing that letter to me is commensurate to a capital punishment crime, which, under our National Penal Code 1462, would condemn you to death by strangulation. However, I would not recommend such a punishment for you, a boy so innocent and of such tender age.*
>
> *My conscience is clean and clear. I know and possess only one son. There is no possibility of other sons, or daughters, for that matter. It is utterly impossible, for I practice the high virtue of our Communistic value, and I live frugally along our Party line. That doesn't mean that you don't have a father or a right to claim one; everyone does. It might be that you mistook me for another general, whom your morally loose mother once consorted herself with, leaving you to live with the sin of bastardry. I know the pain of your heart. Hopeless, with a hopeless tomorrow. Desperation breeds desperate acts, of which your letter is one. I will leave you with this warning, a thing you must heed, if you are as bright as you have described yourself to be, with a desire to go on living. You must never, under any circumstances, repeat such a groundless claim to anyone, at any time, or lawful charges will be brought against you. The Supreme Court of People's Justice and People's Supreme Military Tribunal have been informed of your acts and will continue to observe your future behavior.*
>
> *Young man, please wake up from your daydreaming, which*

is what this is at best and which is why I recommended not bringing charges against you. Rid yourself of the butterflies of imagination and illusion, and learn to live an independent and, more important, an honest life.

Ding Long, Commander in Chief
Official Seal

For days, I felt like a dog beaten by many sticks, limping not in body but in spirit. How could the general be so cruel, erasing the fondest of my memories and the brightest of my hopes, my only hope? Was I not as bright as his other son, as wholesome as he? I went over the letter again and again. That threat of death—what injustice! Citing the penal code?

The world was upside down. Then, slowly, it dawned on me. The Long clan smiled in that photo of perfection with white teeth, combed hair, and neat clothing, while I, the bastard, should never have been born. Even though I had survived—only Buddha knew how—and lived on in this shameful lie of an ill fate, I would never have the right of claiming the father that was mine, who had defiled the Village Bloom. I was but an accident of life, not intended, not needed. Surely not loved, not wanted, not desired, not called for. Not anything! I was the eleventh toe, the second belly button. An anomaly, an abnormality, a dark cloud cursing the blue sky.

What a contrast Ding Long was to my baba and mama, the village doctor and his wife, who had loved and raised me. They were my real parents. But death had taken them and now no one wanted me, except me. So in myself I must trust, utterly and totally. I had only myself to cling to. How very pathetic and undesirable, lonely and alone, a tree without a forest. I had absolutely nothing at all. It would be better if from now on I called myself the son of the tea tree. For that was where I had been caught, saved from death at birth.

From the tone of the letter, not only did he not want me, I was also a burden to be rid of, a dark mold to remove. Surely Ding Long's father-in-law had tried, sending me to this jail of a school upon the knowledge of the general's indiscretion and upon recognition of that blasted necklace. Now this. Both conspired to let me rot with the other orphans and bastards.

But I would not perish. On the contrary, I would stand tall like a mountain, like my name given me by my real parents. Survive, not for myself, but for those who desired me not to, for those who wanted me gone, erased. I, the dark son of the Longs, would spit into their faces, and they would be the ones smeared in the mud of regret and the blood of remorse.

From that day on, I was myself, nothing else. A lone Shento. A man who belonged to no one, came from nowhere. There was no General Ding Long in the princedom of my childhood. No mother who flung herself down the cliff. Only the memory of my dead baba and mama. Only myself, alone, facing the world. On the dock before loading yet another barrow of fish, I tore the letter into pieces and tossed it into the sea. As the bits of paper were swallowed by the water, a part of me drowned with them. In their vanishing, a new Shento was born.

Tan

CHAPTER 10

1977
BEIJING

The death of Chairman Mao marked the end of the disastrous Cultural Revolution. When Heng Tu took the reins of the country, the first thing he did was restore college education. The popular slogan "Knowledge is poison" was thrown into the trash. The "stinking intellectuals" were in great demand now. Suddenly, ten years' worth of high-school graduates, millions of them, were given the opportunity to take the national exams for limited college seats. There was a rage to acquire higher knowledge of science and arts. Lights burned at every household late into the night. Another revolution was on the horizon, one allowing every young man a shot at a better future.

I found Dong Shan Senior High a snobbish old club full of odd and eccentric characters, modern versions of China's royalty and nobility who thus tended to set the trend of fashion both in dress and thinking. Dust-sweeping bell-bottom pants were in style, and the boys wore their hair greasy and long. In the bathrooms, seniors freely passed out cigarettes—but only foreign brands; domestic ones were readily dumped.

Because Father was one of the founders, I was invited to join the most prestigious society in the school of five hundred, the Hammer and Sickle Club. His picture still hung on the wall of the smoke-filled lounge. The original charter of the club was to study the truth about communism as expounded by Karl Marx. But I could not believe what I heard at the first meeting. They called Karl Marx a foreign freak with a beard. Another called him a beggar who had no qualms about riding on the coattails of a rich friend. The young men expounded on all options, trying to find the most suitable political system for China. Eventually, the conversation invariably fell on the democracy in America.

I sat through the first meeting quietly. When it was over, I could not help thinking how paradoxical it was that the children of the Communist elite were discussing alternatives to the very form of government that gave us our privilege and everything we had. It first scared me, for during the Cultural Revolution this meeting would have been seen as a counterrevolutionary act and we would have all been thrown into a dark cell for twenty years without the chance for appeal. But the more I thought about it, the more it made sense—if we didn't do the thinking for the future, who would?

Over the next few weeks I became an ardent participant, an impassioned speaker, and a convincing debater. For the first time, I was thinking hard about the system I lived in. My early exposure to the financial world and now my long talks with Miss Yu opened my eyes. I concluded that there was no democracy here in China because no democracy would have allowed my grandfathers to pick a president for the entire nation. An election for a leader should be left to the people, not politicians. The government should deregulate and release its control over major industries. People should own property and do business as they pleased; only then could the full potential of this big nation be realized. Imagine a billion entrepreneurs. The future of China was here and now. I felt inspired and confident that someday, maybe in the near future, I would be able to put to good use my political view and help my people.

One night the Hammer and Sickle Club challenged the Lenin and Stalin Club, which still dominated the conservative student body, to a debate. I was chosen to represent my club, an honor given to only one freshman before. My opponent was a senior whose father was the minister of propaganda. My opponent argued that China would never be a capitalist country because its people wouldn't know what to do in a free market. But I used the examples of the five little Asian tigers—Singapore, Hong Kong, Korea, Malaysia, and Indonesia—to attack his flaws. I won the debate with a standing ovation. From that day on I was known on the campus as Mr. Democracy. By midterm, I was elected president of the club, an honor Father had not obtained until his senior year.

One afternoon the principal of the school asked me to come to his office. Usually, students were expected to stand in his presence, but I was given the sofa and a cup of tea. "Young man," he said, "politics is like a cloud. You can chase it, but you cannot hold on to it. Your grandfathers did not become prominent politicians because they talked about politics all the time.

"As bright as you are, you should know that life is about solid things. For instance, your grandfather Long was my classmate at Oxford. His trade was economics, a branch of science, by the way. What he has become is not important. Had he not been running the bank, he could have been a brilliant professor. And your grandfather Xia, a true soldier, won more battles than any other in his generation. First he was a fine soldier, then a commander in chief."

"Sir, I fully understand what you are trying to tell me. I shall spend more time studying."

"I knew you would understand."

"Thank you, sir."

"Don't thank me. I am here to make sure that Beijing University, your father's alma mater, will not have to frown at your record and be made to accept you on the basis of your family background."

I left the office determined not to embarrass my parents with my semester finals. I studied day and night, temporarily halting my duty as club president and even my beloved English lessons, with which I was making enormous progress. My average came out better than Father's by a quarter of a point.

That winter holiday Grandfather Xia suffered a major stroke while meeting with President Heng Tu over a thorny military issue. He dropped to the floor, passed out, and was brought to the Beijing People's Hospital. He was in a coma for five days, during which time I visited him every day. The first time I saw him, his pale corpselike figure bore little resemblance to my vibrant beloved grandfather. The second day, I brought my handheld Casio keyboard and played Grandfather's favorite Peking

Opera tunes, hoping to awaken him. The old man did not stir. The third day, I spent ten hours there and only went home after being chased out by the president of the hospital. The next two days, I refused to leave Grandfather's side and slept on a little cot, accompanying Mother, who had cried to the point of no tears.

On the sixth day, I woke up in Mother's lap.

"He is gone," she said. Her eyes were circled with dark rings.

I could not believe my giant of a grandfather would die, but there he was, unnervingly still. I put my head on his chest tenderly. The absence of the rise and fall of his breath was so shocking, I was soon choking with tears.

The funeral was held in a small hall and was attended by the nation's military and civil leaders—ministers, Politburo members, and military attachés of foreign embassies. Grandfather Long gave a glorious yet humorous eulogy to the very deserving man. I cried again when Grandfather Long finished by saying that General Xia's down-to-earth character—humble, simple, a little rough at the edges—made him even greater in spirit and bigger than life. The service ended as I played his favorite piece, "Clair de lune," which the old general had said was the only Western music that could compare to his Peking Opera.

Two old friends of the general in wheelchairs threw themselves upon the casket and would not leave until their nurses dragged them away. They had walked in the Long March and fought hundreds of battles together. President Heng Tu, noticeably missing, had only sent a wreath with some of Chairman Mao's poems written on it.

Back home, a direct call was placed through to the president's office by my grieving grandfather Long. Exactly one hour later, the Central People's Broadcast and Central TV reported the special item that Father had been named by the president to be the commander in chief of China's army, navy, and air force, the post left vacant by Grandpa Xia's passing. All Grandfather Long said upon hearing the news was "I am disappointed that he had to be reminded."

I wasn't particularly impressed with the process in which power was given like a gift. I congratulated Father by hugging him, then went back to my room and stared at the old picture of my dead grandfather, who was in essence just a simple man who liked his pipe.

In the following months, I could feel the tension at home. Father was moody and shouted frequently. He stopped taking me to his headquarters. And he didn't talk about his new position much. There were a lot of sighs felt, though not heard. Something was changing in the household. One day Father raged and threw things in his office.

"Why?" I asked Mother.

"Never ask about his affairs," she told me.

I read about it soon enough in the newspaper: acid criticisms by Heng Tu of the army, and his promise to cut the army budget. Father was missing for days. Mother only said that he was on an official visit to his regional chiefs and that everything was fine. All this affected me little, or at least so I thought.

In the summer of 1977, before fall semester began, I decided to split my time between my grandfather's banking business and Father's military affairs. I sat with Grandfather Long in his grand office at the Bank of China's headquarters near Tiananmen Square, listening to the executives discussing matters of the day. Loans and more loans, top executives screamed with urgency. It was a heady time for the newly freed China. Entrepreneurs were everywhere. It seemed that if you had any capital at all, you could shake coins off a tall tree. Seeing this, Grandfather Long's advice to Heng Tu was caution and more caution, or the shaky start and inflation would kill the budding economy. But his words fell on deaf ears as billions of loans were processed without any credit check or risk analysis. I began to see more new faces at the bank. In the meetings, they began to assert their power and make changes without Grandfather's approval. Grandfather got so angry one day that when a new face told him to calm down he smashed his favorite jade teapot on the table and just walked out. I followed him quickly.

"Who are these people?" I asked, concerned, as he threw open the door to his office then stood at his desk, taking deep breaths.

"Heng Tu's disciples." Grandfather sat down heavily.

"Are they here to oust you?"

"I won't let them just yet. They don't know a dollar from a mark." He forced a smile before looking away. Looking at him, I realized that my grandfather was an old man whose hair had silvered and eyes had dimmed. The glow that used to color so many of our conversations about the world financial market was missing. I blamed it on the death of Grandfather Xia, for I knew that deep down the two had loved and admired each other. Their egos had just gotten in the way. Nothing was the same anymore with the general's death.

One day a report was printed by the government daily news that a whopping 20 million US dollars were missing from the central bank. Next Grandfather stopped going to the bank. His Mercedes-Benz lay idle in the garage, and he started reading Japanese comic books, a passion from his youth, to pass time. Mother and Father admonished me not to bother Grandfather with any questions about the missing funds. It would only insult his dignity and honor as the most trusted moneyman in Asia. Something must have happened, someone must have stolen it, or maybe it was just one big fat lie meant to chase Grandfather out of his governorship. In the old days, he would have called Chairman Mao directly and everything would have been cleared, but there was no Chairman Mao anymore. Things were not the same, and that worried me.

The rest of the summer, at my insistence, I tagged along with Father. The headquarters of the biggest army in the world was the utter opposite of the central bank. It was deader than death. In every meeting that I was allowed to sit in with Father's top men, the word "downsizing" kept popping up.

Generals dreamed about war. It was in their bones to smell the fishiness of blood, which stirred them from one battle to another. The piercing sound of the bugle, the cranking of the tanks, the itching caress of wild grass during an ambush, and the abandoning toast of victory were far cries now. Lazy armies were the worst armies. I was surprised, but not shocked, to see some of Father's men show up at meetings with hangovers. They had nothing to do. No border disputes. Even the worst enemy, Taiwan, wanted to do business with the Mainland. The Cold War was over. So drink, celebrate. As Father told me, some of the military men never stopped celebrating.

The meetings now were all about how to fight the new crop of legislators who were attempting to cut the military budgets. "It's the end of us," the army men cried. "We built this nation. Now that they don't need us, they're dumping us. Who suggested the cut? Tell us who, General Long, and we'll take care of them."

"I walked that fucking Long March with our late Chairman Mao. Doesn't that count for anything?" said one army veteran.

"My army has become state construction workers involved in meaningless labor," China's northeast regional chief said. "Just the other day, we were requested to sweep the streets for a parade celebrating a joint venture between Ford Motors and China's number one automobile factory. What are we now? Janitors for the capitalism we were taught to fight only a few years back when Mao was around?" He looked at the others indignantly.

"My men are now deep-sea-fishing experts," the navy commander joked.

"And mine are performing aerial stunts as a tourist attraction for the Guilin region," said the air force commander.

Every day it was the same complaints. I noticed Father looking more and more despondent. The morale of his men affected him greatly; he was the sum of them all. His men were now janitors, street jesters, and construction workers. They began to receive insults in the streets. People, especially children, would shout, "Dumb soldiers!" Only a few years ago, when there were no colleges to go to, the army was the greenest pasture. The green uniform, one size too big, was any youngster's symbol of success. The army took care of you. The lucky few who rose up in the ranks went from a two-pocketed uniform to a four-pocketer, and soon they could even bring their big-footed country bumpkin wives to the cities where the armies gathered and make ladies out of them. Their kids were pampered army brats with food to flaunt. But now it was no longer. Their stipend was a pathetic sum. One could not even afford to buy the cheapest cigarettes in this go-go marketplace. Father felt their pain more deeply than they knew. He was a soldier who would never jettison his men even in the most dire situation. I wondered how far he would go.

As anticipated, a massive military budget cut was announced in the newspapers. When I rushed into his office waving the news in my hand, Father set his jaw. He soon disappeared again for days and returned looking even more troubled. I saw his silhouette pacing his office at home late into the night.

"What is happening to us?" I asked Mother, who was reading a fashion magazine.

"Politics, as I told you, is no good. That's why I wanted you to be an artist or something else. Anything would be better than this. I'm sorry, son, that you have to see all this."

"On the contrary, Mother. I'm curious to see what Father's next move is. I have no doubt that he can resolve it all."

"Back to your studies. This is not for you."

"But it is," I chided. "I still remember you telling me to prepare myself to be a leader some day."

Mother only shook her head and pointed her proud chin at me.

Shento

山头

CHAPTER II

1978
FUJIAN

My life was disturbed again when Black Dog, after years of absence, returned to the campus. Rumor was that after they had plucked out his bad eye and his wound had healed, he escaped from the army hospital to roam along the coastal provinces, robbing the living and stealing from graves. All his ventures and heists ended dreadfully in failure, convincing him that the world at large was not his to conquer and the only place left for him was the place he loathed, the orphanage where he had been dumped at the age of three. So one day he surrendered to the coastal police, who trucked him across three provincial borders to return the scoundrel back where he belonged.

Black Dog no longer walked around with the same swagger. A noticeable addition to his rebel wardrobe, a shabby army leather jacket, was a black patch over his right eye. Life beyond must have been a paradise for him, as he looked radiant and stronger than ever. Due to the twisted system of the school, Black Dog returned to room 1234, where he lived before. We said nothing to each other. There were no handshakes, no looks exchanged. Though it was calm like the morning sea, I knew that trouble was in store for me. I had seen Black Dog's two crippled friends shooting dark looks my way with the return of their one-eyed boss.

That night, Black Dog skipped curfew and did not return until midnight. I had drifted off with a knife under my pillow, only to be awoken as the door squeaked and the bunk bed shook.

The following morning at breakfast, I saw Sumi surrounded by her girlfriends. They whispered as they huddled together, looking tense like a flock of frightened chicks. Sumi ran to me when she saw me. She pulled me into a quiet corner and clutched my arm tightly.

"Are you all right?" I asked.

"No. Trouble is beginning all over again for the poor girls with Black Dog back."

"What happened?"

"Dog and his friends came to our dorm and took one of the girls to the garden, where they raped her last night."

"What? Weren't there any guards?"

"They're not any better. Last year two girls who became pregnant were sent away to get abortions. They had been raped by the guards."

"That's awful!" I felt my blood rush to my head. "How's the girl? Who is she? Is she one of your friends?"

"It was Ai Lan. She bled a great deal. Now she just wants to die. I cared for her all night."

"That bastard! If he dares so much as touch any of you again, I'm going to take his left eye out."

She began to cry.

"Don't cry, Sumi, I am here. You have nothing to worry about."

The loudspeaker crackled and the much-hated voice of the principal rattled the roof of the dining hall. "Two ships have just arrived. For the next couple of days, school will be canceled until all the tuna are unloaded. Boys and girls, remember, your tuition and food have to be paid for. It is payback time."

There were loud hisses and rude curses among the crowd, which were only stopped when the guards' clubs landed on students' heads. I had no desire to go to school today anyway. I was filled with hatred for Black Dog. The wind by the sea and the salty air were better to lessen my emotions and forget about the cruelty of the world. That morning, I hauled a record fifty barrows of tuna from the dock without any rest. At noon, a sailor from the tall ship, the *Star,* tossed a candy bar from the deck and told me that I had done a good job. The man had a nice smile and a thick beard. Munching on the candy, I waved back to him and bowed my head in thanks.

I continued to work through lunch. By sunset, I had hauled a total of 150 barrows. When I wheeled the last load from the dock, the sailors were sitting on the deck, worshipping the sunset with beer and cigars. They burst into applause and a round of catcalls, which made me blush from head to toe and my aches disappear. As I ducked my head and pushed the barrow away from the dock, I heard a voice from the deck. "Come, young man, join us for a drink. We'll take you away from this hellhole!" The sailors burst into another round of laughter.

Whether he meant it or not, the last part of the invitation stopped me. I turned and looked back at the high deck. The sailors were waving with their bottles. The flag on the mast flapped in the sea breeze, and seagulls circled around the pinnacle of the pole, trying to find a landing but getting blown away by the gale. For a long moment I thought the most dangerous thought I had avoided since receiving General Long's letter.

Away, far away!

I turned and forced myself to walk back to the dormitory. When I returned to my room, Black Dog was sprawled out on his bed, smoking. His eye patch was off. The red hole of his socket resembled a cavity left in the earth after a tree had been uprooted.

"How do you like my rotten eye, darkie?" Black Dog said.

"I'm glad for you."

"Hah! Why is that?"

"Because you still have the other one."

"What's that supposed to mean? You ruined my life, now you'll have to pay!" Black Dog shouted and jumped up from his bed, his spittle flying all over.

I reached under my pillow, my eyes fixed on Dog's solo orb.

"Just you wait," Black Dog leered. "We'll start with your girl, then you, one by one."

"If you touch Sumi, I will kill you. That's a promise, I swear." I pulled a blunt and rough-edged knife out of my pillow and waved it at Dog, who knocked it out of my hand.

Black Dog, bigger and taller, clutched my throat, squeezing tightly. I used one hand to grip his Adam's apple. At the same time, I plunged my knee into his crotch, sending him flying into the door holding his balls. Dog ran out of the door bent low, cursing and screaming. My body felt like a sack of wet sand after the day's extra work. I collapsed and soon drifted off, still holding the handle of the knife. At midnight, I heard a knock on my door. It was Mei-Li, one of Sumi's friends. "Shento, you've got to come. Something terrible has happened!"

I jumped out of bed. "What is it?"

"Dog and his friends have taken Sumi. They're under the pine tree now."

I darted out of my room with the knife in my belt, and told Mei-Li to go back to her room and not make any noise. I ran in the moonlight as fast as I could to the fish plant, broke the window, and grabbed a coil of wet rope, which I hung around my neck. Then, as silently as possible, I ran in the soft grass, my back low, until I reached the edge of the garden. The ancient pine tree was like an old man with long beards hanging down from its branches and twigs, providing shade from the moonlight with its canopy of leaves.

On all fours, I crawled along the short wall around the garden, my ears pricked, listening for every sound. In the darkness, I saw three cigarette lights dancing but couldn't locate Sumi. Then I heard her. Her faint cries were muffled and blurred. It was Sumi, my dear Sumi. I almost jumped out. My blood was boiling and my temples throbbed with the fire of hatred, but I forced my head to clear. I only had one chance at surprise. I had to attack them where they were the most vulnerable. I heard her weak cry for help again.

"Shut up!" one rough voice said.

"I'm going first. My big cock can't wait for her pretty ass anymore." It was Black Dog's voice.

"Yeah, let's do her," said a third voice. They sounded a little drunk.

"You animals!" Sumi shrieked. Hearing the sound of fists hitting flesh,

I climbed over the short wall. Three figures stood under a low hanging branch of the pine tree. Hugging the trunk with my limbs, I climbed upward and crept noiselessly along the branch. The breeze rustled the leaves, covering my movements.

I was almost above the thugs when the moon came out from behind the clouds. What I saw stabbed me like a thousand knives. The two crippled boys were holding down Sumi, who was pushed facedown over a short wall. Dog was behind her, moving at a frenzied speed, letting out animal cries of ecstasy. His pants were down to his knees.

I trembled, my head burning and heart racing. I made a loop out of my wet rope, then I jumped like a mountain cat and landed on Dog's head. The two of us crashed to the ground. I looped Dog's head with the rope and jerked it tight. With a swift move, I pulled the other end of the rope that hung over the branch, hauling Dog off his feet high into the air, and quickly tied the rope around the trunk. Dog dangled, kicking and fuming, clawing at the rope frantically, but his breath was cut off and soon his tongue slipped out of his foamy mouth.

I chased after the two cripples, who had run only a few yards. I caught one of them and plunged my knife into his back. The other one had run a little farther, but he was no match for my long strides. I caught him and spun him around. Speaking no words as the cripple begged, I sliced the knife across his neck before pushing him out of my way.

Slowly, I stumbled back to where Sumi was lying at the bottom of the wall and collapsed beside her. "I kept my promise, Sumi," I said in a small but firm voice. "I killed them all." I said it like the closing of a ritual.

In a tiny, trembling voice, she whispered, "Thank you."

"Don't thank me. Are you all right?" I picked up her hand and held it in mine.

"Please, leave me," she said hoarsely. "I am impure now. Go somewhere far."

"I love you! I still do." I burst into painful sobs, mourning an invaluable loss, the loss of the most innocent and beautiful.

"Shento, you will always be my first love, but you can take back your promise of love. I will forgive you. You are free to find a new love in the world."

I cradled her in my arms and kissed her cold and quivering lips. "I need you," I said in a strained voice.

"I feel so dirty." Tears trickled down her face. "Make me clean, please. If you will have me, I swear to the mother moon that I be wedded to you in the grace of her embrace." Sumi took off her torn blouse, helped me unbutton my pants, and touched my manhood hesitantly. Even so, I swelled in her hands. Carefully, she took me inside her. We were one now, our eyes closed, our hands searching each other. I trembled at her touch, awed by the pleasure and love that could come from such a coupling. We moved in gentle rhythm and harmony while the moon shone shyly until I quickened and collapsed in her arms. Entwined, we slept.

Life could have ceased and it would not have mattered to us. I had no idea how much time passed. It was Sumi who woke up first. She heard footsteps coming from the sandy soccer field. "Shento, Shento," she whispered urgently, shaking my shoulder. "You have to hide somewhere. You have to run, the guards are coming."

I rubbed my eyes and sat up. The distant rush of hurried footsteps came closer with every passing second.

"Go!" Sumi cried.

"Go where?"

"Somewhere far away."

"I can't leave you, Sumi!"

"You must! For me! For us!" She embraced me tightly. "If I don't see your body floating in the sea, I will always think of you as alive and wait for your return."

"Someday I will come for you."

Sumi kissed me for the last time before pushing me away. "I will distract them." Throwing on her torn clothes, Sumi limped to the other end of the garden, where she waved and screamed. The guards rushed in her direction with flashlights and dogs. She began to cry harder, telling what had happened in an incoherent manner. When they finally understood, Sumi fell into their arms and had to be carried to where the dead bodies were. The guards saw Black Dog's body dangling from the pine tree, his two cronies dead, and a bloody knife lying beside them, which one of the guards immediately recognized as mine. They blew a nasty whistle. The campus lights all snapped on.

"Where is the killer? Where is Shento?"

Sumi told the guards that I had gone back to my room. Some went to search my room but returned empty-handed. By the time the guards initiated a dragnet and the students all woke, I had crawled through a dark open field and reached the tall wall erected around the school at the edge of the deep sea. I knew too well that the sea would be my surest way to death, but I had little choice; by now I had learned that there was even less chance of escaping on land with the guards, the dogs, and the bottleneck leading to the mainland. To try by land was to fail. Only by doing the unthinkable would I have a chance of survival.

I began to climb the tall wall, which was made of chunky rough rocks from a local quarry. It was a good twenty feet straight up. My well-formed muscles from the daily toil allowed me to dangle and swing my body upward. I almost lost my grip when I heard more piercing whistles blown. If they found me on the wall, the bullets would spray me to a bloody mess. In a nervous struggle, I climbed the last ten feet at twice the speed, only to find my fingers punctured by barbed wire buried on top of the wall. I sucked on my bleeding fingers and stayed low on the wall, trying to determine where the tuna boats were. My heart jumped as I saw a light on the *Star.* A refreshing sea breeze swept my face.

Just as I was about to dive, the lights on the wall lit up. I had little time to think or respond. I ducked my head and plunged into the dark sea thirty feet below. The contact was painful, for I had little experience diving. I sank an eternal ten feet into the black water before emerging and reorienting myself toward the ship a few hundred yards away. The water was pinching cold. Somehow I swam with my bleeding fingers in my mouth, paddling with my good arm. A few times my toes were nibbled by unimaginable creatures down below. I kicked violently to get rid of them and thought about what the guard had told us about big fish and human-eating mammals in the waters.

Breathless, I reached the shadow of the ship and floated in the water, assessing a way to get on it. It looked impossible. The ship was about another thirty feet high and there was no visible way of climbing onto it. I swam around until I saw a little lifeboat fastened to the ship by a thick rope. I looked up and listened for any sounds coming from the deck. There were none. I grabbed the edge of the small boat and climbed up to it. Then I grabbed the rope. It felt solid enough for me to scale the next thirty feet. Though my muscles ached from ascending the wall and my fingers were raw, I inched up slowly and surely and only had to rest once midway before reaching the deck. I didn't climb over right away. There might be guards or sleepless sailors. I dangled on the rope for a second before raising myself eye level with the deck. Nothing. As I hooked one foot over, a pair of feet came into view. Quickly, I dropped back over the side, dangling by the rope. A sailor hummed as he walked by with a rifle in his arms. When he turned the corner, I jumped over noiselessly and disappeared into an open hold.

Tan

唐

CHAPTER 12

1978
BEIJING

The December winds from the Mongolian steppes made Beijing bleak, shrouding the city in a sandy blanket. Food was tasteless and the piano was but a sad affair. I missed Grandfather Xia. My life was empty without the man's roaring laughter and earthy humor. I had never been thrilled about how his mouth often smelled of garlic, but even that I missed now.

I looked at his old photos and saw the one that had been Grandfather's favorite: me holding a baby rifle, chasing him while he raised his arms in surrender. I smiled, my eyes shiny with tears. Only a grandson whom he so loved could get the proud man to surrender. That man who had been captured more than a few times in his military career would rather die than give in. No wonder he had lost most of his teeth by the age of thirty. He always joked about the fact that he had never lost his tongue. I would ask him why, and the wise old man would say because the tongue was soft while teeth were hard, and sometimes it didn't hurt to be a little soft, a little more flexible than just hard charging all the time.

I felt nostalgic about all things pertaining to Grandfather Xia. I remembered one National Day at Tiananmen Square when he reviewed his troops. He proudly carried me to the platform, and we stood right next to Chairman Mao, whose tummy looked like a little mountain. I remembered that day well—the sea of greenness, tens of thousands of men marching by, shouting, "Long live Chairman Mao!" I wondered why no one was shouting "Long live General Xia!" and was hushed quickly by my grandfather, who warned me never to repeat that question to anyone, ever. Mao was the chosen one, Grandfather said, while he was just a serviceman, a soldier, working for the people of the country. I was smart even then. I knew it was not true. But I did not say so.

On an impulse, I asked my driver to take me to the south gate of Tiananmen Square. December in Beijing was cold and windy, especially for one standing in unobstructed spaces like the ancient square. But it was just what I wanted. I strolled until I reached the northern gate to the Forbidden City. I was counting my steps leisurely when I saw a crowd, one hundred thick, all dressed in heavy cotton padded coats, standing by the foot of the city wall. They were attentive and seemed to care nothing about the dropping temperature and the howling chill from Siberia.

Curious, I blew a mouthful of hot air into my hands and strolled toward the crowd. At the edge, I stood on my toes and stretched my neck, catching a glimpse of a stunningly attractive girl with sweeping long hair and a slender figure. She wore a pair of blue jeans and a red turtleneck sweater that contoured to her body. Her elegant hands waved in the air to emphasize her speech, which was delivered with a slight, almost unrecognizable southern accent.

"Democracy is the air that you breathe. All men are born equal . . ." The wind blew away the tail of her sentence. ". . . we need a constitution that will bind us all, not dictators who tell us what to do and what not to do . . ."

As I came closer, I was shocked to realize that the girl was none other than my English teacher, Miss Yu. From the bits and pieces, I could tell that she was talking about democracy in America and how China should follow its example and give people the freedom of speech. At the end, she posted her speech on the wall next to other postings under a large section titled *Ming Zu Chiang,* the Democracy Wall. She left with a young man on a motorcycle before I could yell out to her. I could see why they were leaving in a hurry—policemen were approaching.

I rushed over and scanned the speech. Miss Yu had signed her name in English as "Virgin" with a Chinese translation by it.

A larger crowd closed in to read her writing. Some even pulled out pens and pencils, straining their heads to copy it word for word. I asked a young woman, "Why are you copying it?"

"My father can't fall asleep without reading the installment of the day. Virgin is a good writer."

My heart was warmed by such outpouring of affection for someone I knew so well.

"I know her personally."

"You know Virgin?"

"Yes."

"Nobody knows her. She comes and goes mysteriously. We don't even know what she does for a living."

Just as I was about to try to convince the woman that I did know Virgin, the policemen began dispersing the crowd with their sticks.

"Go home! Do not gather in public places without permits!" a policeman shouted.

"Why not?" someone said.

"It is the regulation! Who asked that? What is your name?" a policeman demanded, scaring the speaker. He ripped all the papers off the wall, tore them into pieces, and said, smiling, "Now you go home. There is nothing to copy."

I left, but the picture of Virgin lingered in my mind long afterward. I looked at Miss Yu in an utterly different light the following day during our lessons. I smiled mysteriously and wrote the word "virgin" on a piece of paper and asked her, "What is the meaning of this word?"

"Why do you ask?"

"I saw it on the Democracy Wall."

"You did?"

"Yes, and I love the writing."

Miss Yu smiled and lowered her voice. "There is a reason why I write under a pen name, do you understand?"

"You're safe with me."

"I know I am."

"On one condition."

"What is it?"

"Can you bring me to your meetings? I'd like to learn more about democracy."

"You, the son of China's most conservative military chief?"

I nodded.

She smiled and gave me a hug. That night I dreamed about Miss Yu in a manner far too embarrassing to ever discuss with her or anyone at all.

THOUGH MOTHER THOUGHT Miss Yu had the fatal defect of being young and attractive, she nonetheless felt the girl was harmless. Miss Yu's charitable spirit as a volunteer, leaving the comfort of Hong Kong, was also endearing. The driver who picked her up in the mornings and drove her home in the afternoons knew only bits and pieces of her life in Beijing, not enough to prick Mother's suspicion, who by now was much pleased by her son's progress. So, on the eve of the Chinese New Year, when Miss Yu sent me an invitation to a costume party, I was readily allowed to go. I decided to dress like a cowboy, an image my teacher had painted for me in one of my lessons about the Wild West and Buffalo Bill. I wore faded jeans, a black Stetson hat, and a tiger skin vest that one of Father's comrades had made out of a white cat from the mountains of southern China. Mother tied a red square into a necktie, and Father gave me his gun holster to hang around the waist.

Miss Yu picked me up in a taxi. She wore a short red dress with high heels. Instead of shoulder straps, she had a matching silk shawl. We looked at each other and laughed.

"Hello, cowboy! You're very handsome," she exclaimed.

"You look very . . . female."

She laughed. "Did you mean to say sexy?"

"Yes . . . But who are you supposed to be?"

"I am myself."

"But you said it is a costume party where you're supposed to dress as someone else."

"Correct. But you see, in the West, women have the prerogative of being capricious and changing their minds freely. Men follow rules."

There was something sweet and childish about her that night. She was open and laughed a lot.

"Tan," she said as the taxi accelerated, "I am sure you'll like the party tonight. I want you to meet some interesting people."

"I can't wait."

The taxi left the congested streets of Beijing, which remained, despite the howling wind, festive. Colorful lanterns festooned the doorways and firecrackers burst incessantly in the chilly night air. A light snow sifted to the ground, quickly vanishing under the feet of noisy children chasing each other down the narrow streets. We rode along a bumpy dirt road, shooting through a wheat field to a distant village. In the middle of nowhere emerged a farmhouse. Two blinking lights flickered. An old man stood by the door, smoking his pipe.

We walked hand in hand across the dirt yard. Her palm was warm and soft. The darkness shaded my blush.

The old man bowed to Miss Yu and opened the door for us. Inside was another world—gentle lights in quiet shade, soft Western music playing in the background. The furniture was rough, wooden. Along the far wall was a typical northern bed called a *kang,* built from dirt with a stove burning underneath. About twenty people sat on the spacious *kang* with their shoes off. The atmosphere was comfortable and mysterious. Also on top of the bed was a short-legged table where food and drinks sat. Everyone stood to greet us.

"Come meet Tan, everybody. This is Law Professor Ko from Beijing University, dressed as Lincoln. This is our famous singer Lu, the writer Lin, and . . ." She continued around the room. When she was done, Miss Yu said, "Tan is a bright young man and someone to watch in the near future. Now, shall we begin our meeting?"

As we sat down, I asked her quickly, "Why didn't you tell me that this was a political meeting rather than a party?"

"It was a half-lie to get past your mother. Do you mind?"

"Not at all."

Much of the meeting was about the formation of their democratic party and the declaration of its agenda. They heatedly discussed the detailed activities, a magazine, a newsletter, and future branches in other cities. Miss Yu was unanimously elected the chairwoman and the editor in chief of the magazine, whose title the crowd argued over vehemently. When the subject of budgeting was introduced, silence fell. But everyone was charged, nonetheless. With such energy, all the people red-faced and glowing, I couldn't help but think of it as almost a religious experience. Future China might well have been born right before my eyes. Yet I felt a tinge of discomfort that this crowd of freethinking idealists might be undoing the foundation upon which my family was built. I quickly dismissed the inappropriate thought and let myself admire the glowing Miss Yu with a touch of possessiveness.

"Now we party," she said, pulling me off the *kang*.

We danced and drank and chatted. Miss Yu was especially radiant. She danced with Professor Ko and leaned on his shoulders as they moved in a gentle circle. I felt a slight pang of jealousy. Could the professor be her lover; was he the reason why was she dressed so sexily? The two looked unmatched, beauty and the beast, but the look on Miss Yu's face convinced me that she was in love with the man.

As we made our way home at midnight, Ko shared our taxi. Miss Yu kissed me on the cheek and they dropped me off and drove off together. I gently touched the spot where her lips had brushed my skin as I saw their shadows in the back window merging. I felt both happy and sad. The sense of loss accompanied me as I fell asleep that night.

Shento

山头

CHAPTER 13

1978
JIUSHAN ISLES, EAST CHINA

The hold was wet and slippery, and still reeked of the fresh tuna that had been unloaded. I landed on my butt and scuttled to a corner hidden in shadow. No sooner had I settled in when I found myself not the only living creature in the ten-by-ten-foot hold. Half a dozen large ship rats, armed with shiny little eyes and sharp whiskers, took me for the last piece of tuna and started nipping furiously at my wet feet, hands, buttocks, and thighs. The bloodstains on my body added frenzy to the craze. One of them even climbed up my shoulder and gazed at me eye to eye with the most dangerous curiosity.

The rats did not scare me. Instead, I decided to make friends with them. I put one hand out and let the climber on my shoulder walk along it to the tip of my fingers and back. When the little fellow repeated the short journey to my hand, I closed my grip and threw the rat against the wall, which resulted in a sad loud squeak before it fell to the floor, dead and silent. Sensing that there was a larger force at work in the darkness here, the rats all scrambled out through a hole in the bottom of the hold and left.

In the quiet, all I could hear was the sound of waves and the occasional barks of search dogs a great distance away. They must still be searching for me. Would they come to the ship to inquire about my hiding here? If and when they found me in this tiny hold, it would take just two bullets and I would be as dead as the rat lying on the floor.

I prayed and prayed to Buddha, asking him to let me survive the night and at daybreak take me to any port on the face of this earth, any at all, no matter how hard and long the journey might be. With my hands piously clasped before me, I leaned weakly against the fishy, slimy wall of the cargo hold. Fear and loneliness engulfed me.

Time passed and the sea breeze intensified, rocking the ship like a cradle on the soft waves. The mast sang the song of a windmill in full swing. The serenade of nature soothed me like a tired infant and my eyelids grew heavier and heavier. Trying to stay alert, I pinched my thighs, tickled my nostrils with a strand of hair, and finally smeared my face with the gooey slimy substance collected on the wooden floor, the pungency of which could kill a dog under ordinary circumstances. But I only managed to keep my eyes open for another few minutes before I drifted off into a nightmare of fright and ghostly scare.

When morning came, I was awoken by a thunderous noise crashing down from above deck. I blinked, only to witness the pouring of sandy gravel down to the bottom of my hold from the head of a crane. The dust that flew in the bright sunbeams almost suffocated me. I pulled up my shirt and covered my head while crawling swiftly to a safer corner. Through the buttonholes of my shirt, I saw with increasing alarm the speed at which the noisy gravel was piling up in the center and filling the space in the hold. In no time, the area would be filled to the brim and I would either be exposed to the sailors and caught or buried forever under the sharp pieces of rock.

The gravel stopped for a glorious moment and I could hear what seemed to be curt instructions being given to the crane operator. When the pouring resumed, I dodged quickly to avoid burial by the blinding, flying gravel. At another interval, the crane operator mentioned the name of a place, Jiushan Isles Navy Base, but I did not catch the question to the answer.

From my geography class, one of my favorite subjects, I knew well that the Jiushan Isles were a group of islands cast at random like a handful of pearls in the South China Sea, forming an ideal frontier for the coastal province of China. They were the base of China's proudest Pacific fleet, overlooking the Taiwan Straits, the Philippine Islands, Japan, South Korea, and Hong Kong.

It must be their destination! It made great sense, for Jiushan had the best fishing seas along Asia's Pacific coast. Tuna was shipped from there and the ships returned with building materials—a perfect barter in this most inefficient state-controlled economy. I could not conceal my excitement. Maybe I could join the navy there and navigate ships. My peril was temporarily dwarfed by this new prospect and my will to survive doubled.

When the last pouring was done and the lid shut on the hold, I thought I was going to die; the space left in the hold was only enough for me to lie flat. There was no opening in the lid. Light was shut out entirely. In darkness, I tried breathing shallowly at first. When I felt air trickling in from somewhere, I breathed a deeper breath. I could smell the sea. I could live! I could breathe!

I lay quietly, waiting patiently for the ship to start the journey. After hours of waiting, the ship began to stir, tremble, and finally move slowly with a steady motion through the beating waves. Lying on my back with the little gravel pieces digging into my skin, I did not feel the pain or the slight discomfort. On the contrary, my heart was filled with gratitude to Buddha. Hot tears trickled down my cheeks. The orphanage school was behind me now and so was Sumi, my sweetheart.

I had never felt her love more closely and more vividly than now. I promised myself that one day I would come back to fetch her in the grand style of heroes whom I had read about in books. That is, of course, if I lived and became a somebody, which I had little doubt of, even in these circumstances.

I slept and woke and slept again. The sea wind stiffened and softened and the ship encountered a heavy thunderstorm. Raindrops hit the lid of the hold like stones hitting an empty tin can. Some of the raindrops leaked through the seams of the lid and wet my shirt along my shoulders. I caught a few drops of the water and fed them to my mouth. The ship tossed against tall waves caused by the storm and I was shoved back and forth, making me retch with dry heaves. When the storm passed and the wind subdued, the journey resumed its gentle rocking on a calm sea.

As for my hunger and thirst, I had to follow the old axiom of constraint and tolerance my old parents had taught me as a young child. When hungry, draw a cake in your head and pretend to enjoy it. When thirsty, imagine walking among a green field of ripened berries. But such dreaming about the unattainable only intensified my urges, causing my stomach to growl and rumble in vain.

Days went by and nights passed before I felt the ship slowly come to a stop. I heard the voices of sailors. Soon they opened the lid. An old sailor's jaw dropped open upon seeing me squeezed in the corner, covered in dirt. Waving frantically, the old man shouted for his crew, who rushed over and picked me up from the hold. The captain ordered one of the ship hands to wash me down, but I tried to run away. The sailors rounded me up and settled me down while the young ship hand cast a bucket into the sea, hauled up a full load of it, and dumped it on me, which elicited a round of rowdy catcalls from the sailors. I dripped and shook with delight from the refreshing water.

"Hey, aren't you the boy from the reform school?" the captain exclaimed.

"It's the murderer—he got away on our ship!" another shouted.

"Let's turn him in."

I begged the sailors to please help me, but instead they escorted me off the ship to an old three-story brick building guarded by two navy officers. The sailors handed me over to a tall officer, who led me to a small cell that had TEMPORARY DETENTION painted on the door. I was given a prison uniform, then taken to a hearing room where one old navy officer sat and smoked, filling the space with the pungent odor. On his desk a nameplate read JUDGE.

"What is the charge?" the fat judge asked the officer.

"Escape from a reform school in Fujian after killing three classmates."

"Great achievement at such a tender age," the judge said wryly. "How do you plead, young man?"

"Not guilty," I said firmly. "I was justified in the killing. They were raping an innocent girl, Judge!"

"Of course they were." The man waved annoyingly as if it was a lie he had heard one time too many. He shook his head and ordered casually, "You've got nothing that hard labor cannot cure. Retrial after three months. Case is dismissed until then." He slammed his gavel and the trial was over.

I should have received a bullet in my head the day I got to Jiushan. In the simplistic shotgun justice of Communism, I was guilty and might as well be dead. My escape even doubled my penalty. But there was an ordinance in the locality that superseded even the constitution of China, which read that there could be an indefinite stay of execution, even for death-penalty convicts. The reason was hardly humanitarian. Rather, it was a forced result of the pressing labor shortage there. A deep-sea military port and other infrastructures such as railroads and highways were being built. Prisoners were perfect slaves—why kill them?

The following day, bright and early after a breakfast of flat bread, I boarded a truck loaded with other laborers. The driver slapped my shoulder and said, "You are *not* going to enjoy this, young man." He was right. I was one of thousands digging the soil and carrying dirt in bamboo baskets for a mile to dump into a wet land by the sea, making a foundation for a port. The hours were long and the work backbreaking. The sun was hot and humid, and along the lines where the laborers marched, angry and abrupt guards stood with whips, ready to strike anytime they detected anyone slacking. There were many laborers, but we looked tiny compared to the size of the undertaking, like busy ants scurrying around carrying food before a rain came.

The first week, I burned like a boiled crab. The second week, my skin peeled like a snake. By the third week, I boasted a tan like a shiny eel from the sea, especially when sweat soaked me from head to toe. I was only seventeen but stood a towering six feet, with broad shoulders and a narrow waist like my father. My head was shaved like the other prisoners and that baldness made my strong features stand out even more prominently. But what impressed others the most was my work. When the rest walked, I ran; and when they ran, I flew. I held the record for hauling the most dirt off to the wet land. After observing the slow parade of tired laborers scurrying back and forth inefficiently, I took the risk of suggesting to the head guard that if all the laborers were to line up and pass the bucket down an assembled line, it would be a lot faster, and no one could be lazy without causing a breakdown. The next day, ten lines were formed from the hill, reaching to the sea. The same amount of work was accomplished three times faster. I cheered people on with mountain labor songs as I passed out bowls of tea to the laborers in the line. My enthusiasm even affected the guards, who usually struck us. They sang with us, and some even offered smokes to me during my break.

Another trial was held for me nine months later. The government prosecutor read his charge without any expression: "Three murders and one account of attempted escape from justice."

The same judge yawned at the accusation. Then, mocking the wax-like state attorney, he lauded my hard work. I was happy my work ethic had been noticed but disappointed when the judge declared that the case would be retried in another three months while he contacted the reform school for more information to verify my crime.

When the second retrial was just weeks away, a fire of anxiety burned in my soul like the scorching sun at its mightiest. I was facing the biggest trial of my lifetime. I firmly believed that I had killed those rapists justly and rightly, in the same way a thief's hand should be chopped and a rapist's eyes should be popped so that they would not repeat their sins. I believed I had a strong case, and if I could present it in a convincing manner before the fat judge, maybe—no, certainly—he would listen to reason and rule in my favor after weighing the evidence.

Using my charm, I begged the guard in my section of the cell to borrow all the books he could from the library on China's penal code and anything ever written on criminal law. What the guard brought back was pathetically scanty. One penal-code book was unimpressively thin and looked like it had been chewed by rats and lived in by termites. But what I found in its contents was even more unsettling. In its preface, I was told that a criminal, once taken into custody based on suspicion or circumstantial evidence, has a burden to prove his innocence. He was presumed guilty until proven innocent. The argument of self-defense would only be a weak tactic disliked by judges. Besides the judge's adjudicative power to reach a final verdict, he also had the investigatory capacity to collect evidence and build a case in the manner that pleased him. Judges were gods in this case. I would live or die all according to the whims of that fat robed slob. I shuddered at the thought.

I leafed through the procedural matters and quickly turned to the section under death penalties. I was not surprised to find that if I were to be charged with three murders, my sentence would be immediate execution with two bullets in my head. I also had to bear the cost of the bullets. What I also found, to my relief, was that a rapist was likewise chargeable with the death penalty. Hope rose within me. I had indeed killed the three bastards in an heroic act to save a rape victim. I should be lauded by this legal system since I had saved the country not only the bullets, which could be used for its enemies, but also the tedious legal proceedings. I was confident that the judge would listen to this plea and let me go if he were presented with evidence from Sumi, the rape victim in this case.

In the dim light of the moon, I took out the stub of a pencil that I had filched from a napping clerk. I scribbled on rough toilet paper a letter to the girl I missed day and night.

> *Dear Sumi:*
>
> *Thousands of li* away, after an eternity of a journey in darkness at sea, I find myself locked in the damp dark cell of a prison. It is not the place in which I hoped to write to you. Nor is this the tone that I would choose to address my dearest darling, but here I am begging you to do me a favor that might save me from the cruelty of death at seventeen, before all the dreams that we have dreamed can become reality.*
>
> *I am facing a court hearing soon for the possible charge of murder of those three animals who savagely attacked you that unforgettable night. If I could prove to the judge that the killings were prompted by my most justifiable urge to defend you, my*

---

*A Chinese unit equivalent to a mile.

little soul, I do not see why the honorable judge wouldn't sympathize with me, who has so far been praised as an outstanding worker on a huge navy construction project.

Please write in your most vivid and truthful manner the events of that night, which might be embarrassing and hurtful to recall, and mail it to the judge's chambers.

No matter how far I am from you, I feel your love close to my heart. No matter what dire condition I have placed myself in, I feel it only to be my honor and good fortune to be able to save you. Love is only an understatement, Sumi. What I feel for you is the greatest of all love. Simply put, if I do have to die for you, I shall do it with a smile.

Oh, how I long for you. Especially in the face of only despair, darkness, and the possible end of life!

Love always,
Shento

P.S. If I sound pathetic and petty, please do forgive me. Also, remember to write to the judge, not me. Here is his address.

I added the last bit of information and fell asleep with the letter on my chest. The next day, I used all my meager savings from the cheap labor—twenty fens a day—and bought cigarettes to bribe a guard to deliver the letter.

On the day of my trial, I asked to bring along my penal code and stood firmly and straight before the fat judge, who averted his eyes.

"How do you plead, criminal Shento?" the judge asked.

"I am not guilty," I said firmly.

"You know our penal code calls for leniency if one is honest and is forward with confession, and severe punishment if one is found lying to avoid conviction." The judge stared at me. "Now that you understand our policy, please tell me on what grounds do you plead not guilty?"

"On the grounds of defending the rape victim, Judge. I killed the three because they were raping one Sumi Wo, my classmate in the orphanage school. Under the penal code of the People's Republic of China, rape is also a death-penalty crime. If one is justified in causing the death of the rapist in action, he should be exonerated for the death he has justly caused."

The judge was caught off guard by my rendition of the criminal law. He frowned at me and asked in a grave tone, "Do you have any evidence to prove such a defense?"

"I believe you do, your honor." My tone was calm and confident. "I managed to send a request to the rape victim a month ago, and asked that she write an account and have it sent to your attention. Under China's judicial system, a judge's role is not only adjudicatory but investigatory in nature." I quoted the line I had read in the penal code.

"I did receive a letter." His eyes narrowed and mouth pursed.

"So then, please, let me free, your honor," I pleaded, hopefully.

The crowd in the usually quiet room became even quieter. The judge looked around, collected himself, then slammed down his gavel forcefully.

"Young man, it angers me that you are lying right before the court about the events of the night that the deaths occurred. Miss Sumi Wo did write a letter to me." He held the letter in his sausage fingers. "But she was never attacked or raped. In fact, she claims that you killed them out of personal revenge."

"No, Judge," I said, shocked. "It could not be. That is a fabrication. The whole school could testify to that."

"Evidence, young man, since you seem to have read up on the law. Rule number one is evidence. Convincing and useful evidence. Your friend Sumi has given you up in this signed letter to me, at your request. This case is therefore decided. Guard!"

"No, please, Judge. Sumi would not lie about me like this."

"No, she would not. She told the truth. Under Penal Code Section 99, you are now sentenced to death to be executed this day on the high sea at noon."

It was as if a bomb had exploded in my head.

"Judge, you've got it all wrong. Sumi would not lie like that. Please let me see her letter."

"Take him out of my court, guards!"

My knees felt weak and my head faint. The words of the death penalty rang like thunder. I struggled like a trapped animal, fighting to get loose. Then I felt a thumping pain on my head as the guard clubbed me with a thick choke stick.

I WAS THROWN to the deck of a navy boat, unconscious, then handcuffed and chained to the stern railing. When they dumped cold water on me, awakening me for my final moments, I threw myself left and right, thrashing like a caught fish.

I am really going to die this time. I have traveled this far just to die like this? Like a pirate, a thief? I screamed, my lungs bursting with anger and desperation.

The officer loaded three bullets in the chamber of an old revolver and took aim at me.

It is over, I thought. I kept my eyes open, wanting to go out seeing this world, however shabby it was. But the officer lowered his gun and shouted, "Is that a necklace you're wearing?" It had slipped out from beneath my shirt in my struggle.

Two sailors stepped forward to remove it. I kicked and fiercely fought them, shouting, "Don't touch it! I want to die with it on! It is my father's."

"Your father's?" a sailor asked.

"Don't listen to him," the other sailor said. "Get it off him."

"No!" I cried, but was subdued by the two men who yanked the necklace off.

"The character *Long* is engraved on it," a sailor said.

"Let me see." The officer examined the necklace. "It's heavy and looks like real silver. What does the character mean, convict?"

"It is my father's family name."

"And who is this daddy of yours?" the officer inquired, curiously.

"General Ding Long."

"Sure, and I am the son of Chairman Mao," the officer scoffed.

"It is cursed! You can have it," I spat. "Ding Long killed my mother and abandoned me as a bastard."

"Well, well, well. Who is to believe you?"

"I don't expect you to believe me. Nobody believes me. I only wish to die now. Come on, shoot me!"

But the sailors seemed intrigued by the story I told. The naval officer weighed the silver necklace in his hand and a wicked smile came to his lips. "Then again, maybe you are telling the truth. We all admire General Ding Long's libido, don't we?" The sailors laughed lewdly.

The officer went below deck to the lower cabin to radio the naval command center on shore. When he returned, the officer wore a somber expression on his face.

"Let me die! Shoot me!" I struggled again and kicked a bucket, sending it rolling.

"I'm afraid we can't do that," the officer said to me and then turned to the sailors. "Untie him."

"Why?" a sailor asked.

"The commander himself is coming to take him away. Hurry up!"

The sailors did what they were told immediately.

Hardly a half hour had lapsed before a much bigger military cruiser arrived. Out rushed three doctors and an army stretcher. They picked me up and raced away.

"Where are you taking me?" I cried. "And why?"

"You ask too many questions," a doctor said, injecting a yellow liquid into my arm. Instantly, all was dark.

Tan

CHAPTER 14

1979
BEIJING

Every month, Miss Yu passed an envelope to me in school. It would contain the newest issue of *Early Spring,* which was the name of her group's magazine. I read the magazines in the secrecy of my bedroom. Miss Yu's writing was poetic and moving. In one issue, she advocated setting up a press to publish books of essays, and even fiction to broaden their organization's readership. A few months later, the first novel was published. It was written by none other than Virgin, about a girl who fights against the constraints laid upon women by society. I hungrily read it through a sleepless night and cried for the heroine. Soon it became a much whispered about sensation through hand copying.

One day Miss Yu appeared in class with dark circles around her eyes. She had been crying.

"What's the matter?" I asked quietly after class.

"Haven't you read?" she whispered, after the last students had left the classroom. "The police have torn down the Democracy Wall and Professor Ko is missing."

"What could have happened to him?"

"Murdered secretly." There was quiet anger in her voice. "What better way for the government to crush our organization?"

"I am so sorry."

"It's not your fault," she said.

My eyes lowered. "But it feels like it is."

The next day, we sat in the classroom without our English teacher. We waited and waited, then the principal came to tell us that Miss Yu had been arrested and was not expected to resume her duties. Stunned, I left the room immediately and asked my driver to take me directly to Father's office at the army headquarters a few blocks away from the school. Layers of armed guards waved me through without any inquiry. The license plate said it all—No. 5. President Heng Tu's was No. 1. I dragged Father out of a meeting.

"Son, what is so urgent that it can't wait?" Father said brusquely in his office.

"I need a special directive from you to save Miss Yu right away."

"Son, I am afraid it is not that simple."

"But it is, Father. She is only a scapegoat. She is a Hong Kong citizen whose legal right is still protected by international law. You should not do anything to her."

"Let me check with the Public Security Ministry." Father reached for the telephone.

"No, Father, there's no time for that. I am asking you for a favor. Free her and send her home. You could forbid her from coming back, but don't harm her in any way. She is my teacher, my friend, and yours, too, Father. We have to protect her."

"Let me think about it tonight."

"Tonight is too late. Please tell me where she is being held."

Father took a deep breath. "She is on her way to Xinjiang."

"China's Siberia?"

"There is nothing I can do right now. It was an order from Heng Tu himself."

"But he listens to you, doesn't he?"

Father looked troubled. "You don't understand."

"I'm very disappointed with you, Father," I said sadly and left. I asked my driver to take me to the Beijing Police Station. Once there I saw the chief himself, but the man would not give a release either, saying that the truck was in Xibei by now. There was only one thing left to do.

I rushed home and went into Father's office. There in the drawer lay the personal jade seal of the highest-ranking officer within the military. Using Father's stationery, I wrote carefully, then pressed the seal at the end of the letter. I studied my handiwork briefly. The writing could easily pass as Father's to an uncanny eye, for since I was young I had made a point of imitating his calligraphy, the flowing southern-grass style. Then I set off to find the military truck on the Xibei highway, the only one heading west. It was hours later when my limousine finally caught up with the dusty truck. The driver swerved our car in front of the truck, forcing the vehicle to the roadside. I jumped down, holding an official order from the commander in chief. At first, the soldiers ignored me.

"Do you know who I am?" I screamed. "And do you know what I am holding in my hand?"

That caught their attention. They studied the document, then my face.

"If you don't hand over that prisoner, I will have my father, the commander in chief, court-martial you!"

The driver read the paper. Recognizing the famous seal, he folded the document, put it in his pocket, and reluctantly released the prisoner to me.

Miss Yu looked solemn and thoughtful. There was no fear in her eyes, though she seemed to have aged. I hugged her, but she froze in my presence. Quickly, I urged her into the limousine and drove her to the train heading for Canton. From there, Hong Kong was only a bridge away. But the train didn't leave for another hour. Night had fallen. Miss Yu was in tears now. She asked me to send the driver away. In the back of the car, she undressed herself and slowly took off my sweater and unzipped my pants.

I was shocked at first, then aroused. Her breasts were firm and full, her skin like silk. She fed her nipples into my mouth and I suckled them hungrily. My heart throbbed with burning desire and my groin felt as if it were about to burst. Miss Yu straddled me. I slipped deep into her and she rode me, her moans abandoned, as if she was dying. Not long after, we both cried out. Then Miss Yu nestled her head under my chin and sighed deeply. I laced my fingers in her hair and held her close.

After we had caught our breath, she stirred and murmured, "You are now a man."

"Is it all right for a student to love his teacher?"

"You are no longer my student." She kissed me tenderly.

"I have loved you for so long." I stroked her breasts. "I wish you never had to leave."

"Come, lover, make me cry again." The words from her sweet mouth were dizzying. I loved her again with even more passion. Our climax was so prolonged that she almost missed the train. Dressing quickly, we ran to the platform, then hugged. She stepped up into the railcar, then the train pulled out of the station and vanished into the night.

Shento

山头

CHAPTER 15

1979

NUMBER 9 ISLAND

My head throbbed with pain, and my stomach walls seemed to be stuck together, I was that hungry. I must have slept for a very long time. The bed squeaked as I turned. My hazy eyes made out a man sitting in a chair, facing me. Around us stood tall walls painted white, without windows.

"Who are you?" I squinted and studied the man's uniform warily.

"That's not important. Aren't you glad to be alive?"

"I guess so. Who gave you the order to save me?"

"I don't know."

"Where's my necklace?"

"I don't know. Sign this," the man ordered. He held out a clipboard with a piece of paper on it.

"What is it?"

"An agreement. Ask no more questions. I will explain later."

I stared hard at the mysterious man for a long moment, then, stretching my right arm, I signed the piece of paper. "Am I still a prisoner?"

"You will be working for us from now on."

"What kind of work do you want me to do?" I asked.

"Worthy work," the man said.

"What if I don't want to work for you?"

"You owe us your life. I have a standing order for your execution, any time, at any location, from the Supreme Court of People's Justice. You have also just pledged your life to our cause, in writing, and vowed your silence regarding your worthy work ahead of you."

"How comforting to know."

"Sarcasm is not welcomed." He pulled his gun out of his holster and placed it on the table beside him.

"Why don't you just shoot me?" I cried.

"I could." The man casually fired two bullets into the ceiling. The shots echoed sharply.

"Now, boy, let's talk more about our worthy work. Your new life has just begun. We will be leaving soon."

"Where am I going?"

"Number Nine Island."

OUR YACHT SPLIT the blue waters of the Pacific, heading into the bosom of the sea. The wind slapped my skin, making it numb like wax, but the smell of the ocean refreshed me. I no longer bothered to ask questions about the mysterious life ahead. I knew they would not be answered by the man steering the boat. I just wanted to live, for I knew how precious life was, and how quickly it could slip away.

After a long ride on calm waters, a small mountainous island appeared, gleaming against a big yolk sunset. The boat slowed down and maneuvered into a secluded dock, hidden under ancient trees. I was led by a young soldier to a barrackslike brick building, where a middle-aged sergeant with a salt-and-pepper crew cut met me alone. He gestured for me to sit.

"I am Sergeant La, your personal tutor," the man said. "This is a special unit of China's intelligence called Jian Dao, or Sharp Dagger, that few know exists. From now on, you are one of us. You will share that knowledge with nobody beyond this island, and will only bring it to your grave one day." He paused before continuing. "This place is surrounded by water mines and the swirl of the powerful ocean undercurrents. We have our Sharp Daggers everywhere in this world. It is in your best interest to follow our secrecy code.

"Each cadet here is trained individually, according to his abilities and, of course, potential. You will be taught all aspects of your life—your new life, that is—and all forms of combat. And you will learn to use the best and newest weaponry in development. Someday, when you are ready, you will be invaluable to your benefactor."

"Who might that be?"

"I am not at liberty to disclose such a name, now or in the future. All your inquiries will be in vain. We will start at sunrise."

Number 9 Island woke at daybreak. The sea fog simmered at the edge of the island, as if still holding onto the serenity of night. I stood in perfect army posture before my trainer, Sergeant La, who wore a sleeveless shirt and baggy pants tied at his tiny waist by a satin belt.

"You have four years ahead of you. Success or failure, do you understand?"

"Yes, sir."

"I couldn't hear you! Say it again, until you feel your stomach ache!"

"Yes, sir! I understand, sir!" I shouted at the top of my lungs.

"Good."

Sergeant La continued. "I grew up in Henan Province at the foot of the Shaolin Temple. My kung fu is therefore Shaolin style. I can be as soft as water." He moved his body like a snake. "Or as hard as steel." Sergeant La widened his stance. "Now hit me right at my *dung tien.*" Lower belly.

I hesitated, studying La's eyes.

"It's an order! Punch me as hard as you can."

I rolled up my sleeves, found my footing, made a fist, and attacked my master. My fist was a big hard rock that had been known to cause much damage to whoever deserved it. But this time it felt different at contact. His skin was soft like fermented dough and his stomach muscles sucked in my fist before releasing a surge of energy that sent me tumbling ten feet backward onto the grassy ground.

"Be careful there. I could have broken your arm with an ounce more power from my intestines. If you haven't been trained, you are as stiff and useless as a stick. From the size of you, you ought to have the power of a mad ox, but instead what you've got is only a sheep's push. Let's start with strength building. Push-ups." He fastened a bulky belt filled with sand to my waist, then pointed to the ground. "You have one hour. The first quarter hour, ten pounds. The second quarter, twenty pounds. The third and last quarter, twenty-five pounds. I will be observing you from my office. Don't disappoint me."

The first fifteen minutes was bliss. A second quarter passed and I was breathing urgently, my body screaming with pain. The third quarter, I almost collapsed and ate the dirt on the ground. But I persisted. When the time was finally up, I lay dead on the damp earth for a good twenty minutes.

"To your feet." La was back, smiling. "Clean up and go to classes now. This afternoon, we'll climb the steps to the top of the nameless mountain on the island. Be sure to bring the ten-pound weights to strap to your feet."

"Thank you, master." I could only manage a small smile on my sweaty face. I stumbled back to my room to get ready for my morning class, "The Art of War."

The class was taught by an old scholar, Mr. Wang, once a senior adviser in the army. He had a goatee, and constantly smoked a bronze water pipe. His textbooks were brown and stitched together with thread, the pages torn on the edges. His hands trembled as he read from Sun-tzu's classic *The Art of War,* an ancient document, mandated reading. I was one of five students in his class, and I found my teacher's guidance simple but enlightening. His first lesson was the teaching of An Empty Fortress.

Zhu Guo Liang, a well-known strategist, was once surrounded by eight thousand enemies around the city wall. He was ambushed, but he knew that to send a smoke alarm to seek help from a distant ally would only convince the enemy that he was weak and frantic. So he opened the city gate and sat in a chair in the empty front yard of the city, plucking away at his *pi-pa*—a banjolike instrument—humming folk music with his eyes closed. His enemy's scouts were surprised to find Zhu enjoying himself, oblivious to the engulfing siege afoot. Silently, they retreated faster than they had come, believing that the tricky Zhu had set up a counter-ambush and was waiting for them to rush in. Nobody would have believed that Zhu only had two dozen soldiers in the city with him.

It was such an inspiration that I rushed afterward to the library intending to borrow all the books written by Sun-tzu, only to be told by the librarian that the author had only been known to have written that one book. The book was meant to be read slowly and chewed finely and digested carefully. Only after many readings would the truth come to one in full.

In the afternoon, Sergeant La made me run the beaten path, climbing the back of the mountain rising from the center of the island. Seven miles up. Another seven down. That night I slept dreamlessly until I was awakened by an echoing bell at sunrise.

The following day, a young man with a doctorate in computer science from some American university gave me an introductory lesson in a computer lab equipped with dozens of terminals. Within an hour, I fell in love with the machine that could process numerous data with one keystroke. At the end of the lesson, I was offered a portable unit for my own use that could be connected with the network on the island. Fighting sleep, I stayed up until early morning tapping away slowly on the bouncy keyboard, marveling at the magic unfolding at my fingers' touch.

Time seemed to flow by like water in a stream. Summer soon was gone and autumn came with its coolness in the air. My body had hardened with the stringent daily exertion, and my heart regained the lightness that I had not felt since parting from my beloved Sumi. The isolation from my past, from the rest of the world, seemed to cure me.

In the mornings, I immersed myself in the discipline of martial arts practices, learning *nan chuan, bei ti* (southern fists, northern kicks) and *xi ro, dong gong* (western suppleness, eastern hardness). At night, I devoted myself to long hours honing my marksmanship. I preferred big guns like the AK-48 automatic and a rather crude-looking black beauty called an Uzi. All my other hours in between, I was schooled in fields of learning and branches of study in such subjects as Marxist Politics, Chairman Mao's Thoughts, Communist History, and International Affairs. But there wasn't a moment that I was away from my love, that sweet love of mine—Sumi. Each punch I pulled, each kick I threw, each bullet I fired, each mile I ran was secretly an accumulation, an acceleration toward that final goal of succeeding at the worthy work afoot and returning to claiming what was rightly mine—my Sumi.

Three months into the training, I was called into an office where a tailor measured me for a fancy suit and a shirt with French cuffs. The tailor showed me a video presentation of various styles of clothing—all kinds of brand names, cuts, and fabrics. Within five hours, I had a crash course in the world of fashion. The teacher's parting words were "You are what you wear."

My monastic life of discipline and order was interrupted one night when an attractive woman in her late thirties appeared in my room. She had an amazing body; I felt dizzy just looking at her. She introduced herself as a former dancer from a well-known Shanghai ballet company. Only later did I find out that she was serving a life sentence for a double murder, some love triangle, and was now a member of the faculty on the island.

She told me that she was here to teach me some classic and popular dance steps that I might be compelled to perform in future missions. I was a quick learner and we managed to waltz smoothly by the end of the evening. Since it was a private lesson that lasted until the student was well taught, I suggested that she stay longer to review some of the basics with me. She obliged happily.

Around midnight, during our last dance, the teacher pressed her supple curves into my chest. When she stepped back, I could see her hard nipples through her flimsy dress. Her eyes sang a melody. She giggled and whispered into my ear and brushed her lips lightly a few times along my sweaty neck. As the music ended, I was shocked to find one of her hands grabbing my buttock while the other rubbed my pulsating manhood, which had pained me ever since I set eyes on her.

We were glued to each other. I pulled her onto my bed. The feminine aroma from her mature body was more than I could bear. I found myself arching in climax, soiling my own pants. Oh, her devilish fingers. But my youth allowed me a second rise within minutes. She undressed herself, climbed on top of me, and rode me, facing my twitching toes. At the sight of her beautiful rump, I erupted within a maddening half-minute.

"Aiyah! You could have broken the hundred-meter dash record with that one," she pouted, her bottom still gyrating on my limp number.

"You didn't enjoy it as much as I did?" I was shocked.

"I was just beginning to." She yawned.

For the first time, my manliness was challenged, but no matter how she coaxed and teased with her artful hands or lustful tongue, my snake lay coiled, unable to stand up again. The teacher got up on her feet, declaring authoritatively, "For a beginner, you're doing fine. With your potential, you could be perfect in no time."

The second night, my dance teacher showed me a few techniques to control my tendency to arrive early, bearing such names as Choking the Snake and Pull-Hold-and-Plunge, but her inner muscles and gyrating buttocks soon rendered me useless, nonetheless.

The third night, she told me at the beginning of the class that this was serious business and that I had to concentrate more on my technique and rein in my emotions. At times, the ability to please a woman might mean life or death. I not only made her climax but brought tears of gratitude to her eyes.

The fourth night, the teacher completely let go of herself. I made love to her five times. When I was done, she had cried, cursed, moaned, screamed, and repeated all that again, though not necessarily in the same order. We finally fell asleep in each other's arms until late afternoon, when my thrusting awakened her and caused her to spend another hour beyond her schedule. A few classes were missed, but more was gained.

Finally alone that night, I was consumed by guilt until I concluded that it was not love I felt, only lust. Thus no betrayal to Sumi was committed. Furthermore, I believed that my newly acquired etiquette—where the tongue goes and the hands should caress—would make me a better lover for Sumi and that we would be a happier couple when we were finally together. But my mind for the next few days rarely left the scent and sound and feel of the teacher.

My first assignment of worthy work came a year after my arrival, on a misty night. Sergeant La escorted me onto a boat to the mainland, then I was put on a train to Hunan Province and transported in a special compartment labeled RARE DISEASE. I came in a stretcher, my face all bound up like a mummy, except for my eyes and mouth. I was carried by two attendants through a maddening crowd in the train station. As soon as I was on board, a nurse removed my bandages and offered me tea. The train crawled out of the station. An hour later, we reached the foot of a mountain, and the nurse returned with a doctor in a white coat. The doctor, a mustached man with shifty eyes, nodded and the nurse disappeared. He felt my pulse and listened to my heart. Everything was fine, he said. "This is my diagnosis." He handed me a piece of paper. "And this is your medicine." He pointed at a briefcase he set at my feet. "You must wear the sweater you find in there."

I nodded and the man left. In ten minutes, the paper said, the train would pull into a tunnel, where it would stop suddenly. I was to climb out my window, run along the rail, enter the car in front of me, kill the passenger in the sleeping compartment, then jump off the train.

I did what he prescribed. I first put on the sweater, which was yellow and fit me surprisingly well. I sat with my eyes closed, meditating for the tranquillity within. I imagined various faces with my inner eye—young, old, comely, homely, thin or plump—but I had a hard time picking a particular face as my first kill. What would the doomed face look like? Would it be gray in color? Would he be sad or shocked or happy to die? Would he beg for life?

Dear Sumi, let me carry out the worthy work so that I can live to see you again, I prayed.

The train entered the tunnel and screeched to a sudden halt. I jumped out of my window, stumbled along the gravel, slid open the window in the next compartment, and climbed in. To my shock, sitting alone in the compartment was a young woman. Her frightened eyes bulged wide at my sudden intrusion. A woman! It can't be. It was utterly beyond my calculation. My pulse raced and temples throbbed. Sergeant La, how cruel you are to test my courage on such a tender victim.

The girl's next move surprised me even more. Instead of running, she stood up with a cry, her eyes softening with sparks of recognition. She reached for me, her slender arms opening.

You are here to kill an enemy! Sergeant La's voice rang in my head. *It is a trial you must pass.* There was no time to think. The train was moving again. In a blur of dizziness, I pulled out my revolver and shot her between her big, innocent eyes. Red seeped out from her forehead before the impact of the bullet threw her back onto her bed.

A sudden burst of light shot out from the wall, blinding me like lightning. *What was that? A camera flash? Had I been seen?* The job was done. I must go. But something about the way she had collapsed, with her eyes open, tugged my heart. I leaned over and closed her lids with a trembling hand. Then I leaped out the window and ran into the tunnel, not allowing myself another shred of sentiment. At the other end of the tunnel a jeep was parked on the slope with its engine running. At the wheel sat none other than Sergeant La. "What took you so long?"

I didn't reply. Silently, he drove onto a busy road, vanishing among trucks, mules, and children riding on bikes.

Tan

CHAPTER 16

Virgin, virgin. How ironic that my initiation, my maiden voyage, had been a tumultuous ride with a virgin. Oh, what a word. It seemed so beautiful, so simple. But my recollection of Virgin was only partially true to the definition. Virgin in the backseat of my Red Flag limousine was lovely, yes. Poetic, and even spiritual. But innocent, no. Rather, I was vividly reminded of some of the arousing scenes from the literary masterpiece *A Dream of Red Mansions,* an erotica set in the Ch'ing dynasty. Arousal, a powerful word by itself, was something I experienced more and more frequently these days. Everything seemed to arouse me. Everything around me had a deeper meaning.

Lying in bed, my mind still foggy, I heard a knock on my door. "Come in."

Father stood in my doorway in his full uniform, unusual at 10:00 p.m. Surprised, I stood up to meet him. He was here for a reason. Otherwise he would never have ventured into my room this late. I said with a little bow of my head, "Good evening, Father."

Father forewent the greeting and asked sternly, "Did you forge my signature on my stationery today?"

"Yes, I did, but for a good reason." Honesty had been expected of me from an early age, and I had found it to be my best weapon when all arguments collapsed, effective in pulling the emotional strings.

"There is no reason good enough when it comes to forging my authority, son!" Father raised his voice. "Do you understand? Are you aware that I am the chief of all three branches of the military?"

"You refused to help her, and she is innocent!" I protested.

"You still do not see what you have done wrong, do you? There is a warrant for you. The state police are here to arrest you."

"What?" I must have heard wrong.

"Get your things ready. They are waiting for you downstairs."

Father's tone was calm and assured. He meant what he said. I could not believe what I just heard. "Arrest me, your own son?"

Unmoving silence.

"Mother!" I yelled, running downstairs only to find her weeping frantically. "Mother."

She just shook her head helplessly.

Father stood over the ornate railing of the grand house and said, "Tan, this is a military order. No one should or could stop it." He turned into his office and shut the door.

When I saw the two soldiers with guns in hand, I knew it was for real. Everything about Father was for real. Mother held me tightly, as if she would never let me go. "I'm here," she said. "What did you do? What did you do? Tell Mother you didn't do it. You didn't do it, did you?"

"Mother, what I did was to save Miss Yu. I can't go to jail. What I did was right."

"You're not going to jail, son, as long as I live. Father, come out of your room and do something about this! You're the military chief! Get these lowly soldiers out of this house. Get out!" She waved her arm at the two policemen as if they were a couple of intruding animals. "Do you know who I am and who my father was?" she said, imperiously. "When he was fighting for this country, your fathers were still in diapers, you lowly footmen. Get out!"

The two officers took a few steps back, hands on their guns, shrugging and shaking their heads.

"What did he do? He is only seventeen. Leave!" she persisted.

"We have an order in hand," one soldier said. "We have to bring him in."

Father came slowly down the stairs. He put his hands around Mother's fingers and slowly loosened her hold on me. "Let them have him."

"No. What good are you? The military chief! Can't you just cancel the order? What did he do that is so wrong and criminal? We, this whole family, have fought for the country and we can't be excused for a little mischief committed by a minor? What justice is this?"

"Let him go. This order comes from above me," Father bit out.

"Damn them! Damn you! There is no one above you. Who ordered the arrest? Who?"

"The president."

"President Heng Tu, that little dwarf?"

"Shhh. Not in front of these men."

"Not in front of these men? I'm going to the People's Radio and broadcast all over the world what a leech that man is. My father took him out of prison and made him president. Did you know that, officers? He was dying like a dog, rotting in that prison. What a heartless, ungrateful little man he is! What does he want from us? He used us every way he could and now he issues an arrest order for our son? He's going to burn in hell for many lives for what he is doing to my family. Do you hear that, officers? He didn't even attend my father's funeral, that bastard!" She broke down crying again.

"Where is Grandfather? I need to call Grandfather!" It was my last resort.

"Son, you have to go," Father said. "I will resolve this later."

"No, Father. You can't let them take me. Call Grandfather!"

"Let's go, Tan Long," one of the soldiers commanded.

"Wait, I need to call Grandfather Long."

"Why can't he call his grandfather, you ruthless, ignorant animals?" Mother yelled.

"Commander in Chief, please help us carry out the president's orders," one of them begged.

Father stared back at him sternly.

"You don't have to obey that petty officer!" Mother said angrily.

Father bit his lips and forced Mother away from me as I kicked and punched the policemen.

"Tan, you have to stop or we'll make you. Give me your hands," the soldier demanded in a quiet, firm voice, holding a pair of old handcuffs in his hand.

"Is that a joke? Handcuffs? Step back and hand me the phone. Do you know who my grandfather is?"

The soldier pushed me, which surprised me. No one had dared do that to me, ever.

"We do not know and we do not care. Give me your hands or I will have to make you."

"Help! Mother!" I shouted, looking up the wide stairs. But Father had pulled her away. My shouts bounced back from shut doors. "Help!" No one was going to help me. The soldier grabbed my arms roughly behind me and the iron cuffs clicked and locked around my wrists.

Slowly dragging my feet, I followed the men out the door. Where was freedom? Where was democracy? Where was everybody when I needed them?

I felt both anger and fear. Arresting your own son, for what?

They pushed me into the jeep. I didn't even look back at the house that I called home, not once.

The jeep vanished into the dark night.

A CLANKY FORTRESS prison stood silently against the massive Sishan Mountains. I had visited this part of the Beijing suburbs every year, especially in autumn when Fragrance Hills Park was covered with the blazing leaves of the red maples. Once, when I arrived by Father's helicopter, it looked like a red sea or a spreading prairie fire. But today I was a prisoner taken into custody for treason. What a ridiculous accusation. All I did was let an innocent girl go back to her own country. So she had started a little magazine. She had organized political meetings. She might even have sowed the seeds of democracy. Why was she so bad? In fact, she was wonderful, with her ideas, her aspiration, and beauty—she should be lauded as a heroine. I still felt no regrets about helping her, and least of all for loving her.

They took me through layers and walls and flights of stairs before finally arriving at a dark cell. I no longer felt fear but pride. I felt heroic and very romantic.

The prison was quiet after the warden slammed the door on me, and dark except for the dim light in the hallway, from where the shuffling feet of a night patrolman could be heard. I closed my eyes so that they could adjust to the blackness, but I couldn't even locate my bed.

Groping around like a blind man, I found a flat pillow and almost tripped over a bucket, which I took to be my night pot. The walls were rough, with an unfinished feel. Prisoners did not deserve better. It was also damp and wet. The floor, quite smooth but cool, must have been cement, for I could feel uneven seams between pieces. In the far end by my bed was a small table. I lay down and put my arms under my head. The bed was a hardwood, covered with a thin, sweat-soaked bamboo mat. It smelled of the inmate before and the one before that.

I grew up being told, ever since I could remember, that I wasn't ordinary. So tonight, confined in this smelly cell, I still felt that I was special, unlike the convict next door, whoever he might be. When tomorrow came, the sun would rise again and I would be freed. Or if not tomorrow, then in a few days. Presently, I was a rat temporarily trapped in a cage at a scientific lab. I was here as an experiment, to test my constitution. Any great man had to have a stop in prison. Look at all the history books. Prisons tested and hardened men.

In fact, I wouldn't be surprised if dear Mother—I felt so sorry for the anguish I had caused her tonight—rushed here tomorrow and brought some of my favorite foods or even a few books. My banker grandfather, beaming with pride, might also bring some of my favorite reads, such as the *New York Times* and the *Wall Street Journal*.

I had not forgotten Father, who by now had probably planned every move to save me after feeling belatedly contrite about not helping in the first place. In his stiff and serious manner he would come, with his secretary tailing behind, to apologize to me. He was probably suffering insomnia because of my absence and composing the most sincere apology to personally deliver to his only son.

None of my expectations were fulfilled the next day or the day after. I was left alone without any human contact. Mother did not rush in, crying. Father did not send his apologies, not even in writing. And worst of all, Grandfather Long was also silent. What was happening here? I was abandoned. The whole world had forgotten me. Nobody cared about the sole heir to the Long and Xia dynasties anymore.

After three full days, I began to find the prison short of good air, the silence maddening, the desperation deepening, and the loneliness crowding my entire being. If I had to stay in this ancient fortress another day without the slightest movement of wind, I would go insane.

At last, a horse-faced soldier opened my door with a clinking bunch of keys and ordered, "Prisoner number seventeen, face the wall and stick your hands behind your back."

"Where am I going?" I asked the man.

"Inmate seventeen, you are to keep your mouth shut until spoken to. Do you hear me?"

"Loud enough to deafen my ears."

Unexpectedly, the soldier kicked my back with his leather boots and jabbed me with his elbow.

"Ah!" I grunted. "What did you do that for?"

"Verbal abuse is a violation of prison rule number nine."

"You animal! Wait until I get out."

The soldier slammed iron handcuffs into my head. I dropped to the floor, holding my bleeding head with both hands. "Which rule did I violate this time?"

"The rule to beat the shit out of you does not really exist. I just made it up."

The soldier roughly cuffed me and dragged me along the hallway while I screamed for help.

A medic was summoned to the small cubicle of the interrogation room, where he bandaged my head with three pieces of thick gauze. I was still fuming when the honchos came in and sat opposite me at the other end of the table.

"What kind of treatment is this? I want to talk to my father, General Ding Long."

"Shut up and listen," said one of them.

"I am not going to shut up anymore! I am innocent. I did not do anything wrong. Let me go. Let me out off these cuffs!" I demanded.

"Young man, things might be a little more complicated than that."

"Complicated! Why don't you name one crime that I have committed against the people."

"You're an intelligent young man. Why don't you tell us what happened."

"I have nothing to tell."

"Confession will lesson your punishment, and dishonesty will only increase your guilt. You know our criminal policy well, being the son of a great revolutionary family."

"I have nothing to confess."

"Well, this time if you don't confess and tell us the truth, we might have to hand you over to the authorities in Hong Kong and let the International Criminal Tribunal handle the case."

"It would be fine if you did that. I know the judges of that tribunal would think Miss Yu deserved freedom and not imprisonment or being sent to a labor camp in the Siberia of China."

"Young man, you are not understanding us." The taller one of them reached over and slapped a photo down in front of me. "Take a look at her and tell me the truth."

It was a morbid photo of a girl lying in a puddle of blood, with a gaping hole in her forehead.

"Who is this?" I cried.

"Virgin!"

"She's dead?" I felt nauseous.

"Very much so."

"No, it can't be!"

"The medical examiner confirmed that the time of her death was when you were last with her, remember?"

"No, no . . ." I began shaking.

"We have a photo of you copulating with her, and the doctor also confirms the presence of your semen oozing in abundance out of her vagina."

My head grew feverishly hot, my arms numb, and neck stiff. "Who did it? Who would do such a thing to her?"

"We have found our suspect." The man smiled triumphantly. "And we believe he acted alone."

"Who is it?"

"You!"

"Me?"

"Yes. We also found the gun that was used to shoot her to death."

"No, I didn't do it!" The accusation suddenly cleared my mind. I had heard too much about how an innocent person could be made to confess to a crime he had not committed. I was born strong and would not let these skunks get away with it. "That's a fat lie. I did not do it! On the contrary, I set her free and saw her get on that train. You're not going to implicate me. I loved her and she loved me. We made love. How can one so in love kill the other?"

"Who knows? Jealousy? Maybe you knew she didn't love you. She was a loose woman, we discovered, who slept with anyone who shared her belief in democracy. You had motive to hurt her because she was running away, not from the authorities but from you, with another man, and verbal conflicts turned into a physical one. You raped her and then killed her. That's how we see it."

"You murderers! You killed her. I will let the whole world know. I am going to petition the highest authority to prove my innocence. You all should be sent to the People's Guillotine. I need to talk to my parents. Let me out of here."

"I'm afraid we can't do that, or the Hong Kong government will hold us responsible for letting loose a prime suspect."

"Let me out of here!" I had never felt so enraged before. I felt as if heaven had fallen. I needed to be out of here. I needed my parents.

I jumped out of my chair but was stopped by a soldier. Two guards dragged me back to my cell. They uncuffed me and slammed the door, and the lock clicked ominously shut.

Virgin was dead. How could it be? How could Buddha let it be?

How could such perfection be ruined in such a cruel twist of fate? Had my act brought about her untimely demise? She had been *yiaozhe,* her youthful tree brutally cut right at the waist. And all her dreams that promised to blossom in springtime had fallen with the tree. Everything that was Virgin was laid to rest, to rot into dust.

I lay where they had dumped me, on the cool cement floor, breathing jerkily like a wounded beast, no longer a child. A cold, dark tunnel lay ahead, beyond which I saw not light but only darker depths, sucking me down and inward.

In a faint light I awoke. I couldn't remember how long I had slept. I must have cried, because the collar of my dirty shirt was drenched. There were bloodstains on my shirt. Miss Yu's face hovered over mine. Her hot lips, smooth hands. Her eyes crying, laughing, shining through her tears.

I was exhausted from the sickening emotions draining me from within. My mind, a thing so agile and excitable, was numb and tired. Hopelessness only intensified the longing for my family. There had to be a reason the size of the Yangtze for them to stay away from me this long. But what was it? The false accusation must have brought dark clouds upon them.

Another day spent in darkness, in silence, in desperation. All I did was sit, sleep, think, and cry. I knew I had not done anything wrong, but now I could understand those who confessed to crimes that they had never committed, simply because they needed to breathe, eat, and feel alive. I cringed at that thought, shivering. For warmth, I climbed down the thin bed and started doing push-ups. One, two, three, four . . . I could still do fifty. My muscles ached and my breath shortened, but I felt better. I almost felt like myself again. My energy returned, and with that, my conviction to stay clearheaded and alert. How wonderful to be alive at seventeen. I was sure it would be even better at twenty, thirty, and every tenth anniversary after that. I did not want my life to end here. I wanted to go on forever and ever.

On the ninth day, the same horse-faced soldier took me again to the interrogation room. I was clearheaded but pretended to lower my eyes and let my eyes move a little slower. A piece of paper was placed before me. Someone had already written the words of a confession, and had even started the first line by writing, "My name is Tan Long . . ."

"Do you know what the paper is for?" the officer asked me.

"Could you repeat that question again?"

"Confession. You can confess now, young man, then you can go home. Home to your beautiful home."

"Oh, home. I want to go home."

"Yes."

"What should I write here?"

"That you killed the Hong Kong girl out of jealousy. That you consorted with her. She did not ask for it, but you forced yourself on her because she was voluptuous and her dress was short." The officer laughed lewdly.

"Anything else?" I asked slowly, as if my tongue was too thick to move at normal speed.

"Anything that your father or grandfather has done to help you kill the girl, anything at all, put that down as well."

My heart beat faster. Not only did they want to get me, but they also wanted to implicate my family. "Anything else?"

"That will be all for now."

"Can I start writing?"

The officer nodded.

I grabbed the pen and started working on the paper. After a few long minutes, I flipped the sheet facedown and stood up from the chair. "Can I return to my cell?"

"Certainly, if you have completed your confession."

"I have, and you should be very happy about it."

As I was being taken away, the three officers read what I had written. It was not exactly what they had asked for. On the paper, I had drawn a large penis with two supporting balls accompanied by two poignant and self-evident words: "Fuck you."

They weren't amused in the least.

I smiled for the first time since I had been here. It was a small victory, but it proved that I was still alive with intelligence and humor.

That night, I was taken and pushed into a torture room. Whips hung all over the wall. A shirtless man with a hairy chest was puffing on a thickly rolled cigarette. The place smelled fishy with the stench of blood. But they did not whip me. Instead, they stripped me and hung me up by my two thumbs with my feet barely touching the bloody, smelly ground.

"In the old days, we'd have made you a eunuch. But we'll try something new." The hairy man held me from behind. Another man introduced himself as the doctor. He bent over and grabbed my penis. In his right hand, he held a piece of sharp wire.

"What are you going to do?" I screamed.

"Give you some pain and make you wise." They laughed.

I kicked and struggled to no avail. The man with the hairy chest was a giant.

The doctor took aim and penetrated my pee hole like an acupuncturist. He spun once. I jumped, the pain shooting directly through my groin to my heart. But the horror of what was happening was even greater. The wire spun again. I screamed. I had never known a pain so excruciating. I jumped and tried to kick. The devil spun it a third time and the hard wire went so deep, it reached the base of my manhood, burning with fire.

"Confess now!"

"I have nothing to confess!"

The wire spun again.

I cried in pain. "I have nothing to say!"

"How about now?" The doctor jerked the wire around, sending electrical shocks all over my body.

"Please stop," I sobbed.

"You have a confession?"

"No . . ."

More jerking.

"Yes!"

"What did you do?" The doctor spun deeper, and a stream of blood dripped down from my penis.

"I confess! I killed Virgin . . ."

With the wire embedded deep inside me, I was untied and a pen was inserted into my right hand. On the paper, stained with my own blood, I wrote down a confession that I would never have imagined myself writing. When I hesitated, my punisher twanged the wire again. That was when the last thread of my willpower broke.

Sumi

CHAPTER 17

Dearest Shento, my heart, my soul:

I'm writing this entry not for you to read, but for your soul to sense. It is an apology. Such word is light, barely able to lift the weight of my guilt. A sad apology. A sordid, morbid apology.

It was I, my cursed self, who has driven you off your life track to be condemned to die at such a young age. I should have warned you. No, my maker, whoever it was, should have warned the world of my coming, my cursed coming.

A fortune-teller once told me I possessed three bloody killing knives in my fate. The first knife was meant for my father. He took it bravely on the execution ground, shot in the back of his head by a green-uniformed soldier, the agent of my destiny. Father's brain splashed all over the executioner's uniform, reddening his chest as if the killer had bled, a witness recounted. The second knife was plunged into my mother's heart. It was the commune's security officer who performed this deed. My mother had scolded the Communist leaders for wrongfully labeling her and her husband as "Rightists." Feisty life met feisty end. They chose a painful death for her, letting her linger, blood gushing out of her mouth until she choked on her own essential fluid.

The fortune-teller told me the reason I was born to carry the three knives was due to some dark, hidden debt incurred in my parents' last lives. We have a cycle of nine lives, each rewarding or punishing the life preceding, according to the deeds performed or sins committed.

I, the carrier, was the angel of goodness, for I am the one to free my parents' condemned souls.

I was six. I believed. I replaced my tears of guilt with the conviction. Then I grew up, living in this misery that is the orphanage. A certain clarity descended on me, the clarity that comes with suffering, a suffering that makes one strong. I questioned the wisdom, the illogic, the random choice, the foolishness. I wasn't the chosen carrier of those killer knives. No! How could I be? If only one could know how I loved my baba and mama, and how I missed them, gone so brutally, so shortly after giving me life. Oh, damn the maker! Damn the heavens! Damn you, smiling Buddha!

Then you came, and oh, how you emboldened me. At times, I was flooded by your light, your warmth, the rainbow of you arcing over me, making me safe, or so I thought.

I dreamed of a life with you. You, one wheel of a handbarrow. I, the other wheel. Together, side by side, we'd roll along the bumpy rises and falls of our path, carrying whatever load life imposes.

Then that fateful night, when my shrieks tore the campus quiet to pieces, my frugal dream was also shredded.

That fateful night that you killed.

That fateful night that you fled.

That fateful night when the life of another first stirred in the depths of my womb.

Dearest love, now you've been forewarned. If you've left this earth already, you will know who the killer really is. It is I. Yes, the one who so adores you. By my loving you, you were chosen as the receiver of the third and final knife of bloody fate. And as the Old Belief goes, it was really not I, the knife carrier, to blame, but you yourself to blame. A sinner begets the punishment. What have you done in your last life to deserve the blunt of heavenly wrath? What on earth have you done, my dear, dear, cursed lover, my heart?

My eyes are open big every day, watching the sea. My ears never shut, listening to the tides in the wind to this day. No body has popped up on the surface of the sea. No bones washed up the blasted sandy beach nearby. Then again, there are seas beyond the sea, beaches beyond the beaches.

Where are you, my love?

Where are you, my Shento?

Sumi

Tan

CHAPTER 18

I blinked at the glaring sunshine. As if seeing an old friend, I wanted to embrace it all in my sore arms. I had been waiting for this moment a long time. An eternity of ten days.

As I limped painfully away from the fortress, my mother rushed toward me, a blue scarf over her head and dark sunglasses covering her eyes.

"Mother!" I cried, quickening my steps to meet her along the cobbled path. Each step I took triggered sharp, shooting sensations from my groin. The damage along my urinary tract was severe and the infection that followed made peeing an intolerable, bloody punishment.

"Mother!" I gasped, weakened from the pain.

"Oh, Tan, dear." Her voice was hoarse.

We hugged tightly in silence. No need for a single word. What was not said was understood. What needed to be said had already been felt.

The chauffeur, clad in his green army uniform, honked a few times. "Hurry up!" he shouted.

I looked up from her shoulder, puzzled at the sudden rudeness of the soldier who had been with us for the last few years.

"Don't pay any attention. Things aren't the same anymore," Mother said. "We'll talk when we get home."

We got into the car. Mother wiped the tears off my face, staring at me for a few long seconds. "Everything will be all right from now on, son." She gestured for me to stay quiet, pointing her index finger at the young soldier at the wheel.

I frowned. Something alarming was happening. My mother, the queen of Beijing, was scared of what? And why? I didn't have to wait long for the answer.

The guard at the Zhong Nan Hai entrance didn't salute us. On the contrary, he spit our way and whistled to his comrades inside the barracks. A platoon of guards crowded at the barracks windows, laughing and peering at us with curiosity. Mother averted her eyes. The garden, with its sweeping willows and tranquil pond, was overgrown with thick long blades of grass. Weeds that had been kept at bay by the diligent scissors of the old gardener now sprouted from every crack. Some of them had crawled over the furrows and had invaded the lilies and roses. Geese were pecking away at the young peonies, and in the pond, once an oasis, floated discarded bottles and rubbish. The car stopped, but no one rushed to open the door for us. The driver sat at his wheel, lit himself a cigarette, and let his smoke fill the car.

"I'll get some help for you," Mother said, stepping out of the car. The queen of Beijing society helping herself in her own mansion. It was outrageous.

She clenched her teeth and dragged me out of the car with a strength I had not known she possessed. "Old man, come get your son!" she called out as we entered the house.

To my surprise, Father looked haggard, with his beard unshaved and wearing no uniform, just a white shirt, army green trousers, and a pair of sandals. His head was bent and his eyes squinted, as if fearing the sun.

"Father!" I stepped forward. The surge of love made me forget the pain between my legs, and I stumbled. Father hurried down the steps to meet me. I had never seen Father looking so tired and old. Had he been sick?

"Son, welcome home." Father's grip was still firm like a soldier's and I winced. He looked me over worriedly, pausing here and there, as if spotting something different or something amiss.

Father's facial skin sagged where it once was taut. His eyes no longer contained the flames of a bonfire. They were bloodshot, reflecting an uncertain and troubled mood. General Long, who had been a statue of principles and dignity only days earlier, had crumbled into shadows of doubt and suspicion.

"Father, are you ill?"

"No, I'm fine." He managed a small smile grazed with a drip of embarrassment. "How about you? We have all been so worried about you."

"I'm fine. I am really fine." I realized that I had a duty to look and sound cheerful, though I did not quite know why. "Father, I am so sorry that I got you and the whole family into trouble."

"Son, come and talk inside." He managed another weak smile that fell short of his usual echoing laughter that pleased men and tickled women, and helped me up the steps to his office while Mother supported me on the other side.

When the door opened, it was to a sight that I would never have expected to see. All the furniture was stacked up against one wall and a dozen trunks were piled one against the other.

"Are we moving out of the house? And who are these people?" I asked as five young soldiers carried more things into the room.

"Let's go to my music room in the west wing," Mother said.

"I want to go to my room."

"No, it is all cleaned out. We have packed everything into trunks for you, everything that was yours. I made sure nothing was left out."

"Are we thrown out because of my confession?"

"Son, it is much more complicated than that."

Once we were seated in the office, Father sniffled a little, which startled me.

"Please tell me what has happened," I said.

"It's probably better that you read this." Father handed me the *People's Daily.* On the front page, in big bold letters, screamed the headline COMMANDER IN CHIEF GENERAL DING LONG RESIGNS.

Blood rushed to my head. The room spun.

Father resigned? The most promising young general in China's army?

"Father, I am so sorry. It is my fault."

"No, you were just the trigger. We have fallen out of favor in Heng Tu's eyes. There's been a war out there against us all along," Father said.

"What war?"

"Read the next headline."

I scanned it and then exclaimed, outraged, "They're saying Grandfather took the twenty million dollars? It's a lie. Grandfather would never do such a thing. How could they blame him?"

"They did, even though the money could have been stolen a long time ago. There was no systematic auditing at the bank," Mother said. "The reason is simple. Grandfather didn't agree with some of Heng Tu's reform policies and Tu didn't like it."

"But why did you have to resign?" I asked Father.

Father was silent and looked out the window.

"Your father resigned to save both your and your grandfather's lives," Mother said. "They were threatening to extradite you to Hong Kong to stand trial and imprison your grandfather for the bogus embezzlement charge."

"I don't know how to thank you, Father," I said. "You gave up your life and career for me."

Father smiled at me. "Do you remember that poem? Riding on your father's shoulders like a horse?"

"Yes, certainly. In the hope that his son would one day rise up to be a dragon," I finished the poem.

"There is no need to thank me, son. Only the need to fulfill my dreams."

"What would that dream be?"

"Your dreams define mine," Father said.

Choked at the generosity of his love, I struggled up to my feet and embraced him again.

There was a knock on the door. It was Grandfather Long, dressed in khaki, with a pipe dangling from his mouth, a new addition to his stuffy banker image. He raced to me, grabbed me, and pecked me on the cheeks.

"Grandfather, I am sorry."

"Don't be. We are not going to talk about this grievous matter anymore. We're leaving and moving to Fujian."

"Why Fujian?"

"Because that was where my grandfather lived and died. We are moving into my family's old country estate."

"When are we leaving?"

"As soon as you are fit to travel," Mother said.

"Oh, grandson, I have so much to show you in my hometown." The white-haired old man was as excited as a child. Father beamed with relief, and Mother touched me here and there, tears in her eyes.

After a fortnight's rest, my infection eased and my gait recovered. I was fit for the three-day journey south. On the day of our departure, the old servants and maids, remnants of the revolution, left early without saying good-bye, reassigned to serve other important revolutionaries. Their brains would be washed and they would be taught to forget.

I knelt in my room for a brief moment, not to reminiscence, not to be nostalgic, but to mourn the end of my childhood. Good-bye, Number 16 Zhong Nan Hai.

I asked about my schooling. Mother told me curtly that there was a letter from the principal announcing the decision not to take me back. No reason given. No reason needed.

The awards won by me and the bronze soccer trophy, the first of its kind in the history of the school, would be stripped from the showcase. There would be no traces of a boy called Tan Long. As far as history was concerned, I never even walked the hallways of the venerable school. My fingers had never flown along the submissive ivory keys of that old, mellow Steinway on the stage of the auditorium.

I felt like a stranger. If life were a mirror, my reflection would have shocked myself. I was now a sorrowful person eaten up by the guilt of causing catastrophic change to the life that I had known so well. Nothing was certain anymore, least of all myself. My fortress—or rather the imagined fortress of power, wealth, and privilege—had collapsed like a toppled pagoda on sandy ground. I understood finally that anything impossible was now possible.

Father, the power of all power, suddenly was just a loving father, bending over some of his memorabilia from his old days as chief, trying to put away one item too many into the limited space of a trunk. Mother, the whirlwind of temper, the chic untouchable queen of elegance, sat in the corner of the living room tapping her feet, impatiently waiting for the transportation to arrive. Her clothes were comfortable cotton khakis suitable for the long and tiresome travel ahead on the smelly and crowded train, she said. But at heart, I knew that she was dressed to blend in. This was not an occasion when she begged to be noticed. She wanted anonymity. In a single moment, she had descended from the moon and landed on the earth.

Grandfather, who had seen the rolling mountains of England and Trinity Church on Wall Street, sat on the stairs, twirling his beard, rocking slightly with the old clock. Not an ounce of worry in the whole wide world. He could care less that his country's foreign currency reserve had dwindled to a record low or that the government might never recover from the sinkhole budget deficit. He was the old guard ready to stroll the sandy beaches of Fujian. His name might still be on 10-yuan notes, but his mind was far away at his childhood home. He smiled and rocked and waited. He did not seem to have lost anything.

An army van, which was normally used for delivering groceries to the Long household, finally came. Mother jumped to her feet, clapping her hands. I climbed with my family onto the hard seats. There was no salute. Not even a hello. The driver whistled as he stepped on the pedal, lurching and squeaking along the pitted road to the train station. Mother wore a tolerant grimace. Her old self would have screamed at the driver if he accidentally ran over a pothole. Now, in the jerkiest ride that I ever rode in, Mother was smiling. She held contentedly onto Father, while I supported Grandfather, who dozed and nodded. He was all peace and calm.

Nearing the Beijing train station, I turned to my mother and asked, "Why are you so happy leaving behind so much?"

"My dear son, I am happy to have you all close to my heart. Nothing else matters anymore." She smiled, tears shining in the afternoon light.

Shento

山头

CHAPTER 19

A fortnight after my return to Number 9 Island, I was shocked to read about General Ding Long's resignation and the firing of his banker father. Though I jumped at the news, I was nonetheless pained by the fact that someone had deprived me of the pleasure of taking revenge upon the man who had fathered but abandoned me. Relief came, though, in knowing that Ding Long was still alive. The day of judgment from his ill-gotten son would come one day at my choosing. I saluted the portrait of President Heng Tu on the wall and whispered, "You are my unsolicited avenger."

On the first anniversary of my arrival, which fell on the Moon Festival—the fifteenth of August, a day to celebrate the moon goddess of love—I sat down on my favorite spot, a flat rock looking to the west where sunset painted the sea amber. The western sky was dreamy. My thoughts flew to Sumi down south where the Yellow Sea met the South China Sea and the waters turned from brown to a deep blue. I thought of my dear Sumi holding her books, her sleek black hair, her head leaning against her hand as she read and thought about me. I remembered how she was always deep in thought with her big eyes looking into the distance. My demure moon.

Was she still my bride promised to me on that unforgettable night? Was I still her husband pledged by the act of loving her? Where was she?

Thoughts of her in another man's arms or loving another made my chest tighten painfully. I reasoned that if she remained so pretty, which was only natural, and in time blossomed into something curvaceous, even voluptuous, she would be surrounded by men of all kinds and shapes. If I wasn't around, especially if she thought I was dead, she might just fall in love again, if not from her volition then from the weakening of her willpower and yielding to temptation. What would I do then? My mind raced fast for an answer. None of them came in a form or shape that was not criminal in nature. I, of course, would have to kill that lover. At that conjuncture, I pulled a gun from my holster and shot a passing seagull. The bird came whirling down from the sky with ominous squawks, disturbing the silence of the mountaintop.

"I would hate to be that bird," Sergeant La said, putting his hand on my shoulder. I jumped up and bowed deep to my master. "My apologies, master."

"What for? Something must have angered you."

"It was nothing. Just target practice."

"I doubt that. The dance teacher hasn't exactly changed you as much as I thought she would. Missing someone from the south?"

"How did you guess?"

"I know that look. I was in love before, but she married my best friend instead."

"Do you miss her?"

"No, but I miss him. Women are like flowers growing out of the earth in abundance. Wherever you go they're there; each one is different from the others. But best friends are hard to find. Come on, a man like you can have as many women as your heart wishes. Cleanse your mind of her. Cut off all your past contacts. Devote your mind and soul to the great leader. Shape yourself into the sharp dagger you are meant to be. Your future, a bright one, is well within your reach."

Such words calmed me. His promise quieted me. Work hard I must, I said to myself, so that one day I can make good of my pledge to Sumi, to meet her again as a grown man, a man of substance, of glory.

Tan

CHAPTER 20

1979

LU CHING BAY, FUJIAN

The Long family house sat grandly like a local god against the rolling hills of Lu Ching Bay, facing the sea. The hills were overgrown with wildflowers in the shapes of bells, pagodas, and gongs, some the size of a woman's straw hat, others as tiny as ants' toes. Their colors spanned the rainbows that often adorned the blue sky after a sudden burst of shower. Some flowers were bright and brilliant like tropical summer days; others demure and moody like a quiet mountain pond.

It was hard to say whether the house was a part of the slope or if the flowers were an expansion of the house. One began where the other ended, in utmost harmony, in total surrender. The locality smelled of a permanent fragrance mixed with the scent of the rich soil. But that good aroma only lingered when there was not a breath of wind and when nothing in the universe moved, which was at best a fleeting phenomenon, for Fujian, the land of the sea and the land of the mountain, almost never lay still. Life was movement and movement enhanced life.

At noon, when the subtropical sun was shadowlessly straight, white tides gallantly chased the virgin white sand on the beaches in the bay. Big-legged and small-bodied red stone crabs hurried angrily into their holes, swearing not to come back until the moon rose above the ebbing sea. Little shrimps jumped in the delight of sunshine, then washed back into the rocking cradle of the blue sea.

The tides created a palm-shuffling breeze that in turn pushed the rich aroma of the sea inland, up the hills, beyond the ridges, and into the mountains of the west where tigers roamed and monkeys howled.

Grandfather sat in a bamboo chair on the wide veranda with his eyes closed as he inhaled the first breath of the noon breeze, as if he were taking in the spirit of the Goddess Ma Zu, who, in local mythology, watched over fishermen floating in their little sampans on the violent ocean surface.

"Oysters, no, prams, eels, yes. Oh, here you go, the clams, the colorful tiny ones that you suck in after breaking the tails," Grandfather said to me excitedly as he analyzed the elements of the sea with his nose. Then he opened his eyes suddenly and declared angrily, "Now the wind has picked up and all I can smell is mud."

Grandfather was a child of the village again. Smelling the sea was a daily ritual for him. His self-anointment as a man of the sea and a son of the mountains solidified his decision to become a recluse, not caring about life, not caring about anything. But that changed a few days after our arrival when the family woke to the symphonic sound of local folk music—the *dia-dia* of a bronze trumpet, the *gu-gu* of the bamboo flute, the *wa-wa* of the two-stringed er-hu, the *ta-ta* of the plucking *pi-pa,* the piercing *kwan-kwan* of gongs the size of frying woks, and the *tum-tum* of drums made of local buffalo hides. Whacking bamboo poles exploded like firecrackers. Birds flew off their nests on nearby trees.

"The long lost son of the Longs, please come to the door to accept our welcome," shouted a fat man of about fifty, leading what appeared to be the whole village in a two-column parade.

Grandfather lined the family along the veranda, where we bowed to the bowing villagers. I rubbed my eyes while the man introduced himself.

"I am Fu Chen, the leader of the village. We are honored that you have chosen to retire in your hometown. We are here to wash your feet," he announced sincerely, bowing constantly.

"You shouldn't have," Grandfather said gruffly. He bowed back even lower than the fat man did.

"I should indeed. I am the grandson of the Chens. My grandfather used to feed the pigs of the Long plantation."

"And I am the great-granddaughter of the Tangs, who ran the western farm near the river. My whole family was fed well by your ancestors," said an old lady, toothlessly. She was wearing a burning red blouse, and wiped her hands habitually on her apron.

"We are the offspring of the Liangs, the fishermen who rented your family's fishing nets," a strong young man said, bronzed from the relentless sun at sea.

"Quiet," the fat leader announced, before the rest of the village introduced themselves. "We shall begin our feet-washing ceremony now." He took a bucket of brown local brew known as *Fujian lao jiu* and dumped it over the feet of everyone in my family. The pungent smell of the fine-grained liquor attacked my nostrils with a vengeance, and the sticky quality of the brew lingered over our toes.

"The locals believe that the best way to welcome a son home is to wash from the feet all the dust that has collected during his thousand-mile journey," Grandfather said.

"And what is the best way to send one off?" I asked.

"Also to dump a basket of this liquor on your feet."

"Why?"

"To strengthen your feet, for they believe that the liquor chases the chills out of your bones. You could withstand even the strongest storm."

"What else do you do with the *lao jiu*?"

"A pregnant woman drinks a barrel to make a baby stronger and another barrel after the baby is born. And crabs drink it so that men can eat them drunk and raw."

"Is there anything the drink can't do?"

"Nothing."

The music continued and soon began to make sense even to me. It had a *yee-yee-ya-ya* tonality, filled with this particular countryside's energy and life. It had the rhythm of the sea and the rugged edge of the mountains. The flowery renditions made me think of the songs of animals hidden in thick hilly foliage, the whispering of the sea when calm, and the shouting of the ocean when it threw typhoonic tempers. I understood everything: the music, the people who sang it, and the beauty of the land that inspired it. All those elements were a dream, a life, a song called Fujian.

The villagers placed on the veranda jars of their finest local stinking tofu, pickled octopus, thin white rice noodles, and a barrel of *lao jiu.* They did not ask why my family was back. They might have known, but they did not seem to care. They cared only that we were the pure blood of the Longs. One was born a Long and would die a Long, just as the Chens, Lius, Liangs, and Changs of the village remained always in their clans. One could wander along life's path for whatever time, as long as one returned, bruised or triumphant. You were a good son because you honored the land—your return said it all.

The fat Chen invited Grandfather for a light breakfast of fresh jellyfish, loosely tossed with slices of onions and ginger from his garden. The Liangs asked him to come by their home for fresh clams, the colorful ones, baked over an earthen stove off the cliff overlooking the rising sun. The fisherman Lao wondered if Grandfather could make it to the sunset raw-oyster dig, where they could slurp live ones from half shells. There were many more invitations that Grandfather could not remember.

The following afternoon, a group of singing women lined up at our door with brooms and mops, offering to clean the house, which hadn't been lived in for ages. They all wore the color burning red. When I asked why all the red, they smiled shyly and explained, "We are married." A badge of honor.

Only married females were allowed to wear red. Widows didn't have that luck. Any young girl of marriageable age stayed away from the color lest she be mistaken as married and her door remain unvisited by suitors. Widows wore only gray and black. They walked at the edge of the village, spoke only in whispers, never stared at men, and wouldn't speak unless spoken to. They were the shadows and darkness, for the villagers believed they had contributed to the early deaths of their husbands. They had sunk their men's boats, caused thunder to strike their husbands' heads, and even raised the sea to drown their drunken men. It was their bad luck, not their lack of husbands, that made them what they were. In shame and humiliation, they continued living to suffer, and suffered to live. Their next chance to smile and laugh again would only be when their son, if they were lucky to have one, got married. And during that ceremony, the widows were to hide from the celebrating crowd, for again it was believed they might ruin a good thing coming the way of their fatherless sons. They would only be allowed to feed the cripples, the lepers, the blind, and the deaf of the village who were there to beg for a good meal in return for a lucky song for the couple. Such was the little world I had moved into.

I went to many of the issued invitations with Grandfather, who now spent days visiting every household as if it was his duty as a son of the Long clan, which used to reign as the largest owner of land and fishing businesses. Had he missed a home or two, the slighted villagers would bear grudges for dishonoring them. The visit might be for just a cup of tea or a bowl of rice noodles. But it was the tradition here.

Mother turned herself into a model housewife. She cleaned every corner of the old house while she hummed her favorite Chopin sonata. She got up with the sun, put on her colorful apron, fetched fresh water from the sunken well in the backyard, cleaned the kitchen, and scrubbed the bottom of the frying wok before making breakfast. If I was down at the beach or outside in a field of flowers, when the chimney spat smoke, I knew that Mother's food would be ready soon. Then it was time to hurry home, for if I was late and the meal got cold, Mother would give me a stern look.

Father was busy finding a new life. He had heard that there was an abandoned army post not far from here on the Lu Ching Peninsula. For a while it housed an orphanage, but then the government cut the funding and the orphanage was shut down. Father was interested in exploring the possibility of setting up a business in the old complex. Local cadres told Father that there was a tuna-canning facility there, too, that might be for sale. Should he look into it? Where would he get the money to finance such a purchase?

Days became long and nights even longer. I missed my school, but that was not to be for long. A man in his forties, wearing a neat Mao jacket, limped up to our door one day and introduced himself as Principal Koon. His smile revealed a couple of gleaming gold teeth. But his manner soon revealed that he was an educated man after all, not like the fishermen of the village. He used words carefully; a little too carefully, maybe. I found it ironic to be conversing in such a fine manner while facing the sea and smelling the mountains.

"It has come to our attention that you are in your final year of high school. I would very much like to have the honor of inviting you to be the twentieth student member of our proud Lu Ching Bay High."

"Well, thank you, Principal," Mother said warmly.

Father and Grandfather had come downstairs to meet my future educator. Their presence only made the man nervous. "I must hasten to add that even though we enjoy the good standing of a legitimate school, we are missing a few key courses."

"Why?" Mother asked.

"Well, many of the teachers left the school, due to the small salary, to run their own businesses. You see, the new reform policy of our government is killing education, even though education is so important. That's why some of our students never graduated and none entered college. However, I still want to extend the warmest welcome to you," he looked at me, "for your attendance. The other choice of school is miles away, very far. Of course, it is a lot larger." The man looked down at his feet.

"I am sorry to hear all that. How could you make up for those missing key courses?" Mother was concerned.

"Well, we need more teachers."

"How many teachers do you have?"

"One."

"And plus you, that would be two?" she asked.

"No, just me."

"Just you?"

"Yes, and I am so sorry it took so long for me to come see you. I have been making a chair and table for your son."

I felt flattered by such an act.

"What teachers would you be needing?" Mother persisted.

"I teach Chinese, English, geology, and political science. I have been praying for a math teacher, and if we are lucky, we may only have to wait until next semester for a music teacher."

Grandfather smiled and said, "How would you like some volunteers? I can teach math. My son was a history major at Beijing University, and my daughter-in-law a concert pianist. Tan would be proud to be your twentieth student."

Principal Koon was deeply moved. "I can't believe it."

"If you do not have any objections," Grandfather said, "we will begin tomorrow."

I shook my head, looking at my family members, who were congratulating one another happily. "I might as well be learning at home."

"Tan, we want to make you the first college man from Lu Ching Bay," Principal Koon said.

"And not just any college," Mother said.

"Beijing University," Father said.

"A history major," Grandfather said.

They had been silent for so long about my future, but now they were all chirping like morning birds. Hope was palpable in the salty air.

When my family and I reported to Lu Ching Bay High School the following day, we saw the three most important officers of the town in one sitting: the principal, the Communist Party secretary, and the head monk of the village. Mr. Koon held all three titles. He smiled and explained, "I'm a teacher by profession, a widower by fate, and a politician because no one wanted the title. And I get a double salary to make up for the low one as a teacher." He shrugged and continued. "This used to be a temple. During the revolution, the commune wanted to tear it down, but the superstitious town people resisted. So, as a compromise, they changed the temple into a school and hung up a shingle, also making this the headquarters of the Communist Party." He looked around his six-room bungalow proudly.

I was amazed by the convenience-store mentality of grassroots communism. What would Mao have thought of sharing a pillow with good old Buddha? A frightful thought. What would Buddha have felt about molding the man who had a jacket named after him into a temple altar boy?

Mr. Koon showed Father the history books, Grandfather the giant abacus to be used for class, and Mother a wooden upright organ that was silently collecting dust behind the gilded shrine of Buddha. When

Mother stepped on the foot pedals, a bellowing sound hissed out from the hollow pipes.

"Oh! Shhh. Not in here, please. We might disturb His Holiness." Mr. Koon, the monk, clasped his hands and bent his head. "Let us please move this thing to the room farthest from his presence."

"Why?" I was curious.

But the monk was busy praying with closed eyes. I only caught the end of his prayer. "Forgive our sins, please." A genuine monk, indeed.

I told myself to be silent for the rest of my stay. I saw and listened and learned. This was all new to me. The school was the temple, which was also the Communist headquarters. So, for one offense, you could be expelled from school into the Communist jail.

The new Long family faculty taught the younger students, and Koon oversaw the oldest ones. He limped into the senior class like a bobbing sampan in a rocky sea, smiling. He opened the class, uncharacteristically, with a silent prayer.

I began to wonder whether he was more one than the other—Communist or Buddhist. Each part of him should have contradicted the other, yet in this crippled man they somehow coexisted in harmony.

"Class, I have good news for you. We have a very good student joining us today from the city of Beijing. Please welcome Tan Long."

The class he was addressing was six members big, without a single female. The boys sat lazily like a loose army. Like their fathers and brothers, they smelled of the fish they netted, stored, ate, and dreamed about. Their clothes were torn and patched together, and their manners were those of tired fishermen. One of them spat in my direction.

I stood up politely and bowed to them. I thought of Mother's advice about never being too polite.

"What's the matter? Working too hard unloading the overnight catch?" the teacher asked, waving for me to sit down. Slowly, he hobbled over to the first student. Grabbing him by the ear, he dragged him all the way up to his feet.

"Ouch! Stop it!" the tall boy screamed, rubbing his red ear.

With the second student, the teacher pinched his nose and brought him up so that he stood properly. The third one the teacher whacked with the back of his hand. The fourth didn't have to be told what to do. He stood up and said politely, "Yes, Dad, you don't have to smack me."

"All right, son. Next time stand up when a guest is here," the monk said.

The lucky fifth got kicked by the teacher's bad leg and shot out of his chair, protesting.

It must be the Communist acting within the teacher now, I thought. All the monkishness had gone out the window. I had never seen one person wear so many hats.

The teacher smiled wickedly and ordered, "Now, students, say, 'Welcome, Mr. Long, to our town.'"

Silence.

The teacher cursed. "Do I have to get my acupuncture needles out to cure you all?"

Quickly, the five pupils muttered their welcome.

"Now we can start our English lesson." A smile wreathed Koon's face. "Today we are going to learn the irregular plural forms of some nouns. First of all, what is the plural form of 'fish'?"

No response.

"Wait a second. Why are you all silent? You don't know the word 'fish'?" he asked the class. "You answer it." He pointed at the tall boy.

"I don't know."

"Of course you don't know. You never open your book. But you should know it, for you smell like a fish. Who knows the answer?"

"I do." I raised my hand. "The plural form of fish is still fish, f-i-s-h."

"Good. That's why I said it is good news that Tan is with us, otherwise the class wouldn't even move. Do you see how good his pronunciation is?"

Just before the hour was over, a tall, slender girl pushed the squeaky door open, entered gingerly, and slipped into the seat next to mine.

"Well, well, well. See who is here now." The teacher turned his attention to the girl. Dragging his bad foot, he rocked over to her side, touching her shoulder with his hands. "What's the matter? Babysitting duties get in your way?"

"I'm sorry I'm late."

"You are excused this time. Meet our new student—Tan."

I extended my hand to her. She looked up, managing a smile, but did not take my hand. Instead, she bowed low to hide her face, which turned red like the mountain flower she wore in her single braid.

I hesitated, not knowing what the custom was in meeting a girl who did not take my hand. I tried bowing, once, twice. On the third bow, I caught her eyes stealing a look at me. What a face: long with high cheekbones and a straight, tall nose. The blush, so shy, only added to her charm, an unspeakable charm, pungent with fragrance. I inhaled. Her scent entered my nose and intoxicated me. I forgot to look away, as local custom required a strange man to do. But so did she. Our eyes lingered, spoke with lights that danced in them. Time was forgotten. The world was forgotten. Yet it was only a very brief moment in real time, as evidenced by the fact that the teacher didn't seem to have noticed anything unusual.

"In case you're wondering, this is Sumi Wo, the only student here who might be your competition," the teacher said with a proud, fatherly grin. "To give you an example, while the rest of the class is still doing the plural of 'fish,' she, our Miss Knowledge, is doing book six of English. Sumi, can you please say 'Welcome' to Tan in English?"

Sumi. What a name it was.

She shook her head slightly to clear the bangs from her fine forehead as a shy yet challenging look crept into her big eyes. Her lips parted slowly and in an almost perfect accent, she said, "Welcome to Lu Ching Bay High School, Comrade Tan Long. It is an honor to meet you."

"The honor is all mine," I answered in English also.

"No, please, it is all mine."

"Your English is very good."

"Yours is even better."

"You know how to flatter."

"You deserve it."

Sumi and I had lost the whole class, including the teacher. The students, with their mouths open, listened to us conversing in a language that was so alien, yet soothing to their ears.

When the dialogue ended, we were both trembling with excitement.

She smiled, her face an exotic mountain bloom. I smiled back, a silly awkward man looking for his lost mind. Time flew by as I sat next to Sumi the entire day.

She seemed absorbed in her studies, while I looked for any excuse to talk to her. She only smiled back, each of my attempts rejected or failed, like mosquitoes flying into a kerosene lamp. But I, being of strong mind, managed to squeeze a note into her hand before school was over. She put it in her pocket and waved good-bye to me. Longingly, I saw her walk away into the fading day.

Sumi

CHAPTER 21

My dearest Shento,

I could barely hide my blush when I set my eyes on this city boy, Tan Long. Those dimples, the broad face, that nose, the manliness—I'd only seen present once before in the other boy of my past: you, my dear one.

Why are you and this city boy so alike, not just in appearance but in spirit? That generosity, like a shining sun, free for all to share, open to the meagerest.

Why am I blushing again, thinking of him? Why am I feeling the same rabbits running in my chest that I felt when I set my eyes on you the first time, my dear Shento?

Love seeks its own shadows. Is Tan Long your shadow, a twin that you sent in your stead to soothe me? If so, are you then forfeiting your claim on me? Remember. You said we would never part, in life or death.

Now I'm here, alive, and you are dead, as the school's bulletin said, shot to death in the back of the head, eating three bullets for three lives taken.

Why the city boy? Is it your doing? I ought not to be blushing. It is unbecoming, isn't it? It's unfair. You killed for me, and I live and blush in the presence of another boy. Is it fair? Am I fastened to your yoke forever? Am I not?

Sumi

Tan

CHAPTER 22

With the influx of us Longs, the formerly lifeless Lu Ching Bay High School seemed to regain energy. Chopin's concerto flowed silkily from the bellows of the wooden foot organ, filled the bamboo ceilings, climbed along the curled roof of the school temple, and hovered over the palm trees that stood nonchalantly along the vantage point of the bay.

Mother polished every inch of the instrument. It shone brightly in the sunshine filtering in through the window as she made music ooze from its belly. Toothless village children swamped around her, rubbing their noses, scratching their naked butts, their hearts filled with a joy that was not known to them before. Even their infant siblings, straddled to their backs, were quiet.

Father refound his passion in history, all that glorious Chinese history, some of which our family had played no small part in making. His pupils followed him to lunch by the cliff, strolled with him by the pond, and even followed him to the outhouse, where bamboo poles blocked the wind but not the view, for this was mainly a boys' school and girls were rarely present, even though the village had no shortage of them.

The local people did not believe in educating girls. They were the assets of their fathers before they found their men, and then the assets of their husbands after marriage. In case of an unfortunate widowhood, they became the property of their sons, who would boss and use them until the day the women died. Women were here to sweat, suffer, and still die happy. Education for them would be a complete waste.

Grandfather, carrying his abacus back and forth, made math so much fun that his pupils all went home and asked their fishermen fathers for some pocket change. Grandfather had set up a hypothetical bank, and his students were required to make deposits. He helped them calculate the interest accumulated day and night. When one of the boys asked him how the bank grew interest, Grandfather made the analogy that it was like planting young rice. One seed sowed would amplify into a hundred grains. So on and so forth. The kids were quick to grasp the concept, yet were puzzled by the fact that their fathers always put their hard-earned money under their pillows. Why didn't anyone start a bank here so that their fathers didn't have to lock their bedrooms when they were out on the sea?

Frowning with his thick eyebrows, Grandfather often wondered the same thing. A bank for the flourishing fishing town might not be such a bad idea. He talked to us about it, and we all shot him down. The thought, however, had taken root in his mind. And the old banker was more stubborn than his age. In fact, his age was to blame because the older he got, the more hardheaded he became. The seed kept growing.

Sumi, the shadowy girl, had also planted a seed in my mind. I thought about her often, especially when the sea lulled with its gentle murmurs and the moon shone as it touched the universe with its light.

I did not see her at school for a few days. Then she came in late and ran home early. I tried to catch her attention but she just smiled, and that was that. She did not return my note, which had simply said in English that we should study together. I could not ask other students about her. They all seemed busy with their lives. They came to school smelling like fish after helping their fathers unload the catch from the previous night, and dozed off during class, only to be woken up by the teacher.

I studied day and night, trying to catch up with lost time. My peers in Beijing were well on their way to a college dream. They had tutors to guide them through their books and servants to pour them tea. I had nothing, and nothing was probably better for me because I wanted everything back. To start from nothing is to fight with your back to the water. No room for mistake. No luxury of retreat.

I didn't have to be told by my parents. I knew. Their gestures, their eyes told me that this village was only a mirage and that I only had one choice in life—Beijing University. Anything less was to shame my father, my father's father, and more. I wanted to show my parents that I could rise again, like the mythical phoenix from its ashes, to fly even higher. I understood, and so did they, that we were hiding here, and it was only a temporary safety. If Heng Tu's people looked for us, we could disappear into the mountains on the west or hop on a fishing boat and sail to where the isles of Taiwan lay gleaming. That was the plan, a beautiful plan.

The time to test my manly courage was now. For that, I pushed aside my thoughts of Sumi, my only weakness, and tried to occupy my mind with the formulas of math, chemistry, physics, and English. But each day of school that she did not appear, I felt strong disappointment. Despite my busy schedule, I often wondered when I would see her again.

One fine day, I was sent off to buy some fish sauce from the old lady who ground baby sardines with a handheld mortar and pestle, making the finest sauce my family had ever tasted. The store was by the main street of the village. The road was cobbled with pebbles, another gift of the sea, and dusted with loose sand that came off the fishermen's ankles when they returned from the water. Grain sellers lined their storefronts with large jars of wheat, oats, fat yams, and thin rice. The candy man doubled as the blacksmith, and the barbershop showcased large bundles of incense and paper money to burn to Buddha. The liquor store boasted the largest barrels of colorful brew I had ever seen. Surprisingly, there were no fish stores. However, there were three butchers, each one shouting louder than the other when I passed by. One butcher ran over to me in the middle of the street, gave me a leg of lamb wrapped in a banana leaf, and said, "Pay me when you can."

I took it and paid him right there. My favorite meat, though, was tender goat meat, sliced and dipped in a hot pot, to be slurped down with spicy sauce. The butcher saw a willing buyer, so he offered, "How about the sheep head? Very nutritious, and it's very good for men to eat the brain. You know what I mean." He winked. "I bet your mom would cook that for your dad."

I smiled and walked away. As the children carrying their little siblings raced by, I finally came upon the fish-sauce shop, which also sold vegetables. I stood before an old lady who frowned over her wrinkled nose. "The Long grandson. I will give you free," she said, moving her toothless mouth as if chewing air. That was another thing that I noticed. There were so many people without teeth. Where were the dentists?

"No, I have money. You should charge me."

"I know you got dough; your grandfather was a banker. I just wanted to thank your folks for helping with the school."

"It is our duty to contribute to the community," I said sincerely.

"I like it when a kid so young sounds so much like his father. And so good-looking. Listen, son, since you're paying, I'm gonna give you the freshest bottle. This old hand is no good anymore. I'm not grinding as quickly as I used to." She shook her head and her silver earrings jingled.

I thanked her with a bow, as was the custom here. Everyone bowed, and everything was cooked with fish sauce. After all, it was a fish town. As I turned to leave, I heard shouts and screams in the street where the kids had been playing.

"Those kids." The lady stuck her head out along with me. "It must be the snake again." She withdrew and sat back.

"But I don't see any snake," I said.

"The dogs might have eaten it."

"They seem to be chasing someone."

"Oh, that poor orphan. It must be her they're chasing after."

"Orphan?"

"Yeah, the girl . . . What's her name?"

I saw a group of kids throwing sand at a fleeing girl who covered her head with a scarf.

"My useless head, I can't remember that poor girl's name." She hit her head with her fist. "Aha! . . . Sumi, that's it."

"Sumi Wo?"

"Yeah, the poor orphan. She was assigned to our village after they did away with the orphanage school by the sea."

"Go on."

"Why are you so interested?"

"Go on," I urged, without looking back at the old lady, who seemed to enjoy chatting. The kids were ruthless. They threw stones at the girl as she ran along the gutter toward the end of the street, where a pile of watermelons stood. She stopped for a brief second to see if the kids were still chasing her before taking off again. It *was* she.

"Why do they chase her like that?" I asked.

"Like widows, orphans are a curse of our village. But I do not think so. Our ancestors here said that widows and orphans are bad luck; they are a curse to their families. That they're half devil and half human. But I don't agree with that, either. The older you get, the stranger you get. I don't believe anything anymore. They're just humans. And the girl, what's her name?"

"Sumi."

"Yeah, Sumi, the sweet thing. When she first arrived here, she stayed at the temple, where the school is. They said she got raped or something. The head of the village, Mr. Chen, the fat merchant, bought a hundred yuan worth of incense and paper money, and hired a local opera company to perform for Buddha, hoping to cleanse her of the curse. But Chen had an evil thought about her. You see, he has a crazy son who eats his own crap for meals sometimes, and no one—I mean no one—in this town or any other town would have their daughters marry him, no matter how well off his father is, and believe me, he is well off. Look at his belly, so big, and a big belly is a good sign of one's wealth, isn't it, young man?"

"Also a good sign of one's poor health."

"Young man, where did you get that idea? Anyway, so he took her in and has her take care of his boy, who is about five years her junior, hoping that the son will one day be better and sleep with her, that she will bear a child, hopefully a boy, so that the Chen name would go on, you know?"

"Unbelievable. How can you buy a girl and have her sacrifice her life for someone like that?" I paced around the little store.

"Well, Fat Man thought he was doing it out of generosity. Money can buy things."

"But not human beings."

"Oh, yes, it can. At the beginning, he let her go to school. I heard she is a good student, but now rumor has it he doesn't want her out in the street because her breasts are as big as mother clamshells, and her eyes are roving. Men can smell her ripeness from miles away. Her hips are widening, you know what I mean. I should probably not tell you this. How old are you, by the way?"

"Old enough."

"I'll take your word for it. So he's locked her up, and she doesn't like it. He beats her and threatens to have her married legally to that half-wit son of his, having marriage papers drawn by that weasel of a teacher you got in the school."

"That's inhuman."

"I would say, but it's a little more complicated than that. Fat Man thought he was doing her a favor by taking care of her bastard son. It was sort of a bargain, an arrangement, shall I say. Otherwise the young boy would have died." She moved her mouth again, chewing air, and her neck, with all that hanging flesh, moved like a turkey's.

"Sumi has a son?"

"Yeah, she got raped somewhere and got pregnant. They all wanted her to kill the baby, but she refused to abort it and hid in the mountain. So Fat Man said to her, 'I will raise your bastard son and you take care of my son,' and of course never did he say anything about marriage."

"How can the whole village accept that?"

"They live and they breathe. They only wish that that sort of thing doesn't happen to them. They go their separate ways. Especially because Fat Man has a company, a fishing company, and he hires people in the town to work for him. His eyes are on her every day. I don't think she can sneak to school anymore. And villagers are afraid of him because he lends them money, and if they say anything he doesn't like, they're finished."

"How do you come to know so much?"

"I live and I breathe. Gossip keeps me alive. Look at me, ninety and still not dead. The goddess of life doesn't need me yet, but the day will come, I am sure." She smiled, and her face looked like a bundle of wrinkled sticks. Her eyes disappeared, and all I saw were her nostrils and her turkey neck.

"Could you please tell me where her house is?"

"Who could miss it? The red roof with the stone walls."

I stumbled home, my heart heavy with the weight of Sumi's tragedy. I felt sad for her. No, sadness didn't even begin to tell the tale of my sorrow. How could a beautiful girl like her be saddled with such a ridiculous feudal fate? What shocked me even more was that on the surface, the village seemed so calm, not a ripple, not a wrinkle. No one seemed to care or notice that there was something wrong in their midst. The myth of Sumi only got deeper and wider as each day went by.

Sumi. I said her name tenderly into the wind from the sea. Sumi! What I feel for you—a mixture of millions of little feelings, a zillion of them. Sumi, oh, you poor girl.

That evening, alone in my room, listening to the waves, I grabbed my pen, pulled out a piece of white paper, and composed the following poem:

The mountains could only sigh and the sea moan
The heart of a lover breaks in the night
Gather your shoes
For the thousand-li journey
Will start from under your feet
A wisher by the mountain

Utterly irregular in rhythm, sound, and pattern. An atrocity that Grandfather would tear apart as a gushing of rampant emotion. But it satisfied me. I felt limp from such expression, a load lifted from my heart. Tomorrow, I would wait for her by the road and pass the poem to her. If she didn't show, then the day after tomorrow, and the day after that. The sun could set and the sea rest, but I was determined to give this piece of burning fire to her, unedited, the way it was written, with all the misspellings, to show the contour of my heart at that particular moment, and the skyline of my lofty hope for her.

THE MULTIFUNCTIONAL Mr. Koon coached me, one-on-one, as the single seed of this town to contend for the trophy of a college seat. He had written to the county miles away to ask for preparation materials and guidelines for the all-important National College Exam. As I made great progress, Mr. Koon grew excited. His bad leg swung a little wider, and sometimes he forgot that he was a monk and cursed like a fisherman to praise my efforts.

One day after all the nappers in class were gone, Mr. Koon told me, "I have registered two names for our school to take the annual college exams. Here is the confirmation." The excitement was obvious in his eyes and fidgeting bad leg. He waved the piece of paper from the College Exam Committee.

"One would be me. Who is the other one?" I asked.

"Sumi Wo."

"But I haven't seen her for weeks. How could you register her?"

"I will visit her and talk to Fat Man Chen," Koon said.

"That's a great idea." My pulse quickened. Mr. Koon surprised me. He didn't just live and breathe; he cared. But did he dare? I asked, "Aren't you afraid of Fat Man Chen?"

"Don't forget, I am the top Commie in town."

"That doesn't mean much these days, does it?"

"Well, it does when the fat man wants my official seal on his paper to do business outside the county. It's still a Communist state." I never saw Koon so animated.

"Could I go with you to visit?"

Koon considered my request, then nodded. "Why not? Let's go now."

I bagged my books, jumped to my feet, and followed the cripple down the narrow path leading to town. My poem was folded inside the pages of my English dictionary. The red roof, the symbol of my yearning and forbearance, was now going to swing open its forbidding door because the top Commie dog of the village desired so. I mused over my good fortune, and could not help smiling at the two shadows we cast on the road—mine, straight and tall; Mr. Koon's swinging with an assured and purposeful rhythm. Dust danced at his feet, and there was a light bounce to his gait.

The house was sturdy stone, its face washed by the rain, looking whitish green. The red roof resembled fish scales, vibrant with color. It was two stories, but it huddled closely against the slope like a sea turtle clawing to the earth. Nothing, not even the wickedest typhoon, could lift this shell off the slope. The thoughtful owner had planted leafy *bailan* trees to shield the wind. And the entrance, framed by the rarest green rock from the mountains, was made from the finest lumber, seasoned and cut according to the flow of its grain.

Koon knocked on the door, and a dog appeared from a small hole at the foot of the door—two sizable balls swung between his legs, telling us that he was the hunk of the town, and the rest of the female doggies were just his dispensable concubines. He wore the air of his owner—fat, wealthy, well fed—not a wild dog that chased crabs and fish down at the beach or snakes in the street. This dog was impatient; his eyes asked the questions, not his mouth. They looked lazily and slowly at the two of us as if we were but another pair of money borrowers, pathetic poor fishermen of the town, whom he often had to chase off the property. *Get out of here, I am going back to sleep,* he seemed to say.

"Anyone in there?" Koon asked.

The dog began to growl, obviously angry at our intention of breaching protocol. His hook eyes rolled with the same meanness that would have reduced female counterparts into squatting submission.

I took two steps back, but not the cripple, who shouted again, "Anyone there?" Koon's voice seemed to displease the beast, and so it lunged at him. But Koon wasn't a fool. He spat, squatted down, and swung his bad leg, causing a half-circle of dust to rise, which made the dog sneeze and claw his dusty snout with his paws.

A woman's voice answered from inside the shut door. "Who is it?"

"The Commie director," Koon shouted back.

"Oh, wait a second."

The door swung open. A chubby woman of about forty, in burning red, smiled like the mountain flower stuck in her greased hair.

"Hello, Mrs. Chen." Koon bowed.

"Yes, can I help you?" She had to be the fat man's wife, for she, too, was heavy at the waist and small on both ends. Her tight blouse and skirt contoured plump breasts and a fat behind. Fat was good in this town. All the rest of the townspeople were thin, working sticks who ate three *liangs** of food and lost four on their way to work. She had to be the most glamorous and sexiest woman in town. A well-kept woman was a fat one with makeup.

"I am here to talk to your husband about Sumi."

"What do you have to talk to him about that he doesn't already have an answer to?" She was short and rude, her hands resting on her waist.

"I don't know the answer. That's why we are here."

"She is not going to school."

"Says who?"

"Says she."

"Can I ask her myself?"

"No, she is busy."

"I have to ask her myself before leaving. I have to have an answer from her."

"Who says you have to?"

"I say so."

"And who the hell are you to step onto our doorway with this alien son of the Longs to threaten me, a poor little housewife. You get out!"

"Sumi, come out," Koon shouted, knowing that he was not getting anywhere with this fat lady.

"You're wasting your time. I'm going to tell my husband and you will be sorry."

"No, you will be sorry. I'll report this to our commune and see who wins."

---

*Three *liangs* equal about half a pound.

"Mr. Chen knows all the *tao kai** in the commune and in this province. You don't scare us. Fat Man does what he wants to do, and nobody bothers him. You hear that?"

"I'm afraid it is not going to be so simple," Koon said.

"Yes, it is that simple. If she goes to school, who is going to take care of her bastard? You tell me."

"She can bring the baby to school, and no one would be bothered by him." I jumped in, trying to be helpful.

"Who are you to tell me what to do?"

"I am her classmate."

"I know who you are, and where you came from. You are on the run from the government yourself, everyone knows. The whole family is shamed and disgraced. That's why you're here. Don't you get cute with me. Know your position or you will suffer."

I was stunned by the outburst. They knew everything about me? Then why did everyone act as if everything was fine?

"Don't start with him. He didn't come here to fight with you. You fight with me," Koon said. "Let me talk to Sumi or I will file a complaint."

"Get lost!" She turned and slammed the door.

The two of us were left speechless. As we wondered what to do, the door opened again. It was Sumi. Her face was bruised on one side, and her eyes were red from crying. In her arms she held a beautiful bouncing boy with big eyes and a tall nose. He was crying because his young mother was crying. She bowed and said, almost begging, "I'm not going to school. Thank you for inviting me again."

"You are registered to take the National College Exam. Here, this is the confirmation," I exclaimed.

She looked up, wiped her teary eyes to clear her vision, and stared at the piece of paper in my hand. "Is it, really? Am I registered to take the test?" she asked urgently.

"Yes, see for yourself."

Hungrily, she read the brief description of the test and saw her name. "I can't believe it."

---

*Leaders.

"You must. We'll help you prepare," I said. Koon nodded in agreement.

I saw a teenage boy rush toward Sumi from behind, a wooden chair in his hands raised high to strike her. The boy was followed by the fat woman, who obviously had gone inside to instigate him. "Go get her! Go get her! They are here to take away your bride!" the woman shouted.

"No one take my bride! No one take my bride!" The retarded boy couldn't pronounce the words clearly, but I understood him and stepped up, pushing Sumi aside just in time to dodge the strike. But the boy was strong. He picked up the chair again and struck at me. I caught the chair in the air and squeezed the boy's right arm so hard that the little demon screamed like a sheep, crying for his mom. "Mama, Mama! Hurt, hurt!"

"You are bad people coming to hurt us. This is war! Wait until Fat Man is back. You hurt his only son. Oh, you're going to pay!" The woman drummed at my chest and cried.

"Please, you should go. Please go," Sumi begged us, her baby wailing. But she grasped the confirmation firmly.

Koon pushed the fat lady indoors and told her, "We're going, but you must send her back to school."

"Never! You are no monk! You are so rude, intruding into our family affairs. We bought the girl. It is none of your business. Get out and go. And the young Long, don't you lay your hands on my son's bride, you bastard."

Koon grabbed me and we ran off like a couple of beaten soldiers. I knew I had gotten into trouble with the most feared man of the town, but I had gained something. I had gotten to see her again, and had slipped my poem to her, too.

"We've got to do something," Koon said. "I am sorry to get you involved in this thing."

"It's only right, Master Koon."

"But you've got to watch out for Fat Man. He lashes back like a poisonous snake."

"I am not afraid."

"Good. But he will strike you when you are most unprepared."

I could still hear the dog barking and the fat lady shouting. "I'm worried about Sumi."

"I am, too."

"What will happen to her?"

"I can't imagine."

"You think we made things worse off for her?"

"No, I think we did the right thing."

"Master Koon, we are really fortunate to have you as our teacher."

"It is my good fortune to have you here by my side."

We shook hands. I looked back. The red roof now looked more like a fortress, a prison.

The following day, the school wall that was usually pasted with political slogans was covered instead with a large green poster that looked as glaring and as out of place as an ugly birthmark on one's face. It announced that Mr. Koon was officially removed from the position as the head of the Communist Party of Lu Ching Bay Village. The salaried position was to be taken over immediately by Lou Fu Chen, Fat Man. It went on to say that Mr. Chen, a prominent businessman, had joined the Party as of today, and would be taking care of the village's political affairs as promulgated in the Party manual. Mr. Chen had promised to take on the job without a salary, a selfless act much to be praised. Almost like a footnote, it mentioned that Mr. Koon had been fired for the possible embezzlement of Party dues. The notice was signed by the county's Party chief, with a glaring official seal at the right bottom corner.

I had known the power of Mr. Chen, but had not anticipated his reaction to be so quick and adverse. I saw my classmates in the crowd standing before the poster. They grinned and patted each other's shoulders. "I told you the cripple was creepy," one of the students said.

"The Party crap is old news. Who cares whether Fat Man or the cripple is our political leader?" another boy said.

I hurried in to my classroom. There sat Mr. Koon in his usual corner with the contented look of a peaceful monk. He smoked his tobacco roll, letting the bluish spiral climb along the morning sun that shone through the windows. He was humming a local tune, much like the way he chanted in the shrine. His head was shaven, though the roots of his hair were not burned like a real monk. He looked his usual self.

"Master Koon, I am sorry they fired you," I said. "Is what they said true?"

"Yes and no."

"What do you mean?"

"Yes, they fired me. No, I did not embezzle the money. The Party dues I collected were spent buying lumber to make new tables and chairs."

"I believe you. What are you going to do?" I asked, concerned.

"I could always float in a wooden basket in the shallow waters and dig clams in my spare time. What really hurts is that they took away my largest salary among the three titles. Fat man knew that if I lost the Commie job I would naturally think it unprofitable to continue teaching and take my dead wife's father's offer to sell boxes of incense in another town. But you know what? The more he tries, the more I want to stay and make sure that Sumi goes back to school. He could buy the Commie job, but no one is going to drive me out of this town."

"Can I help you in any way?"

"You already have. I don't want you to be more involved than you are. Fat Man is known around here as a serpent, a miser, a demon. He fights dirty. How do you think he got hold of a fleet of fishing boats?"

"What did he do?"

"Nothing that Buddha would approve of. No wonder all that money couldn't buy him a healthy son to carry on his name. Remember, virtue is the best cure for evil, but only the virtuous know that rule."

"So you'll stay?"

"Until you and Sumi are gone to college."

"Thank you. I will help as much as I can."

"Your only mission is to get into college, son. Don't waste your time. You're meant to be somebody, you know."

Standing before this crippled giant of a man, I felt small and petty. Then I worried about my own punishment coming from Fat Man.

FATHER HAD OBTAINED more news about the seaside tuna factory. Another army veteran told him that with some investment he could export anything through unofficial channels by boats that negotiated the waves of the Taiwan Strait or went down south to the colony of Hong Kong—in other words, by smuggling. One day, Father came up with a brilliant idea: herbal medicine. Start cheap, grassroots, get some local doctors. But Grandfather said that modern medicine outside China had advanced greatly, and there was not much of a market for herbal medicine. Why not try raising oysters, or start a pearl farm? Father could hire all the army veterans in the region, and have a profit-sharing venture. Hong Kong and Taiwan could use plenty of pearls, Father repeated to me each night as we sat out on the porch. Just imagine the pure gleam from a genuine pearl. Father started to read up on the pearl business and visited the oyster farms along the coast.

Grandfather continued to pursue his idea of starting up a bank to service the coastal cities of Fujian, and went to the county government to inquire about getting a banking charter. A bank was what this growing fishing town needed. He was told that the only condition for getting a charter was a required 250,000 yuan as capital reserve. He sighed, disappointed. Where would he get that kind of money? If he had a bank, he would be able to finance his son's oyster business, but without the seed money, he couldn't even start a bank.

As the men of the Long family got more and more involved with their different ventures, they found themselves sighing a lot more and talking less. Grandfather could often be found looking at the distant dock where the fish were unloaded and traded for cash. Truckloads were transported nightly to the city. He would count on his fingers the number of loads each day. All this money could be put in his bank and made to grow more money, and he could use that money to finance even more ventures. Soon a capitalist township would grow like the sparks of a prairie fire. And no one could stop it.

Grandfather remembered the great concept that he had learned at Oxford about leveraging. It did not take long for him to find the answer.

One day he jumped up from the silent dinner table and declared, "I want to mortgage this old house for the seed money."

"Our house?" I asked.

"Yes. I will go to Fat Man to borrow money, and use our house as collateral. What do you think?"

"Great idea. Would he do it?" Father was excited about anything that could bring him some hard cash for his oyster business.

Mother sat silently, smiling. She was happy to see her men happy. The last thing she wanted was to have them rot away in silence.

"No, no," I protested vehemently. "I don't think it's a good idea. In fact, I think it is a terrible idea. You see, he wouldn't lend the money to you because you'll compete with his lending business, or he will charge you so much that it wouldn't be profitable for you. He's a serpent, you know."

"A serpent? I have never heard that before. They all say he is a fair lender," Grandfather said.

"He might be, but you have to be very careful." I had not told them about my brush with the man's tricky wife. Grandfather, not knowing the situation, would only be inviting revenge that was late in coming. I only had one solution to the problem. In fact, the timing was a godsend. It was now or never.

Shento

CHAPTER 23

1980

NUMBER 9 ISLAND

Train a soldier for a thousand days only to test him in one day's trial. Such was the motto of Number 9 Island. One year had passed, the tides had ebbed and flowed, and the leaves of the island trees had fallen and rebudded.

Every day I followed an advanced regiment of martial arts tailored especially to fit my progress and my growing muscles. Mind punishes the body. Body enhances the mind. In that cycle, the mind strengthens, the body toughens, no matter the thunderstorms, the scorching heat, or the winter cold. In the end, my mind succumbed to a numbing, disconnecting my body from the earth beneath me, the sea surrounding me, the sky above. I was a cleansed monk, light of weight, clean of earthly burdens.

Such was the essence of martial arts, propelling me to rise above it all, unsoiled by the mud of living, marking me a slim lotus bloom that stood tall and alone from the ordinary and plain. Time, when uncontemplated, flowed freely by like an unwatched river, measurable not by the minutes or hours lapsed, but by a will formed and firmed. Mine was a will like no other, a will of iron, of hardened steel.

On the second anniversary of my arrival, Sergeant La bestowed upon me the citation of Light One, the third-highest honor in his discipline and style of kung fu, after Transcended One and Unburdened One.

Light One I might be, but unburdened I was not. We remained parted, Sumi and I, and the agreement I signed and my vow to the worthy work of Sharp Dagger compelled me by the code of honor to refrain from writing to her or inquiring about her.

The code of honor was one thing, missing Sumi another. On a few dark days, I went as far as making the feeble attempt to send a message in a bottle. The idea wasn't that far-fetched, for I also thought if I included some money with the letter to Sumi, when a fisherman or a water boy found it floating in the sea, he would be enriched by carrying out the act of forwarding my message to the designated address. And Sumi would know that I survived. Was it too much to ask for? The letter was written, not once but many times. Bills were rolled outside a slender letter, clear bottles sought with secured caps that would not leak or smear the ink. But the act of tossing the bottle into the sea was never carried out. The code of honor and Sergeant La's knowing eyes stopped me. I was a Jian Dao, and the blade was double-edged. The hollow bottles lined my windowsill instead.

Tan

CHAPTER 24

When dawn was just breaking, I walked as nimbly and light as a cat down the squeaky stairs of the old family house, carrying my trunk, the one I kept hidden under my big wooden bed. I had borrowed a bicycle from Mr. Koon, who had given me the day off from school and agreed to lie for me if my parents inquired about my whereabouts.

The bike was practically an antique, with a few spokes missing. I figured that if the road was not too pitted and rocky, the remaining spokes would be enough to sustain my weight. I wore a straw hat on my head and a long-sleeved white shirt buttoned at my neck, my cotton pants were pressed straight, and my leather shoes were freshly shined. All were a rare sight in Lu Ching Bay and a possible source of laughter in the village, where men's favored wear was their bronzed skin, coarse shorts, and bare feet. Men here would rather die than be caught wearing so much.

My destination was twenty miles away, the county seat of Linli. To my misfortune, the sun was biting like bees and the wind was blowing south, causing me to ride vigorously against a stiff headwind. The trunk I tied to the back of the bike only added to the weight. By the time I got to the People's Bank, a two-story brick building in the middle of the town, I was soaked in sweat. My formal wear now looked like the feathers of a fallen seagull in the water. But I didn't take it off. Meeting a government banker, like any professional occasion, required that I act with the utmost politeness and rigidity, especially since I was a mere seventeen-year-old.

The town of Linli in the summer heat at noon looked like a tired sand castle on the beach—empty, irrelevant, with the possibility of collapse at any time. Hungry-looking stray dogs with sunken stomach walls and scars from unsuccessful heists lay in the shadows of dirty market walls, seeking mercy from the sun.

A hatted old man with wrinkles that shelled his sweat like a terraced irrigation system squinted at me from his onion stand, which displayed his sleepy produce. He told me that the bankers were all napping at their desks at this time. When they woke up, they would only be at work a little while longer, playing poker to kill the time and heat.

I parked along the front steps of the bank, sweaty and thirsty, waiting for the siesta to end. The whole universe seemed to have settled down, motionless, barely breathing. The drowsiness made me yawn. I took off my shirt, hung it on the bike's handles, and let it dry in the sun. Then I kicked off my shoes that smelled of the road I had traveled.

I went over my lines again and again. My biggest obstacle was to convince the banker that I was the rightful owner of all the bonds that I had in my trunk. The bonds had matured, and I intended to redeem them all. But there was a staggering amount. A thousand or two would not make a dent in the bank, but a million yuan?

When the heavy wooden entrance to the bank opened, I stood upright. My white shirt was only a little stained with sweat under the armpits. My shoes were well laced, and I had washed my face in the river that ran nearby. I was met by a yawning bank clerk who puffed his smoke while scratching his ass, his cheek creased with the uneven grains of the rough desk at which he had just been sleeping. "What do you want?" he barked.

"I am Tan Long and I am here to do business with your bank. Can I see your manager, please?"

The clerk pulled up his trousers, which kept slipping off his skinny frame. He rubbed his eyes and said, "The manager is busy and only takes care of the big accounts. What is your business?"

"I demand to see your manager. You will not regret asking him for me."

"My manager only deals with clients with assets exceeding ten thousand yuan, no less." He lifted his eyebrows with disdain.

"Then he will have a hundred reasons to see me, sir." I briefly opened my trunk, which was filled with the bonds I had collected in my childhood, giving the clerk a quick glimpse.

"This way, please."

To my surprise, the manager of the branch was a woman of forty, handsome and forward. For a woman to gain that position in this male-dominated culture, she had to be at least ten times smarter than the next man.

"To what do I owe your presence, young man?" she asked me respectfully. She offered me a filtered Sphinx, a brand smoked only by a privileged few in China. "Do you smoke?"

"I certainly do," I lied.

"A young man who smokes and comes in with a suitcase of mystery." She was a poet. "Tell me where the goodies came from, how much, and how I can take care of you." She was a fast talker as well. She leaned over her lofty desk, lit my cigarette first, then hers.

I dumped my suitcase on the desk. "I need to redeem a million yuan worth of matured Patriotism Bonds."

The lady stood up, threw away her smoke, and almost crawled over the desk to bite me. "A million? A farsighted investor. How did you gain that confidence of yours?"

"By inheritance. From my grandfather."

"Uh-huh. How do I know you came into possession through a rightful manner, so to speak?" she asked, thumbing through a stack of the bonds.

"You can't," I said candidly. "And I don't have to prove my ownership. This is a negotiable instrument, as indicated on the backside of the certificate."

"Fine print."

"I read them and so should you."

"Young man, that's not what I meant." She slid out of her chair and walked to the door to shut it. Her hips, tight and round, swayed left and right with a blood-quickening rhythm. Her breasts, drooping a bit, still bespoke of a wanton lust. She turned slowly and shut the curtains, and in the process, displayed a slice of heaven as her creamy thigh peeked through the slit of her *chi pau*.*

"What do you mean then?"

"I meant them." She lifted a corner of the curtain, letting me see the sign for the police station. "You don't want to go to them for the certification of your ownership, do you?"

I was shocked at the innuendo. A dangerous woman. I stood up, ready to run out of the office, but she blocked the door, tossing her head of dark hair to one side. "And yet, if there is no need to worry, then an apology is in order. What did you think I was going to do? Turn you in?" She laughed.

I knew what she meant, and she had meant the worst. Why was she playing with me? "You can't fool me. There is no such requirement for cashing in the bonds."

"We make the laws here," she said, "to protect the bank's interest. What if the certificates were stolen?"

"They were not stolen," I said.

"I believe you. In fact, I could vouch for you. For a price." She smiled at me.

"How much would it cost?"

"Half of what you've got there."

"Half? Not in a million years."

"Think of the possibility that you might not get anything for them."

"You're threatening me again."

"No, I'm merely negotiating. The cut is well worth it, for it comes with other services," she said, taking off her jacket, revealing pointed nipples beneath her silk blouse. "Related or unrelated."

"For a price?"

---

*A Chinese formal dress with buttons running down the right side.

"You're a quick learner."

I quietly considered. "Ten thousand yuan for you if I walk out of here today with a cashier's check."

"Twenty," she said.

"Fifteen. I have a long way home."

"Deal."

She extended her hand, but I didn't take it. She grabbed my hand anyway and sandwiched it between hers. "Lena Tsai. By the way, who is your grandfather?"

"Make the check first."

She summoned the clerk in to weigh the thick chunks of bonds.

When the clerk reappeared, Lena happily made out two checks, one for 15,000, the other for 985,000.

"You think my share was expensive?" she asked.

"Lifelong earnings for a teacher in half an hour? You tell me."

"You wouldn't think so if you had to deal with those pigs across the street. Now tell me like a good boy who your grandfather is. I've been dying to know."

"Hu Long."

"The former governor of the Bank of China?"

I ran out the door and rattled off on my bike almost a million yuan richer. The wind had changed with the tidal waves. I had to face another headwind on my way home. The bike finally succumbed to my weight, and the front tire flattened over a hidden ditch. I threw the bike into the sea, letting it sink to the bottom of the Pacific. I whistled and ran all the way home. I made a small trip to the village's postman, where I bought a thick envelope, stuck the check inside, and whispered to have it delivered at my home the next day again without revealing who had sent it. For that silent service, I squeezed a 10-yuan bill into the postman's hand, who grinned from ear to ear at the bonus, the size of his monthly income.

At the dinner table, my family sat with long faces. The meal lay untouched. It was a whole fish, mackerel, steamed with ginger slices and garlic sprinkled along its succulent body. There was fishball soup, the kind ground from fresh catch, mixed with glutinous rice and some local spice.

Grandfather was puffing silently on his old pipe, which he had made out of a sea tree grown under the water, believed to give the coolest smoke. Father was reading a wrinkled, yellowed document with fading red ink and an official seal. Mother picked at her rice, feeling lonely in the silent group.

"What's the matter?" I asked.

"Where have you been?"

"On an errand for Mr. Koon."

"We might have to be out of this house soon," Grandfather said sadly. "I went to Fat Man early this morning about mortgaging our house."

"And?"

"Fat Man was kind enough to talk to me, and thought it was a good idea till he came back in the afternoon to say that there was a deed hidden in the Party chief's real-estate cabinet, which had effectively given the ownership of this house to a poor farmer in 1949 when the Red Army first took over the village."

"But it has always been in our family," I said. "And besides, the new reform policy is to give the property back to original owners like us, making the Communist transfer null and void."

"But Fat Man said he, as the head of the Party in this town, had no proof of that return policy. There is no precedent in enforcing that policy, and he said he was not going to do that for us. I can't understand why he acted like that, as if he had a grudge against us," Grandfather said, puzzled.

It was obvious revenge against me. Now my family had to suffer for this most inconceivable claim.

"We might need a good lawyer to fight for us," Mother said.

"No, let me talk to Mr. Koon. See if he can be of any help," I said.

After the meal, I ran off to Mr. Koon's home.

Koon lived in a bungalow overlooking the sea. He and his son welcomed me at the door. "What brings you here, Tan?"

"To pay the price of your bike. It felt off the cliff, and now it is swimming in the sea. Here." I took out a folded 100-yuan bill, which was rejected vehemently by Koon, who said, "I picked the bicycle up one day, strolling down the beach at low tide. It came from the sea, it has returned to the sea. Please keep the money."

"No, I insist. I threw it off the cliff."

"A fitting place for it. Now tell me why you are here and not studying? Sit."

We sat on short stools at a round stone table. I told him the whole story. All Koon said was "I will take care of it for you." He followed that remark with a small chuckle. "Just wait."

The next day, my gloomy family got two pieces of news that made them smile again. An envelope arrived with a check for 985,000 yuan to the attention of Grandfather Long. The letter accompanying it said that it came from a silent partner in a banking concern. Grandfather danced around the house like a drunkard. The second piece of news came in the afternoon when Mr. Koon showed up at our house with an official government document, stamped with the red Communist seal. The document briefly stated that the original owners of all the houses taken over by poor farmers were entitled to the return of such property. Mr. Koon had signed it. He had also made a deed reverting the old house to the Long family. No one in the village would know that he had predated the paper and slipped a copy of it into the cabinet in the Party chief's office at midnight last night. Afterward, he had thrown his spare key to the office into the sea. No one would ever know.

AT LU CHING BAY, change wasn't a constant; stagnation was. For thousands of years villagers worshipped the same sea, the same mountain, and the same land upon which the village had patched itself. Occasionally, when life did change, villagers did not digest it well; it was much like eating spoiled fish that caused their intestines to revolt. Such was the case with the changing of guard of this insignificant position from Mr. Koon to Fat Man. They disliked it not because Fat Man bought the power with his bloody money, but because he failed to offer the same kind of services that Mr. Koon had offered and provided with a smile. A marriage certificate now had to wait until Fat Man was back in town for his signature. Marital discord was left unresolved. Wives ran crying all the way back to their maiden homes, leaving their grumpy husbands stranded, at a loss. Property disputes, petty theft . . . the list grew longer and longer. The troubled villagers skipped a step and went directly to the county seat. As time went by, the Party chief there smelled a rat. An official investigation was issued when an abused fisherman's wife threw herself into the sea, where big eels picked the flesh off her body, which washed ashore days later.

The father of the dead woman was a pig broker who also made a living castrating male piglets, and he threatened to do away with Fat Man's slimy balls. Had Fat Man investigated the complaint, she might not have been beaten, and had she not been beaten, she might not have taken her own life in shame and dismay.

Surrounded by children of the village, the father waited at the red-roofed mansion of Fat Man, whetting his equipment, a nice-looking crescent-shaped knife that shone brilliantly in the sun. Occasionally, he would toss a blade of grass and slice it in midair. He was the man known along this section of the coast for doing a painless job. But anyone who had seen him at work knew it was but an illusion. It was as if all the piglets could smell the man miles away. They dragged their hind legs, hid from him, and shook in his presence. When their heads were forced into a bamboo tube to stifle their poor screams, one was left certain that it hurt, that it hurt real bad.

Fat Man, frightened by the crowd at his front door, called the county to request that a team of militiamen be sent to investigate the sticky situation. They took the angry pig broker off Fat Man's grounds, but the grief-stricken man came back at night, shouting, "Eh, you. Come down here. It will be painless, you fat pig!" The siege continued for days before Mr. Koon persuaded the old man to cease and desist.

No one knew what Mr. Koon whispered into the ears of the pig broker. But everyone could guess. In this backward town, men compared the size of their balls blatantly in the open, under the sun. For accuracy, they weighed them, measured them, and let you grab them to test their solidity. Hard testicles were superior to soft flowy ones. The big and hard ones were everyone's dream. Most believed small and hard were better than big and soft, but there were different schools of thought. Big balls, hard or soft, were a big deal, no matter what. Hence men frequently waded into the sea, sat on the sandy bottom, and let their balls be pecked by tiny fish, believing that the bites would make them grow.

A man who did not have a son was a man who could not have a son. Therefore there must be infirmities in his balls, no matter how big or hard they were. That was worse than having no balls. And based on that theory, the pig man might have been persuaded to give up his pursuit. Because Fat Man obviously had shamed himself by having a half-witted son, and in the village, having a half-witted son was equal to having no son. With Mr. Koon's help, the pig man might have decided that Fat Man was a ball-less failure not worthy of his pursuit.

The pig man collapsed before Fat Man's wall, delirious. Even as he was being carried away, he was heard to murmur, "Resignation or your balls!"

Still frightened, Fat Man sent in his resignation the following day. But it was not to be so easy. It showed his intention to forfeit the Party, which was questionable behavior at the very least. And the Communist Party didn't want to lose this capitalist fat cow, or any cow at all, especially at this time when its membership applications were falling like a running tide. As it was known to all, nothing Communistic was ever easy. A sincere resignation was seen as an act of betrayal. They hanged these people and let them dangle. They called them cowards, traitors. And if they could make that person suffer in any way, they would.

Fat Man had chosen the easy way out, deciding to protect his worthless balls and ignoring the advice of the county Party chief, a wicked man in his own right. The chief was then immensely humiliated. No one, he said to himself, had ever in his political career wanted to quit the Party because of a pair of balls. He let the case hang on the excuse of the slowly considered resignation process and kept Fat Man in his job, hoping that the crazy pig man would recover soon and take up the knife again in pursuit of what was hardly visible between two fat legs. In the meantime, the county Party chief issued an order to neighboring counties not to give work permits to Fat Man to do any more business of any kind.

Soon Fat Man rarely ventured out of his red-roofed mansion. If he did, it was always at high noon. Kids made fun of him by shouting the name of the pig broker. Fat Man would look around nervously and run. The shine of his face dimmed, and his gait, once bouncing, had slowed a bit. While he once made deals on the dock every day, with a calculator in one hand—an invention no one in the village trusted—and a small abacus fastened around his hefty waist to appease the locals who insisted on checking the accuracy of the calculator, now he sent his wife out, and she ran back and forth from the house with slips of offers and bids for loads of daily catch from returning ships.

FOR DAYS THERE was no possibility of seeing Sumi. It frustrated me a great deal, and Fat Man, though a subdued man, was not a contrite one. There was even a rumor that he had made Sumi his concubine to breed his own third generation. The village was simmering, but no one lifted the lid and let the steam out. I knew that eventually the newness of the matter would ebb, and everyone would talk about it as if it were the happenstance of yesteryear. The townspeople would see Sumi pregnant, a midwife would pluck the fruit from her womb, and the baby would cry. Behind his back, the villagers would call the baby the son, even though Fat Man would present him as his grandson. With his insistence, the line would be blurred eventually. Sumi would be kept as a vague fixture of the household and live to receive rolling eyes, whispers, and the inglorious title of Little Bedroom versus the first rightful wife, who would be called Big Bedroom.

I stormed into Mr. Koon's office. "Isn't there a law to prevent such a thing from happening?"

Koon knew what I was upset about. He shook his shaven head and said, "Law does not allow it, but tradition does."

"That's a terrible tradition. I'm going to help her with her studies. I know for a fact that with the new government policy, she could get help once she excels at the college exams. And if Fat Man still wants to drag her back, the government would intervene and put her on the train," I said. "That's her only way out."

"It makes sense. The new policy to modernize the country is really about finding talent. It might work. But she has missed so many classes, and she doesn't have time to study for the test."

"If we smuggle all the materials to her, the choice is hers to make."

"I know that she would like the idea. She is one of the brightest girls I have ever met. She certainly belongs out there."

"How can I find a way to talk to her?"

"She is locked in, except for an hour a day, when she is allowed to pick vegetables from Fat Man's backyard garden at dusk."

THAT EVENING I hid behind a hairy old pine tree, with a bundle of books bound together by rope tucked under my arms. In the graying light, I saw the profile of a young girl bending over furrows of bok choy and pungent leeks. It was Sumi, holding a bamboo basket in the crook of her arm, picking the tenderest of the crops and dusting dirt off the stems.

"Sumi?"

"Who is that?"

"It's Tan."

There was a moment of silence before she looked around her shoulder, and then she moved hurriedly toward me.

"What are you doing here?" Sumi asked, her big eyes even bigger.

"I've heard all these rumors about you. Are they true?"

"No, they are only an evil rumor spread by Fat Man to blacken my name," she said, sighing.

"Your only way out of here is by getting into college," I whispered. "These are the books for you to study."

"How do you know that is the only way out?"

"You have another idea?"

"Yes, I am writing a book about my life at the orphanage. If you can help me find a way to have it printed, all my headaches will be over."

"You're writing a book?"

"Yes. I've been doing this since the day a boy died for me. I promised myself that his story will be told."

"What boy?"

"It is a long story." Her eyes were downcast. "I want to thank you for the beautiful poem. I was touched by its robust youthfulness."

"You talk like an old lady."

"I feel like one, old from within. You will know what I mean if you read my book. The next time you bring over some materials for me, I will give you my manuscript. Do you see that window?" She pointed at a small opening up in the attic of the house.

I nodded.

"When the lantern is on at night, you will know I am studying with you."

I smiled and pointed to my house clinging to the hill. "If you see a light on there, it is my bedroom. I will be reading your book."

"We can talk even in darkness now."

"I am looking forward to seeing your light tonight."

"Me, too."

My chest heaved with excitement, the effect of her attraction vivid and palpable. I wished I could touch her, feel her, sit by her, or something. Anything.

That night, I studied with increased energy. I moved my table to face the window, my candlelight flickering in the sea wind. I was there early so that I could catch the first glimpse of her light. The clock struck midnight but still she wasn't there. I got impatient, blew out my candle and relit it. Her window lit up. She had been watching. I blew it out again. So did she. It was she. Almost simultaneously, we both relit our candles.

I did not see her light go out till the next day when silvery light radiated from the eastern horizon. I had fallen asleep, but not her. I rubbed my eyes, wondering what she had been doing—writing her book or studying. She had stayed up all night. Oh, my lady of the night.

Sumi

CHAPTER 25

Dear one,

My heart is sweetened as it has not been since my honeyed days with you, when you were still alive and vibrant. It is the city boy, a self-imposed hero, casting himself to save the horrid me. It has to be your doing. Nothing without the engine that is you could move the earth or part the sea like the Western god, Jesus.

You must detest this, my writing of another boy vying for my heart. If you were still standing, this would lead you, no doubt, to another killing. But you aren't. I'm sorry. Did I say I'm sorry, dear Shento?

The truth is I've been holding myself clean, clean from the hands of many lustful beasts, Fat Chen included, while managing to live and make living possible for our son, Ming—my radiance. I've been cut, bruised, beaten, and spat upon. But no one can make me lower myself. I must live marginally, in shame of having to seek shelter under Fat Chen's roof, but dignity I still possess. It is what makes me walk with my back straight and head high. It is what allows me to look at myself and not want to snatch the broken mirror and cut my own throat.

Now you are dead and above living. Good for you. You don't have to lift a finger anymore. You've an eternity of time. May I pose a question to you? A question that might seem a little jarring. A question that has been hard for me to ask.

Can I ever love again? Do I have your blessing if I choose to open my heart to another?

Sumi
Loving you always

Tan

唐

CHAPTER 26

When Sumi traded her manuscript to me for more textbooks, she said, "If you think poorly of it, blow the candlelight out once. If you think it is any good, blow it out twice. And a third time for excellent."

That night, before reaching for her book, I made myself first study for three painful hours. At last I got to Sumi's manuscript, which was a bundle of yellowish paper written densely to the margins with a pencil. But her Chinese calligraphy struck me as elegant and powerful. The memoir was written in the form of a diary. "I was not aware of my beauty until men's eyes told me so," I read. A girl of six, scared and lost, was left at a seaside orphanage, a dark hole filed with cockroaches of cruelty.

My eyes glided along the lines with urgency, and I flipped through the pages quickly. Fifteen minutes later, I had read through twenty pages, which is what I had set as a nightly ration. But nothing could hold me back from stealing ahead to tomorrow's allotment.

I had never read anything so real to life, so honest in narration, and so intimate in feeling. All other books, in the grand tradition of Chinese literature, were flowery and pompous, a showcase of a writer's breadth of knowledge, his command of language, and maneuvers of fancy styles. The memoir penetrated my heart from the very beginning, gripping me until I broke all discipline and read the whole book. I knew she was watching me; her light was on. At four, when I finally closed the book, planted a kiss on her signature, and put it away, I blew out the candle not three times, but ten. I watched her lantern light go out and wondered what she was feeling, this extraordinary girl.

AT OUR NEXT meeting in the garden, Sumi was delighted, and I, more in love than ever. Red-faced, she asked me what I had liked so much about her manuscript. "Everything" was my answer. I told her that she might be starting a new genre in China's suffocating literature. She asked what that might be. Telling the story the way it actually happened, I said. Less was more, like Hemingway—the most widely read American author. She was flattered by such comparison, and wondered what she could do to get it printed.

"There is a way. Leave the printing to me," I said firmly and mysteriously.

She smiled. "My head tells me not to believe you, but my heart does."

"Listen to your heart. When I get it printed, I want something from you in return."

"What would that be?"

"A first kiss."

"I like that word, 'first.'"

The college exam was only three months away, to be held in the brutal heat of Fujian in the middle of summer. I began to feel a knot in my throat every day as I plowed through my books. I had to take six exams within three days, and I had to make it to the very top, as my father had been the top pick of his year at Beijing University.

Every night, my lady of the night studied with me until early morning. When tired, I would lean over the windowsill and count the stars. Sumi was another star in the sky. She would blow her lantern out to let me know she was there. When she blew it out twice, I would blow mine three times. She would do five, and I, six. Sometimes when the night was very quiet and the sea sleeping, I could almost hear her footsteps on her squeaky wooden floor as her shadow moved back and forth. I knew she was reciting the English vocabulary, and I would feel recharged and plunge right back into my studies.

I did not forget my promise to Sumi about her book. I wrote a short, concise letter to Lena, my banker, the cadre woman who had skimmed no small percentage of my deposit. Within a week, I received a letter back from her, addressed to my school—no small feat considering that the cumbersome postal service lost more mail than it delivered. I read it and smiled. Long live currency, any sort of currency. There would be a book.

The same day, Grandfather received a letter from the same woman banker. At the dinner table, he waved the piece of paper and told us happily, "It seems that I have made the first loan as the chairman and chief executive officer of the Coastal Banking Corporation."

"To whom?" I asked.

"A publishing concern." The old man smiled proudly. "What do you know? This woman banker sent me the capital for the bank. Now she's also brokering loans for us."

"What do you think of the publishing business?" I asked.

"A government monopoly. But it could be a potentially huge growth business. Media could be the next big thing."

"I think you are a very wise old man," I said.

"I am wise, but not quite that old. I feel young, being my own boss."

What Grandfather didn't know was that I had set up a holding company—Blue Sea Publishing—to borrow money to publish Sumi's book. I also instructed Lena to hire a retired editor to work on Sumi's book.

Coastal Banking made a second loan to Father the day he received a business permit from the county government. The loan gave Father the seed money he needed to lease the whole peninsula where Sumi told me the orphanage used to be. Father was frustrated to hear that the land had been bought only a week earlier by an undisclosed developer, who handled business through the female banker. Nonetheless, the lease was for ninety-nine years and the terms were more than favorable under the current market price. And, even better, the undisclosed owner asked for a stake, in lieu of immediate deposit and rent—50 percent ownership.

"Hah, he sure drives a hard bargain," I said.

"He seems to be a kind man trying to help me out," Father said, "and a shrewd one with an eye for upswing potential."

WHEN THE TEST date arrived, I made a bargain with Mr. Koon. "If you are able to get Sumi out for three days to take the test with me in the county, I promise you a brand-new gold coating for Buddha's statue, and a handsome set of basketball hoops."

Koon looked at me in disbelief. A coating for the smiling Buddha would easily cost a thousand yuan. And two basketball hoops another thousand. Nothing this nice had ever happened to this temple. He readily accepted the challenge, without knowing how he might achieve it. Koon, the monk, prayed that night, alone in the quiet shrine, and an idea came to him as if the smiling Buddha himself had planted it there. On the counter sat a dozen sacrifices for the Buddha—a painted chicken, roasted ducks, flour pigs, and a steamed octopus. Koon picked up the octopus and brought it home. The next day he hand-delivered several large slices of the sea beast to Fat Man's household.

"I am here to deliver the precious leftovers from the sacrifice," he said to Fat Man, who confronted him at the doorway without a smile. The sacrificial leftovers, when consumed, were thought to bring good luck.

"To what do I owe this honor?"

"I came to thank you for your generous temple offerings," Koon said sincerely.

Suspiciously, Fat Man took the octopus and went inside the kitchen, where Sumi, child on her hip, was preparing dinner. When she saw Koon, she cut a piece of duck breast and extended it to the teacher. Accepting the meat, Koon slipped another package of octopus meat into her apron pocket. He didn't say a thing—it was all written in the package.

That evening, the news spread that Fat Man was sick with bursting diarrhea. So was his family. The monk was informed, for he had resumed his duty as Party chief. He called an ambulance from the county. The whole family, including Sumi, was shipped to the county hospital.

"Who's going to watch her baby?" I asked.

"Who else?"

"You?"

Mr. Koon nodded. "A teacher and a babysitter. Do your best to deserve me."

Koon had put in enough laxative and herbal sedation so that Fat Man slept for three full days. Sumi, though believed to have eaten the same meat, had in fact only swallowed the good meat in the special package. The following day, she stepped out of the blue patient gown and walked to the middle school at the county seat.

I was overjoyed by Koon's ingenuity but worried that when Fat Man woke up he wasn't going to let the monk get away with it. I didn't know what Koon had under his wide sleeves, but I was sure that Buddha would fend off whatever was coming our way.

Sumi and I held hands for the first time as we waited nervously for the test. The youngsters from the county town were all dressed nicely, most riding in on bicycles and some driven in cars. But I wasn't intimidated. I told Sumi, "Remember, we will succeed."

"I am so scared."

"Don't be. Just think of me and the name 'Beijing University.'"

Sumi did, through three tiring days. We compared answers after each test and could only smile. When the test was finally over, Sumi pecked me lightly on the cheek, and blushed before she disappeared back into her hospital gown. I stood there for a good five minutes before I got on my bike and rode home, whistling with a tailwind.

BY NOW, my banker had become my alter ego and commercial proxy. Lena, an amazing combination of mature beauty and wit, made a perfect representative for me. The summer holiday allowed me to ride into the county seat to chat with her.

"How is my book coming along?" I asked her.

Lena lit two cigarettes at the same time and gave me one. "Not so smoothly, I'm afraid. Blue Sea Publishing is going down. The cash flow has dried up, the workers haven't been paid, and they print lousy books that even monks wouldn't read."

"So they might shut down?"

She nodded, but her eyes lit up as she continued, "I see opportunity here. Let's acquire them."

"But it is a government entity. I will have to inherit all the problems, such as pension and housing for all the retirees."

"Not so if we only acquire the equipment and titles that were copyrighted to them."

"Asset purchase. Brilliant. Go ahead and negotiate the deal. I'll pay you ten percent commission for the transaction."

She smiled. "That's generous. I will initiate talks with Blue Sea Publishing about acquiring them. As you know, they are my clients here at the bank. Also, Coastal Banking will be receiving ten new loan applications that I have pushed their way. As for your father's manufacturing business, I recommend that we make it a joint venture with the Agricultural Import and Export Agency of Fujian Province."

"I do not fancy any joint ventures. I want total freedom."

"This is the only way to export your products legally, since the provincial agency has the export quotas, and we don't."

I nodded. "One more thing," I said. "Can the memoir be printed a month from now?"

"Consider it done."

Three days later, I got a letter from Lena informing me that for a hundred thousand yuan, I was now the owner of Blue Sea Publishing and that I was able to borrow the entire sum for the acquisition from her branch of the People's Bank without any down payment. Neither Lena nor I knew that what we bought would be worth so much more in the future. We held in our inventory a long backlist of copyrighted vintage editions of Chairman Mao's works, and the translation rights of all the Communist leaders. I told myself that from now on, I would never buy anything with my own money. Lena had taught me the first lesson in leverage.

At times, I would ride to the city of Linli and stay in the library until sunset, reading any newspaper that I could get hold of. After much research, I summed up the current China in two words: Golden Era. All government companies were losing money. All government banks had been given a loose leash to make loans, and these were mostly risky loans to the newest generation of capitalists after the dormant Cultural Revolution. Almost every industry needed infusion and efficiency. The state economy was collapsing, and an infant market economy was emerging. It all came down to three words: Opportunity. Opportunity. Opportunity!

The next day I made another trip to Lena's office and told her I no longer wished to operate as an undisclosed partner. Instead, I was naming my enterprise Dragon & Company and wanted Lena to be the president. I asked her to resign from the bank and act solely in this new capacity.

"But you do not understand, sir. It is my current position at this lowly government bank that gives me the power and the leeway," Lena said.

"Wrong. I have just created a new breed of business executives who do not need to rely on their Communist contacts solely, but on their instinct to survive and succeed. If you think you are that new breed, then take the position."

Without any further hesitation, she accepted my offer.

Dragon & Company thus was founded with a handshake and assets of close to a million yuan, the equivalent of US $50,000.

Sumi's book was to be the debut title of the reborn Blue Sea Publishing House. The editor in chief, Professor Jin, a victim of the Cultural Revolution himself, personally copyedited the slim manuscript. As the publication date approached, Professor Jin called Lena to tell her that he had cried many times while reading the book, and that it should sell well in the market. But he was afraid the traditional distribution channels would not be available because the heart-wrenching account exposed too much ugliness of Communist China, and the authorities would stop it from reaching the usual chain of bookstores.

I told Lena to hire trucks, tractors, and bicycles and have people hand-deliver the books into the hands of the small bookstores throughout the province. If it proved successful, I wanted them to do the same nationwide.

The old editor then asked me if he could have free rein to acquire books of the same nature. He predicted that there would be a strong demand for more exposé books about the Cultural Revolution, which government publishing houses dared not acquire. But Blue Sea could. Nonetheless, he cautioned me that there was enormous risk involved. All I told him was no risk, no profit.

THE TEST RESULTS came one day in August, arriving at the office of Mr. Koon, who dutifully ran to my home. With his bad leg dragging on the road, I could see the rising dust announcing his arrival before I could see my teacher waving the envelope. As he neared the house, breathless, the monk asked me to kneel down on the porch. I tried to grab the envelope, but the monk slapped me, and asked me to pray with him before opening the result.

"Buddha, help us."

"Buddha, help us."

"Please bless this boy, who has paid for your new gold painting so that you shine brighter, and the basketball court. And do bless the girl, Sumi, who needs your help so very badly."

"Come on, let's open it," I urged.

The monk kneed me with his bad leg. After a lengthy chanting of unintelligible prayers, Koon opened the first one.

"Four hundred and fifty for Comrade Tan Long," he announced. Then he read on. "Here, it says you have tied with another for the top spot in the province of Fujian. Congratulations!"

I was stunned. Number one in the province? My head went hot and cold, my temples thudded. I was going to Beijing University Law School! But who had tied me?

"Let's see how Sumi did," Koon said.

This time it was I who opened the letter. "She scored 450!"

I knew instantly, without reading the rest, that it was Sumi who had tied me. I jumped up along the wooden porch like a frog. "Sumi got in! Sumi got in!"

The monk screamed and jumped with me, bad leg and all.

"Thank you, teacher. I cannot thank you enough," I said, holding his shoulders.

"No, thank you. You do not know what it means to me to have produced two Beijing University freshmen in the same year. I must have topped all the teachers in this province. I am ready for a promotion."

"Let me deliver this," I asked.

He handed me the envelope, smiling.

That evening, I gathered my family around the dining table and declared that the third generation of the Longs would go on, and that Beijing University Law School was my destination.

"Why not the history department like your father?" Grandfather asked proudly.

"Lawyers make the best politicians and businessmen," I said. "I'm sorry, Father."

"On the contrary, son, I am very proud of you for choosing law. Times have changed. Law has its use now. At my time, law was whatever Mao said."

"It is now whatever Heng Tu says. That gives me even more reason to go into law."

My whole family laughed. Mother opened a hundred-year-old maotai liquor. We toasted again and again until everyone was drunk. Then we all started crying.

"I am going to miss you so much," Mother said.

"You have to be careful going back to Beijing," Grandfather admonished.

"Just be yourself. BU is the right place for you," Father said. "But do not give them reason to take you into custody again. You cannot afford that."

"For the first time since we left Beijing, we're truly happy," Mother said, wiping away a tear with her handkerchief. "Happy to our bones."

"Please, do not cry," I begged.

I saw Father squeeze her hand.

EARLY THE FOLLOWING day, I rode my bike into the county town. There, on the desk of my new office, a lime-walled, red-tiled building that Lena had quietly purchased across the street from the bank, lay Sumi's book. I rushed to it and held it in my hands. It was beautiful. A slender volume with an elegant cover design. "What is the first printing number?" I asked.

"Fifty thousand. A record high for an unknown author," said Lena.

"But it will fly," I said, leafing through the pages.

"We're shipping them out, as you suggested, at midnight tonight. Bicycles, trucks, tractors, and even handheld baskets," Lena said. "Congratulations on your first book, Mr. Publisher."

That same afternoon, I carefully slipped the test results into the back of Sumi's book. Finding her picking vegetables for the garden, I hid behind the pine tree and whistled like a *gu-gu* bird to her. She looked around and made her way toward me.

I held the book behind my back, a big smile on my face.

"Do not let me guess. What have you got there?" She chased me, and I turned and ran to the far end of the garden, where swinging willows hung low and thick.

Suddenly I stopped, causing Sumi to bump into me. We fell onto the soft grass, with Sumi on top of me, her chest against mine, her mouth an inch away from mine. I stole a kiss from her tender lips and she didn't protest. Our tongues touched and tangled in a gentle wrestle. Our breath became urgent and our chests rose and fell in a crazy rhythm. She trembled and I held her tighter.

Dizzily, we caressed each other with the intensity of summer heat, our light clothing no barrier. Only when we caught our breath did she notice the package.

"Is it my book?" She tore the wrapping off. "Oh, my book! I can't believe it!" She opened the pages reverently and inhaled deeply.

"There is more."

"What?"

"Your test results." I pulled the paper from where I'd hidden it.

Sumi's eyes widened upon seeing her score. "Oh, Tan! What is your score?"

"I tied with you. Congratulations."

We melted into each other with another kiss.

"Beijing University, here we come!" I managed to squeeze in.

"Beijing University, here we come!" Sumi murmured between kisses.

Love was blinding, suffocating. We were lost in another tight embrace when heavy footsteps approached. I opened my eyes.

"You son of a whore!" Fat Man stood over us with a sharp spear. "Take your hands off my son's bride. Get out of here before I pierce your heart."

We struggled to our feet.

"No, you animal!" Sumi cursed. "I'm not your son's bride. Neither will I ever be your concubine."

"Step aside," I said to her.

"No, he can't do this to me anymore," Sumi cried. "I am going to college, and there is nothing he can do about it."

"You little whore, you're not going anywhere. I'll kill both of you," Fat Man said, swinging his spear toward us. With all her pent-up rage, Sumi threw herself at Fat Man, pushing him onto the ground. Fat Man tossed her aside, struggled to his feet, and raised the spear. I tackled him. Backward he fell, his head coming down hard on a rock. This time, Fat Man lay limply on the ground. Sumi stepped on the fallen man's beefy chest and jumped and jumped. I'd never seen her so angry.

Fat Man didn't fight back. He was twitching, his eyes rolling, his mouth foaming with spittle, gasping for air as he clutched his chest. Sumi said in a trembling voice, "He is dying. Run now! You are innocent. I will take all responsibility."

"No, I am responsible."

"No, you are not responsible!" Sumi grabbed my collar and shook me. "As someone going to law school, you should understand that this is self-defense. He was trying to kill me! Rape me! There is no place for you here! Do you hear me? Run, please!"

"I have to help you."

"You have helped me enough. Run, you fool."

Run I did, in the direction of the sea. Behind me I could hear Sumi scream frantically for help. "Fat Man is trying to kill me! Help! Fat Man is trying to rape me!"

Hearing the footsteps of villagers, I dived into the sea and swam along the coast for a while before heading home.

That very night, Mr. Koon came to tell me the wonderful news. "Fat Man died from a failed heart while trying to rape Sumi in the garden. She can go to college now."

"Thank you for the news."

"Thank Buddha. He is the one with the scale of justice," he said, looking to the sky.

OUR LAST SUMMER in Lu Ching Bay was filled with poems and love. Emotions ran high and low like the coastal tides. The receding heat of the season and autumn, with its lonesome buffalo moos, brought us even closer to each other's heart.

Yet I never forgot my business. Lena reported that book sales were brisk along the coastal towns of Fujian. A nice twenty thousand had been snatched up by eager readers. In the middle of August, Lena reported that we were getting orders from government-owned bookstores throughout the region. Those money-losing stores had heard of the runaway bestseller, and the Communist officials blinded one eye and let the other see, so that they could make some money, too. The new reform policy allowed store managers to take bonuses if sales were good.

"Amazing," I said to Lena.

"Do you want to hear something else?" Lena asked. "Those who cannot afford the book take turns hand-copying it, page by page."

"Hand-copying?"

"And in some high schools, they're forming reading clubs. They read and they cry for the poor orphan. But, most important, they cry for her lover who died for her."

I was silent on that point. I decided not to let that little flaw bother me. A dead man was, after all, a dead man. Dead men usually took a larger share of credit and a bigger portion of greatness than they deserved, just because they were dead. I was now the love of her life. The reason her lover was such a hero was not due to his bravery but her beauty. Her rarity made all men brave. She was the pearl that made those around her shine.

I WAS NOT surprised when Sumi and I were both admitted into the venerable Beijing University. I was to learn the rules of the gavel and dark robes, while Sumi entered into the shrine of China's literati. When it was time to leave for school, Sumi and I took a pair of quacking ducks with red bows tied over their wings, a thick bundle of broad-leafed tobacco, and two bottles of mao-tai liquor to Mr. Koon in his humble home.

The monk was so moved. "Do you want to hear something? They are promoting me to be the Party chief of the county's Education Board," he said proudly. "But you see, a teacher is only as good as his students. I have chewed over that phrase many times since I heard the news. How true it is! How very true! I thank you both for coming to our little town." The monk untied the quacking ducks and let them fly down the slope. "Go! Fly!"

In the setting sun, framed with light, he looked golden. He, who had worshipped Buddha, had in some way become a Buddha. His smile was that of a sinless savior, and his gestures were full of love. He understood, he forgave, he accepted, and he aspired to higher things like the mountains behind him.

"Good-bye, Teacher." Sumi and I hugged him in a tight circle.

"Good-bye to you," he said gently. "Remember, you are the mountain, Tan. And you, Sumi, are the sea."

The monk passed a bottle of water to Sumi and a bag of sand to me. "Take this, and when you arrive in Beijing, spread them on the land. Then you will prosper."

"Oh, I nearly forgot. Here is five thousand yuan." I pushed a small red envelope into Koon's hand. "Our business is growing. Grandfather, Father, and Mother won't be able to help you anymore. They wanted to give you this to hire three new teachers next year. And every year afterward, you will receive the same amount so the school will remain open for the children."

Koon gave me three deep bows. "I thank you, the children thank you, and Lu Ching Bay thanks you."

FATHER'S OYSTER-FARMING business employed mostly army veterans at minimum pay, but Father promised them a cut of everything when the business turned profitable. Fat oysters were hot commodities around Southeast Asia, and pearls were the envy of the world. Gone was Father's fear that he, who used to plan for wars, would not fit in this small village. He fussed over every business detail as if he were commanding military strikes.

Grandfather's banking firm had made ten loans now—he told us more than once how fortunate he was that the city banker named Lena sent business his way. He predicted he'd turn a profit the first quarter.

Their successes made me happy. The more the better, for whatever they did, I would gain 50 percent of their bumper harvest. I enjoyed my role as silent partner; I could sleep while my seed money grew. And that was only a small part of my enterprise. There was my own Dragon & Company. I had big plans for it, but for the time being, Lena would guide it with her able hands while I attended college.

Two days before I was to depart for Beijing, my grandfather took me for a stroll along the mountain ridge to see our ancestor's tomb, nestling against a lush hill carved out in the form of an armchair and facing a flawless vista of the serene Pacific Ocean.

"Look, grandson. This is perfection, in terms of feng shui. The ocean promises endless abundance of good fortune. The hill behind backs us with the solidness of the earth. This is the feng shui for an emperor. Our ancestral book prophesied that in the sixth generation, there would be two emperors born of the Long clan. You are the sixth generation."

"Me?"

"Yes."

"But you said two? I am the only son."

"All it means is that if you had had a brother, he, too, would have ruled," he said after a brief pause.

"Do you believe such a prediction?"

"It is in our family fortune. It is meant to be."

I weighed Grandfather's words carefully.

Grandfather hugged me and I kissed him on his wrinkled forehead. All this was done in silence of the mountains, surrounded by a calm sea.

On the eve of my departure, my family sat on the moonlit porch, enjoying a gentle breeze from the shimmering coast. We drank, and Mother brought out the freshest ocean delicacies—burning-red crabs, succulent oysters. We chatted about my childhood, laughing and crying until the moon fell behind the pine trees. Only when the first rooster crowed and the air turned cool did we reluctantly seek our beds. Soon I would embark on a journey of a thousand miles, and that journey, in the hearts of everyone, was their return to the city that had deserted us. Everything I did from this point on would impact us all greatly. The battle had to be won, yet the only one to fight it was I—the sixth generation.

I slept with that thought in my mind. I was that fortunate son. Had I not left Beijing, I would have laughed at such superstition; but now, having tasted the saltiness of the sea, felt the grain of the soil, and smelled the fragrance of this fertile land, I knew not to laugh. I was the sixth generation, the bridge of continuity. I saw my place in history now.

A few hours later, Lu Ching Bay was alive with the sound of drums, gongs, firecrackers, and the happy *yee-yee-ya-yaing* noise of a traditional ten-piece band. The whole village was at our doorstep. The married women who had not lost their men to the sea wore their festive red. The men, who had not gone to the sea that day, smoked their thick pipes. Children ran around, chasing dogs that chased the squirrels. Numerous gifts—baskets of eggs, bags of peanuts, roosters shaking their red lobes, ducks quacking in confusion, long-legged jumping frogs stitched together by their mouths—all lined our porch.

"Get up, you lazybones, we are here to send you off to the big city." It was the voice of Mr. Koon, the organizer of the festivity. "The tractor is waiting."

They pushed me up onto the back of a muddy tractor, which was by far the fanciest ride in the village. As I sat there, waving to my family and the villagers, I saw another line of celebration coming from the red-roofed mansion. It was Sumi, smiling. She had pinned a large mountain flower in her hair, a symbol of the village. She would forever be their proudest mountain bloom.

In a teary good-bye, we, the first pair of college students in the history of the village, started our journey from the cobbled street of the town. The tractor cranked along, coughing and sneezing, puffing its thick smoke, scaring birds into the sea. The music receded and an incoming tide swallowed up the cheers. I nudged Sumi and pointed to the sea. "Take a long look, for it will soon be no more."

"Wrong, Tan. I have grown up with the sea. I will never forget its waves, its beaches, its mystery," Sumi said, "no matter where I go."

As the tractor turned and Lu Ching Bay disappeared, Sumi held Ming's hand and whispered, "Good-bye, Pacific."

I took the boy into my arms and said, "Why don't we give this big fellow a nickname—Tai Ping, the Pacific."

"Tai Ping. I like that. That's what we will call him, so that he will always know the sea, too."

Shento

CHAPTER 27

1983

NUMBER 9 ISLAND

On the fourth anniversary of my arrival on Number 9 Island, Sergeant La summoned me to his office and said, "Your training here is over. There is no more I can teach you. Tonight, we are sending you back to the Mainland to a new post."

I knelt on the ground before him. "I am most grateful to you."

"Grateful is good, but useful is even better. You are leaving at 0700."

I flew to Beijing that night. The city gleamed with lights. As the plane descended, my chest tightened with emotion. The city of Ding Long. But no longer. Now it was my city. The city of my revenge, my rebirth.

I stepped down the ramp and took my first breath of dry air in this northern city in its golden autumn. Bright lights illuminated the red leaves surrounding the airstrip. I reached out my arms and symbolically embraced my new destiny, then, on a whim, carefully pulled off a perfect leaf from a maple tree near the gate. I placed it in the middle of my diary. Someday, when I had found Sumi again, I would give this to her.

"Comrade Shento!" A soldier saluted me. I saluted back. "Please follow me." A jeep idled nearby. I stepped into the backseat. The soldier tied a blindfold over my eyes.

The ride took me through what I assumed to be the inner city of the capital. I soaked in the noises—the *ding-ding* of a thousand bicycle bells, the grumble of buses, the shouts in quaint accents that reminded me of village bazaars. The smell—my keenest sense—told me that the sea was far away and the mountains forgotten. We traveled up a slow hill and then down again before we entered a quiet place where nothing except birds could be heard singing. I was dying to open my eyes and see the world. But I had to wait till I was guided into a room where a soldier took the blindfold away. I was greeted by a middle-aged, olive-shaped officer who smiled at me kindly. "Welcome, soldier. My name is General Wu."

"Are you my savior who spared my life on the boat?" I felt a surge of gratitude and knelt humbly before him.

He pulled me up from the ground. "On your feet, soldier. We will speak not of your past, but only of your future. Your path to redemption, to glory, lies in your willingness to serve your future benefactor with absolute loyalty."

"I shall not disappoint you, General."

"I hope not. You come with the highest recommendation from our trusted Sergeant La. Do you have any idea what you are here for?"

"No, General."

"You are here to protect the president. Are you ready for that responsibility?"

Chills climbed up my spine. I couldn't believe my ears. The president! The man who had undone the power of the Long clan. I saluted. "Yes, General!"

COLONEL PAI of Beijing's Garrison Force was a monk. I did not know what to make of him. Should I kowtow to him or salute him? The colonel got up every day at five and went to bed at nine. He chanted and meditated, and ate his vegetarian meals alone in his room, with the smell of incense flowing from his windows. The colonel called himself a bachelor, not a monk, which was not a fortuitous label in this Communist power structure. He reminded me of a royal eunuch of a bygone dynasty.

The colonel was a serious man, his eyes darker and clearer than others'. When he looked at me, I felt as if I were the only person in the world. His thin physique made me think of long-legged hungry dogs I had encountered along windy mountain paths, with sunken pelvic walls, tall ears, and alert eyes, always watching out for prey and, more important, predators.

The colonel was the best and worst teacher. Inferiority, he spit on. Superiority, he sang praises for. He silently watched us new recruits with our bulging, sinuous bodies and bubbling intelligence. We were the cream of the country, skimmed from millions of inferior stock. A chosen few of us would be the thousand-*li* stallions that he could count on to deliver absolute safety to his god, the president.

On the third night, fifteen recruits out of our one hundred were returned as damaged goods back to wherever they came from, after the colonel raided the barracks and found their shoes randomly strewn under their beds. His logic? With the extra minutes it would have taken them to find those stinking shoes in an emergency situation, the president could have been lost.

The next few weeks, we new recruits were tested like rats in a lab—our blood, lung capacity, endurance, reading skills, and command of various dialects. Everything testable and measurable was within his realm. One moment, the monk would narrow his cold eyes and focus on a man; the next moment, that soldier was out. The colonel claimed that his inner core gave him signals about his targets.

On the eve of our third month, the colonel opened a bottle of mao-tai, a fine brew, and sprayed it on everyone's head. "You have my blessing now. Tonight, I want you to go out and have fun. You have passed every hurdle. Congratulations. Now go out and enjoy. Each of you will find a wallet full of bonus money under your pillow."

The fifty-one remaining men jumped and cheered, then rushed to their barracks. I counted my money, which was neatly folded in my new leather wallet. One thousand yuan. The crisp bills smelled new. The sun was setting and the western sky burst with colors that matched the excitement of the night. We had been living like monks for the last few months. Hard work, tension, and stress had filled our days, which began at the crack of dawn and ended whenever the colonel said so, usually around midnight. This night fun awaited.

A veteran member of the Garrison Force volunteered to bring us to the hottest spot in town—the Wildflower Club. He herded everyone into a bus and honked for me to join them. "Come on," he shouted, as the others shouted and whistled.

I stayed, waving them good-bye. I did not feel in the least lonely. I had been alone for too long. I decided to compose a letter to Sumi; this was probably the only time I had before my assignment came. A few other men also opted not to go. I wondered if they, too, had loved ones in their thoughts.

I sat at my desk, jotting down a short but pointed letter addressed to the commune in which the orphanage school was located. As far as I knew, Sumi believed that I was dead. I had to reach her as soon as possible. I couldn't stand the thought of her mourning me for the rest of her life, or, even worse, that someone else might steal her heart. Where was she now? The rest of the night I spent dreaming about the day we would meet again. How I wished it would come soon.

Just before dawn, the thrill-seeking crowd crawled back—drunk, noisy, smelling of perfume. One short fellow was so drunk and disoriented that he fell on his face after peeing in his pants. Another kissed my face and woke me, declaring, "Sweetie, come to Papa."

I pushed him away. "It's late."

"You missed a great deal, Shento. The girls, they sang and they danced and I tell you, they've got such lush bosoms, I almost didn't come back," another declared in a loud drunken voice.

I covered my head and went back to sleep. A couple of hours later, the sound of the bugle woke us up. The colonel appeared at the door of the barracks with a list in his hand. "When your name is called, please step out." I, together with another nine, were called.

"The rest of you, start packing to go home."

The confusion was put to rest when the colonel continued, "Those whose names were not called flunked the last test of willpower. You failed miserably in the face of a little temptation, young men."

I looked up to the sky and said under my breath, "Sumi, dear, you have been a blessing to me."

That morning, I was summoned to the spartan office of the colonel. What the monk had to say would change my life forever. "I am sending you to accompany the president to Beidaihe beach for a weeklong holiday."

"Guarding the president?" I said with delight.

"Such a childish exclamation is not to be repeated." The colonel frowned. "From now on, you will have to live our motto as his guard. What is that motto?"

"To die for him without a moment of doubt!"

I WAS AMONG the entourage surrounding President Heng Tu as the private train shot out of the city like a bullet. I beamed when the president casually nodded in my direction as he was escorted into his compartment. In an unexpected ceremony, the colonel then took me to the private compartment and introduced me to the great man.

"Shento is your new soldier, my president," Colonel Pai said, bowing.

"Welcome, young man. Where are you from?"

My head bowed low, almost touching my knees. "I am from Jiushan, dear president."

"I thank you for coming to protect me," President Heng Tu said. "You are an old-fashioned fellow." He smiled.

"I believe in old virtues, and I will protect you with my life. Thank you for the honor."

The president nodded, and Colonel Pai took me back out. My head was so hot from the excitement of meeting Heng Tu that I had to throw a handful of cold water from the bathroom sink onto my face to cool down.

The train traveled through flat terrains of green fields. The mountains of the north appeared and the train puffed its way through tunnel after tunnel, crawling slowly up hills. The crew ate lunch while the entire president's cabinet, also on board, met in the middle compartment.

A massive mountain appeared in the horizon. The train ducked low and disappeared into another tunnel. It crawled and hissed, then suddenly stopped. The lights in the train went off. Darkness and muggy heat wrapped the express train snugly, and the foul smell from the rails attacked my nostrils. My instincts told me to move, so I did. I broke though my window and jumped onto the dark, rocky ground. From my hip pocket I pulled out a small flashlight, but didn't turn it on. I ran as noiselessly as possible, counting the compartments from mine to the president's. The third one, I remembered. I fell once in the dark, scraping my knees. I got up and ran again. When I reached the third car, I smashed the window and crawled through the jagged pane. In one hand I held my pistol, in the other the flashlight, which I used only once to illuminate the face of the startled president. I slung the short man over my shoulder and slipped out the door. Shots were fired as we ran down the dark tracks in the tunnel.

"Are you all right?" I asked the president.

"Yes, I am. Are you the new fellow?"

"Yes."

"Thank you," President Heng Tu said with dignity, despite his awkward position.

I scrambled down to the slope on the side of the rails, President Heng Tu bouncing on my shoulder. More shots were heard behind us. Then the lights of the train came on.

I set the president down and shielded him with my own body as footsteps came our way. It was Colonel Pai.

"Are you all right, Mr. President?" the colonel asked urgently.

"Yes, not a scratch. This young man saved me."

"Mr. President, we must get back to the train," the colonel said.

"No, we should not go there," I protested.

"Follow my order!" Colonel Pai snapped.

"Please," I begged, my feet dug firmly into the ground.

In the next moment there was a loud blast and a fireball rolled toward us from the end of the train. Quickly, I threw the president over my shoulder again, and turned and ran in the opposite direction. If I did not make it out soon, a second bomb might go off, and we would be dead and buried under rubble. The ceiling of the tunnel cracked and chunks of debris rained down on us. The ground shook. The tunnel was collapsing. I sprinted even faster as the president screamed with fear.

"We will make it," I panted. "I will bring you to safety."

After an eternal breathless dash, I saw light at the end of the tunnel. When I reached the mouth, I pushed myself further, climbing up the hill to a good vantage point. Hiding Heng Tu behind a rock, I scanned the area and saw a trail of dust rising from a mountainous road. Two cars ground their way down the slope, escaping from the scene.

The attack had been engineered by the allies of the retired general Ding Long, I was later told. Nine soldiers had been buried beneath the rubble, and two ministers had been shot to death and their bodies burned to charcoal. The president would have been the third had he not been taken to safety by me.

"How did you guess?" Colonel Pai asked me.

"I didn't guess. I felt it," I replied.

Without any ceremony, I was promoted to the rank of colonel, and President Heng Tu awarded me a gold medal for my heroic act. "Son, I want you to be in charge of my personal security from now on. Would you agree to that?"

"Yes, Mr. President." I bowed low. "It would be my honor."

When Heng Tu was told that I needed a few silver hairs on my head before I could be counted on to run the security for the presidency, his reply was dry: "He will grow some soon. Don't worry."

Sumi

CHAPTER 28

Dear One,

I'm turning over another chapter of my life.

You know where I am going. I know you do. You've been busy, playing Buddha, lending me the strength to extract the last breath from that hateful man. Aren't you proud of me, that this time I didn't run away or let others defend me?

Now all the ugliness is over. I'm an independent woman. Not just in spirit, but in life. I am not only going to college, paying my way, but also able to afford a caretaker, Nai-Ma, for our son, whom I'm bringing with me. The money, though I am ashamed to mention such a banal word, comes from publishing my memoir. It will also pay for a small rental apartment outside the campus. My own place—what a dream it is. I know you can appreciate that.

Truth be told, your void is partially filled by the presence of your son—what a big boy he is now, and how happy he is to be going to the big city.

Bless me, come with us, always be wherever we journey.

Sumi

Tan

CHAPTER 29

1980
BEIJING

Beijing University sat on the western end of the capital city. Its architecture was much like that of the Forbidden City, with golden roofs, red tiles, and stone lions guarding the carved entrance. There was something secretive and brooding about the old style—distant from reality, still dreaming of the glorious past.

I imagined an ancient Confucius sitting on a bamboo mat, surrounded by disciples, chewing on philosophical questions of his day over brewing tea, not knowing days and weeks had gone by. Tuition in those times was slices of dried pork; and the disciples' goals, to spend their lives as itinerant scholars, spreading the truth of their teacher. The philosophy of their time was still alive on the campus—harmony among all and obedience to our leaders. Without such good philosophy, I couldn't imagine how ten pairs of stinking feet could coexist in a sixteen-by-sixteen dormitory room by night, and how, by day, the same crowd could squeeze into lecture halls like sardines, listening to venerable, toothless professors spouting the same slogans they had once shouted in the streets—the Communist truth.

"I can't stand these endless lectures of virtuous Communist propaganda anymore," Sumi declared one day not long after our arrival, as she walked with me along Weiming Lake. "I'm supposed to be studying literature, philosophy, and foreign and Chinese classics. Instead, all I do is read propaganda material in the library."

"Have you heard of the Poison Tree Club?" I asked. "It's a secret club where members trade forbidden books."

"Really? Let's join."

"You have to contribute one or two books before you can join in the secret circulation."

"You know I've got one," Sumi said, smiling.

"Right, *The Orphan.*"

That night, I took her to a wooded hill in the back of the campus. The round moon shot its rays through the thick foliage, and a refreshing breeze made the leaves dance like butterflies. In a clearing sat a few dozen young people listening to a bamboo flutist playing an ancient tune that matched the mood of the moon and the rhythm of the wind.

Sumi and I sat at the edge of the gathering. There were jugs of beer sitting on the grass. I was surprised by how much college men and women drank. They smuggled beer into the smelly dorms, stole it into the cafeterias—no small offense if caught—and often danced on the tables, drunk. They had beer for birthdays and holidays, and a great deal of them drank it any day.

The music ceased. The crowd clicked their mugs loudly and started mingling.

A tall fellow came over and greeted us. "New here? Have a drink. Next is a reading from *Anna Karenina.*"

"We wish to join. This is Sumi, a freshman literature major, and I'm Tan Long, first-year law student."

"Fei-Fei, philosophy major, senior. I am the president of the Poison Tree Club. It is a pleasure to meet you both." He stuck out his hand. Sumi and I extended our hands simultaneously. Fei-Fei took Sumi's first, holding it a little longer than necessary. "Pretty one." He smiled at her, then shook my hand. "And you are the handsome one—a perfect couple. But you are forgiven for your perfection," Fei-Fei said. "What book do you bring with you?"

"The Orphan," Sumi said.

"How about you?" he asked me.

"The Orphan."

"How amazing. Same title on the same night by the same couple. Could you comrades be more married? Frankly, I have never heard of the book before." Fei-Fei gulped another mouthful of beer. "But I am curious. Why the same book?"

"I'm the author."

"And I'm the publisher."

"Well, well, well. Now we are talking."

Sumi passed the book to Fei-Fei, who leafed through it carelessly.

"Let's see, Blue Sea Publishing House. I have heard of them. Now, Miss Sumi, would you be kind enough to read from your own book for us? But only the first five pages, please."

"Not even a chapter?" Sumi asked.

"No. Remember you are competing with the likes of Tolstoy, Nabokov, and Dumas." Fei-Fei jumped onto an empty beer crate in the middle of the guzzling crowd. "Friends!" he called out. "Fellow book lovers! Tonight I have with me my acquaintance and soon-to-be friend, Miss Sumi Wo, the author of the book *The Orphan,* which I have not had the privilege of reading. I want to give her ten minutes of our time and let her be heard. Agreed?"

"What about *Anna Karenina*?" someone asked.

"Tolstoy is not here, but Sumi is," Fei-Fei defended.

"She is no Tolstoy!"

"Not even good enough to be his chambermaid!" another shouted.

"Young man, I would not bet your beer on that, for our Sumi is quite a beauty. Even our bearded Tolstoy would have gotten a yen for this one."

"Come on, then, make it as quick and painless as possible."

"Yeah, get going. You talk too much, Fei-Fei."

"And you drink too damned much," Fei-Fei retorted. "Next time you pay for your own beer."

I shook my head, fearing for the future of China's literati. Fei-Fei bowed out and Sumi took center stage. The moonlight landed perfectly on her face, and the mostly male crowd fell quiet, a temporary lull that soon filled with catcalls and whistles.

"What major are you? You can sit with me anytime at my chemistry class," one boy said.

"I've got a story for you to write. Come have beer with me tomorrow, Building Number Five."

"Shut up, you lousy drunk," Fei-Fei shouted, throwing an empty mug at him.

Though it was the first time she had read before a crowd, Sumi was calm. She began in a quiet voice.

> *"I did not know I was beautiful until men's eyes told me so. I had no parents to comb my hair, sing me lullabies, and tell me to look at myself in the mountain brook. Beauty was not important, but living was. For I, at the age of five, had to live alone in an orphanage. It perched on a lonesome peninsula, reaching unwillingly into the Pacific Ocean. When I arrived, I was given a rusty iron bowl chained to my neck and a spoon made of wood, too thick for my lips and too big for my mouth. If I lost them, I would have to eat with my hands, the principal told me.*
>
> *"My shirt was cut from an old rag two sizes too large. It once belonged to a grown woman who had jumped into the river, and whose clothes no one in the village wanted. My shoes were a pair of wooden sandals carved out of two pieces of pine planks, nailed with two pieces of cloth. My hair was cut down to the roots, but it was still no cure for the fleas and lice. Pus oozed from my bubbling skull.*
>
> *"One day, the principal slapped me for stealing two slices of pickled vegetables. I did not cry. He asked me why no tears. I told him my tears had all dried up. But the truth was, tears did not bring you food . . ."*

The crowd was quiet. Five pages passed, then ten. When the first chapter ended, Sumi stopped and wiped her tears with her sleeve. A thoughtful applause, started by Fei-Fei, slowly rippled into a standing ovation.

"What a shitty life. Is this fiction?" a voice asked.

"No, the little girl is me, and the life is mine. Let me introduce the man who had the courage to publish this memoir—Tan Long. He is also my boyfriend, by the way."

"Lucky man, stand up," Fei-Fei shouted. I did so and held Sumi's hand.

"Where can we buy this book?" Fei-Fei asked.

"Yes, where?" asked another.

"By special order only," I said. "It is currently only in Fujian bookstores."

"What do you have there, an underground publishing world?" Fei-Fei asked, interested.

"We do what we think can make a difference in life," I said.

More people surrounded Sumi, each wanting to borrow her copy and inquiring about her dormitory address, notwithstanding her public announcement of her romantic link with me. A star was born right in front of my eyes. She belonged out there, to everyone who loved her and her writing. I watched her with admiration and respect. She blushed at the outpouring of attention, yet she often searched me out and waved to me, smiling. She seemed to be saying, "I love you. You are the only one."

After the last of the crowd dispersed, Sumi stood before me. Her eyes were two gleaming pools of love. Her cheeks were flushed with desire, and her look, a lingering caress. Together we ran into the silvery moonlit woods and embraced, the moon our witness, and the silent trees our testimony.

THE FOLLOWING DAY, the lanky Fei-Fei stopped me on my way to breakfast. "I know some of the most talented young writers in this country," he said, "but they cannot find a publisher."

"What kind of work?'

"All kinds. Poetry, prose, short stories, essays, novels."

"I am open to new ideas. Beer is on me anytime you want to talk books."

"Agreed," Fei-Fei said.

Fei-Fei not only had the eye for a good book, he was also the writer of seven such books that could not find a publisher. He was one of those older students sent to the countryside during the Cultural Revolution who had paid his dues through backbreaking labor and now was pregnant with things to say. Schoolwork was but a joke to him. His father was the editor of a major newspaper, and his mother a dancer. He could have any job. The government owed him. But no job under the Communist rule seemed to fit him. His bitterness showed eloquently in all his works, the most outstanding titled *Under the Blazing Sun,* a poignant tale of hardship in northern China during the Cultural Revolution. It detailed how the cadres had raped his classmates, sodomized his friends, and stolen their money, their lovers, their bodies, their youth—their dreams. No wonder Fei-Fei acted the part of a man who had lived it all and hated it all.

I shipped Fei-Fei's work to Lena and asked her to publish them as soon as possible. After receiving glowing reviews from the Blue Sea editor not long afterward, I called on Fei-Fei with a 1,000-yuan advance, and offered him a job scouting and editing works for Blue Sea's northern China venture.

"Editor in chief of Blue Sea Northern China?" Fei-Fei smiled wickedly. "I beat my father with this title."

"And soon you will beat him again with the kind of money you will make." I knew the right lever to press.

The Poison Tree Club blossomed like a young tree in spring with Sumi as its featured member. A chain of similar clubs grew like wild mushrooms after a rain throughout Beijing's hundreds of campuses. Monday nights, she read at Aerospace Technical College. Tuesdays were Beijing Medical College, Wednesdays, Art College. Thursdays and Fridays, she studied with me. Saturday afternoons, we took Tai Ping to the Summer Palace and rowed a pleasure boat in Qunming Lake. The boy was blooming like a young ox. He'd grown a few inches taller and wore a well-padded cotton coat. His eyes were big and his nose taller. Many times, curious passersby would say how much father and son looked alike. When Tai Ping burst into my arms one day, calling me "Baba, Baba," I felt a surge of warmth spread through me. The child was so innocent and trusting. But I was curious as to who had encouraged the child to call me such a name.

"I thought it might be nice for him to call you Baba," the grandmotherly Nai-Ma said. "You are even better to him than a real father."

THE ORPHAN slowly became a national bestseller, though there was no official list of any sort. But I knew it was so when Nai-Ma said one day, "I know another person called Sumi Wo. The author of the book that my granddaughter is reading, *The Orphan*. The silly girl hand-copied the book herself."

I rushed to the nearest post office, pulled out a hundred-yuan bill, and had the clerk telegraph the following message to Lena:

> *If you haven't done so, please immediately reprint 100,000 copies of* The Orphan *to be distributed in northern China through our usual distribution manner. Tan*

Five days later, I went to the Beijing Railroad Station to personally supervise the unloading of the first batch.

That night at the Beijing Hotel bar, Sumi and I celebrated the shipment—or rather, the safe arrival without any unwanted detection and intervention—of her book in its new territory. It was our first taste of bubbly wine, and we both agreed we could get used to it.

Shento

山头

CHAPTER 30

I cherished the singularity and purposefulness of my mission to guard the president, a calling that was sacred beyond the din of a dusty, changing world outside the red walls of Zhong Nan Hai. I was wired to every detail of this mission, every day of the year, every second of the president's day. Nothing escaped me. I checked out every minister and adviser coming and going through the entrance. Some complained that I had taken the word "security" a little too far. But I knew that once trouble was in, it would be forever too late.

"Are you sure you're not overdoing it?" President Heng Tu asked me one day while walking in the gardens.

"The worst assassin is your friend."

"You fear too much."

"You fear too little, my president."

I reviewed the Kennedy assassination film once a month to remind myself that I was living on the edge of a cliff. One slip of my concentration and my president would die. Each time I saw the film I felt chills run down my back. I swore it would never happen here on my watch.

Day in and day out, I created a routine for myself, tasting the president's three meals before he ate. I conducted background checks on every staff member periodically, even though some had been with the president for years. Soon I possessed enormous knowledge, in great detail, of all the staff's friends, and even their most remote relatives. Names, ages, jobs, homes, and associates—I knew it all. Once a junior gardener reported that he was to leave early for his mother-in-law's birthday. I replied, "Unless you have remarried, your current mother-in-law, a dentist by trade, was born fifty-five years ago one fortnight ago."

The young man was speechless.

"However, do not cancel your rendezvous with your mistress, that waitress friend of yours, aged twenty-seven."

"I do not wish to go anymore, sir."

"But you should. You are fired."

I considered it my good fortune to be only inches away from the president when he suffered his first heart attack. I stayed at the president's side for the entire three days he was in intensive care, refusing to sleep a wink. The man looked old and dwindled, even smaller than his usual short stature.

When the old man finally woke up, I told him, "I will give you my heart if you need it."

Heng Tu smiled and patted my shoulder. "Not yet, at least."

Afterward, I worked closely with his personal doctor to enforce the old man's strict diet. And what a job it was. The president was a cheater. Once I caught him at midnight in the kitchen, helping the chef fry greasy kung pao chicken, a favorite of the president's, for he came from the pepper-chewing corner of the country known as Szechuan.

"Mr. President, I am afraid I can't do my job if you do not do yours," I said.

"Come on, son. I am an old man. Dieting is not what I desire."

"Do you want me to follow your orders?"

"Well, certainly."

"Well, then, your order to me was to protect you." I took the frying pan and dumped the contents in the trash. "This is following your order."

"What have you done to my delicious chicken!" the president exclaimed.

"Your heart will not take that generous handful of salt your chef just threw in. And that oil your chicken was soaking in will pack your veins like the hairballs in your bathroom sink."

"I'm hungry. The tasteless food you have been feeding me is killing me!"

"No, this is killing you. I demand that you return to your bedroom. I will bring some healthy food to you. Thank you."

Heng Tu shuffled away like a child as I lectured the chef. "You will murder our president with that food, do you know that?"

The president took a detour into the pantry and was about to grab a handful of raw peanuts when he heard my voice again. "That is not good for you either, Mr. Tu. I said the good food is coming."

Heng Tu had been healthy ever since, and the country was thriving with his Open Door policy, the economy growing at a nice double-digit gait. More private jobs were created as state jobs were cut. People were living better. The world was watching this dinosaur nation turn around and stand up from the mudhole it had been mired in for many decades under Mao's rule. Heng Tu was the monkey who rattled the system. He deserved all the credit.

In 1984, President Reagan invited President Heng Tu for a state visit. For the first time, I embarked upon a trip to America. I had sent a request to the CIA and the FBI that a team of Chinese agents be allowed to inspect the route of Heng Tu's tour months before the trip. My request was rudely rejected by a pompous Treasury Department representative. Once foreign dignitaries set their feet on US soil, they fell under the CIA's protection, he explained. Chinese agents were but a trivial supplement to the American security detail, which had extensive knowledge and experience.

I did not like the idea of playing second fiddle in the mission, so I flew to Washington, DC, and also Dallas in the guise of a military attaché at China's embassy. I was rudely stopped at JFK Airport in New York City by a customs officer, who asked me to walk a narrow painted red line to the tiny office of Immigration and Naturalization Services.

"Why?" I asked through an interpreter.

The INS officer, Mr. Smith, did not pay any attention to a Chinese-speaking traveler. He ransacked my simple luggage, then leaned his head to one side, trying to match the passport ID picture with me. He frowned, chewing gum and blowing bubbles.

"What is the problem?" I asked.

"Just a second! This is Customs. You have to be patient." He turned to the interpreter. "Tell him to shut up or I'll send him back where he came from."

Only after a lengthy phone conversation with the Chinese Embassy in Washington did they finally let me through customs. I detested my experience at the airport. People were rude and the crowded airport was dirty.

My stay in Washington went no better. I was mistaken for a waiter in the bathroom of a Chinese restaurant. A well-dressed white man gave me $2, and asked me to hand over some towels to wipe his hands. When I did not know what he wanted, the American snatched the two bills back. "Lousy service here," he said, and left.

Lousy service, indeed, I thought, on the flight back to China.

When President Heng Tu arrived at Andrews Air Force Base in Washington, DC, one week later, I was standing nervously right behind him. President Reagan made a welcoming speech, but as soon as Heng Tu began his arrival speech, demonstrators from behind the police picket line began to shout.

"Down with Heng Tu!"

"Down with Reagan, the Commie lover!"

"Down with Communism!"

"Free China! Free Tibet!"

I criticized the CIA for letting this happen. The director's ridiculous response was "Our Constitution allows legal demonstrations. As long as they behave within the guidelines of the law, we can't do anything about it. Freedom of speech, you know."

"But they were cursing China's great leader."

"And they were cursing President Reagan as well."

"What good is being president if he can be shouted at by his own people?"

"What good is it if he cannot be shouted at by his own people?" the CIA director retorted.

President Heng Tu's next stop was Dallas. I could not sleep that night. The sheer mention of Dallas made my stomach roil as the Kennedy assassination footage came rushing back at me. I could almost smell the blood in my own mouth.

The day of Heng Tu's visit, it was a warm early winter day; the sun shone and flowers covered the streets just like the day JFK was taken down by a bullet to his head. Just like then, too, the president rode in a motorcade, heading to meet the governor. I had arranged for another ring of protection by scattering Chinese agents thickly along the route. I almost had a heart attack when a demonstrator threw a banana, which I mistook for a hand grenade. When my men failed to catch the banana thrower, I lectured the agents stationed at that spot until they broke down with sobs.

"We could have gone home without our president. You want that?" I shouted.

"But it was only a banana."

I slapped the soldier across his face and stormed off.

The rest of the trip went smoothly. My face was captured in a photo behind the president as Heng Tu waved good-bye to Reagan. The photo appeared on the cover of *Time* magazine, which named President Heng Tu as Man of the Year.

MY JITTERS FROM the American journey had hardly faded when the president made another impossible request. Facing his seventy-fifth birthday, Heng Tu was seized by a sentimental desire to journey to his birthplace, Szechuan, at the foot of Tibet.

"Fallen leaves should return to their roots," the president told me. "The older I get, the closer I feel to home."

"Your wish is our mission, Mr. President." I saluted.

"Good. For this trip, I want you to stay away from my entourage and merge into the crowd, into the people of that province. Hear them out. Find out what they're thinking and what they are really saying, and report to me directly. I want truth that reflects the reality."

"Sir, you are surrounded by advisers and ministers."

"That is the very reason why I am asking you. They never tell me the truth."

On the first day of the trip, the president broke all the rules that I set for him. He ordered his chauffeur to stop at random and walked unprotected into the cheering crowds, shaking hands with villagers who had known his family for generations. He was happy, smiling with tears in his eyes. People came up to him and wished him well. At times, the little man lost himself completely in the thick throng.

On the third day, I suggested that the president's tour to his ancestor's tomb be canceled.

"Why?" the president wanted to know.

"It's unsafe."

"I need to pay homage to my father, and his father's father. Let me do it. If I can survive the trip to America, I should do well here. I am surrounded by my own people."

"Mr. President, I have intelligence indicating trouble," I said, waving a sheaf of paper.

"What trouble?"

"Death threats."

"I am going to prove to you that it is only a threat."

"Please, Mr. President, you will be taking a severe risk."

"I must see their tombs."

"If it is so important to you, would you consider changing the time of the visit?"

"No. Sunrise is the traditional time to visit the dead. When the sun sets, they all return to the dark. I can't change that."

I agonized for a moment, then softened. "If it is that important to you, I will personally make it safe for you."

The burial site was impressive. Though I knew little about feng shui, I could still sense the site's beauty as the rising sun caught fire on the unblemished horizon. A green mountain sat behind the tomb, providing a shield at one's back. The tomb faced the east, catching the flow of good *feng*—wind. The site overlooked a large lake filled to the brim with gleaming water, fulfilling the element of *shui*—water, indicating perpetual abundance. When the sun broke through the morning mist in the east, it was magical.

The threat had been sent in writing two days before. Nothing specific, but worrisome enough. My men had combed and sifted through every inch of the tomb ground overgrown with wildflowers and thorny bushes, but only found the usual green frogs and garden snakes in the fertile soil.

A large crowd waited for the visitor but was kept two hundred feet from the tomb where the president was to kneel before his ancestors. When he arrived, the president talked and waved to the crowd. Suddenly, screams were heard from among the well-wishers. My men jumped into the panicking mob while I stood my ground and stayed close to Heng Tu. One of the villagers was having a seizure, I was told, and was suffering badly with his tongue bitten and bleeding.

"I do not believe it. Everybody, stay on guard! Do not, I repeat, do not leave your positions!" I shouted into my walkie-talkie.

"We need a doctor. Can we ask the president's physician to care for him?" an agent asked.

"Absolutely not."

"Why not?" Heng Tu asked.

"It is an order!" I said firmly. "Get the limousine ready! We're aborting this operation!"

There was a cry from the crowd, begging for help.

"Help them!" Heng Tu demanded. "Shento, help them! These are my people."

"We must return to your car now."

"No. I haven't knelt yet. We should help that suffering man."

"We can't. You need to leave immediately."

The tomb site was chaos; my men were distracted by the commotion. Heng Tu's back was not being watched. Fear gripped me as my eyes swept left and right.

The president slipped away, grabbed his physician, and rushed over to the sick man.

"No!" I shouted, dragging Heng Tu back while ordering another agent, "Help me, soldier! Get the president out of here!"

As we rushed the kicking old man away from the crowd, there was a loud explosion behind us. People screamed. I pushed the president into the car and ordered the driver to speed down the rough country road. I cursed under my breath while covering Heng Tu with my body, afraid the scare might trigger another heart attack. Through the walkie-talkie, I learned that I had lost ten of my best men. The sick man had turned out to be a suicide bomber and had blown himself to pieces.

I reported to the president, "Another mission accomplished."

"Son, I should always listen to you," Heng Tu said, gripping my shoulder.

Disguised as a migrant worker, I later returned and mingled with the poor villagers who had swamped to the cities. What I learned disturbed me greatly. Young girls from families who wanted sons were abandoned or sold into prostitution, and farmers hardly had enough to eat. Capitalistic success descended upon a rare few. Beggars and orphans crawled all over the mountainous land. Most troubling were the hundreds of thousands of army veterans wandering every village and packing the congested city after they had been dismissed from the downsized military. They were unskilled, lost, and mad with indignation. They drank, gambled, and fueled prostitution, and were ready for a revolt. The suicide bomber had been one of them, a little detail I kept from the ailing president.

My report on the people of the city of Chengdu soon landed on Heng Tu's desk. The old revolutionary, who had risen up from a poor peasant family and had always seen himself as the people's leader, cried bitterly. His tears blurred the words.

"Son, thank you for telling me the truth. Something will be done about it. Now I need you to do something else. I am going to put you in charge of revamping our army. You seem to have compassion for the soldiers. I want them happy, for without them I am nothing, and the republic will crumble to the ground."

"But who will guard you?"

"Someone else could watch me. You belong in a bigger place, doing a bigger job, son."

"But there is nobody I would trust your life with."

"Nobody would argue with me except you and I like that. It is because of that that I am sending you on the most important job anyone could do for me. You are like my dam. I need you to hold back the flood." He paused. "I want to hear every detail of your findings and solutions, and the logic behind them."

"I fully understand, Mr. President."

"Your new title will be special assistant to the commander in chief, which is myself."

ARMED WITH THE scepter of the aging president, I traveled alone to far corners of the vast land, making unannounced inspections on the regional chiefs of the eight military districts. Dressed in uniform, I appeared purposeful and dignified despite my youthfulness. Women felt comforted by my presence, and men seemed lifted by my confidence. But that did not spare me from cold and even rude treatment at some of my ports of call.

My first stop was at the headquarters of the Southwest Command of Qunming, Yunnan Province. My heart sang as I flew over the tall mountains. All my childhood memories came flooding back to me. I was certain that I saw the cliff from which my mother had flung herself to her death. The wild, yellow flowers that bloomed in the warmth of summertime—they were the tears and laughter of my childhood, my only reminder. The village was gone and the land had returned to wilderness. One day I would return to do what was expected of me as a filial son—build a mausoleum, burn some paper money, and plant some sticks of incense to awake the spirits of my baba and mama to let them know that I had lived and prospered. One day when I gained authority and glory.

On the street of Qunming, I stopped many times to look at the children. They smiled at me, some without teeth, others with running noses. I could see my own shadow fluttering like a butterfly in the garden of my memory.

The regional chief, General Tsai, was a beefy man with eyes that disappeared each time he smiled. He was a racist who frequently referred to the Tibetans as barbarians in the presence of the lone token Tibetan deputy, Hu-Lan, a short, stout man with dark, pocked skin who had little actual power and even less backbone.

"We are in total control," the chief boasted at the banquet. "Last year we had to jail a hundred or so monks." He laughed, chewing on minted roasted beef.

"Don't forget the ten that we had to execute, Chief," Hu-Lan added.

"You killed ten last year? For what?" I demanded.

"Religious rebellion. They organized strikes and demonstrations to stir the local sentiment," the chief said. Sensing my anger, he changed the subject to what the half-million soldiers in that region were doing besides beating up locals.

"We make money." The chief smiled again. "That's why we got what we got. Look at the wines and furs. These are all our businesses. We're even thinking of setting up an army travel agency to attract the mountaineers of the world. Tibet is popular now. Just imagine the helicopters that are now idle being used to carry climbers to the camps. What quality and assurance these white climbers would have, with the trusted name of the People's Liberation Army. We wouldn't even need to advertise."

"We could corner the market and put China's travel agency out of business," Hu-Lan added, referring to the government's monopoly.

I wanted to strike the two smug men, but I was in their territory, their fiefdom. The emperor was far away and they did what they wanted.

At night, a female member of the army hotel staff knocked on my door, a bottle of local brew in her hand. She lingered, showing her long legs by lifting the hem of her short skirt. I sat her down on the bed and asked if she did this for everyone who came by this army resort hotel.

She smiled, coiling her body, and said, "You ask too many questions. Many of them just screw me and fall asleep."

"Thank you for telling me. Your job is over for the night." I dismissed her.

The girl left, puzzled.

The next day, the chief winked at me. "How do you like the local flavor? She's a descendant from Tibetan horsemen. She surely knows how to ride, does she not?"

I smiled. "Come over here, Chief. Let me adjust your collar."

"What is wrong with it?" The pudgy man leaned over and I ripped off the golden rank badges from his uniform.

"You are a disgrace to our army and our people!" I shouted. "I recommend that you hand in your resignation. You have reached retirement age."

"I am not old enough."

"But you are rotten enough."

As for Hu-Lan, the Tibetan deputy, I recommended that his rank be lowered to corporal and that he be assigned to guard the fabled temple where the Dalai Lama once sat.

The Northeast Command was no better. It bordered Russian Siberia and it had become the land of smugglers. The chief met me in his well-appointed office, with animal heads mounted on the wall. "The Russian border troops are a bunch of poor drunks," he said. "I bet I could buy millions of acres of their Siberia with cases of the local beer that our army brews here."

"But they are still our enemy. We do not have a formal diplomatic relationship with them."

"Now we do. The trading between the Chinese and Russians is so brisk that I have turned our army into tariff collectors."

"You should not relax your vigilance. Our border security and national defense might be jeopardized."

"The Russians don't want to fight anymore. All they want is to make money and more money. Every day hundreds of them take the trains to our side to buy jeans and cheap watches. This is big business."

The chief drove me in his Mercedes to tour the border. It had grown into a sprawling bazaar, crowded with thousands of traders speaking Chinese or Russian or a mixture of both. To the north, trucks, cars, and mules carried jeans, umbrellas, and sacks of watches from the Chinese side, returning south with Russian furs and jewels. The border ceased to exist.

The next day I changed into civilian clothes and returned for a second inspection. I was stopped only briefly by a Chinese border guard and was allowed to cross the border after I paid the young solider a hundred yuan—the price demanded clearly and loudly by the man with a rifle.

When I returned from Russian soil in the afternoon, after a day of rambling around the bazaarlike border market, the same price was demanded by a different guard. But this time I was offered something, too. "Wanna fuck some white girls?" the guard asked me. He reeked of sour beer and was much in need of a shave.

"Sure," I said.

"One hundred yuan in cash."

"Where do I do it?"

"Where else?" The soldier led me through the gate to the back of an army office. There, in semidarkness, with Russian folk music playing in the background, sat a dozen young Russian girls, who stood up at my arrival and greeted me silkily, speaking simple Chinese while caressing me all over.

"All Chinamen like me. I got big breasts, you see?" a tall and well-endowed one declared in accented Chinese.

"I am sure they do."

"How about you, handsome? I'm game for a good fuck, you horny Chinaman. Like me talk dirty?"

"No, I just brushed my teeth."

"You funny. What service you buying?" She puffed a mouthful of smoke in my face.

"Military style," I said, reading off a price list posted on the wall.

"We got that. Nuclear warheads." The girl grabbed my buttocks and rubbed against me.

"How much?"

"One hundred, as army man said. But that only for him. I fuck for living."

"I have to pay more?"

"One hundred for straight nuclear warhead. Two for rear-entrance permit."

"Your Chinese is good."

"I fucked enough to get the hang of it."

"You work for them?"

"No, they work for me." She cast a glance at the guard standing by the door.

"Do you know the chief?"

"Do I know him? What joke is this? He our biggest protector. This his business."

I paid her 200 yuan and returned to my hotel room to write my report. When I returned to his office and handed a copy to the Northeast Command chief, I warned the man that a long jail term was awaiting him.

"Never threaten me on my soil," the general said. He spat at me as I stomped out.

The trip was not entirely fruitless. I was impressed by the Northwest Command near the Gobi Desert, the hotbed for China's nuclear research and development. The military scientists in that sandy and barren isolation seemed entrenched in a long, forgotten Cold War. They bubbled with enthusiasm at meeting the special envoy of the president. One young scientist named Dr. Yi-Yi took me on a tour of the underground silos.

"How powerful are we in terms of nuclear warfare?" I asked.

"Powerful enough, sir. Without going into great detail to bore you, we could press a few buttons and all the major cities on earth would go up in a puff," he said with glee.

I was pleased that I did not have to demote anyone.

The last leg of my inspection trip was to Fujian, where my orphanage had been—the Southeast Command. The chief insulted me by not seeing me at all. He was too busy, his secretary said. I saw no point in pushing for a meeting. I visited the Pacific Fleet, which was supposed to be guarding the East China Sea against Taiwan. The fleet, which had once been China's only and last defense against the hawks of the Cold War, lay idle, looking lonesome in the Taiwan Strait. Many ships were rusty and worn, and sailors complained about being left out of the money-making frenzy on land, though a few had found their own venue—intercepting smuggling boats between Fujian and the island of Taiwan. What disturbed me most was when I caught a group of young naval officers crowded into a sordid cabin, watching a pornographic video on a ship that was named after the great leader, Chairman Mao.

"You like this movie?" I asked them, sitting on the floor with them, after swiping away a few empty beer cans and cigarette butts.

"Like? We live on it," one of them said, without turning.

"What would you say to Chairman Mao had he been alive and visiting the ship?"

"Join the orgy." The entire cabin burst into rowdy laughter.

Disgusted, I again asked for the chief, who again had his secretary tell me to get lost.

"Where is he?" I demanded.

"He is busy with some military emergency," the secretary said, looking up from her desk.

"There is no such thing."

"It is confidential."

I found out back in my hotel room, while watching local television news, that the chief was at a ribbon-cutting ceremony for an army joint venture with a Taiwanese company that made imitation Italian shoes.

"Making shoes with the enemy. That is indeed an emergency." I wrote my last ticket for the chief, recommending that he be stripped of all rank.

UPON MY RETURN, I was asked by the president, "Now that you have recommended firing half of my military chiefs, what is your next move?"

"To reorganize the whole military into one unit. The way they are now, the chiefs are warlords. They have too much autonomy and no accountability. The left hand doesn't know what the right one is doing. In times of war, we will crumble like a sand castle. We need a smaller but better army."

Heng Tu nodded. "I know how to make it smaller, but how do you make it better, my young colonel?"

"We need to buy the best fighter planes from America, and upgrade and modernize our fleets. But our greatest strength is our nuclear power, Mr. President," I said with excitement. "We have a world-class arsenal to fight any superpower."

"Even the Americans?"

"Yes, and the Japanese and Russians."

President Heng Tu had an amused smile on his face, which disappeared with his next question. "What do we do about the millions of soldiers you would like to see discharged?"

"My proposal is to legitimize those army-related industries that have cropped up, even start new commercial ventures, and let the veterans buy into the companies as shareholders. When the companies are listed on the stock exchanges, the veterans will all be abundantly enriched and have a means of living. That way they will not deteriorate into a loose army, threatening your power."

"How do you go about doing that?"

"Give them special permits and generous lines of credit from the Bank of China. I want them to remember us. And they will."

"Quite a fruitful journey, then."

Not fruitful enough. I had searched in vain for Sumi. The orphanage had long been destroyed, they said, and records lost. No one knew where all the orphans had gone. No one cared, either.

WITHIN A MONTH, my newly formulated plan for the three branches of the military was officially presented to the president. The eight regional districts were to be shrunk into one.

"That sounds good," Heng Tu said. "But my desk is covered with complaints about you from all the regional chiefs. They went over your head and came to me in protest."

"I fully expected that. But once they are relieved of their positions, they will be powerless. What can they do?"

"There is a lot they can still do, young man. They have been entrenched in their position for a long time. These letters, in the subtle terminology of the military, are no less than a prelude to a revolt. The Northeast Command chief calls you a scoundrel. The Southeast Command chief calls you a young fool. The rest of them awarded you the title of 'the bad toe of my rotten foot to be cut away.'"

"That's a compliment."

"The Northwest chief says that if you ever dare return, he will have your eyeballs plucked out and your eardrums broken, so you can neither see nor hear again."

"But the nuclear researchers seemed to appreciate my visit."

"Two-faced." The old president shrugged. "They all are."

"What do you think of the complaints?" I asked.

"When they insult my foot, they insult me."

"We should act quickly before we lose our military."

"I am going to call in all the chiefs in a fortnight, and make them accept what is coming their way."

On the morning of December 26, 1986, a light snow dusted the icy ground. Some flakes stayed on my fur collar. The cold, a bone-penetrating chill, made me alert. And alert I needed to be, for today the eight regional military chiefs were gathering here for a special session, the kind that had been called only twice before in the history of China—once when the Russians lined the northern border, the other time when Vietnam was invading Cambodia.

Each of those titans of China, with their armies, could start an empire by themselves. Many things could happen from an explosive meeting such as this. A coup was an easy guess. They could run tanks into Beijing. Or they could split China into two—the north kingdom and southern empire, to be divided by the mother river, the Yangtze. It had happened before. The mildest option was maintaining the status quo.

I had no idea what speech the president had prepared to deliver to these corrupt men of guns. I had been told to just stand by. But I had to do something. My men took over the airport where all the chieftains arrived. On each plane that carried the military chiefs, I planted a mole to monitor every move they made. Their limousines were wired with the most sensitive listening devices, thanks to the KGB—or was it the CIA? Anything they said would be used against them as evidence, in case of their prosecution.

A red flag adorned the conference hall. On the wall hung the forever benevolent Chairman Mao, smiling his Mona Lisa smile. President Heng Tu forsook the wheelchair he often used now for his arthritic knees, to limp in with a straight back. Reluctantly, the eight waiting chiefs stood up and applauded the entrance of the man who was the angry father they did not want to meet.

Heng Tu's first session, held in a solemn chamber in the Forbidden

City, was with the Southeast Command chief, the ribbon-cutting man. General Fu-Ren was a short fellow who crossed and recrossed his stumpy legs nervously. His diamond ring shone glaringly in the president's eyes. Fu-Ren kept trying to loosen his collar, without success, for his fleshy neck overflowed even the unbuttoned collar.

"See, Fu-Ren. When you have not worn your uniform for a long time, it does not fit you anymore," the president said.

"I much prefer the Western suit and tie, which you can loosen for air, not this damned buckle." He frowned unpleasantly at the collar that usually made a military man stand tall and proud.

"Son, when we were at the Long March, you were a small boy that I carried on my back."

"That's history, Mr. President. We need to move on with our agenda." Fu-Ren shrugged his thick shoulders. "Do you have an agenda?"

"Yes. Tell me what you have been doing with your army and its precious resources. This is your opportunity."

"I have been guarding the South and East China Seas diligently."

"Again, my soldier, I trusted you with our south gate facing Taiwan, Hong Kong, and Macao. You should be honest with me. It is your time to come clean. I have stacks of reports of your unsightly conduct."

"You tell that fool colonel of yours—what's his name?—to get off our backs. We are soldiers, and soldiers have certain ways of living and earning our deserved rewards."

"Stealing and slicing?"

"Mr. President, who would you rather trust? Your soldiers, who keep this place safe for you while you sleep here up in comfort, or your young colonel?"

"I only listen to the truth."

"I am telling you the truth. Everything is fine."

"Come close, Fu-Ren. You've got a little dirt on your chest. Let me dust it for you."

"Where is it?"

The president grabbed the short man's jacket and buckled his collar tight. It snapped closed and the fat man's face turned red. "I can't breathe," he gasped.

"Good."

"Unbuckle it!" He tore at the collar frantically. "Help me, help me!"

The president limped out of the room without looking back. "You can help yourself. Get out of here before I have you thrown out. You are a disgrace!"

Fu-Ren's mouth foamed. It took him a good minute to tear his collar apart.

Through my hidden closed circuit camera, I could see it all. "Congratulations, Mr. President," I murmured.

Heng Tu limped into another conference room. This time it was the Northwest Command chief. "The Nuke Chief" was his nickname.

"Have you any idea," President Heng Tu asked, "how many warheads are missing?"

"Nothing is missing." The Nuke Chief acted surprised.

"I have a list here in my hand. I demand nothing less than the utmost honesty from you now, or it may forever be too late."

"Mr. President, why are you being harsh with me? I guard the most vulnerable division of our military, after all. Without us, we would be breakfast to the United States and lunch to the Japanese."

"Maybe you can tell me about the profit you have been reaping through the mysterious disappearance of more than fifty warheads."

"It is a lie! That deputy of yours!"

"He was my envoy."

"He sneaked around without our permission!"

"Without him, I could never find out the truth about you."

"Mr. President, you seem to have made up your mind and have chosen him over us," the Nuke Chief said bluntly.

"Us?" Heng Tu challenged.

The chief looked down, avoiding the president's eyes. "I meant 'me.'"

"I have," the president confirmed.

"What are you going to do about it?"

"Many things. But first of all, you have a little hair growing out of your nose."

The Nuke Chief frowned.

"Here, let me fix it for you." The president ripped the stars from the man's collar, then spat in his face.

The chief recoiled. "You spit on me."

"You have earned it, son. Your father would have agreed with me."

Limping, Heng Tu walked out and into another meeting. By noon, he had talked to them all. He was fuming with disgust as he gathered them again in the hall of the Central Command headquarters. By now the chiefs all looked like rats that had been drowned. Some were dazed. Some had their heads bowed low. Others looked worried. There was a general sense that they had failed. They all waited for the president to speak about their fate.

Finally, the old man opened his mouth. "I have a complete reorganization plan for all three branches of our military forces. The author of the plan is your friend Shento, someone I take pride in presenting to you now to explain the finer points of our future."

I bowed only slightly and saluted them all, then spent the next hour going through the logic and necessity of the changes.

Heng Tu's parting words to them all were "Go home and study these plans. In six months, we will pick a leader from among you to lead this army into the twenty-first century. Your compliance with this new plan will determine your future. I want to give you another chance. Even horses deserve a second run."

Sumi

CHAPTER 31

Tai Ping asked me, Why do roads fork and rivers split?
Why do young birds leave their nests to build their own?
Why does Baba Tan only visit us?
He said, Mama, why do you sleep alone?

Sumi

Shento

CHAPTER 32

My life inside the deep silence of Zhong Nan Hai, the presidential residence, was like riding six stallions at the same time. Each horse demanded my total concentration, yet to give any one a single-minded devotion would only cause me to fall in this dusty, roaring race. I knew I had to master them all if I was to arrive and conquer.

Every day, I rose before sunrise and studied the reports from all thirty government ministries. By daybreak, the previous day's events were summarized, bound with leather, and laid on my mahogany desktop.

Of them all, I had a weakness for the most voluminous from the Finance Ministry. Their reports carried good news—a double-digit growth in the GNP, the blossoming of the Shenzhen Special Economic Zone. Exploding export figures from Fujian showed a record high number of private firms being opened. Foreign firms seeking business opportunities petitioned for thousands of joint ventures. The list ran as long as the Yangtze River. It brought sunshine to my face, even in the cold winter days of Beijing.

I next reviewed the daily dispatches from the Foreign Ministry. All nations, including some former hostile states, smiled at China now. The chill of the Cold War had thawed. New treaties were being proposed and diplomatic relations suggested. I particularly liked the report on how Taiwan, which used to be part of China's territory before the Nationalists fled the country in 1949, had sent a petition to the ministry, asking us to permanently cease the daily shelling on their golden gate island.

"Tell them to invest in our future here," I told the foreign minister. "Then we will stop."

The Agricultural Ministry reported that a million acres of farmland had been converted into housing projects. All over the country, ancient trees were being pillaged to keep up with the building boom. The Agricultural Ministry lauded this phenomenon as a heroic act, but the Environmental Ministry declared it a disaster, claiming, "We are losing our priceless environmental protection faster than ever. Please make laws to stop this rampage." My only comment about this predicament was that men needed shelter to live, and trees would grow again.

The file from the Public Security Ministry always sobered me up with a dose of cold reality. I had an aversion to anyone who wore that uniform, for it reminded me of my dark secret prison past, and with it my nightmarish close call with death. But I had to face those reports because they revealed all the holes in this dam called China, which, if not mended, could bring the flood of chaos. Every day there was the usual list of illegal crimes and moral sins that humans could not seem to live without from the time of Peking man—prostitution, gambling, drinking, wife beating, murders, kidnapping, drugs from Laos, and smuggling in the Golden Triangle. Nothing new, nothing as bad as one particular entry titled "Dissidents and Their Antigovernment Report." More than 350 democratic clubs had been organized throughout the country. One thousand antigovernment magazines were being published. Quite a few prominent protest leaders had surfaced. Among them were some writers whose names I had never heard before. I had a simple solution for all those little champions of freedom and democracy: send them to wind-blasted Xinjiang, where they could talk democracy to the wolves of the desert and freedom to the cold, high mountains.

WHEN I WROTE the first draft of my new military plan, I had omitted telling the president one small detail. On my tour of the country making my inspection rounds, I had compiled a list of young army officers at those faraway posts who seemed genuinely ambitious and far from happy watching their barracks slide into the fortress of popular commerce. These young officers had one common thread linking them together: They were soldiers at heart.

In clandestine meetings with them, I had shared my vision—to revitalize our army and proudly rule this world. I never talked about rewards. It was understood. To mention it would have only instilled impurity in their search for glory.

I called my secret organization the Young Generals' Club, a title all of its members had the ambition to secure but not the luck of obtaining so far. I placed a weekly phone call to each member, conducted in utmost secrecy. If discovered, they, who were reporting on their own district chiefs, would end up with a bullet in the head or a knife across the throat.

My phone calls usually started with Captain Ta-Ta of the Tibetan district. He was a big-boned Tibetan who knew the dangerous trails up the Himalayas. I had been approached by him after I had sent away the prostitute in Qunming. Ta-Ta knew from that single act that I was a real soldier. Our phone calls usually began with a casual exchange of pleasantries, and then serious matters would start to flow.

On this particular occasion, I wanted to know the reaction of the chief after meeting the president. Ta-Ta informed me, "The chief is flying inland somewhere."

"Find out the destination and call me back. What is the mood there?"

"Tense."

Immediately, I rang my friend Don Tong in the coastal region of Fujian. He was a short, well-built sergeant serving under Fu-Ren, the most corrupt chief of them all. I had found Don Tong sitting in the sun, polishing his pistol with pride while the rest of his comrades fought over a pornographic depiction of a young girl wearing nothing but a pink bud on her belly button. I had come over and patted him on his shoulder. "I am here to fight the Japanese, Americans, and Russians. My comrades only want to fight over Hong Kong porno. It disgusts me," the young man had uttered matter-of-factly.

"Good spirit. You will fight your enemies someday," I told him, and recruited him on the spot.

Today, I cut right to the subject. "Where is your boss?" Don Tong was the chief's private-duty soldier in charge of walking the chief's dogs and fetching his son from school. He was well versed in the details of his superior's daily routine.

"He left early in the morning with his first secretary on a plane," Don Tong said. "No one knows his destination. Tuesday is usually his fishing day, and at night he goes to dance clubs in disguise and sits there drinking his favorite Japanese sake."

"The poor man has broken his routine, is that what you are saying?"

"Yes, it is very unusual. And there is an order for us to stay where we are."

"Find out where the chief went."

"Certainly."

When I made my call to the northern district, Hai To, a captain in the border army, told me, "The chief was rushed to the hospital."

"Really? For what illness?"

"No one knows."

"Is his wife at home?"

"She is."

"How odd that she is not at the hospital by her husband's side. Find out which hospital and call me back."

Something was brewing right under my nose. Two chiefs breaking their daily routine of corrupt and lavish living. I could almost smell it. My suspicions hastened me to make the fourth call to the nerdy technical sergeant of the northwestern district, Dr. Yi-Yi.

"Extra security has been put on the silos," the PhD in nuclear science reported to me. "But our chief is here. His plane is sitting on the airstrip."

"How do you know?"

"When desert sand is blown into your bowl of rice, everyone knows the chief is going somewhere."

"So, no sand in your bowl today?"

"Yes. Lots of it. Other planes are arriving, similar to the one used by our chief."

"How many?"

"Seven."

I did not have to make the rest of the calls. I knew. My suspicions had been confirmed.

Tan

唐

CHAPTER 33

1984

BEIJING

In the summer of 1984, both Sumi and I graduated with honors. I was named Graduate of the Year at the crowded graduation ceremony. Any government job was mine for the picking—Supreme Court clerkships, prosecutorial positions, army postings—but I chose to work for myself. Sumi, having received no job offers due to the university's awareness and disapproval of her writing, decided to devote herself to her writing as well as running a charity organization called Poison Tree Foundation that she had set up to help the poor and underprivileged.

My first act as an independent entrepreneur was to make Beijing the headquarters of Dragon & Company. I envisioned that one day soon, I would be dealing with international corporations such as IBM, Coca-Cola, and GE, so it made sense to seat myself in the capital. Another consideration was that historically, any dynasty that made Beijing its capital invariably lasted longer than those that did not. Dragon & Company was an embryo of a dynasty, and I chose wisely not to repeat an error by those who only read history but never digested its lessons.

Upon his graduation three years earlier, Fei-Fei, my North China Blue Sea editor in chief, had acquired a printing facility nearby, rather than depending on the southern plant in Fujian. In addition, he had published fifty titles. "All of the books are bestsellers," he boasted to me.

"I paid no advances to reduce the risk, and I buy only books that people want to read but the government won't sanction."

"You've got to cut your long hair."

"Mr. Long," he addressed me formally. "This is part of my mystique. My hair says, I am Fei-Fei. I am the free-spirited editor. The day I lose my hair, you might as well fire me."

"Very well, the hair stays. But your free spirit disturbs me."

"You mean my girlfriends?"

I nodded.

"I can't help it. They are all unmarriable."

"And you drink too much."

"You want me to be a monk? It's part of my persona. Writers relate to me because I act as if everything is acceptable. When they feel that way, they pour out their hearts to me. And some, even more."

"You mean your young female writers."

"Better me than you, boss. You make sure that your bottom line is covered and fattened, and I'll take care of the other things."

"Times are changing. The government will be onto us soon if we keep publishing what we publish. Do not let your personal life worsen your plight when it comes. That's all I am concerned about."

"When the wind blows the other way, I will act in accordance. Remember, I have survived the Cultural Revolution; that should count for something."

Lena reported that the southern operation was flourishing like a willow tree. Dragon & Company's 50 percent interest in Coastal Banking had already tripled its investment. Coastal Banking's total loan value had reached the mark of 100 million yuan. Grandfather Long insisted on a percentage of each business he financed. My stake in the hundred-plus businesses to which he had made loans could thrive into a modest empire all by itself. Grandfather Long, a loyal student of the House of N. M. Rothschild and Sons of London, was now the merchant banker he had always yearned to be.

Lena also wrote that she had hired the best graduates from Xiamen University's economics department to assist her. And, she was pleased to report, our 50 percent stake in Father's investment had yielded a phenomenal return of more than 20 million yuan.

Father's firm, proudly named Veterans & Company, had formed a joint venture with a Taiwanese chemical plant to produce fabrics and building materials for the housing boom in the south. My holding was enough to vote for or veto a venture, but so far Father had not given me any reason to exercise that right. If anything, Father deserved the manager of the year award for his enormous business expansion, and more important, for his contribution to all the veterans who had been discharged by the military.

All these developments were best described in Mother's letter.

Our Dear Son,

We miss you as always. Grandpa is busier than ever playing the financier to the needy and enterprising. The locals call him the "Silver Abacus."

Your father now has over five thousand employees working under him. Since all his workers are veterans, they call him "General," deservingly so, and he likes it. Both your father's and grandpa's businesses are prospering so well that we have decided to invite you to join us. They have both agreed to offer you a minor partnership share of 25 percent of their respective ownership (as you know, they have silent partners who own 50 percent). As you progress, which is to be expected, you will become an equal-share partner with them both. We think this offer should provide you with more than enough to start a family.

The future of China is in the south. The people, the land, our access to the southeastern Asian countries—all have convinced me that you will thrive here rather than up north, where bureaucracy still rules. We know you have great ambition and even bigger aspirations. My advice to you is that you have to start somewhere, so why not here? Besides, this is home. What better place to start than with the family.

It would give us such great joy to have you back here to take part in such unexpected good fortune and abundance that Buddha has offered our household.

I hope that you will give our invitation serious thought.

Love,
Mother, Father, and Grandfather

"I am already your partner," I said to myself.

What perturbed me were Mother's frequent hints about starting a family. She ignored the fact that I was with Sumi. Never did she mention Sumi's name or inquire about her, even less her little boy, Tai Ping.

"Oh, that wild girl with a past and a bastard," I could just hear her say, had I told her about my engagement to Sumi.

I did not want to torture Mother sooner than necessary. Sumi and I had agreed to marry two years from now. My plan was to reacquaint the two most important women in my life slowly over time. I was sure, given time and reason, they would come to love each other—if not for themselves, then for me.

IN THE ROARING EIGHTIES, as I thought of them, Beijing was a go-go town of new rich, old *guansi* (connections), novel hustlers, and daydreamers who thought money should fall to earth from the tree of capitalism. Money was all anyone talked about. The sex appeal of capitalism oiled everyone's slurping tongue. Since Communism was still the domineering force, one had to tiptoe around its limits. There was a sense of mystery and adventure and the extra attraction of tasting the forbidden fruit of money. Fortune seekers formed their own secret circles, and their clandestine clubs redefined the order of society.

I mingled with these colorful new go-getters with relish, and they sought me out because I had genuine power of my own—a staggering amount of funds from an unknown source. More important, I possessed the rare blue-blood pedigree, which made me a trustworthy fellow, for they were, after all, for the most part of the same stock. My last name, Long, still echoed the power of China's chilling past. My family's recent downfall only made me seem more heroic. I was their Count of Monte Cristo, the comeback boy. I spoke with a touch of the now popular southern accent, that of a Hong Kong man. If occasion required, I could effortlessly switch to English with an accent that one American described as a mixture of half-baked Cockney and full-blown South China lilt.

It was my English that led to my acquaintance with a tall, thin fellow named Howard Ginger of the *New York Times,* and a ruddy-faced, mustached Virginian named Mike Blake, whom I regarded as a drinking buddy.

Howard ran his one-man bureau from inside the tall wall of Friendship Hotel, living a James Bond life of a freedom fighter, an unwanted foreign troublemaker. In short, he was the enemy of the country by the mere fact that he reported the truth. He was a foreign devil, perpetually tailed by China's secret agents, who tried to curtail him from contacting locals for embarrassing leaks about the inner workings of the government.

One day we met in the posh hotel bar at the Beijing Hotel, the place to see and be seen.

"I dig dirt on Communism and for that I am awarded better protection than President Reagan," he said to me, laughing at his predicament, sipping his martini. "One day I was at the Shanghai airport. The men's room was busy, so I decided to go into the ladies' room. You should have seen those agents' faces when I came out to find them blocking a long line of antsy females who wanted to kill them. These goons are everywhere I go. You shouldn't be seen with me too much." He chugged down his drink.

"I have my protection, don't you worry," I said, referring to my SOBs—sons of bosses—friends whose fathers were the powers that be.

"One of these days, even your SOB friends will not be able to save you." Howard was a man of perpetual doom and gloom.

"How do you mean?"

"President Heng was named Man of the Year by *Time* magazine. Soon he will become his own enemy because the people will expect more from him and he will grudgingly have to give more. But there is only so much he can give before he feels threatened. I think he's reached that point now."

"What should we do?" I asked.

"Ask for more."

"But you said it would only trigger a tragic setback."

"If you don't ask, you will never get it."

"A perpetual struggle."

"Tan," Howard slapped my shoulder. "You could be a forceful freedom fighter with all your abilities."

"I want nothing to do with politics," I replied.

"It's your destiny. It's in your blood. Inescapable." With that he dashed off to meet his American journalist friends.

Conversations with Howard always made me think deeper and see farther. And, invariably, they prodded that old sore deeply buried at the root of my manhood. Though it had been years since my torturous and unjust imprisonment, a fiery anger still smoldered in my soul. One day, I feared, the flame would fan itself into a storm—a storm to erase all the hate sown and tears shed. But for now, I told myself, it was commerce to which I must devote my life. I would be a Chinese Morgan, an Asian Rockefeller. And this banality of commerce would not be in vain. It was the foundation of a modern-day arsenal, a means to a noble ideal. I would accumulate them all—dollars, yuans, yens, marks, pesos, lira, and pounds. One day they would all be converted into an inevitable force to topple the likes of Heng Tu and the other tyrants to come. Democracy would come, I concluded, not from the barrels of guns, but from the hushed vaults of mammoth banks.

After a month's absence, Howard suddenly turned up at the Friendship Hotel club in dusty khakis and fedora, smoking a cigar. He gave me a copy of that day's *Times.* In it, I read a disturbing report about a major military shake-up coming our way.

"It was not reported in the Chinese newspaper," I exclaimed.

"That's why they pay me well." Howard tilted his old hat with a wicked smile.

"But even my SOBs haven't heard of this."

"Because some of those SOBs are on the outgoing list themselves."

"Where did you find this lead?"

"Driving roads and trailing a very mysterious colonel named Shento."

"Shento?" Wasn't that the name of Sumi's first love? I frowned, quickly dismissing the unwelcome thought.

"He will be my next feature. Stay tuned. Now buy me a drink."

I waved to the bartender, ordering a double martini.

I met my other American friend, Mike Blake, at the Friendship Hotel watering hole that same evening. Mike's usual spot was the tall stool at the entrance, upon which the Virginian, to my amusement, seemed to spend all his waking hours.

"What is a busy investor doing all day long at a bar?" I asked Mike as a greeting.

"Saving exorbitant office rent," Blake replied, stirring his cold drink. "Besides, who wants to sit in an office? I get more done with a drink than with a hundred phone calls." He waved at the waitress for another stiff one. "What are you up to lately?" he asked me.

"As a businessman yourself, if you have to ask me that question, you are too late."

"Come on, come on," Mike urged. "Share."

"I've received a lot of business proposals, but nothing grabs me. I need something big to do. Something that measures up to the legacy of my father and grandfathers. Something that will endure and last. Something that will throb my heart."

"I got just the thing for you," Mike said, grabbing my shoulder. "A heartthrobbing idea. Women's wear."

"Do tell." While I did not always share Mike's tastes in life, his business ideas were always refreshing, if not outright revolutionary. There was something pungently American and wickedly resourceful about Blake that I found compelling.

Blake leaned over, as if conferring a secret. "Ever since I arrived here, I have been noticing that all Chinese women—short, tall, southern, northern—are beautiful, but they all lack one thing, one fatal element that would make them unparalleled."

"What is that?"

"Ten out of ten Chinese girls that I have been with possess dull-colored boxy undergarments and coarse, chunky brassieres with old-fashioned, rusty hooks."

"Shhh. Not so loud," I said, embarrassed, glancing around the long oak-wood bar crowded with foreign and local patrons.

"Take that beauty at the end of the bar." Blake pointed his chin at a slender local girl sitting between a Japanese businessman and a German with a blond mustache whom I vaguely remembered was a managing director for a leading German bank. "Her backside would be so much more seductive clad in the seamless, silky lingerie we make in the West. The worst moment comes at the best of times, when a woman reveals herself to her lover. If anything can kill the mood, it's those Commie boxers. They work like some cursed chastity belt meant to chase men away."

"They didn't chase you away, did they?"

"No, I happen to be a genuine Don Juan with a truly romantic heart and discerning eyes that can see through the Great Wall of Chinese lingerie and behold the beauty within."

I could only shake my head.

"Every single man here can attest to their plight. So here is the idea. I have decided to be the Underwear Emperor to all the grateful women of this land. Imagine half a billion women in sexy lingerie!" His eyes glowed with dancing lights. "Think of all of them screaming for the satiny touch. Think of all the men. I am a gift from God!"

"And a curse to all the husbands," I said. "How are they going to afford this?"

"For a visionary, you are unusually shortsighted. We all know Hangzhou, that beautiful city in the south, the birthplace of silk and satin; they could make these garments cheap and fast. All we need to do is collect the slinkiest designs available; we could license these from the leading designers in the world."

"You mean pay to use their name and design, but make the lingerie locally?"

"This would save not only the cost of labor and materials but bring glamour and fashion right to our consumers. What do you say? Shall Dragon and Company and Virginia Inc. join hands in this venture? You take care of the manufacturing and I the licensing, designing, and marketing."

"It's not quite what I'm looking for."

"But it's something, isn't it?" Mike said.

I shrugged and said, "I didn't hear you mention the C word."

"Ah, capital. How could I forget?" Mike sipped his drink. "That, you, my favorite dragon, will have to come up with, before this idea can be fruitful."

"It is a risky business, not to mention outright anti-Confucianist, contrary to the principles of decency and the virtues of modesty."

"Virtues, principles . . . what nonsense are they? Doesn't Confucius believe in comfort, elegance, and beauty? What is the essence of Confucius anyhow?"

"Harmony."

"That's right. Harmony within a woman's heart, within a bedroom, which will breed harmony within the state. Oh, young Mr. Long, you will be lauded for such a revolutionary endeavor. Your ancient emperors will smile in their tombs over your beautification movement."

"Let me think about it."

"Don't take too long. Money waits for no man. That's the only thing you ought to think about now in China. Politicians come and go—Mao Tse-tung, Liu Shao-ch'i, and Heng Tu. They will all be gone, and despised even more in death. But fortunes stay. When you visit New York, you must go see Rockefeller Center, in the heart of Manhattan. It's my favorite place, the symbol of capitalism and a forever-lasting legacy. Do not stray into the path of politics. It's suicide."

THE FOLLOWING DAY, Mike met me in my office, which was situated in a three-story stone building overshadowed by the monumental Beijing Hotel.

"Have you seen anything this beautiful before?" Mike spread photos of assorted silk lingerie worn by blue-eyed blond models on the long, lacquered table. I glanced at them briefly before turning to look out at the foggy Tiananmen Square.

"Have you given any thought to my idea?" Mike asked.

"Yes, I have."

"And?"

"I could hardly stop thinking about it," I said, still staring at the square. "I only slept three hours . . . It's such a rare and brilliant prospect."

"I told you so."

"It will be grand and tall, stretching to the east from here."

"Are we still talking about lingerie?" Mike asked, puzzled.

"No, I am talking about your other idea."

"What other idea?"

"Rockefeller Center. I am thinking of building one myself."

"A Rockefeller Center in Beijing?" Mike scratched his head.

"Dragon Center, a monument to all high ideals." I squinted, seeing the future rising before my eyes. I swiveled around in my chair and stared at Mike intensely. "Tell me it can be done, my American friend. Let's build this Dragon Center together. Drop your lingerie idea and come work with me. I need you. After all, it was you who planted the seed in me. You possess the craziness that I have long admired, the intrepid vision of an American. Please, my friend."

"That will not be a problem, but you know I am broke."

"Say no more. Will this sum convince you to join me?" I pushed a piece of paper before Mike's eyes.

"This sum would make me feel very well indeed," Mike said, smiling. "Where will you build it?"

"Last night after our conversation, it was as if lightning had struck me. I went to Si Dang Bookstore and I found this book." I pushed forward a thick photography book entitled *Architectural New York,* opening to the pages on Rockefeller Center. "It's an inspiration looking at this flagship building, the skating rink and the smaller buildings surrounding it, forming a group of architectural giants to guard Midtown Manhattan. What grandeur. I have chosen this site." I pushed the photo book aside, unrolled a local map of Beijing, and drew a circle around two city blocks bordering Tiananmen Square on the east that housed dilapidated courtyard estates, formerly spacious brick mansions of Manchurian princes, now divided and resided in by multiple households.

"I want to buy up the whole area," I said.

"That's ten acres of prime real estate, right at the center of the capital city! What do you plan to do with it?"

"First of all, there will be the Dragon headquarters. We will take the entire top floor from the tallest building among them. I will give my friend Howard Ginger a nice space right under me. That way I'll have the eyes and ears of the *New York Times* only an elevator ride away. Then there are the American blue-chip companies, which will vie for such a fabulous address as this—GE, GM, Coca-Cola, Ford, Exxon, and IBM, to name just a few."

"You're out of your mind."

"There is more. I will build a beautiful hotel, maybe a few of them, right within the center. There will be shopping centers with fancy stores for your lingerie, and maybe theaters showing the newest Hollywood motion pictures. I also wish to donate a sizable space for children to run around in—playgrounds, gardens, man-made lakes, and boat rides. During holiday seasons, I will hire leading opera singers to sing those Christmas songs."

"We call them carols."

"Christmas carols. And I love clowns, those big, red-nosed guys with huge shoes. I saw them once in a foreign magazine. We'll have to have them as well."

"And make sure that you have plenty of public bathrooms for tourists as well," Mike said dryly. Beijing had a severe shortage of public toilets.

"That, too. I am not finished."

"You don't say."

"Big juicy steak houses with Chinese cowboys and cowgirls serving everyone with coiled lassos. Good, clean fun. Pubs and bars. German beer, French whiskey, California wine. I can see the center going up, higher and higher, reaching for the sky like the dragon it is named after."

"That all sounds very grand, but where is the dough?" he asked.

"Of course, I have the dough."

"I mean a lot of dough."

"I have a lot of dough."

"Not this much," Mike said. "You need loans."

"Vision begets visionaries. This is the best of times and the worst of times. Everything is possible."

"Forget Dickens." Mike rubbed his fingers together. "Money."

"Leave the loans to me."

I had a confessed distaste for most SOBs, abhorring their banal attitude toward life and narrow outlook on the world. I treaded carefully around them, treating them as what they were—the necessary evils of our era, eyes and ears into the inner sanctum of our secretive regime. But not all SOBs were roughs. It behooved one to look closer. There were indeed gems to be found, albeit decidedly few in number. David Li—the general manager of the Bank of China's Beijing branch—was one.

Li, a sturdy man with a square face, was the son of the minister of public security. He had fashionably taken an English name, David, after earning a bachelor's degree in economics at Princeton and a law degree from my alma mater. His current position was the result of a barter system that not so secretly existed among the old generation of revolutionaries, demanding that their heirs be put in key positions so that when these sons inherited the power seats, it would look like their rise to power was earned. David had gotten his current job because his father had secured a position for the treasury minister's son. A little Communist nepotism went a long way.

After sending off Mike Blake, I picked up the phone and dialed Li's number. "Good morning, David," I said.

"I find it flattering, getting a phone call from you, Mr. Long," David replied.

"Remember you mentioned a while back that you wished to do business with me?"

"Yes, in fact I was going to call you about the financing of your women's wear business that Mike Blake mentioned in passing."

"I am impressed. You are again one step ahead of the game."

"I am born to be a banker, and I will die one."

"It is not a bad way to go. Talking about life and death, one cannot help thinking about immortality. I've got an opportunity for both of our names to go down in history in a monumental fashion."

"I am all ears, as always."

"Have you heard of Rockefeller Center?"

"Yes; my fellow bankers at the Bank of China, New York branch, often boast about it. I went ice-skating there once."

"So then I take it that you know who the Rockefellers were."

"Indeed, they were once the richest oil princes in the world."

"But would you have known of them, had it not been for the existence of that center that attracts millions of tourists every year?"

"No, I would not," he confessed readily.

"And homage is not the only thing they pay at Rockefeller Center."

"Go on, please, Mr. Long."

"The center commands the highest rentals per square foot in this world," I said, citing a line from *Architectural New York.* "And they own it forever. All future Rockefellers will live on the rents, which will only increase every year."

"So you wish to build a Rockefeller Center here?"

"Yes, I want one built, but I want it built even better. It's going to be called—"

"Let me guess . . . Dragon Center."

"Mr. Li, we think alike."

I told David my detailed plan. The other end of the phone was silent except for occasional enthusiastic yeses.

"Everything I have told you must remain confidential between us," I warned.

"As a banker, I have my canons and ethics. I am prepared to bring many of my clients' secrets to my tomb, Mr. Long."

"Ha! You will need a very big tomb."

"If not for the secrets I have been entrusted with, then for the big dreams that inhabit my soul."

"Men are only measured by the size of their dreams."

"How true that is, Mr. Long. I wish with every grain of my being to be the financier for your Dragon Center. But on one condition. I wish to have a little bronze plate inlaid at the front of the site citing the Bank of China as the financing bank, and me, personally, as the manager of the transaction."

"Granted. You will have a big plaque with your name in gold, and a bronze bust of yourself sitting at the entrance."

The line was silent.

"What is the matter, David?"

"I am touched by your generosity."

That night, when I returned to our new home, a spacious town house in a residential development south of Beijing, I found Tai Ping already asleep after a long school day and Sumi writing at her desk, waiting for me to return so we could dine together. She had prepared four dishes, all seafood—fried prawns, steamed carp, sautéed squid, and boiled snails. The sea was her specialty, and she could do wonders with generous sloshes of soy sauce and simple slices of fresh ginger.

"I feel like a newlywed," I said, sitting down at our Ch'ing dynasty–style dining table.

"So do I," she said, scooping a bowl of steaming rice for me. "You should have come home earlier."

"Busy. Very busy. Remember when I ran out to the bookstore last night?"

"Yes." She filled my dish with food.

In between hungry bites and busy shovels with chopsticks, I told Sumi about my plans for Dragon Center.

"What is going to happen to the people who live there now and the companies that occupy those old buildings?" she asked.

I was not surprised—it was in keeping with her humane spirit. "I am going to build them the most beautiful residential villages, Sumi, right off the suburbs of Beijing," I said. "Direct buses will carry them back and forth from the city so that they will not have to pedal their bicycles anymore."

"But they could not afford the houses."

"Have you heard of barter trade?"

"An apple for an orange?"

"Indeed. They will have new houses, new schools, and new shopping centers, and I get to acquire their old houses in the city. I will let them trade with me. I will even offer them jobs at the center once it is opened up. They will be my priority."

"You do have the people in mind," she said, pleased.

"Money isn't everything. But I will still make plenty just creating those satellite villages. Soon, I will own half the city."

Sumi sighed.

"What's the matter?" I asked.

"I'm afraid you are slipping into a capitalist hole, all money and no conscience."

"But you haven't heard the rest. For the companies whose buildings I tear down, I will offer them space inside the center. If they cannot afford it, I will help them relocate into the suburbs, where the future will be. There will be a huge bookstore on the street level, and your books will be put on display right in front."

"That's nice. But you do not need to pander to me. Just please do not betray the people."

"Never." I took her hand. "Listen, tomorrow I will try to come home earlier, before Tai Ping is asleep."

Sumi gave me a small but pleased smile.

HOWARD GINGER burst into laughter when I mentioned the idea of Dragon Center to him the next day over a drink at the Friendship Hotel bar. "You have gone mad."

"Why?" I asked.

"Money. It will take billions."

"We will find it. I already have a major bank lined up."

"You'd better. You're going to need plenty."

"But what I need from you, my friend, is a feature story about the project."

"Are you asking me to dent my journalistic integrity so that you can get free international publicity?" Howard asked jokingly.

"Yes, and you will not regret it."

"What's in it for me?"

"Office space. You will have your pick. After all, you represent one of the finest media companies in the world."

"Will we have to pay rent?"

"I am shocked at the bluntness of your journalistic greed. This is a colossal project to signify the arrival of China's capitalism. Isn't that enough of a scoop for you?"

"Of course it is. And I promise you a front-page feature, above the fold, when the time comes. I will be honored, Mr. Rockefeller." He loosened his tie, then stirred his drink. "I had a long day trying to dig more news out of that mummified propaganda minister about the military cutbacks."

"How did it go?"

"They almost had me arrested," he said quietly.

"For what?"

"For writing that report on the not-yet-announced military reshuffling. They said I had violated an absurd penal code of leaking military secrets, while at the same time denying everything that I have written."

"I would hate to lose a friend like you. You better be careful."

"You, too," Howard said. "Remember, the bigger the dream, the darker the peril."

WRITING WAS A thorned rose for Sumi. Her adoring fans—the petals—showered her with thousands of fan letters and inquiries about her next book. The cruel government critics—the thorns—called her the "Teenager Whore," her life a voyage of sin, and her book a concoction of little literary weight and even less moral value.

"The government hates me, yet the people love me," she lamented one dreary day in the fall, throwing away that month's literary review by a very harsh Communist critic. "I am perfect sandwich meat."

"I wonder which you cherish more, the love or the hate?"

"They are both the highest literary praise for any writer on this land."

"And the most powerful factors pushing your book over the five million record." I'd just gotten the numbers from Lena.

"Really?" Sumi could not help getting excited over the enormity of the number. To her, a million was like the sum of all the stars in the sky. Five million . . .

"You know I do not write for the money," she said, firmly.

"You certainly do not write for money, but money comes because you write."

"Money and money. You are ever a businessman."

"I have to be, for millions of your readers are waiting. Without me, they would never have read your words. Speaking of money, I just received an unpaid invoice from a food factory claiming that you forgot to pay for a truckload of food you ordered. They took the liberty of sending it to your publisher." I fished out a folded sheet from my briefcase.

"Oh? Let me see." Sumi glanced at the invoice and stuffed it into her pocket. "This is my business."

"Your business is mine. Would you please tell me what is going on?"

"I am broke," she said sadly.

"Broke? But what about all those royalty payments?"

"I have been spending all the money on an orphanage near Tianjin. Winter is coming and those kids have little to wear. When I send money for clothes, their food runs out . . . There is always something."

"What happened to the government aid?"

"There is none. The city of Tianjin has long wanted to get rid of the orphanage. If they do that, where will the kids go?"

We were both silent, remembering the brutal treatment she had received in the house of Fu Chen.

"So you have been sending your royalty checks to them?" I asked quietly.

Sumi nodded guiltily.

"How many kids are there in the orphanage?"

"Exactly three hundred, after three were lost to pneumonia."

"Oh, darling, you should have told me about it. I would have helped. What else have you been hiding from me?" I looked into her clear eyes. She lowered her long lashes.

"This." Sumi walked over to her desk and pulled out a thick stack of paper from a drawer.

"My dear Sumi!" I leafed through the pages. "Your next book?"

"It's about the Tianjin Orphanage. It has cruelty, romance, and, this time, corruption, big-time corruption of the government," she said proudly.

"I like corruption. In fact, I love corruption; it sells. I propose to purchase the world rights."

"I included the names of major government officials," she said seriously.

"You name names?" I sat down on the couch.

"Are you backing off?"

"No, but who is it that you are pointing your finger at, exactly?"

"Too many names and too long a list," she said, sitting down beside me. "I have evidence of their illegal acts, and, if I am lucky, half—or more—of the Tianjin government will go to jail. Are you scared?"

"No. I just want to be prepared." I kissed her soft cheek. "To show my appreciation of your heroic literary talent, I am proposing to up your advance."

"I will accept your offer if my text is printed as written." She brushed her lips over mine.

"A bestselling author with an attitude. Nobody is good enough to edit you anymore?"

"No, that's not it." She held my face in her hands and said earnestly, "I only care about the authenticity of the children's voices. They are not educated. They speak in certain ways, with certain accents and a syntax that an educated editor would deem unprintable. But I insist that the language be printed as spoken. The rough words and broken sentences will carry the ring of truth."

"Agreed, if you accept my condition."

"Which is?"

"That in case of need, you must accept the protection I offer," I said gravely.

"You men think only of cold and harsh things, don't you?" Sumi stroked my hair tenderly.

"We do. That doesn't mean we are coldhearted." I kissed her neck, inhaling her scent.

"Come to bed, my love," she said softly. "Tai Ping is out shopping with Nai-Ma."

She laughed with delight when I swept her off her feet and carried her into our bedroom.

THE COMPLETION OF her second book took longer than Sumi anticipated. She traveled often to the orphanage for research and to talk to the children. Tai Ping and I were fine. Nai-Ma, who lived with us, cared for the boy, and I was occupied with the details of Dragon Center. But a soul is missing when the mistress of the house is away. We, the two men of the house, made the best of it, filling the void by doing the things we did together—strolling in the nearby park, playing soccer at the playground, reading each other our favorite picture books, and singing the lullabies that induced our dreams, as we waited for Sumi's return, for the house to be restored to its former exuberance.

One day at the orphanage, Sumi was visited by Mr. Ta-Ti, the bespectacled president of the Tianjin Writer's Association. She was surprised when the old man told her that she had to have a membership in order to write there or to write about Tianjin.

"But I am a writer, free to write anything and anywhere."

"Not according to our rules and regulations. We know who you are. Your writing style and the kind of material you write do not qualify you as a writer. Besides, you only have written one book, while most of us have been prolific."

"But people enjoy my work." Sumi did not say that people hated the novels that the association's authors had been commissioned to write.

"Of course they crave it, such perversion. On page one hundred, you vividly described your own body in the most disgusting manner that only appeals to men's prurient desire."

"You have read it. Thank you."

"Yes, and hated every word of it. With your lowly style, we do not welcome you to Tianjin. Less do we want you to write about our fine city. You have to leave Tianjin within a month or the police will arrest you." The man spat a plug of yellow mucus on the floor and stormed out.

That night she called me and cried, telling me about the incident. I begged her to return, but she said the insults and threats only hardened her conviction to stay and edit the book to its finest shine.

WITHIN THREE MONTHS, Dragon & Company had secretly acquired two-thirds of the land needed for my dream project. The acquisition was first met with suspicion by many owners of the old, gray-brick houses known as *si he yuan,* four-roomed residences with front yards. But they were sold by my vision of the heavenly existence I was building in the suburbs for them—apartments with running water, private bathrooms that did not stink, kitchen stoves that came alive with the strike of a match, and flowery rolling gardens that one could wake up to every sunny morning.

For the housing complex, I chose a scenic village nestled in the rugged western mountains. Land there was cheap. The villagers plucked their mental abacus, calculated in and calculated out. Corn was good and rice precious, but nothing beat cash stashed under a warm pillow. It was a perfect site for my future village, one of many to come. A shopping center here and a theater there, a school all the way through senior high, and, when many satellite villages were up and orbiting within my imagined universe, maybe a university, with all the necessary or unnecessary academic degrees.

"It sounds kind of eerie, Tan, and sickeningly clean," Sumi said on the telephone a few days before the new year. She was holed up in her small hotel room hundreds of miles away in Tianjin. "There is always going to be poverty, crimes, and hate."

"You've been dealing with those orphans for too long, my little soul. I want you back for New Year's Eve."

"I can't. I want to organize a New Year's party for the children," she said with lament. "Just a few more days and I will be yours forever."

Yours forever. Why not now? I thought to myself.

Ding Long

丁龙

CHAPTER 34

1985

FUJIAN

It had been a good year for Tan's father. Very good indeed, Ding Long thought, reviewing his year-end business ledgers laid neatly on his mahogany desk in his home facing the Amoy Sea. The profits were up and the employees doubled. Ding Long lit a cigar, the only one of the day, rationed by his wife, and inhaled deeply. He was about to reach for his half-empty wineglass when he heard a noise from the adjacent study. Ding Long quietly pulled out his old gun from the top drawer, crept softly to the door, and pushed it open slowly. A man was sitting in an armchair, silhouetted by the moonlight through the window.

"Why the darkness?" Ding Long asked.

"I desire no unwanted eyes," the man said, standing up. The moonlight gave away his build, tall and broad-shouldered.

"What is your business?" Ding Long asked.

"I mean no harm to you, General. Please close the door." The intruder remained still.

Ding Long eased into the room, his gun still trained on the stranger.

"I am sent by your old friend, General Fu-Ren, the Fujian chief. He requests your presence at this meeting." The man passed him a piece of paper. "You must be there. It concerns a matter of great importance. Please read the detailed information." The man slipped out the window.

Ding Long flicked on a light. "Lan Xin Airstrip at 9:00 p.m.," the note said. "Destination: Lanzhou. Burn this after you read it."

The note sent a chill down Ding Long's spine. Something was brewing at the military camp. He knew there had been discontent with the president among the chiefs. But what was this request? Why did it concern him?

LAN XIN was a camouflaged landing strip, hidden within a mountain range and built during the coldest years of the Cultural Revolution to counter any attacks from the Nationalists in the Republic of Taiwan, which was only a short flight away. The place smelled of the Cold War. Ding Long saluted the pilot, who saluted back like a good soldier.

"Commander, welcome back to the force," the old pilot said.

"Have we met before?"

"December 1969. Ho Chi Minh City."

"You are the young man who flew me back through enemy territory when I was injured."

"I am, and have been proud of it ever since."

"Then I am in good hands."

"The flight time will be two hours."

"See if you can cut it in half."

The pilot did. When they arrived, two guards escorted Ding Long underground, into the well of a deeply buried silo. In a generic white conference room, the eight military chiefs sat around a round table.

"To what do I owe this honor, generals?" Ding Long greeted the men and saluted. They saluted back with enthusiasm.

The eight men were dressed in full uniform with solemn faces. Ding Long remembered them when they had been younger and thinner.

"Our military has reached a dire state. Old commander, we need your wise counsel," Fu-Ren said.

"I am a civilian merchant now, not someone from whom you should seek military counsel. Unless you have something you wish to sell me, I am leaving." His glance swept across the chiefs' faces.

"Please stay and hear us out. We want to reinstate you as our commander," the Lanzhou chief said.

There was an uncomfortable silence.

"Are you all mad?" Ding Long said sternly. "You are talking about a coup!"

"We have been wronged by Heng Tu."

"You had better stop now," Ding Long said. "I'm leaving. If Heng Tu hears of this, he will hang us all."

"That's why we have to ax him before he strikes us down, like he did you," Fu-Ren said.

Ding Long's face twitched. But he took a long breath, calming himself, and walked to the door. He pressed the button. The door did not open. "Let me out."

"One either leaves here our friend or dies our foe," Fu-Ren said.

"This is a trap," Ding Long said.

"No, we are here to take revenge against your enemy," Fu-Ren said. "What Heng Tu did to your son is unforgivable."

"My son killed. I deserved to resign."

"I have evidence to prove otherwise. Bring the man in now."

A young man with a gaunt face entered the room. He looked ill and ill at ease, shifting on his sandaled feet. The light paled him.

"This is Mr. Lo, official photographer with the Beijing Police."

The man bowed and gingerly pressed a photograph into Ding Long's hands.

"I've already seen it," Ding Long said angrily, tossing the photo away as if it were poison. He would never forget that morbid picture, the sole evidence incriminating his son.

The man picked up the picture from the floor and again passed it to Ding Long's hands. "I've blown it up. Please take a closer look and see if it really is your son."

Ding Long stared at the photographer, then reluctantly examined the enlarged picture. The young man in the photo wore the same yellow sweater his son Tan had worn on that tragic day. But this bigger, clearer photograph lay bare what had been hidden in the original photograph. The boy in the picture had a squarer jaw, darker skin, and a darker soul.

Ding Long's breath suspended. *My son was framed.* "Who is he? Who is this killer?"

The photographer trembled, his face growing paler. In a stutter, he confessed, "A . . . a young cadet from the Jian Dao unit of Number Nine Island."

"What is his name?" Ding Long asked.

"Shento."

Ding Long stood there transfixed, stunned by the name. "Who asked you to take this picture?" he demanded.

"The man at the very top."

Ding Long lunged at the photographer, only to be stopped by the Fujian chief. "The photographer is only a victim himself. He is not the real enemy," Fu-Ren said. "Why don't you join us and fight our real enemy? Remember, Heng Tu would have killed your son had you not stepped down, giving up your glorious career for a crime your son didn't commit. You see? It was all a dark plot against you, my dear commander. How can you stand by, idle, letting this tyrant breathe another second? Consider it, please, General."

Ding Long spat on the frightened photographer and walked out. This time the door slid open for him before he could even smack the button on the wall.

He sat straight in his seat the entire flight home. A good soldier accepted defeat, but never deceit. Once home, he woke up his wife. Sitting on the bed, he quietly told her the horrific truth of that unfortunate night many years back.

Mrs. Long was silent. "I have my own confession," she said in a low voice. "Some years ago, your secretary passed to me an unusual letter addressed to you by an orphan named Shento from Fujian. He claimed to be your son. I wrote him back, turning that bastard away . . . I am sorry. He threatened our future . . ." She leaned against her husband, and he held her tightly.

When she finally fell asleep in his arms, Ding Long tiptoed to their bureau, took out the five-starred badge, the token of his military commission, pressed it to his heart, and made the phone call to his comrades awaiting his word in Lanzhou.

Shento

山头

CHAPTER 35

Dr. Yi-Yi's Coke-bottle lenses made his shifty eyes look apologetic and timid, forever waking but not awakened, adding innocence to the thirtysomething scientist. With his habit of talking to himself and making friends with the trees that he greeted each morning on his way to his office, Dr. Yi-Yi was considered an odd but devoted and trusted insider in this fertile field, overgrown with nuclear warheads.

He surprised everyone when he filed his petition to become a Communist member at a time when membership had dwindled to an insignificant trickle. Even more surprising was his teary ceremony and vow to tithe his entire salary to the Party. No one realized that his cultish devotion to a thing of the past indicated a mental crack as big as a river gorge. He swore that one day his bombs would blast the Russians, who had taken his grandfather's northeastern lands. He would ruin the islands of Japan, whose soldiers ravaged his grandmother in the Rape of Nanking, and annoy the Americans, who split his father's head with bullets in the Korean War, rendering Yi-Yi an orphan.

He certainly wasn't happy when his command chief decided to open the nuclear base as a rocket-launching business for the very nations that had raped and pilfered his family. He sat in his office for days, not eating, not sleeping, hallucinating about genuine nuclear warfare. But the dreams ended when he read a report that China had joined in the Nuclear Non-Proliferation Treaty, an agreement signed by many, but meant by none. He vomited until his guts were hanging at his throat, hurting and hating, until his cursed ulceration acted up, causing massive internal bleeding. His comrades sent for the ambulance, and his turbulent soul calmed down during an uneventful stay at a seaside sanatorium, where he spent his days gazing at a dreary sea.

When he met me during the inspection tour, he knew that we spoke the same language, that our hearts beat the same rhythm. My clandestine agenda fit Yi-Yi's sneaky existence just fine. In his weekly report, Yi-Yi listed all the distrustful officers who took on side jobs and the derelict scientists who sat idle, playing poker in the white silence of silos.

When my call went through, asking about the chief's whereabouts, Yi-Yi vowed that he would get to the bottom of things, and he did. He climbed down to the silo through a secret passage and pasted himself thin and small behind the curtain of the silo's command center, where images of all the facilities flashed across the monitors. There he saw eight men gathered in secret. But it was the unexpected ninth face he reported whose appearance jabbed my heart. *My accursed father, I have finally found you.*

I delayed reporting this secret meeting to the president. I took a long breath, calming myself, then dialed the number of my Young General in Fujian and issued a simple order: "Get me all the files you have been compiling on Ding Long."

THE FOLLOWING AFTERNOON, I received the lengthy facsimile of the former general's crime list. My heart tightened as I glanced over the summary. I marched to the presidential wing and nodded to the guards who saluted me.

"He has company, Colonel."

"Clear it, if you can."

"Yes, Colonel." The guard disappeared into the office. After a moment, the door reopened to reveal the president in his wheelchair, a little perturbed by the intrusion.

"You had better have something good to tell me, son," Heng Tu said.

"I would never have bothered your meeting with the chess master had it not been for a compelling reason."

"What is more important than my game? Tell me, young man."

I wheeled the old man behind his heavy desk of power—it had once belonged to Emperor Ch'ien-lung in the Ch'ing dynasty.

"A secret meeting was held in Silo Number Eight at Lanzhou last night."

"Who were the attendees?"

"Your eight command chiefs."

"Meeting behind my back? What was it about?"

"To meet your old friend, General Ding Long. A photographer from the Beijing Police was also there to show Ding Long a certain old photograph."

The president shifted uncomfortably in his wheelchair. "Some things die hard."

"Some things never die."

Heng Tu grabbed the wheels of his chair and spun around to face the window framing the setting sun. "You never fail to surprise me, son. What should we do about this?"

"I have a network of people watching the entire Long clan. Ding Long has been preparing for his return since the moment he was banished to Fujian. The Long family has been busy building an empire. The Coastal Banking Corporation, headed by the elder Long, has total assets of two hundred million yuan."

"Where did he get the money to start their venture? The old banker must have stolen that twenty million dollars."

"We will look into that again, but my source revealed that the senior Long had a silent partner who is being represented by a former government banker named Lena Tsai. There is other disturbing news. The Coastal Banking Corporation finances all of Ding Long's activities. Ding Long first started on some manufacturing ventures, but now he has branched into military and infrastructure projects—trading weapons, buying up our old airplanes, and acquiring electric power plants. His total fortune stands at the rough estimate of one hundred million yuan. All his employees are army veterans who still call him 'General.' The American CIA file on him lists him as a suspected arms dealer along the Golden Triangle in the South China Sea. It could be that he was buying warheads from our Lanzhou arsenal."

"Throw one net to catch them all," Heng Tu said. "But remember, angry soldiers make hard enemies."

MY YOUNG GENERALS now numbered over fifty. They penetrated horizontally and vertically in all levels of the military. Major cities were my focus, but I never let symptoms of any illness run amiss, even in the smallest of towns. My Young Generals were like night bats. They dived low, made the kill, then flapped their ghostly wings, shrieking back into the darkness.

The mutinous silo meeting of all the command chiefs only heightened the activities among my bats across the land. I had ordered all the chiefs to be tailed and bugged, and, if necessary, eliminated. But the latter would be an option of extreme necessity.

I knew every move each of the eight men made. No detail was too minute—what they ate, whom they slept with, and, of course, their long, long telephone logs.

On top of my watch list was Ding Long. I educated myself with every detail of the Longs' businesses: their purchase of a military airport, their weapon trades, their kickbacks, and their bribery. The more I knew about Ding Long, the more I hated him. The more I hated him, the more I craved to know. The obsession drove me to madness.

With three days left in this waning year of the fruitful 1988, I met Lieutenant Bei, the Beijing Young General, in my office. He was a tall fellow with a degree from Beijing University, currently holding a position in the Beijing Military District as propaganda officer. A man good with words.

"What caused the delay?" I asked.

"My apologies, Colonel. But there are a host of things this young Long is up to."

"Yes? Go on."

"He obtained a degree from Beijing University—my alma mater—with distinction."

"Just like his father."

"He rejected all the offers of plum government jobs on graduation, and he is now the chairman of Dragon and Company, a holding entity that also partners with Coastal Banking of Fujian, which his grandfather owns, and acts as a silent investor with his father in his growing trading and manufacturing enterprise."

"How did you find out all of this?"

"It took a bit of unraveling, but it's all in the government business-registration offices. But most significant of it all, Tan Long is about to submit a proposal to build a monumental complex in the middle of Beijing."

"How monumental?"

"Like a mountain that would block the slanting sun. The best-known architects of the world have been contacted and are bidding to design it, including I. M. Pei. This information comes from an American newsman, Howard Ginger, a friend of Tan's—and mine as well."

"Do you have anything good for me to use against him?"

"Yes, indeed," he nodded deeply. "The young Long owns Blue Sea Publishing."

"He is printing books?"

"Yes. Very disturbing books and magazines. Antigovernment rubbish and pornographic literature written by blacklisted authors that our government publishers would never touch. Their most sensational book, *The Orphan,* launched the publishing house and made a pile of money for them. It was written by a girl named Sumi Wo, who—"

"Did you say Sumi Wo?" I rasped.

"Yes, Sumi Wo. The book is a memoir about her life as an orphan in Fujian. And there has been talk of adapting it into a feature film."

I gripped my chair, feeling dizzy.

"What is the matter?"

"Nothing. Are you certain the author's name is Sumi Wo?"

"Oh, yes. She is famous."

"Can you find her?"

"That's why I was delayed. She is in Tianjin right now, working on her second book."

"Find her. Now." My words were barely audible.

Sumi

CHAPTER 36

1985

TIANJIN

New Year's Eve rendered my heart hollow and empty. A chilly northern wind from the sea swept the dirty, cracked streets of Tianjin, deepening my hollowness, away from Tan and my son, until it threatened to swallow me altogether. Too many lonesome holidays lived and lamented. I often wondered what it would have been like to have a father or maybe a mother, a really good one who came home every day, smiling, hugging, inquiring.

In this moody sojourn, on this last day of the year, I thought of my baby sister, Lili, whom I was told had been given away and adopted into a well-to-do family somewhere in the south. She had big eyes and a nose that always ran, little teeth, deep sweet dimples, and the scar that I, the big sister, had left behind her right ear in a fight over some toy. Lili must still bear that scar. Where was she now? Was she still alive? Famine was rampant, and simple infection took many lives, young and fragile. It was odd that I myself had lived. I wished sincerely that my sister, wherever she might be, still lived. And lived well.

The memory of Lili inevitably brought out those equally broken images of our young parents. Father—tall, handsome, swaggering, with a big smile and big teeth, smelling like the summer sea. Mother—petite, beautiful, with the scent of early spring. Then one day they never came back. Gone. Faded into memory. Beginning nowhere, ending nowhere, the island of memory, wrapped in isolation, at the tip of my foggy, distant past.

I had difficulty touching that dark hole of fear and sadness even now. I had long learned to close the eyes of my mind and face reality—the life of an abandoned animal within the cage of the orphanage. I learned to swallow all sorrows, big or small. I invented a process of dumping any sad feelings into an unknown spot at the bottom of my belly. Bury it and kill it with sheer determination. Once that was done, I felt better.

Sitting in the hotel ballroom where the New Year's party was to be held, I was surrounded by children from the Tianjin Orphanage, who were busy putting the final touches to the party decorations. I looked up from my flower arrangement of lilies, sunflowers, roses, and my favorite—yellow tulips with a tinge of orange. The grandfather clock ticked slowly toward four as the alluring aroma of food seeped through the door cracks. Dinner would be ready soon. I smiled. Red Red, a diminutive boy with long, tousled hair and two fingers missing, was suddenly standing before me. "Missy, you look like another flower."

"Oh, Red Red, keep the sweet compliments for the girl there in the yellow dress," I said, bundling the tulips together.

"I'm hungry. This aroma is killing me," he said, drawing in a deep breath.

"Be patient. It will only be minutes before dinner's served. Why don't you try guessing what the smells are," I said, meaning to distract him.

"Pork with ginger, beef with cilantro, crabs with garlic, and some jellyfish in vinegar." Red Red's eyes were closed, his imagination vivid, as he paused to swallow. "The oxtail is getting burned just a touch, and there's steamed fish."

I was amazed. "Good nose."

"From years of begging and smelling the chimneys of the rich, and scrubbing the pot bottoms of the poor. You learn to like the smell more than the food itself. Some of the food I've never had, but I know how it would taste in my mouth." He closed his eyes again.

"Stop it. You will have the food soon."

A bell rang. A rotund chef in a colorful clown costume thrust the door open and announced, "Dinner is ready." He danced around, tinkling his bell to the rhythm of the waltz being piped into the hall. His big webbed shoes flopped around while the orphans surrounded him, cheering and pulling his red suspenders, dancing into the dining room with him.

Inside there was a long table covered with food that Red Red's nose had precisely discerned. Well-simmered pork knuckles piled thick and tall on a giant plate. Oxtails gleamed with drips of oil. The chef burned them deliberately for the flavor that gathered within the thin crust as the oil was sucked out and the juice sealed in. A three-foot-long carp that had swum the Pacific only a short while ago now lay steamed and almost dead. Its unmoving eyes, looking but not seeing, lay in a bed of ginger slices and scallions. Its tail extended stiffly beyond the boat-shaped plate, occasionally jerking, signaling its dawning finality.

While the rest lined up for the food, Red Red remained in a corner with his eyes closed. I went up and hugged him, pecking him on his forehead. "You can open your eyes now. I promise the food is going to taste even better than its aroma."

Red Red opened his eyes a crack. "I am in heaven?"

"Not yet. There are better things awaiting you in life."

"I wouldn't mind if there aren't." Red Red rushed off to the serving table.

It would be a good New Year, I thought, watching the children exclaim and eat with excitement, their squeals of joy swooping in the air like flocks of birds.

Tan

唐

CHAPTER 37

I rented the lavish reception hall at the Beijing Hotel and hired the Beijing Chamber Orchestra to play in the room now decorated in the spirit of winter, with reindeer, Santa Claus, and fake snow. A banquet would be held in the adjoining hall. French champagne was smuggled in from Hong Kong, Shandong salmon swam in the hotel fish tanks, Fujian crabs crawled around with thick and juicy legs, and there was *de zhou pa ji*—roasted chickens each weighing no more than one tender pound.

Editor Fei-Fei, with surprising epicurean talent, orchestrated the whole event. The guest list, another painful yet necessary achievement of Fei-Fei's, ran like a Who's Who of Beijing—businessmen, cadres, artists, actors, writers, and a few army officers. Some I knew; others I didn't.

"But you need to know them," Fei-Fei insisted.

"This is ridiculous. Some of them are like fire and water. They should not be together."

"You'll be amazed what a couple of drinks can do to men," Fei-Fei said. "We've also invited officials from the City Planning Bureau. I would not be surprised if your Dragon Center project is approved on the spot tonight."

"Keep your fingers crossed and don't drink too much yet. I need you for the rest of the night."

"Who is going to pick up the surprised bride-to-be in Tianjin?" Fei-Fei asked.

"You."

"Me? Why does everything have to be me? Where is your managing director, Mike Blake?"

"He is helping the architects with the final touches of the Dragon Project presentation. Besides, she is your author."

He acquiesced. "Very well."

"You will leave at five in the afternoon by helicopter. She will be glued to the hotel in Tianjin all day, preparing a party for the orphans. The flight takes fifty minutes. Have her here by eight. That will give her time to be surprised and dressed and wedded to me by nine."

"Sounds good, but what are you going to do with those poor kids?"

"Bring them. I've rented a military cargo plane for that purpose. They're very special to her. She will not come without them."

"Only you could pull off something like this."

"A compliment, I presume."

"No, a criticism. Bringing orphans to your wedding."

We hugged, and Fei-Fei gripped my arms. "Take good care of her. She is my favorite author. I rise and fall with her."

"So do I," I said.

MY FAMILY CAME bright and early on my wedding day. I sat them in my living room and paid my respect to them by performing the Becoming a Man ritual. Mother washed my face with a towel, Father combed my hair one last time as a child of the family, and Grandfather shaved my beard. Then I poured them each a cup of tea and served it with a deep bow. A child had grown, and now I was ready to grow my own family.

Mother cried, saying that she would never have set foot in this city that had rejected us had it not been for this special day of mine. She managed to avoid mentioning Sumi's name, but she seemed to have accepted my decision, and I was certain she would shed happy tears when Sumi and I finally wed. Father would smile, and Grandfather would hope aloud that we breed a lot of little dragons to run around his knees and pull his ears and that goatee of his. As a great-grandfather, he would be even more enthusiastic when he taught his great-grandchildren the value of compound interests and the significance of the Dow Jones Index.

Everything would be fine come the night. On my way to the hotel, I said the word "wife" carefully, as if tasting an unknown recipe. I nodded, liking the flavor, and repeated it, smiling. Wife, she is, and husband, I will be. My heart choked with abundant gratitude as I entered my hotel room to prepare for the evening. I checked my watch. Four p.m. Five more hours and we would reach another milestone.

Shento

山头

CHAPTER 38

The watch on my wrist read four. I frowned at the whirling dust as the helicopter lowered to the landing pad at the Tianjin Navy Base. Seawater wrinkled as the propellers whirled and fanned the air. A navy officer flagged us in and the helicopter came to rest on the eye of a painted circle.

"The Tianjin Hotel, officer," I said to the driver as I jumped out of the chopper and entered the waiting jeep.

"Yes, Colonel. The ride will take twenty minutes."

"Make it ten."

"Yes, Colonel." The driver floored the car and shot out of the parking lot, nose-diving into the veins of the cemented city roads.

As the city flew by, I picked up the mobile phone in the jeep. "On land now. Update, please."

"Our men are on every floor of the hotel. All exits are blocked. The children are eating and singing."

"What is she doing?"

The phone crackled.

"Hello? Talk to me."

"Colonel, it's the bridge we are passing through," the driver said.

"I am back," said the voice on the phone.

"What is she doing?" I asked again.

"The target is talking to a boy and dishing more food onto his plate. In fact, it is a fish head, Colonel."

"I will be there in a few minutes. Then we take action. Don't let her get away."

"No, Colonel."

"And make sure she is not harmed."

"Never, Colonel."

I was taken to the operation's command center, situated on the second floor of the office building across from her hotel. I silently grabbed the binoculars from my Tianjin Young General and took in a long breath. My whole existence ceased. I felt like a wisp of cloud, floating, without roots, dreaming. My head was hot, my mind a mess. My eyes searched hungrily. Then I saw her and held my breath—the cascade of her hair, the face of love and beauty, her body, a little fuller now, and that smile. The scent of Fujian rushed back to me; her fragrance lingered in my head. I felt lifted by it. My mind went blank for a second. I looked on, begging silently for her to look up at me.

She laughed, ladled out more food, patted the children, and turned her back to me, continuing her work at hand. Then she stopped, frowned, and looked up. She searched around. Suddenly alert, she stared directly into the lenses of my binoculars.

"Take her now," I ordered my man in an unsteady whisper.

Sumi

CHAPTER 39

In the noisy dining hall, a little girl ran over and pulled on my dress. I crouched down to face her. "What is it, sweetie?"

"There is a man looking for you," the girl said. She was missing many teeth.

I looked up and saw a tall man in his mid-twenties approaching. He wore a serious look.

I wiped my hands on a towel, and went to meet the man. "Can I help you?"

"Yes, miss. I am the city fire inspector. There is a fire reported downstairs. We need to evacuate all the children here, as soon as possible."

"What should I do?"

"Do not shout. Just follow me. My men will take care of the evacuation in an orderly manner."

"I need to stay here and help."

"No, you will slow down the evacuation. Come now."

A dozen firemen surrounded the hall. The children were surprised to see them. "Is there a fire?" one of them asked.

"Yes. We need to evacuate right now."

The kids turned into a hive of bees.

"Where are you taking me?" I asked.

"Across the street," the man said.

Suspicion began to rise. "Are you arresting me?"

"No, of course not. It is safer there."

I was taken into the building and into an empty office and asked to wait. I thought of my orphans, whose first New Year's party was being ruined by this fire, and sighed.

Shento

山头

CHAPTER 40

I adjusted my uniform, smoothed my hair, set my hat on my head. I didn't know what my first words would be or what I would do. She was only a few feet and a thin wall away from me. I turned the knob and opened the door, my head held high. And looked straight at her.

Sumi stood up, at first startled. Then she drew in a long breath, one hand on the arm of her chair for support, the other covering her mouth. But a little cry got through. I could see her body sway dangerously.

I ran over to her and cradled her in my arms. *Oh, Sumi.* I kissed her randomly, madly, blindly. With the same passion, she kissed me back. We spoke nothing. Everything that needed to be said was expressed in the way we clung to each other.

"How?" she said. She reached up and touched my face—unbelieving.

In tears and laughter, I told Sumi about my escape by sea, my pending death in prison, my long search for her and the lost records of the Fujian Orphanage. I was coherent at times, illogical at others—it was a mad wash of words. I left some sentences unfinished, lost in thought, but when she tried to jump in and share her story, I would hug her and seal her mouth with mine and went on deliriously about my life and why I was here. When I had said everything, an old weight lifted from my chest.

"I knew you would be a great man someday. I knew." Sumi's eyes gleamed with admiration and love.

"You haven't told me anything yet."

"You didn't give me a chance."

"I'm very sorry, my love. My ears are all yours now."

She seemed to melt when she heard me say "my love." She began her story in flashbacks, in spurts, formless, like a poem, image on image, the complex symphony of her life since that night when I saw her last, petrified in the moonlight. At times, with symphonic complexity. Other times, in a whispered, haunting melody. She pillowed her head against my chest, which heaved with the rhythm of her sobs. I shed tears I did not know I had. And there was also laughter.

"Oh, but Shento," she said, smiling. "I have the best gift of all." She took my hand.

"What might that be?" I asked.

"Tai Ping. You have a son."

I stopped breathing. "I have a son?"

"Conceived from love on that sad night of your flight."

"I have a son," I repeated incredulously.

"We have a son."

"We have a son." I held her close, kissed her, my heart a tangle of gratitude and possibility.

"Are you happy?"

"Oh, Sumi," I managed to say. "So happy."

Sumi kissed me gently, a simple song. I kissed her back, hot and urgent, with fierceness. She softened, responding to me. I tore her dress open, unintentionally leaving light scratches on her tender skin with my blunt nails, and she ignited. I pushed down my trousers and lifted up the hem of her dress. She was shaking for me to be inside her, and I ached with the pain of passion. In a ritual of love, I sucked in the fingers of her left hand, gently at first, then hungrily, one by one, with my eyes closed. I grabbed her right hand to repeat the delicious chore, then stopped as something caught my eyes.

"What is this?" I asked, lifting my head. "An engagement ring?"

She opened her eyes, as if emerging from a dream.

"Are you promised to someone else?"

She blinked as if coming to herself and nodded.

"Who is he?"

"I met him long after you left." She wrapped her arms around me.

I was silent.

Sumi continued quietly, "I waited and waited. Then came the investigator from your prison, and later the notice of your death. I felt so broken. Every day, I stood by the edge of the sea—me and the sunrise. I wanted to end my life. I wanted to die with you, and meet you again in heaven . . ."

I held her tighter. "Where is the man now?"

My words did not sink in. Sumi's eyes were misty and distant, staring back into painful days long gone. ". . . but I couldn't. Every day I felt the Sea Goddess, Ma Zu, opening up her arms and smiling sweetly to me. 'Come here, child,' she said. 'Come to me.' Each day I felt drawn closer. I waded in to the depth of my waist on a stormy day . . . a rocking sampan. An old fisherman caught me in his net. I couldn't die, I decided. Ma Zu didn't want me to. Then I began to throw up and yearn for pickled vegetables. I craved anything salty. One day I stole some moldy pickles from the school kitchen. The principal, the little man, told me, 'You are expelled.' Ha! To be expelled from an orphanage—how much worse can one get?"

I continued holding her, letting her talk, open up, remember, cry so that she could laugh again. The past had become a black wall, blocking our eyes, separating our hearts. She was removing that wall now, brick by brick.

"Do you know why?" she asked.

"Why what?"

"Why I was expelled?"

I shook my head.

"I was pregnant . . . with your son." She drew back and looked into my eyes. "Your beautiful son. Everything he is, is you. The way he talks, walks, his scent . . . What a grand name, the Pacific."

"He must be a big boy now."

"Seven," Sumi said.

"I can't believe I have a son."

"Then my fiancé saved me from the paws of another devil and helped me get into college. He published my memoir and raised our child . . ."

"I understand."

"No, you don't. You don't understand the pain, the curses. I gave birth to Tai Ping in the gutters of a hospital that threw me out. They spat on me. I nearly bled to death."

"Sumi . . . I am so sorry."

"Then a man came, the only light in my universe of darkness . . . his grace, his generosity, risking his own life. You don't understand, and you don't know how I felt, seeing him. It was like seeing you."

"I understand."

"No, you don't. Many times, in those dark days, I wished we had traded places. That I had taken those bullets in my head, and that you were the survivor, walking with our child in the mountains, climbing over the peaks with Tai Ping on your strong shoulders to see the sunshine of tomorrow. I would have been happy and content being a silent ghost, watching over you, wishing you a happy life, hoping that you would find Tai Ping a mother to care for him and a virtuous wife to love you as I would have. She might have even been better than I in many ways, and I would have been jealous but not angry, for I would be dead, living in the dark side of life, and you all belonged to the light . . ."

"I do understand. Please, I do. I am grateful to you. I want you to guide me to that generous man and to my son, and I want to thank him for what he has done."

"And then what?"

"Then I want you and my son back," I said in a firm whisper.

Her big eyes searched mine intently.

"Do you still love me?" I asked.

"I do."

"Do you love him?"

"I do."

"As much as you love me?"

"How I wish there were two of me. One for you and one for him."

"What is done can be undone."

"Love is unforgettable, my dear Shento."

I took a long breath. "You were mine first and still mine now. I need you. You have to come back to me or my existence is meaningless."

"Oh, Shento." She stroked my hair soothingly, like a mother. "Please, I beg you to give me some time. I am still in shock that you are alive."

"The world is once again ours. You are the famous writer that I said you would become."

"And you are in the military, commanding thousands as I predicted."

"I want to talk to the man you are engaged to."

"Oh, he is a good man."

"What is his name and where does he live? I can meet with him tomorrow."

"He lives in Beijing and his name is Tan Long."

I released her and stepped back. "Tan Long?" It was like a knife in my ribs.

"He is a very successful businessman."

"The owner of Blue Sea Publishing House," I said hoarsely.

"You know him?"

I looked away.

"What is the matter, dear Shento?" She reached over, stroked my arm.

I struggled to understand. Rich boy, poor girl, publisher and his favorite author. Two intelligent minds, lonely, searching for their counterparts in Fujian, where the rich boy had been banished. One romantic, vulnerable, a wild mountain flower; the other a city boy, struck by her beautiful soul and ripe fragrance. My head throbbed with crazy thoughts and montages of Sumi and Tan Long holding each other, sitting on the cliff of that dreamy little fishing village at the end of the world, dreaming big dreams, falling in love, deeper and deeper until she yielded her vibrant self to his hungry one.

"Shento, say something."

I shook my head to clear my mind. My throat felt dry. A rock had fallen on my heart and breathing became hard.

"Are you all right?" Sumi asked.

I looked back at her, my eyes filled with suspicion and distance. An intolerably long moment stood between us. I pulled up my pants and buttoned my uniform, with the austere silence and efficiency of a vigilant soldier. Never for a second did my eyes leave her. I buckled my collar and put on my hat.

"It is not kind to answer my love with silence, Shento." Sumi stood up, buttoning her dress. "Why are you leaving so suddenly?"

I gripped her face with my hand. "Love has brought us together, but fate has already torn us apart."

"I beg that you give me some time," she said, pulling away.

"Nothing can repair a hurt this deep, and my love for you only deepens the wound."

"Why, Shento? You said you understood." Sumi started to cry.

"I could with any other man, but not Tan Long."

"What do you mean?"

"His father could tell you why."

"His father?"

"Yes, his cursed father! I am his bastard son, and Tan Long is my half brother!"

Sumi seemed uprooted by this sudden revelation, caught in the moment of great impact. A lull lapsed before she said thickly, "How could this be?"

"It is fate," I said calmly. "But I will fight it."

"Fight it? How?" Sumi asked, wiping her eyes.

"The Longs have given me no breathing space in this world. They killed my mother and sent me to die in that orphanage. And now his damned son is taking what is mine. It is time I made things right."

"What are you going to do?"

"To you, nothing. But to them, everything. Sumi, this world allows only one dragon son, him or me. It is your choice."

"The fortune-teller was right," Sumi said woodenly. "I am not destined for happiness."

"He is wrong. You could be happy again. The whole world that we dreamed of is just beginning. Come back to me. We'll build a family. Let me take care of you and our son. I have powers beyond your imagination."

"I'm sure you do. You have demonstrated that very vividly today. But for our love and your son's sake, let me talk this matter over with Tan."

After a painful hesitation, I nodded. "But you have to promise to come back to me."

She searched my face and promised, "I will."

Such a simple reply. I was moved. My lips trembled as I squeezed out a helpless smile, a sad one, the best I could manage, my eyes burning.

"Have faith in me, please, Shento." She wiped my tears with her sleeve.

I nodded obediently, fighting hard not to take her into my arms again.

"When the sun rises again, I will see you in Beijing," Sumi said.

When she left, the night faded with her, and the warmth of her fragrance was soon replaced by a chill. I took the helicopter back to Beijing muttering just one word: "War."

"What did you say, Colonel?" my Young General asked.

"Nothing. Nothing at all."

Tan

唐

CHAPTER 41

The mood in the reception hall of the Beijing Hotel was pregnant with anticipation and the excitement of the night. The crowd parted for me and applauded as I made my way to the podium. I rubbed my hands, nodding and acknowledging the warm reception. Half of the most powerful men of the town were here. The other half did not matter. How did I get so lucky, I wondered, as my eyes rested on my family.

In the crowd, Grandfather toasted me silently with a glass of something bubbly. Father waved his unlit cigar, an old habit from his army days. Mother looked aloof with half-closed eyes, smiling at half the people here, condescending to the rest.

With Lena on my right, and half a dozen of my executives on my left, I nodded to the conductor. The music trickled away. I tapped the microphone. Someone shouted, "Sing us a song, please."

"I'm afraid I might scare you away."

The crowd laughed.

"We have come to surprise number one of the night. Standing by me, as you all have been itching to know, is indeed the honorable I. M. Pei."

The crowd erupted with thunderous applause. Mr. Pei took a step forward and bowed humbly.

"And he is here for a very important reason," I said. "Ladies and gentlemen, we are proud of our thousands-year-old culture. In this best city of the world called Beijing, we have the Great Wall, the Forbidden City, and many other wonders of the world. But that is the past of Beijing, a glorious past. Tonight, I am here to unveil to you the future of this city. Ladies and gentlemen, may I present to you, Dragon Center."

Lena lifted a satin sheet from a table before me to reveal a sprawling model of Dragon Center glowing with brilliant little bulbs. Atop the tallest building was a dragon displayed in blue light. It was elegant, sublime, breathtaking. The excited crowd burst into applause and rushed to the display.

I made my way to my family. "Mother, Father, Grandfather. This is the future of the Longs. Now you can see it with your own eyes."

"Son, this is unbelievable." Father beamed.

"Grandson, this is going to cost you."

"Are there going to be fashionable department stores?" Mother asked.

"The answers are yes, yes, and yes." I hugged my family. "And Grandfather, don't worry. Even as we speak, money is lining up at my door—J. P. Morgan and Company of New York, Sumitomo Mitsui of Tokyo, Rothschild of London, Deutsche Bank of Frankfurt, Hang Seng Bank of Hong Kong, the list goes on and on. And Mother, all the fashion houses of the world—Paris, New York, and Milan—have inquired about anchoring their Asian flagships here."

"J. P. Morgan and Company should lead the syndication," Grandfather said.

"Why, Grandfather?"

"Other banks might have more money, but Morgan has the best credibility."

"There are a few things I am concerned about, son," Mother said. "Did you realize that your Dragon Center will cast a shadow over a third of Tiananmen Square when the sun is setting? And all the buildings in your center have pointy rooftops. The shadows insult the square, and the pointy roofs insult the almighty heavens. Chinese are superstitious for a reason."

"Mother, this is the future of Beijing. All these buildings reach for the sky. They symbolize the human spirit soaring higher and higher. Besides, they contrast beautifully with the golden curled roofs of the Forbidden City."

"Check with a feng shui monk before you start," Mother suggested.

"I have complete trust in I. M. Pei."

"Is he the same man who designed that spiraling Bank of China Building in Hong Kong?" she asked.

"Yes, why?" I asked.

"Hong Kong traditionalists were very upset about that, predicting that one day tragedy would descend upon the entire island because of that defiant building."

"Mother, throw away the superstitions. Do you see how the people are reacting to the glamour and glory of the design?"

"They know nothing about spikes and shadows."

"Thank you, Mother, for your advice, but this dragon is going to fly no matter what."

"Son, this is not discouragement, but caution. I am the only one in this crowd bold enough to tell you the truth. Your father and grandfather have already fallen at your feet. They do not talk sense anymore. I do."

I hugged my mother again and reluctantly pulled away to greet the cheering crowd. Their words of congratulation bubbled like the champagne being poured and drunk. The mayor broke through the crowd to shake hands with me. "We, the city, will throw our weight behind you to have it completed. Beijing needs something like this."

Reporters from magazines and newspapers from all over the world came up to interview me.

"What is the statement you are making with this project to the world?" the one from *Newsweek* asked.

"The message is simply that the sick giant of Asia is standing up again and the dragon has taken off."

The reporter quickly jotted my words down. "How soon do you think China will be able to overtake the position that Japan holds and become the leader in Asia, and, for that matter, the world leader?"

"Aren't we already?"

A round of applause followed my answer.

I looked at my watch again. Time was running out. Where were Fei-Fei and Sumi? Had he been drinking? I had told Fei-Fei not to start his first gin and tonic until after he returned from Tianjin. It was now 7:55. Fei-Fei should have been back at the hotel by now. What was causing the delay?

I looked around. There was no Fei-Fei. I told myself to wait patiently. These prewedding jitters were getting to me more than I expected.

It was eight o'clock. The tuxedoed hotel manager discretely came up to me and whispered, "Where is she?"

"My question exactly."

"I'll hold off everything until she arrives."

"Good idea."

At 8:15, a disheveled Fei-Fei finally appeared. My eyes lit up upon seeing him. I pulled the thin, lanky man to my side and said, "Where is my bride?"

"We need to talk," Fei-Fei said.

"You need a drink?"

"Yes, and so do you, a stiff one." Fei-Fei dragged me through a door to an empty room. "We could not find Sumi."

"Come on, I know you, the editor in chief and his favorite author pulling a prank on the publisher."

"I'm serious. Sumi is missing!" Fei-Fei shouted, shaking my shoulders with urgency.

"It is true?"

"We searched all over the hotel. There was a reported fire, the kids were evacuated, and then she was gone. Her hotel room was intact. Everything she has is there—her manuscript, her clothes, everything. One of the kids said she walked out with a fireman. We contacted the fire department. They said no fire was ever reported to them, nor did they send anyone out to that hotel this afternoon. In fact, all the firemen were drinking, gambling, and celebrating the New Year at the firehouse."

"How about the police?"

"We checked with them—they knew nothing about it."

"It must be a secret arrest," I said.

"No, if that were the case, they would let the public know after the arrest was made. I threatened them, and the police chief said I was making a mistake. They hadn't taken in anyone. Then I accused them of tailing Sumi while she was there in Tianjin, kicking up dirt about the city's corruption. They said I was right, but the investigation had been dropped for the holiday. Only one man had been left to tail her, but he was pulled off by an order from above."

"An order from above?" My heart tightened. "And the mysterious fireman. I am going to my suite now. Get me David Li. He's the son of the public security minister. Bring him to me."

"Yes, Tan."

I went up to my hotel suite and threw off my tuxedo jacket. When David Li entered a short while later, I took the banker's hand and begged, "I need your help."

"Another billion-dollar loan?"

"I wish it were that." I passed the phone to him. "Call your father and find out for me who kidnapped Sumi Wo in Tianjin this afternoon."

The smile vanished from David's face. "Give me a minute."

I ran into the bathroom and splashed some water onto my face.

"Mr. Long," David said, after fifteen minutes on the phone.

"Tan, please."

"Mr. Long, the news isn't good. The order came from the Garrison Force. That's all we know."

"The Garrison?"

"The president's men, to be specific."

"Is there a name or a reason? Anything?"

"The Garrison needs no reason. They are China's KGB."

"There has to be a name. David, my loan arrangement with you depends on what you can do for me tonight. Take all the time you need and find out."

"But I have tried."

"But it is not the right answer."

"Mr. Long."

"Please, David. I'll tell your wife that you are on the phone with a foreign banker discussing some important loans."

David Li, the banker, the son of the most feared lawman in this country, was proof that all doors could be opened for a price. Twenty minutes later, David found me downstairs.

"Shento," he said.

"Mountaintop?"

"It is the name of a young colonel."

"Does he have a last name?"

"Not that I could find. I have done my utmost for you."

"Thank you. As you know, I always reward back double what has been given me."

"I am grateful to be of service, Mr. Long."

"Please, call me Tan from now on, because we are friends."

"Tan." The banker loosened his tie and grinned. "Friends. I like that."

When I shepherded my family into my suite and shared the news of Sumi's disappearance, Grandfather reached over to pour himself another drink. Mother said, "I told you so. She is trouble." Father's head bent low as he stared at the floor.

"Who is this man Shento? Have you heard of him before?" I asked Father.

There was a long silence, then Father said, "He is your half brother and your worst enemy."

"My half brother!" I said, incredulous.

"A long time ago, I met a girl in Balan. She killed herself when a child was born. That child was Shento." Father's voice was sad and somber. "He believes I abandoned him, but in truth I thought him dead when his village burned down. He fell into the hands of our enemy, Heng Tu, who used him to frame you for the crime you did not commit. It was Shento who killed your teacher, Miss Yu."

It was a few seconds before I could speak again. "Why haven't you told me this before? Why?"

I downed three shots of brandy and stormed out of the room. I needed to work. I told Fei-Fei to cancel the helicopter, telephoned my men to continue the search in Tianjin, and had a driver pick up Tai Ping. I returned to the party, pretending nothing had happened, slapping shoulders here and there, chatting with my guests, even toasting with them, getting more and more drunk.

Then I took Fei-Fei aside and whispered into his ear.

"Are you sure you want to take this route?" Fei-Fei asked.

"Do you have any other ideas?"

"Then it is war."

"Indeed. Let it begin." I downed another drink as Fei-Fei rushed out.

As the guests slowly filed out of the reception hall, shaking hands with their gracious host, Fei-Fei stood at the end of the line, passing out a typed press release to all the journalists, foreign and domestic, as they left the party.

Shento

CHAPTER 42

I spent a sleepless night missing Sumi. When morning came, I was awakened by my personal secretary clutching a stack of newspapers. "Colonel," he said urgently. "Please read the translated headlines."

I sat up in my bed and read the first in the stack. The *New York Times*'s front page screamed, "Democratic Leader Kidnapped by Chinese Government." I quickly skimmed through the rest. ". . . Sumi Wo, national bestselling author of *The Orphan,* was reported missing on New Year's Eve. Sources indicate that she was illegally detained by the notorious Garrison Force in a covert operation in the city of Tianjin, led by a young colonel named Shento." There was picture of her, the same photo that was on the jacket of her book. The British *Financial Times* predicted that China was headed for another crackdown and Sumi was but a chicken being slaughtered to scare the monkeys.

I threw all the papers on the floor, hurriedly dressed myself, and went to my office, where my Beijing Young General, Lieutenant Bei, was waiting.

"Who do you think leaked the information of our involvement?" I asked him.

"I am still checking on it."

"It had to have come from Tan Long. Give me a list of the attendees of his party last night. You do have it, don't you?"

"Yes, Colonel." The lieutenant quickly flipped through his notes. "Here it is. Three hundred of his closest friends, with their titles and political affiliations."

"Why don't you pick a name? This is your territory." I returned the list to him without looking.

"Yes, Colonel." He darted his eyes along the list and paused. "The possible leak might have come from David Li, the son of the public security minister. No one else could have known. David is also the manager of the Bank of China and Tan is his client. They are close."

"It's time we cut some of the toes and fingers that work for this Long boy. Make a list of all of Tan's business associates and friends."

"Yes, Colonel."

"We will weed them out one by one, until he feels all alone in this world. And don't forget to give our Fujian friends a call. A big part of his Dragon empire is there," I said.

"Oh, just one more thing," Lieutenant Bei said. "The general manager of the Beijing Hotel informed me that Tan Long unveiled a plan to build a monumental Dragon Center at the party last night. It is a one-billion-yuan project. I heard that the petition for construction approval is being filed even as we speak."

"Dragon Center, is that what they are calling it? Very auspicious, indeed," I said dryly. "Order the City Planning Bureau to withhold any decision concerning this particular filing, and rewrite their ordinances to prohibit any shadows over our beloved square."

"I'll see to it right away, Colonel," Lieutenant Bei promised and left the office.

My next move was damage control. I made sure my uniform was free of wrinkles, folded the newspapers carefully, and strode into the president's office.

The old man was sitting in the sun. The nurse saw me come in and left quietly.

"An auspicious New Year, Mr. President," I said.

"Young man, you took the girl, didn't you?" The president did not turn.

"I can explain it all. The girl, Sumi Wo, has been on my watch list for the last few months. She is a potential danger to our stability. Her first book sold five million copies, not counting what's been hand-copied. Our sources reveal that her second book will be an exposé about the inner workings of the Tianjin government, and will threaten the orderly operation of the city government. She is the spokeswoman for numerous prodemocracy organizations and magazines—"

"Sounds like a nice girl." The president gestured for me to stop. He swung his wheelchair around, catching it against the table. I helped him turn around until we faced each other. "Be more discreet next time. All the major newspapers in the world are protesting. It does not sit well with my image as a reform leader. You used to do better. Where is she now?"

"Released."

"Then why did you arrest her in the first place?"

"Because I want to rat out the snakes behind her."

"And who are they?"

"Your old friend, the Dragon empire."

"Ding Long?"

"Tan Long, his son. He is the publisher of Sumi Wo's book and many other forbidden titles through his firm, Blue Sea Publishing."

"Too ambitious to be any good. I thought he went back to Fujian with the rest of the family when they retired."

"The little dragon made it to Beijing University Law School, rejected all government job offers, and started his own business. He is proposing to build a monumental Dragon Center, which will overshadow our beloved Tiananmen Square."

"Monumental? Overshadow?" The old man frowned. "That can't be good. That's a direct insult to me."

"I have already blocked the project at the city level. A new ordinance is being written, even as we speak, prohibiting any shadows over our square. Also, Ding Long was here last night. I would not be surprised if he was behind all the trouble."

Heng Tu sat up, his eyes blazing with anger. "The weeds are spreading. We should have cut out the roots in the first place."

"It's never too late."

THAT AFTERNOON, in my spacious but spartan office, I was surrounded by the propaganda minister, the public security minister, the Communist Central Committee political commissars, and a dozen attentive journalists from the major state papers.

The veteran scribe from the propaganda ministry, well versed in the art of Communist sophistry, read aloud the piece he had painstakingly composed to be released by the leading news agency, Xinhua, to all the government newspapers across the land.

At the behest of the president, I was to finalize every word to be published. The subtlety of China's political protocol was displayed by the fact that I was in the center, sitting in the big chair behind the big desk, not the two elderly ministers, who could hardly keep their eyes open as they sat on a couch in the dozing warmth of the setting sun. They were there because I needed them in this battle of words, a precursor preceding another political purge, an occurrence as common as sunburn in the summer and influenza in the winter.

The speech was peppered with moldy phrases such as "bourgeois elements," "anti-Communist currents," "anarchists," and "chaotic state of a rotten democracy." It was an old tune given new meaning. I loved every word of it. The two ministers were napping. "What do you think, Propaganda Minister?" I prodded.

The propaganda minister suddenly woke up, wiping his drool with his sleeve. "I second it. I think the tone is strong enough to send a warning out to the rest of the world about any more attacks on our Communist leadership."

"Yes, it should shut them all up," the public security minister added, roused by the other minister's sudden outburst.

"Then it is ready to print, comrades," I said. "Our president thanks you for a job well done. Remember, front-page editorial, exact wording."

"Yes, Colonel." The newspapermen each picked up a copy and left.

I patted the scribe's shoulder. "You haven't lost your edge."

Gratefully, the man bowed to me. "Honored to be at your service."

I asked the public security minister to stay after everyone else had left.

"What else can I do for you, Colonel?"

"Not for me, for the president," I said, sitting on the arm of the sofa.

"What else can I do for our dear president?" he amended.

"Advise your son, the banker, to stay away from Tan Long," I said gravely.

"My son?" the old man asked, alarmed.

"Your son made the phone call that led to all this mess, didn't he?"

"I am deeply sorry, Colonel." The minister bowed, trembling.

"Children are young and innocent. But they must learn."

"Yes, yes, they must. I will punish him myself. Please give him a chance."

"That I will, Minister. I respect you and your long service with our revolution. It would be a shame to see your son hurt in any way. His future is so bright."

"Please allow me to right the wrong, Colonel." The man bowed out as if fleeing a ghost.

Sumi

CHAPTER 43

The sea churned like a madman, drunk. Its waves tossed and turned and shouted incoherently. Seagulls flew the contour of the stormy wind. Some were blown out off course and fell to the surging whitecaps, their cries haunting and hallowing.

My heart sang the sad reprisal of the sea. Everything around me matched the darkness of my mood. Since I had left Shento, I had roamed aimlessly along the shore, surrounded by darkness that was broken by lonely lampposts, whose dim lights only deepened the depth of the night. My heart yearned for the sea, as if it were calling to me: *Come to me, my child.* How I wished I could walk into its bosom and all my pains would ease.

In love with two brothers. I cursed my own fate, the three knives hidden in my fate. Whom should I choose? Shento, with the rawness of the mountain and his desperate thirst? Or Tan, with his loving heart that soothed my mind, leaving sorrow and loneliness no space, leaving me wanting nothing? One would die for me. The other could not live without me.

Somewhere in the recesses of my soul, a little blade of regret had already grown. How could I have made that promise to return to Shento? Yes, I felt love for him. Yes, he was alive and beautiful. Yes, he had become a man with power and a future only fathomable by the reach of his ambition. But how could I forsake Tan, the love of my life now, my rock? I wished time would stop and I would be no more. I was tired, my feet were cold, and my back ached. My eyes blurred watching the monotonous roaring sea.

I leaned against a rusty public phone and dialed the number I knew by heart.

Tan

CHAPTER 44

I held Sumi in my arms. Sunlight flooded us as we sat on the sofa in our living room. Her eyes were closed, and she occasionally jerked and twitched as she slept, dreaming. Thank Buddha, she was back in my arms, safe in my world. After her call from the seaside phone booth, I had flown over to Tianjin and picked her up. Wet and shivering like a beaten animal, she had been silent all the way to Beijing. I told her what I'd done, how I'd alerted the press about her abduction. She had shaken her head ever so slightly and fallen asleep.

That morning, the first day of the new year, I received a pile of newspapers carrying Sumi's story—the *New York Times,* the *Yomiuri Shimbun* of Tokyo, the *Financial Times* of London, and some French and German papers. The list was long. The power of this new weapon was the oldest sword of mankind. Heed thy words, the wise men always said. Words could kill. They were right.

Why not start more magazines and newspapers myself? My own venues with which to inform the people of this nation. Maybe even television and radio stations. I could install a TV network and radio towers right on top of Dragon Center. What a perfect fit. The sky was the only limit to my vision. No, in fact, the sky would be my extension.

Despite everything, I felt excited by my plans for the new year. I wanted to share my latest scheme with Sumi but let her rest. When she finally opened her eyes, her first words were "Do you love me?"

"Of course, Sumi. Always. In fact, last night I had planned something very special for us. Your no-show meant a huge wedding cake melted and three hundred people feasted on a banquet without the bride."

"Wedding cake?"

I showed her the velvet ring box and opened the lid. Inside was a glistening diamond. "I was going to give this to you last night."

"A wedding ring?"

"Yes, I was going to surprise you last night—I planned a whole wedding."

"Oh, dear, dear Tan." She reached up and kissed me. "I am so sorry. Can you forgive me?"

"In a heartbeat. If I can wed you in another."

Sumi looked away.

"What is the matter? Everything is going to be fine now. That Shento fellow won't touch you anymore. I have shown him that my authors are not to be detained or tortured. Furthermore, I am preparing a lawsuit by the best civil rights lawyers to pursue this case. It would generate . . ."

"Stop, Tan. It's not that simple."

"Of course it is. The government should give more freedom to us all. We need it, the people demand it, and I am going to champion for it with you—"

"Stop! You don't know the real reason for my detention."

"Because you are like a throbbing toothache to them."

"That was only a cover." She reached for my hand. "I have something to tell you."

"So do I. This Shento, that Garrison colonel, might be my half brother. Can you believe that?"

"He is your half brother," Sumi said. "He told me, but there is more. Do you remember the boy who died for me?"

"Yes . . . his name was Shento, too, wasn't it?" I frowned.

"It is the same man. He is the Shento whom I knew. He found me yesterday in Tianjin."

I stood up and started pacing. "That boy—your old lover—is my half brother? Shento? But he was executed, you said."

"He was spared at the last moment. Someone saved him, heaven knows who. My dear Tan, fate played a trick on us. I don't know what to do."

"This is our problem. We will solve it together." I sat down, holding Sumi.

She whispered, "I am moving out of here."

"What?" I leaped up. "You're going back to him?"

"No. I am going somewhere far away, away from both of you." There was a soft finality in her voice.

"What about us?"

"I will love you always."

"Do you love him, too?"

She hesitated, then said softly, "Yes, I do."

"How can you?"

"How can I not?" She shook her head. "Had he not lived, I would have been so happy being your wife. I am leaving you only to save you—"

"The monster threatened that?"

"He is capable of carrying out his threat."

"I will not yield to him and give you up."

"This is not a contest. I am leaving so that you both can live on peacefully."

"You can't just leave," I said, frustrated.

"The hatred of the last generation should not continue," Sumi said. "You both are great men. To fight each other is to waste. Tan, I have made up my mind." She went to the door and called out to Nai-Ma to ready Tai Ping to leave.

"You see what I have risked for you?" I waved the newspapers. "People all over the world know about your detention. Shento will tremble at this international condemnation of terrorism tantamount to the acts of the Gestapo."

Sumi picked up the *Times* and her face went pale. "You shouldn't have done this."

"Oh, there is a lot more. Do you know that his was the hand that killed Miss Yu, the crime that I was framed for and the trigger that caused the downfall of the Long clan? How would he like that to be on the front page tomorrow?"

"You cannot do that! You must not start a war. If not for me, then for Tai Ping's sake."

I turned away, facing the window, and heard the door close behind me as Sumi left quietly.

Shento

CHAPTER 45

Midday at the grand entrance to the Garrison Force of Beijing, an army jeep picked up Sumi and my son and drove them through layers of vast courtyards, past old pine trees, ponds with colorful fish, and columns of young soldiers marching back and forth, patrolling the seat of the government. On the doorsteps of my palatial office, I stood in uniform, ready to meet my son.

The door of the jeep opened—mother helped child out. Tai Ping looked up at me. "Who is this big man?" he asked his mother in a clear, high voice.

"Your father," Sumi said.

"My father? But I already have a father . . . at home."

"Tan Long loves you very much. But this man is your real father."

I squatted down and examined my son. "And who is this?" I asked.

The boy seemed struck by sudden shyness.

"Your son, Tai Ping," Sumi said, proudly.

My son stared at me for a long moment before his round face broke into a sweet smile. I smiled back and held him in my arms, feeling his young heart thumping against me. What a moment. What a moment to savor. When my son started to squirm, I let him go reluctantly and stood up. I rubbed my hands nervously, not knowing what to show Sumi and our son first. I led them inside. "This used to be the office of the prime minister in the Ch'ing dynasty."

My little boy was impressed. "It's nice."

Next to my office was a chamber with an elegant display of ornate swords, arrows, and daggers used in the Ch'ing dynasty.

"Did you know, the last emperor was a boy like you," I said. "That room"—I pointed to the chamber—"holds the weapons he used. Would you like to see them?"

"Really? Can I, please?"

"Of course, you can." I nodded.

Excitedly, Tai Ping ran off by himself.

"You're here to stay?" I asked Sumi.

"No, I am here to say good-bye."

"What? What about your promise?" I demanded.

"I can't belong to two men at the same time," she said sadly.

"So you're going back to him?"

"No, I am going back to nobody. I am going away from both of you."

"But I need you. I need to love you."

"I am lost now. I need calm to find myself, my own destiny."

"Your destiny is with me. I won't let you out of my sight again, ever."

"Is that a threat?"

"No, it's my desire. It's what has kept me alive all these years without you."

She was quiet, seemingly moved by the power of my words. Then she spoke. "Let me go, or you will lose me forever."

"How can you deny me my one happiness?"

"Can you fathom my sorrow, my pain? Do you have any idea what it feels like to be torn between two loves? Do you? My heart has shattered in pieces. You men will never understand. I only want to die!" Her voice pierced the courtyard. A couple of guards came rushing in. I gestured them away and brought Sumi to the sofa.

Little Tai Ping rushed in. "What did you do to my mama? Leave her alone!" He started crying and pounding his small fists at me, refusing to calm down until Sumi pulled him into her arms.

I left the room, not knowing what to do. I waited outside, worried that Sumi had gone mad. Only after a long lull did I tiptoe back in and ask, "Will you return?"

"I don't know," she said, shaking her head.

"If you must go, please stay the night and tomorrow will be yours," I begged.

"Promise you will end this feud with the Longs."

I nodded.

We ate supper in silence, then we lay in bed like man and wife. She was cold, her eyes closed, as I soiled her angelic perfection with my abject lust. When I could bear her aloofness no longer, I buried my face in the sweet valley between her breasts. I'd never known such despair—for Sumi to simply tolerate me was unthinkable. And then, her hand found my head and began to stroke my hair. At last she awoke to my ardor, lifting my face to hers, kissing me softly at first, then hungrily.

When first light crept upon the curled golden roof of the palace, Sumi took Tai Ping and tiptoed around a sleeping guard. They left in twilight, their shadows long on the brick courtyard. The only remnant of Sumi's presence was a wordless message lying on my desk: the trace of a light kiss etched in lipstick on a piece of stationery.

Tan

CHAPTER 46

January 2, 1986

BEIJING

The morning was damp with the drizzle of a wet snow; the sun was nowhere to be found. The gray of the day when I awoke only darkened my mood. I missed Sumi, and missing was even more intolerable on a day such as this. The wind howled, chasing the garbage lurking in the street corners, and wept with the rhythm of a ghost as it beat swinging power lines and leafless tree branches. Dark days like this invited evil. Misfortune befell the unfortunate and bad luck invaded households. People laughed less and cried more. Drunks climbed the moon, and the crazy dived into the sea. Such was the mood I was in when I entered my office that morning. All my managers were lined up at the door to my office, their faces reflecting the color of the day.

"Sit down, my friends. What's the matter?" I asked.

Fei-Fei looked at Mike Blake, who looked at Lena.

"What is it?" I demanded.

"Read this, please, boss." Fei-Fei laid the *People's Daily* on my broad desk. "The *People's Daily,* the *Guangming Daily,* and all thirty or so official papers of this country have the same front-page headline."

I sat down and read the opening lines of the article.

FALSE ANTI-CHINA REPORT CONDEMNED

The recent false report accusing China's Garrison Force of kidnapping popular writer Sumi Wo was a fabrication motivated by anti-China elements that exist within and outside China. This slander, intended to smear China's perfection of socialist democracy in the face of our phenomenal economic growth and good human rights record, will be thoroughly investigated. The bad elements involved will be brought to justice to protect the integrity of our nation . . .

"This doesn't scare me," I said, looking up.

"Boss, lay low for a while," Fei-Fei pleaded.

"Lay low? What kind of rhetoric is that?" I asked. "Coming from you, the leader of the liberal-thinking camp?"

"There was an emergency meeting of the cabinet and all the propaganda personnel at the provincial level," Fei-Fei continued.

"There is another purge coming. It always starts that way," Lena said, concerned.

"And it always ends with a rooster being slaughtered to scare the monkeys. I am afraid that this time that rooster is us," Fei-Fei said. "Nobody is safe here." He looked at everyone present.

"You could always return to your boat-selling business in Virginia, Mike," I said to my American friend. "And you can go back to running your bank in Fujian, Lena. But I will stay right here. Once before I was driven out of this city in which I was born. Nothing"—I pounded the desk with my fist—"nothing is going to move me an inch from here this time."

"We only want you to be careful," Mike said.

"Why doesn't everyone try to be helpful and useful instead of careful?" I said bitingly. "I have worse news than this. Sumi and I have . . . We've gone our separate ways . . . temporarily, that is."

"What happened between you two?" Lena asked.

"Something that no one here would want to know," I said with resignation.

Lena came over and hugged me. Mike shook his head and said, "Sorry, buddy. Let me pour you a drink."

"You never thought my marrying her was a good idea anyway," I said to Mike.

Mike shrugged. "That's my generic answer to the general question of marriage, but I didn't intend for you two to fall apart."

"Let's get down to business. Sit down," I said.

"Business can wait. We can come back some other time," Fei-Fei said.

Mike and Lena nodded.

"No, stay and listen. I had this thought yesterday. Dragon and Company should enter more venues of the media business. We've got book publishing, but I'd like you, Fei-Fei, to start a dozen new magazines—political, lifestyle, fashion, business, everything. And newspapers on every subject printable. I always cherish the simple motto that the *New York Times* prints on the top of their front page every day: All the News That's Fit to Print. I like that. Everything fit to print."

"But this isn't the best time," Fei-Fei interrupted.

"On the contrary, it's the best time. Economic growth begets more freedom of speech. A suffocating regime will kill people's will and halt the boom we have here. Traditionally, the government controls the media and tells the people, all one billion of us, what they want us to hear or read. We need to change that. It's up to us. I want to print and broadcast the truth. People have the right to know the truth, as guaranteed by the constitution."

"You know what a joke that is, your constitution," Mike said.

"You're right. It is a joke now. But I want to change that as well, to enforce the sanctity of the rule of law, not the absurdity of our corrupt rulers. Change starts from us, not them. I want us to have our own television stations, cable, and radio. And do you know why I like the idea so much?"

"Why?" Mike asked.

"Because while we're doing something very important for this country, we will be making money, a lot of it. Media is going to be a big industry in the next century. Food, drink, and all the basic necessities of this world have been provided already. One billion people of the world are hungry for food for their souls. They want to read, see, and hear new and meaningful things. Go out and find me a team of editors and writers with new ideas and refreshing styles. I want people to crave our printed materials. I want to establish a brand name, much like the *New York Times, Forbes* magazine, and the *Economist.* I want people to be proud of reading our papers and magazines, and to feel privileged and enriched by our work. They will never leave us if we capture their hearts. Fei-Fei, I want you to check the licensing requirements for starting up TV and radio stations throughout China."

"I will, Mr. Long. But government censorship will be our biggest hurdle."

"I have faith in all of us to do the impossible. What is possible is already done. You, Lena, please talk to David Li, the Bank of China manager, to see if Communist money can finance some more of our capitalist ventures. Sell the idea to him, as you always do so well, Lena."

"I'll get right on it."

"And Mike, have we sent in the petition to the city of Beijing for the construction permit for Dragon Center?"

"It was hand-delivered to the office of the general director of the City Planning Bureau yesterday. Another copy was also sent to the office of the honorable mayor. I expect to receive a permit within a week. The taste of your good food, fine cigars, and liquor should still linger in their minds, if not their mouths."

"Thank you, Mike. Leave all the worry about this government to me. We've got some of the best legal minds on our side. We'll fight until the end. Happy New Year to you all."

Shento

CHAPTER 47

For the first time in my long military life, I overslept. Rubbing my eyes, I blinked at the sun that flooded the bedroom without invitation.

Sumi was gone. She had been mine, wholly mine, but only for the night. I jumped up from my bed and clung to the window, hoping to catch a glimpse of her, knowing well that even her shadow was no more. She had gone somewhere far beyond the high imperial walls that divided my world from hers. I kissed her silent note, touching the faint red trace of her lips with mine, then folded it, and put it carefully away. In silence, I pondered the meaning of her note. Was it a long kiss that meant the world? Or a curt kiss meant to end it all? Was it a bribe to open my heart or a lock to seal my soul? Such simple ambiguity.

But this mystery of hers wouldn't stay wrapped for long. My desire dictated that nothing in this world would be left undetected by my vigilance, and Sumi's existence was of utmost interest to me. Her garbage would be checked, her phone calls listened to, her door watched day and night. What was power if it could not be given concrete form or solid shape? What was power for, if not to serve yourself in the way of serving others and the country?

Knowing that Sumi, my little bird, was safe in my cage, I returned to my world, a man's world full of reality. "What is the first order of the day?" I asked my young secretary.

"Two investigators have been waiting," the man responded.

"Bring them in."

Two men from the Public Security Ministry came in and sat down.

"What do you have for me?"

"All the foreign reporters involved were asked to leave their posts effective immediately," the taller man said.

"And?"

"We have also received protests from their papers, claiming we violated their freedom to report."

"There is no freedom to report here. Don't they know?"

"One reporter did cave in. The girl from *Yomiuri Shimbun* of Tokyo turned in the typed news release handed to her by Fei-Fei Chen, the editor in chief of Blue Sea Publishing, on the night in question. Everyone received a copy. That's how word got out." He passed the folded copy to me.

"Exact wording." I smiled.

"With this, we could bring some serious charges against the instigator behind this damaging report. Leaking government information to a foreign citizen—treason, punishable by death or a life sentence without parole, among other things. He could also be charged with violation of Public Security Code Number Eighteen—damaging national pride and reputation—and Numbers Nineteen, Twenty, Twenty-one, Twenty-two; if we stretch our imagination a bit, all the way through to Clause Thirty-five."

"In short, you could throw the book at him."

"Yes, Colonel."

"Stick to treason. I like big ropes. Are you a prosecutor?" I asked the lanky fellow.

"Yes, I am a lawyer by training. Four years at Beijing University Law School."

"How would you like to handle this case and make a name for yourself?"

"It will be an honor. But I am an investigator working under the

Public Security Ministry. The prosecutory power falls under the Justice Department."

"What formality. Your transfer is effective immediately."

"Yes, Colonel." He stood up and saluted me.

"You seem to be near Tan Long's age. Do you happen to know him from your law school days?"

"Yes, Colonel, I do."

"You're not his friend, I figure."

"No, not at all. He stole the class presidency from me back in elementary school."

"He did? What is your name, Investigator?"

"Hito Ling."

"Hito, we could be friends, you know."

"I would like that, Colonel."

"Good. When can you bring your charges against Tan Long publicly?"

"Sir, that will come later. I would suggest taking in Fei-Fei Chen first. If he cracks, he can implicate his employer, Tan Long."

"*Art of War.* The strategy of inducing the snake out of his cave," I said.

"Precisely, Colonel. If his men are charged, Tan will make more mistakes in their defense. Then we will rein him in."

"You have studied his character."

"Yes, he lauds loyalty as the highest virtue. The New Year's Eve incident is a perfect example. He will do anything for his friends. That will be his downfall."

"While you are at it, I want to have a case opened for the entire Long clan at the Taxation Bureau in Beijing and Fujian for any hints of evasion or irregularities. Check with the corporate licensing authority for any regulatory violations, and with the Banking Commission for any misuse of funds. Last but not least, have the National Guard and Customs search for possible smuggling charges against the father," I ordered.

"I would like to supervise the investigations that you mentioned and lump them together," Hito said. "We're looking to bury three generations in one tomb."

"Granted." I nodded, pleased. "Law is powerful."

"If it is on your side."

"It is always on my side, Hito."

Only when night came and my uniform was shed would I allow Sumi to return to my world. Nothing regarding her or my son was too trivial to note. She had secretly rented an apartment on the west side of the city—Apartment 4, 28 Ximung Street—neighbor to a white-haired retired teacher. Her daily routine started with walking my son to school a few blocks away from her nest, then writing at her desk, facing the south window, then picking up Tai Ping, and cooking a meal for two. She made few phone calls and only one trip to the post office, dropping off her second book—envelope opened and reglued. There were no men in her life.

To fill my lonely nights, I reviewed the photographs clandestinely taken of her—Sumi surprised by a basket of apples at her apartment door one day, another of her reading a greeting from a nonexistent neighbor that drew a genuine smile from her—and precious snapshots of big, stuffed animals Tai Ping had brought home from school. How I cherished listening to the tapes of Tai Ping insisting that they had come from his teacher rewarding him for his good work, and of Sumi calling that very teacher, who, of course by my design, confirmed everything she had been told. All those stolen photographs of her and my son became my companions in my dreams, giving me reason to live and breathe, allowing me the patience to wait for another day, another week, another month.

Tan

CHAPTER 48

Life lost all its color after Sumi left. Her hugs, kisses, smiles, and tears, the contents of my life, were but memories. I sat in my office overlooking the business district of Beijing, trying to re-create the feeling I used to have, watching her do the simplest things. I could play and replay the way she kissed Tai Ping's nose, the way she'd chew on a pencil and stare into space, searching for the perfect word. The way she brushed her dark waterfall of hair in the morning sun, with her long creamy back to me. The wonderful scent hidden in her most private places. How I yearned for her.

Although I was lonely with my memories, I respected Sumi's plea that I allow her time to sort herself out. It was sincere and profound. I would wait out this perplexing suspension, hoping each day would be shorter and each night warmer. Like any man, I went on with my separate life outside the realm of my personal life. It was a life celebrated by laughs and drinks. It was about conquering, hunting, about the catch of the day. I could win in this game of life, but I also knew that I could lose. I knew the risks; it was within my calculation, and I was prepared. I could even toast a loss, for I knew that with the next round I might be toasting a win.

Life lived without Sumi and Tai Ping was nonetheless eventful, even colorful, in other aspects. Each morning I opened piles of national newspapers to find myself labeled as the elusive, rotten element and formidable mastermind behind the New Year's Eve smearing incident. Without naming names, I became that dark force behind a nationwide subversive movement against the Communist government. Absurdity atop absurdity. It was a war of words against the Longs, and traces of Shento, that madman, were everywhere.

Other bad news began trickling in as well. Lena reported that David Li had been mysteriously fired from his position. Bank financing for the new magazines would have to be evaluated by a new executive who was clearly just a cog in the propaganda machine. I immediately placed a call to Li's residence.

"It was that phone call I made on New Year's Eve," David said sadly. "It was my fault. I imposed it upon you."

"Say no more. I made the call as a friend for a friend, and that was that."

"I owe you everything. Come work with me. You won't regret it."

"I am grateful for your offer, but an old friend has already asked me to join him in a business venture in New York, and I have accepted the invitation."

"A new life? How wonderful. When are you going?"

"Tomorrow."

"Then I have to see you now."

I had my secretary prepare a cashier's check and drove to David's residence in the center of the Beijing, twenty minutes away.

"Please accept this small token of my gratitude to you," I said, passing David the check.

"Twenty thousand dollars," David exclaimed.

"I'm sure you've seen bigger checks than that."

"I can't take this."

"You can only reject this gift at the risk of losing a friend."

David clasped my hand. "Then I will keep it."

"Someday when the sun rises, we will work together again."

"Before I go, I must tell you something. Your Dragon Center is never going to get approval from the city. I think you know why."

"I haven't heard anything."

"And you won't. It has been shelved for good."

"We worked so damned hard on it, you and I."

"Tan, you are a wise man. So do what a wise man would do—be firm, but not hard, or they will break you down to pieces."

Again those words. "Why should I?"

"The tide is against you. Please."

We hugged, a comradely hug, and parted.

I drove off in my roadster, dust flying in my wake. I wanted to drive directly to the City Planning Bureau for an explanation, but I turned around. Dumb anger, dumb solution. I headed back to my office, my mind plotting my next counteroffensive.

Two police cars, marked with the noticeable Beijing Police insignia, were parked in front of my building, their alarms blaring and lights flashing. A dozen policemen armed with automatic rifles stood in two columns at the building entrance, their eyes scrutinizing everyone coming and going. A large crowd gathered, thick and tight, watching the drama unfold. I handed over my car to the valet and quickened my steps. As I passed by the officer at the door, he asked for my identification.

"I am the chairman of Dragon and Company. Let me through," I said.

"Good. They are waiting for you, Mr. Long," the man said. "You need to come with me."

"Who is waiting for me?"

"You will see." The officer gave me a little push. I stared at him angrily. We got into the elevator. Two plainclothesmen joined us. Silently, we rode up. I wasn't surprised to see even more policemen surrounding my office. My employees were flocked together in a corner. Fei-Fei was handcuffed, slumped in a chair.

"What are you arresting him for?" I barked at the officer.

"Who are you?" the officer demanded, eyes narrowed.

"Tan Long, the chairman of this firm. On what grounds are you arresting Fei-Fei?"

"Antigovernment activities. Treason."

"What is the evidence? What?"

"You ask too many questions. Go to your office and answer to the man waiting for you." The officer shoved me away with both hands.

When I pushed him back, another officer slammed a rifle butt into my head, cutting my right temple.

"Tan, be careful!" Fei-Fei shouted. The other employees screamed.

"Fei-Fei, I will get you out soon," I shouted, covering my head with my hands. Blood trickled down my jaw.

"Tan, don't worry. I will be fine. I . . ." Fei-Fei was pushed out of the office by three policemen, who had cuffed his hands so tightly they had turned dusky blue.

"Fei-Fei, I will fight these Gestapo until the day I die!" I shouted.

"Please look out for my father."

"I promise, Fei-Fei."

I was forced into my office to face another government official sporting a sneer on his long thin face. "What an odd place to meet again, Mr. Long."

"Who are you?" I asked the man who was sitting in my armchair.

"I guess fortune does make one forget. I was your classmate twice. In elementary school, you stole my class presidency. In law school, you defeated me in the moot court championship competition, twice."

"Ah, Hito. Get out of my seat."

"Very rude, Mr. Long."

"I am only kind to my friends. To what do I owe this visit?"

Hito pulled out a piece of paper. "This is a warrant. It lists over thirty counts of possible tax evasion, fraud, and an assortment of other charges. But we are not here to make an arrest. We need to further establish our case."

"No arrest? How generous of you."

"No arrest at this time, but you can be assured that when all the facts are established, you will have your day in court."

"Let me get this right. You have already determined that I have committed tax evasion on no evidence whatsoever, and now you and your men are here to fish for things that might prove you right."

"Well put."

"Admirable fairness and justice, Hito. I'm surprised you lost to me twice."

"You are lucky. In other cases, we arrest men, beat them, make them confess, then put them in jail."

"Somehow I don't feel so lucky. Does this investigation have anything to do with Shento?"

"I take orders from above. They say do this, I do this. They say do that, I do that. In this case, they said raid the office and leave him alone. I am doing exactly what I am told."

"No imagination."

"No room for imagination," Hito said. "This office will be temporarily sealed. "

"This is in violation of the constitution, depriving me of my private property," I said.

"And what are you going to do about it?"

"I will bring suits all the way to the Supreme Court to stop this persecution," I said. "And I will let the whole world know the truth."

Hito waved to his men. "Get him out of here and make sure he doesn't take anything."

With a roar, I lifted my heavy mahogany desk and upended it. Hito sat unmoved, a sly smile still on his face.

"Get out of my office or I will kill you!" I shouted.

A dozen policemen jumped on me and dragged me out of the office, kicking and struggling. "Nobody is taking my things! Nobody!" I kept screaming until I was thrown into the street.

"You're lucky. I could have shot you just for this," a policeman said.

"Go ahead, you Nazi dog!"

"My order is to let you suffer."

Once again a rifle butt came flying into my face. Pain and darkness drowned me.

WHEN I WOKE UP at nightfall, I was in bed at Beijing People's Hospital with a dull pain lancing my head and bandages wrapping my skull. Lena sat by the bed, worried.

"Lena," I said weakly.

Lena rubbed her brow. "We're finished."

"No, we're not."

"They froze all our bank accounts."

"We'll get them back."

She nodded, looked over her shoulder, and whispered, "The moment they came to our office, I phoned your father in Fujian to warn him."

I squeezed her hand.

"Excuse me," a nurse said. "There is someone to see you."

It was Sumi standing by the door, looking haggard and worried.

"I saw the whole event reported on the Government Central Television Channel, Tan," she murmured, rushing to my bed.

Lena bid me good-bye and excused herself, nodding to Sumi on her way out.

"Why are you here?" I asked Sumi.

Sumi knelt down on her knees by my side, her cheek touching mine. "Oh, my dearest."

"If I had known you would come back to me for this, I would have hurt myself a lot earlier."

We kissed gently, then Sumi pulled away and announced, "I know whose fault it is. I will right the wrong. I have been composing this essay in my head ever since I saw the news on TV—self-indulgence of public power."

"No, you should stay out of it. Shento's political ambition will swallow you whole."

"The madman has to be stopped. He arrested Fei-Fei, sealed your office, and beat you up. What is next? I can't let him do this to me, to you, to the people. I cannot sit in silence anymore."

"You're risking your life, Sumi."

"I don't see it that way. You, Fei-Fei, and my readers, millions of them, made me what I am today. I am their voice. I can't be silent."

"You sound like Lu Xun," I said, referring to a turn-of-the-century writer known for his fight against social injustice.

" 'Locking my eyebrows, staring coldly at the condemnation of the elite,' " Sumi quoted.

" 'Bowing my head, willing to pull the plough like a cow for the ordinary people,' " I softly recited back.

"So you are behind me?" Sumi asked.

"By your side, always." I sat up painfully, leaning on my elbow. "I will print your essay into a bound pamphlet, and distribute it to the entire city, the whole country. Go home and write it. Our printing plants won't be allowed to stay open much longer."

"If I go home tonight, I may never see you again."

Under the dim light of a fifteen-watt bulb, Sumi leaned over her makeshift desk—a pillow on top of a windowsill. She bent her head, forgetting time and space, and her right hand scribbled urgently over her notebook, thoughts quicker than her hands. She rushed to put down in ink what had transpired in her mind. She tilted her head, pondering a fleeting thought, and blinked, catching a sentiment in flight. She shuddered, cried, then filled her chest with a deep breath, and scribbled on. Between her fingers, the pen, and the paper, poetry was conceived and magic born.

"This is my story. This is my tale," Sumi said. She handed the pages to me, then buried her face in my arms.

Shento

CHAPTER 49

I was overjoyed by the catch of the day. My men had locked Fei-Fei up in the most notorious and disgusting prison in Beijing, beaten up Tan, and sealed my half brother's little empire. My taxmen were hard at work, poking through the corporate files, and my Young Generals in Fujian, acting on my orders, were ravaging through two other related entities—Veterans & Company and Coastal Banking. No arrests were to be made there, I ordered. A little charity. A little generosity. A little patience. All this would lead to my eventual windfall, when I caught that big fish in the pond—the devil, my father.

My noontime report to the president was simple and to the point. Heng Tu gave me a nod of approval, but this time he did not end my report with his usual "time for a nap." Instead, he gave me a warning. "To kill the weed, take their roots. I don't want to see my enemies upstaging me again in my lifetime," he said and wheeled himself out to his favorite napping spot in the sun.

In my office, I had my maid, a porcelain-skinned young girl, brew me a cup of rare tea for celebration. Its flavor was subtle and mellow, reminding me of a mild autumn day. But my serene moment was disturbed by the intrusion of a phone call. What I heard caused me to throw the antique tea set against the wall in a rage. "Call in Hito Ling immediately" was all I could manage to say to my secretary.

Hito materialized instantly before me.

"Get an arrest warrant for Sumi Wo and take her in," I ordered.

"On what grounds?" Hito asked.

"You are the law man. Go make the law as you see fit. I want her before she runs away. She is at the Beijing People's Hospital now, our nurse there informs us. Get your men ready. I am coming with you."

"Yes, Colonel."

"One more question. Where does Blue Sea Publishing print its books?"

"At its Western Mountain Printing Plant."

"Good man. Let's go now."

Sumi

CHAPTER 50

By the time I left Beijing People's Hospital, night had fallen and darkness loomed. Drizzling snowflakes added a gray tinge to the sky, and the streets surged in the slow motion of slosh and slush as thousands of tired feet shuffled blindly for their destinations.

I hugged myself, arms across my chest, a red scarf around my neck flying in the wind. I felt tired, hurt, and angry. The chilly whirling wind reddened my eyes as I searched for the blinking sign of a bus stop. I found it without difficulty. A large crowd had formed around a red-and-white-striped trolley with a tangle of ugly wire on top, fighting to squeeze into its narrow doors. A small child screamed as his fingers were caught in the temperamental door. An old lady's smile signaled her small victory at the end of the long day—finding a seat. An old man fought but missed his step, and sat in the slush with hands waving in the cold air as the crowd ran after the next overloaded bus, which skipped the stop altogether.

I helped the old man up to his feet. He looked at me, his smile full of gratitude. "I almost got on," he said.

"You did," I agreed, helping him up.

"Thank you, angel."

"You're welcome. You look cold."

"It is a little nippy," he said, his beard frosty.

My heart softened for him. I took off my red scarf and tied it around his neck. An army jeep sped down the splashing boulevard and screeched to a halt in front of us. Startled, I looked up, blinking in the blinding headlights. A green-uniformed soldier jumped out of the side door of the jeep and ran toward me. I let go of the old man and ran as fast as I could, but the soldier grabbed me within a few steps. I kicked and shouted. People looked on nervously and silently except for the old man, who shouted, "Let go of her! Let go of her!"

The soldier stuffed me roughly into the backseat.

The old man kept on screaming, "Let her go!"

The jeep clawed away from the slushy street, heading into the night. I cursed and shouted in the backseat of the jeep. "Leave me alone!"

"Calm down, Sumi," a familiar voice said, restraining me in his arms. It was Shento. I threw him off with a strength that I did not know I possessed.

"What do you want from me?" I demanded.

"What did you write and give to Tan Long in the hospital ward?" Shento asked.

"Nothing."

"You have betrayed me, haven't you," he said quietly.

"Betrayed?" I said, my voice rising. "You arrested my editor without reason, sealed my publisher's office without cause, and beat Tan Long, an innocent man, unconscious. You abuse your power, avenging yourself. You are turning into a monster. I will fight you till the people are awakened. I will fight you till you threaten us no longer."

"What about us?"

"The Shento I loved has died. I am in mourning, can't you see? I will stop at nothing to expose you until the world knows who you really are."

"That day will never come," Shento said with a chuckle. "I am taking you somewhere serene, where you don't have to be this crazed freedom fighter anymore, where you can be a woman, my woman forever."

I slapped him across the face.

Tan

CHAPTER 51

In the night, dark and cold, the printing staff at the Blue Sea plant chanted their favorite tunes to fight the fatigue and drowsiness of a double shift as they printed copies of Sumi's freshly penned condemnation of Shento. They sang and they smoked. They sweated and they laughed. Supervisors poured tea and passed out snacks to the men. No one took a break. There was a sense of frenzy under the roof.

The workers were generally a happy bunch: happy to be employed by a publisher who paid good wages and offered the assurance of lifelong employment. Happy because they sweated and got compensated according to their ability. Happier even still because their beloved editor in chief provided them with medical insurance and housing for all. So when they heard that he had been arrested, they were angry. They cursed the government and volunteered to come in and print the thousands of pamphlets needed to fight the powers that be. They had a simple belief—that if they worked hard and got the printed materials out to the streets, Fei-Fei would be released and everything would be fine. So they resumed their good spirits, innocently indulging themselves with songs that kept their mood lifted, for the night was long ahead of them.

Downstairs, where the furnace and other dark oily machines sat, the old guard, Mr. Mei, squinted up at a stranger standing before him.

Another stranger lost in this part of the country, he thought. The printing plant was situated on the edge of the Beijing suburbs. Night after night, truckers carried fresh produce from the deep fertile country into the city. They started early while the stars shone and returned home late when the moon was up. Many lost their way around here, with the knot of newly constructed highways complicating every journey. The old guard, who had lived here for the last thirty years, always helped them out. Occasionally, the drivers would leave a basket of apples or oranges to thank him. Day and night, he was the only waking dog around this ten-mile radius. The light from his living quarters, a small nest next to the machine room, shone like a beacon to all those lost in the night.

"Lost your way?" Mei asked the stranger, a young man wearing a brown leather jacket, whose hair was cut low and flat to his head.

"No, old comrade," the young man replied, looking beyond the old man's shoulders.

"Then what can I do for you?"

"I want you to hold this for me." The young man passed him a compact package wrapped in red.

"What is it?"

"A gift from your old friend," the stranger said.

"What is his name?"

"He would not say."

"This late at night, you deliver it to me?" The old man studied the gift and smiled. "Well, I do have a lot of friends that I have helped, but this is a surprise. What is your name?"

The young man hesitated. "It's not important. Your friend asked that you carry this gift close to your chest and go directly to your bedroom to open it."

"I will." The old guard bowed to thank the smiling young man and was turning to walk away, amused by the mystery at hand, when the young man pulled out a gun and aimed it. He pulled the trigger three times. The first two bullets hit the old man hard, throwing him to the ground facedown on top of the package. The third bullet ignited an explosion in the can of gas wrapped inside the red paper. A fireball spread over the oily machines in one motion. The silence of the engulfing fire gave way to more explosions, then a bigger, hotter fire, making the basement a sea of looming flames.

The young man jumped into the Garrison Force jeep waiting for him, which sped onto the highway heading west.

The fire soon devoured the wooden beams that supported the massive three-story printing facility, and the ceiling caved in. The workers ran amok, looking for a way to put the fire out, but it was impossible. The flames rushed upstairs, surrounding the faithful employees in an encroaching inferno. As they tried to escape through the windows and doors, they heard a final roar. The explosion shook the plant like thunder, uprooted every beam and column, brick and stone, and sprinkled pieces of the newly printed pamphlets into the dark night, so that they rained down like heavenly flames.

Shento

CHAPTER 52

At 2:00 a.m. in my quiet office, Prosecutor Hito Ling's report was brief. "Object completely destroyed."

"No trucks left the plant yet?"

"None."

"How about the old guard?"

"Blown to pieces."

"Make sure you retrieve the three bullet shells fired."

"That will be hard to do."

I stared at him silently.

"Yes, Colonel," Hito amended.

"One more thing. Is this printing plant insured?"

"To the price tag of twenty million yuan."

"By whom?"

"The People's Insurance Company."

"We have frozen all the young dragon's assets. What would a desperate man do to stay afloat?" I asked.

"Burn down his building and cash in the insurance policy." Hito jotted down quickly on his notebook: insurance fraud.

I nodded.

"Working for you has been the most inspiring experience of my whole legal career," Hito said.

"It will be the most rewarding as well."

Visibly excited by the statement, Hito could only manage a meek "Thank you" and a deep bow.

"Now go get him."

"Yes, Colonel."

Tan

唐

CHAPTER 53

After two long days in the hospital, I fought to be released. But the head nurse, a big-boned lady, strapped me to the bed, fastening the buckle across my chest. "I have served your father before and your grandpa before him. No one runs away from my ward, you hear me, Long junior?" she growled.

After she left, I unbuckled the strap and wiggled out of the restraint. Swiping a doctor's white coat from the wall, I slipped down the dimly lit stairs, two or three steps at a time. One flight from the exit, busy feet started pounding down the stairwell. I jumped over the railing, ran down the remaining flight, and dashed into the busy street. I hailed a cab outside, only realizing that I was still wearing the white coat when the driver politely asked, "Where are we going, Doctor?"

"Willow Bay District number 141, please."

The cab overtook a couple of cumbersome buses and sped west toward my township. A hundred feet behind me, two army jeeps jumped into traffic.

LENA WOULD NOT stop crying when she met me at my home.

"What is the matter?" I asked.

"Someone burned down our printing plant. Old Mei, the guard, and six factory workers were burned to death."

"I'm going to drive there right now," I said.

"You can't go there. It's fenced off."

"Nothing is going to stop me, Lena."

"I will go with you." On the way there, Lena counted our woes as I maneuvered though the traffic. "We lost the first legal battle to get Fei-Fei out on bail. They demanded two million yuan."

"We couldn't afford two million yuan?"

Lena bent her head low. "I have tried, but no banks will lend us that much money."

"What about our deposits?"

"All frozen."

"Then sell my house," I said.

"The mortgage payment on your house was due yesterday."

"I thought I bought it with cash."

"No, you asked me to exercise our borrowing power."

"So we are broke? We've generated tens of millions of yuan in revenue and now we are broke. Anything else we could sell?"

"Nothing."

"What about my watch, your car, my car? And where the hell is Mike?"

"He was put under house arrest in his hotel room and is awaiting deportation."

"Why?"

"He was at the City Planning Bureau this morning asking some questions about the Dragon Center proposal. The guard threw him out. He went to the bar next door, got drunk, and stormed the place, trashing it. He was bailed out by his embassy."

"Fight to keep him."

"Our lawyer refused to do it. He said if he did, he could be charged with aiding and abetting foreigners."

"Find another lawyer."

"Nobody else will represent us. Mike has been labeled a persona non grata and will be deported along with all the foreign journalists that reported on your New Year's party."

"Why don't they just arrest me?"

"Well, they have begun that already. Your family's businesses are all sealed as well, as of today. The same government official, that horse-faced fellow, paid them a visit, along with an investigator from the Customs Office for possible smuggling charges against your father and banking irregularities against your grandfather."

I slammed on the brakes suddenly, narrowly missing a truck loaded with produce. I took a long breath and gathered my concentration before I floored the gas. "Anything good to tell me at all?" I asked.

"Nothing. I'm sorry I haven't been able to help."

I put my right arm over her shoulder and hugged her. "As long as we are breathing, we'll be fine."

She nodded in silence, tears smearing her makeup.

At the plant, the air was thick with the choking stench of death—death of wood, death of flesh and bone, death of paper. The printing house was ravaged as if the ghost of war had passed through, leaving a trail of decay.

The police had encircled the site with yellow ribbon, warning the arrest of any trespassers. An officer waved his rifle and shouted, "Stop where you are!"

I could see him and hear him, but I did not care. I floored the gas pedal and the car drove over a pile of rubble, broke through the tape, and stopped before a burned tree stump.

"I will shoot you if you do not leave this crime scene!" the officer shouted.

"Go ahead," I said. "I own this place. I have every damn right to stand here!"

"You are breaking the law."

"So what? Isn't it enough that you bastards burned this place to the ground, along with seven innocent lives?" I walked up to the policeman and pushed him. "Isn't it? Tell me, you bastard!"

"I will shoot you!" he warned, backing up.

"Shoot me? Sure, go ahead. You couldn't do worse than those murderers who torched this place."

The young officer raised his rifle. Two bullets hit the ground before me, making dirt and ashes dance. I kept walking closer.

"Let's go home. Please, Tan," Lena begged, desperately tugging at me.

"You're crazy! What do you want?" the young soldier asked.

"I want to see the dead old man. I owe him," I said, my chest heaving. "Where is he?"

"There," the officer pointed. "The pile of bones by the wall. Go see them, then get off the grounds."

I kicked the ashes as I walked toward the wall. Strewn at the base were an assortment of bones. I knelt down and sadness swept over me. It could have been the bones of wild animals from the nearby mountains. I picked some up and examined them carefully.

"You can look around but don't take anything," the officer warned.

The little bones must be fingers, and this, a rib. I lifted a skull and with trembling fingers assembled the bones together. Lena hid behind me, too scared to even peek. "That's enough, Tan. Let's go home," she begged.

"Wait," I said. The whole middle section of the man was missing. Three feet away, I found it, a hip bone. In its center was a perfect round hole that could have only been caused by a penetrating bullet, nothing else. I glanced over my shoulder. The guard was lighting a cigarette, his head turned to block the wind. I stuck the bone inside my shirt, then, waving a silent good-bye to the officer, walked away.

Before I got into my car, I knelt down on my knees briefly, head low, hands clasped, and mumbled a simple prayer, wishing my loyal old guard a last good-bye.

Only after we returned to my home did I say to Lena, "The old guard was shot first."

She gasped. "How do you know?"

I pulled out the hip bone. "This has a bullet hole in it. This is evidence."

Lena covered her eyes with her hands. "Keep it away from me."

"You're going to bring it to Dr. Min."

"Our author?" Lena asked, gingerly holding the bone.

"He's the best forensic expert in Beijing. Have him look at it tonight."

Lena nodded. "What about Sumi's article?"

"Contact all the other printers in Beijing and have them print the article as soon as possible, tens of thousands of copies, at any cost."

"Do you still have the original?"

"Right here in her own handwriting." I pulled out a folded sheet.

"But I don't think anyone would dare help us now."

"They should. We've helped them before. The manager of Eastern Printing, and the one from Beijing Printing, they all know me. Call them up. Tell them I need their help now."

THE FOLLOWING DAY, Lena was at my house early. "No one will print this for us."

"But they are all our friends!"

"Not anymore. The manager from Eastern Printing warned me not to talk to anyone else about printing this article. There is a directive from the Garrison Force to arrest anyone who cooperates with Blue Sea."

"I'm not surprised. Did you hear anything from Dr. Min about the bone?"

"Yes, here." She passed an envelope to me. The note from the doctor simply read:

> CONFIRMED BULLET PENETRATION. GUNPOWDER RESDUE FOUND ON THE SURFACE OF THE BONE.
>
> LU MIN, M.D., BEIJING MEDICAL SCHOOL
> FORENSIC MEDICINE DEPARTMENT

"See, he confirmed everything," I said angrily. "Shento's men did this."

"What are you going to do with it?"

"I am going public about this killing and the cause of this fire. I have the evidence to prove it."

"Tan, the doctor specifically begged me not to reveal his name. He doesn't want to end up in a labor camp again."

"I understand. I will respect his wishes."

I devoted the rest of the day to writing my editorial about the persecution of Dragon & Company, Blue Sea Publishing, and my family, and the arson and murder of my employees. The writing was simple and direct. How I wished Sumi was here to help me. She had such a way with words, an ease for reaching the hearts of her readers. But I did not know where she was. She hadn't called for two days. She had promised to come back to me, but where was she?

I stayed within the confines of my house, painfully aware of a car parked across the street, under a shady willow tree. Why only one car? I'd expect Shento to order at least a dozen to detail every move I made, every breath I drew in.

When night fell, I had Lena put on my overcoat and drive away in my red Mercedes. After the car parked under the tree roared off after her, I slipped out of my house, wearing Lena's green fur-lined coat, the collar standing high to block the wind and my face. I moved along the city wall slowly, trying to walk like a woman. The streets were deserted and wind blasted the dust. I vanished onto a crowded bus and got off at Long An Boulevard, near my office building.

As suited businessmen and women glided by, laughing in twos and threes, I slipped in through the revolving doors of my office building and took the stairs to the third floor. The hallway was deserted. I ripped off the police seal and opened the door with my key. A foul smell permeated the office. No one had turned off the heat and the place was a furnace. I dialed down the heater and headed for the copy machine. The office was a mess, with papers scattered everywhere and furniture overturned and broken to pieces.

I loaded blank paper into the Xerox machine and started copying my editorial and Sumi's article. I would stay here for as long as it took to make as many copies possible. Then I would spread them around this mad city like snowflakes sifting from the sky.

LIKE A THIEF loaded with loot, I walked out into the quiet Long An Boulevard, a large bag over my shoulder. The streetlights shook in the blast of the March night and power lines howled like lonely wolves in the mountains. At 4:00 a.m., the city was an abandoned jungle, all creatures asleep. A bus wheeled around the corner dispiritedly, as if unwilling to face a new day. When I got on, the driver nasally inquired, *"Nai zhan xia che?"* Where are you getting off?

"Wherever you go," I replied, huddling on the seat near the rear door.

He pulled out a small bottle, gulped a mouthful, and let out a burp. "Sit over here, you fool, and have a drink."

I moved to a seat next to him and took the bottle he passed me, a local cheap liquor, Gao Liang. I took a shot and almost threw up.

"Now tell me what you got in the bag," he said.

"Some pamphlets."

"Aha! You're one of those freedom fighters that live the night and dodge the day."

"I . . ."

"Don't be afraid. I will make all the stops necessary for you." The driver chugged another big mouthful, then choked and coughed so much that he had to lean his forehead on the steering wheel for a moment, regaining his breath. The bus weaved into the other lane and then weaved back.

"Are you all right?" I asked.

"Sure. You spread your pamphlets and I drive my bus." He floored the gas pedal and the bus flew. "You got to leave a little more near here," the driver pointed out at one station. "The teachers who live here read." At another, he opined drunkenly, "The coal miners here never read. Your stuff will just become toilet paper."

I leaned out the window, throwing out a handful at a time, while the driver sped along Long An Boulevard, the Pond Park, the People's Museum, the Forbidden City, the Tong Dan commercial district, the Si-Dan district, Tiananmen Square, and the Hai-Dian district.

"What a pity you're not going to the Summer Palace," I said.

"I'll make a special trip just for you. We mustn't miss all those tourists. Oh, and I'll drive you to the famous College Road, where all the curious liberal-minded college boys and girls are. Our last stop will be the Beijing People's Hospital."

"That will cover the entire city," I exclaimed.

"For the price of fifty fens."

"I don't know how to thank you."

"You already have. You're good company. Bottoms up." He drained the last drop from his bottle. He sang the name of each college as he stopped. "Peking U, Medical U, Techy U, Language U, Agricultural U, Geology U, and Music U."

I ran up and down the stairs of the bus that had become my own delivery truck. The three thousand copies had dwindled to a small bundle by the time Beijing People's Hospital, my last stop, swung into view.

"Please take this." I passed a hundred-yuan bill to the driver.

"You mean to insult me with this, young man. Take the money away from my face and just thank me as a friend."

"Friends it is, then. My name is . . ."

"Don't tell me. I never carried you on my bus and you never shared this bottle with me. Fight on, son." The driver raised a fist in farewell. I got off and the bus zigzagged away into the dawn air.

I saluted the brave man. The street corner was quiet, with only a few patients at the gate.

"Saluting a bus? Are you mad?" A small homeless old man stood up from the bench and threw a rock at the departing bus. "They are the worst bunch alive. Get out of here, Bus 331. I don't need you . . ." He fell onto his face, motionless on the cold ground.

I bent over to help him to his feet, only to be shouted at by the old man. "What are you doing here so early in the day?"

"I'm here to leave you some pamphlets," I said.

"Oh, show me. I'm eager for something to read, anything." The old man rubbed his ungloved hands and adjusted his burning-red scarf, the only thing on his body that had any recognizable color.

The old man hungrily gazed at the paper, stopped, and blinked, remembering something. He turned and caught the tail of my coat. "I saw that angel's face before. I know her," he said, pointing at Sumi's photo in the pamphlet.

"She is a well-known writer. I'm not surprised that you recognize her."

"No, no, young man, be patient. You youth are always hurrying. Slow down and talk to me. I'm not carrying any infectious germs like them." He pointed at the hospital. "She was trying to help me get on the bus. Two men, big and tough, grabbed her and pushed her into a car. I shouted and shouted but no one else cared."

"Are you sure?"

"Are you sure? Are you sure? I'm sick of you people repeating that to me. No one believes me. I'm old, not dead. She gave me this scarf."

Sumi's red scarf! I looked at the label. Chanel, my gift to her on the anniversary of our engagement.

"Do you believe me now?"

"I do. Thank you, grandpa. I must go now." I bowed to the old man in thanks.

"Hey, wait, you impatient young man. Take this scarf and give it to her when you see her."

"It is cold. You keep it."

"No, that nice girl might need it. Besides, I am used to the cold." The old man pushed the scarf into my hands.

I took it and raised it high, shouting into the empty night, "It is war, Shento! It is war!"

The baffled old man shook his head.

Lan-Gai

CHAPTER 54

On the campus of Beijing University, a young man of twenty named Lan-Gai was troubled by the announcement of Sumi's and Fei-Fei's arrests. They had been early members of the school's Poison Tree Club, of which Lan-Gai was not only a current and ardent member but also the president. Angry and on edge, unable to linger in his warm bed, he got up early and hit the frosty trails in a morning run around Weiming Lake to clear his mind. He had been running for half an hour and was ready for a break when he stepped on a damp piece of paper, one of many strewn along the bank. Squatting down, he picked it up and studied it. The name Tan Long immediately caught his attention. He read the paper carefully. It was a piece of beautiful prose. It was also a powerful prosecutory brief, finessed by concrete evidence and delineated by clear arguments. The account inflamed Lan-Gai, and the forensic report of the bullet-pierced bone made him want to scream at the top of his lungs and wake up the whole campus of fair minds and just hearts to the atrocious betrayal by their government.

Sumi, Fei-Fei, and Tan Long were his idols; to him, they loomed as big as titans. Now Fei-Fei had been arrested and Tan was a hunted man. Lan-Gai was disgusted by such outrage—something had to be done.

He gave up his morning classes to make more copies of the precious pamphlet and distribute them to his classmates. By noon, when Lan-Gai stood on the central table of the biggest cafeteria, making a speech, blood was boiling. Many angry shouts could be heard throughout the ancient university; even some faculty members could be seen among the students, listening and cheering. Lunch was forgotten as students, without invitation, took turns standing on tables and making speeches. Quickly, they organized a Free Our Alumni committee and made Lan-Gai its chairman. He proposed writing and sending a communiqué to their sister clubs throughout the nation that very day.

"FREE FEI-FEI! Stop the tyranny! Democracy and free election!" the students shouted that evening, marching before the leafy campus's administration building under the watchful eyes of the campus police.

Disobeying curfew regulation, Lan-Gai climbed out of the dorm window, hoisted himself over the campus wall, and rushed to the telephone company to contact the leaders of all the other Poison Tree Clubs in the thirty-some provinces of China. In a hushed tone, he told his comrades, "Sunday at noon, we're organizing a memorial for the old guard, Mr. Mei, and his fallen comrades. We'll rally there, at the ruins of the Blue Sea Publishing printing factory."

"We will organize one on the Shanghai riverbank simultaneously," responded the leader from Shanghai's Fudan University, one of the country's largest universities.

"We will hold a demonstration by the sea," promised the Xiamen University leader in Fujian.

Later that night, Lan-Gai rode his rattling bike to a secret meeting near the Summer Palace attended by the student leaders of all the universities in the Beijing area. Gathered in knots, in darkness and the cold night air of Beijing, they fervently discussed the details.

The Beijing Music University leader, a long-haired pianist, promised that his school's brass band would provide live music. The Art College would decorate the burned ruins with the most mournful festoons. Qinghua University, a technical college, would make effigies of President Heng Tu from straw and bamboo poles. The Medical University students generously offered to bring emergency kits and provide the first aid services needed for such an event. The Language University took on the responsibility of simultaneously translating speeches into as many languages as required by the possible listeners. The Telecommunication University students would transmit their messages through radio waves to all corners of the land.

"But most of all, we need people to fill this event; the more, the better," Lan-Gai said. "I will promise five thousand from Beijing University. How about you?"

"I promise one thousand," the Qinghua leader said.

"Ten times that," Lan-Gai urged.

"I'll try."

Others raised their hands in the twilight.

"Five thousand."

"Two thousand."

"Seven thousand."

"Three thousand."

"I thank you all for your support," Lan-Gai said. "Now we have to decide who will be the keynote speaker for the event."

"I wish Sumi were here," said one.

"I wish Fei-Fei were here," said another.

"How about Tan Long?" someone suggested.

"How will we find him?" a girl asked.

"If he is a fighter, he will find us," a boy replied.

Tan would be a perfect speaker, Lan-Gai thought. His editorial had been so powerful, and his status as a fugitive of the law would bring the memorial service to an unparalleled emotional height. How he wished that Tan was here among them. Lan-Gai sighed, then concluded the meeting by announcing, "We will read Tan Long's editorial and excerpts from Sumi's book. Each one of you prepare a speech to deliver as well. Now get some rest. We will meet again on Sunday."

Tan

CHAPTER 55

I pulled an army hat low over my head. A green padded cotton coat covered my back. The collar, lined with tiger fur, stood tall to cover half my face, up to my eyes. The clunky army boots completed the ensemble. Thus attired, I sloshed along the muddy streets of western Beijing. I hunched over, as if cold. I tried to look small, but my bigness failed me.

I had purchased this green outfit from an old veteran who had fought in Korea and lost a leg in Vietnam. And Shento lost no time in pursuing me. My picture was all over the city—on street corners, over kiosks, on public-toilet walls.

I shuffled along a narrow lane to a courtyard inn that housed vegetable merchants from inland, tiger hide traders from the mountains, ginger sellers from the north, and shrimp peddlers from the coast.

No window, no bathroom, eight beds, one desk. Travelers slept on their luggage as pillows, using pillows to prop up swollen feet. Eight strangers smoked and swapped stories of faraway provinces and tales of various regions.

I remained wrapped in my greenness, resting my feet, knowing that all the major highways and stations were thick with police patrols looking for me. The little hotel was situated near Beijing University, an area I had combed through hundreds of times in my law school days.

I had called Lena, needing money, asking for as much cash as she could get her hands on. I waited, sitting in the smoke-filled, windowless room. There was no telling whether it was night or day under the dim fifteen-watt bulb.

Midmorning, Lena arrived at the inn with her scarf wrapped around her face, revealing just her almond-shaped eyes. I had never seen her so nervous and shaky. I pulled her into the empty hallway.

Blowing hot breath into her cold hands, Lena whispered, "The police and their tracking dogs are all over your place. I have been walking, losing my tail, for the last three hours. There are arrest notices for you all over the town. You'd better leave here for a while."

"I will. You have to take care of yourself, Lena."

"I'm not afraid of them. I am innocent, and so are you. Oh, a student leader named Lan-Gai called, looking for you—he wants you to speak at a memorial service this Sunday for Mr. Mei, the old guard, and the other workers. It will be held at the ruins of the printing plant. He said other colleges all over the country will be holding demonstrations as well to rally against the government, demanding the release of Fei-Fei."

"What courage," I said. "Tell him I will be there."

"You shouldn't. The police will be there."

"Then we'll need to work out an escape route."

"Tan, it's not worth risking your life."

"But it is. This rally could be the beginning of an unstoppable revolution," I said. "Help me one more time. Tell them I will be there."

Lena nodded reluctantly. "Here is your money, twenty thousand yuan. That's all I have."

I thanked her and stuffed the bills in my pockets. What a faithful friend she was.

"Here, I got this *People's Daily* for you," Lena said. "You should read it." She handed me the newspaper, then pulled up her collar and disappeared back into the narrow lane, snowflakes falling on her back.

I opened the paper. The front page shouted:

Antigovernment elements Tan Long and Sumi Wo fabricated the life story about our revolutionary hero, Colonel Shento. The young revolutionary colonel was orphaned at the age of three, joined the army at twenty, saved our great leader's life, and was promoted for his dedication and loyalty to the Party and its great leader. Colonel Shento has never personally known Sumi Wo, the liberal writer whose fame came from her nakedly absurd, invented memoir. The act of falsification was a flagrant attempt to extract her fiancé, Tan Long, from financial ruin and imminent bankruptcy. Tan Long's latest fraud is an act of arson—burning down his own printing plant and killing seven of his own employees in order to claim the 20-million-yuan insurance coverage by the People's Insurance Company. The Justice Department has begun an investigation of this crime.

On another front, Sumi Wo, who abetted her fiancé in this scheme to frame a national hero, was arrested recently on the charge of bourgeois liberalism. The chief felon in this defamation case is still at large. We advise our people to be vigilant and assist our people's police force in Beijing and the rest of China in capturing Tan Long to stop this random act of subversion from spreading.

I crumbled the newspaper into a ball and threw it into the garbage. A fellow inn dweller, a northern farmer, ripped off a portion of the paper. Rolling a thick tobacco roll with it, he lit it with a sizzle and inhaled his smoke to the hiss of burning ink.

IT WAS A BLEAK SUNDAY. The wind blew, the clouds frowned, the sky hung low, and the land stood numb and motionless—suitable in every way for a memorial for the seven whose lives had risen to the sky in a puff of smoke. By noon, the wind, peppered with flakes of snow, was choking and shaking the leafless trees. Twigs broke, trunks howled, tigers sobbed, and wolves froze in fear and sadness.

Without legs or wings, word had spread of the forbidden memorial. People, like soulless ghosts, roamed about the site, ten miles west of Beijing proper, sad and heartbroken. They donned black headbands and pinned their coats with threads of white in memory of those dead but not forgotten.

By noon, thousands of the students had arrived on foot, by bus, and by bicycle—riding single, double, and triple—singing angry songs, shouting bloody curses, chanting vengeful slogans. Thousands of workers from the country's hundreds of dirty, smoke-filled factories came in loads, some on the backs of trucks, others standing on the nose of tractors. Their uniforms were white and blue, both neat and dirty. They smoked their rationed cigarettes and drank draft beer. Their free hands drummed anything drummable and their feet stomped the ground. They came because the dead had been their brothers. In life, students and workers might have spat at each other, but in death they united. Workers of Communism, the proletarians of the world, owned nothing, so they owned everything. Karl Marx had told them so. The old ragged tune of "The Internationale" had whispered so. *Fight until your last drop of blood for a better tomorrow.*

Lines of police wove in and out of the human flood—guarding, controlling, kicking, and at times stomping, hoping to contain the leaking dam from growing inevitably larger. On the nose of an armored truck, crackling loudspeakers blared: "All illegal demonstrations are banned. Demonstrators will be arrested."

"Shut up!" the workers responded in unison.

"Go home, citizens! This memorial is illegal! Beijing police will take action against anyone disobeying this order."

When a young soldier poked at a female art student, she screamed and snarled at the soldier.

"You touch her again and you will eat dirt!" her long-haired boyfriend threatened.

At the stroke of noon, the slight student leader, Lan-Gai, jumped onto the temporary stage built with half-burned planks and scorched tree trunks. He wore a white robe and a black band around his head, the mourning attire reserved for close family. He was quiet, his head low, eyes closed. In silence, Lan-Gai begged those dead ghosts to descend upon him, giving him strength.

A haunting dirge composed by an art college freshman flowed like a string of tears. Loudspeakers were hidden behinds rocks and under tables, so that the police could not easily dismantle them. A team of student speakers, representing each college and university, stood hand in hand, surrounding Lan-Gai, guarding him in a five-layered circle, the only protection against the officers' guns.

Lan-Gai gestured for the music to stop and waved to the looming sea of young people surrounding him—sitting on icy rocks, squatting, carrying boards with slogans. Intellectuals with worried faces mingled with raunchy workers, who formed the outermost circle. Narrowing his eyes, Lan-Gai started to speak.

"Heaven thanks you, and earth kneels before you. We, the living, today come to weep for your departure, brutal and untimely. My fellow countrymen, comrades, students, teachers, fathers, mothers, and uncles, we live in a tyranny that is long overdue to die. A tyranny that has grown moss that now poisons its people.

"Today, we are here not only to mourn the dead, but to fight for the living. This devil called Shento is the evil responsible for their deaths, the ongoing purge, the financial ruin of Dragon and Company, and the arrests of Fei-Fei Chen and Sumi Wo. Not content with this, he also hunts the innocent Tan Long.

"Comrades, countrymen—today it is only these dead, but tomorrow it's you, you, and you . . . then the whole country. It is time we rid our beloved motherland of those who push the wheel of history backward toward darkness, and not to the light of the future."

The crowd reacted, shouting at the top of their lungs: "Long live the people!"

"Down with rulers!"

"Free election!"

A second speaker, a drama major, held a copy of Sumi's *The Orphan.* In tears, she recited a passage from the book.

> *". . . so the waves of despair swept at my feet as I walked along the cold beach, my heart, a hollow of hopelessness, my head, bruised evidence of human cruelty, unrelenting, destroying. In*

that moment of desperation, I found hope in the vast cold sea. I yearned to taste the bitter tongue of death. The shells along the beach would be my company, and the silent grains of sands, my pillow. I felt weak at my knees, holding the baby of my love—the remnants of his beauty, the glow of stars vanished. I felt comforted that my child's life would end because I was tired. His tug on my young nipples produced only scant beads of sweetness. But he smiled, as if he knew I would be happy dying, not living. Mama is leaving. Good-bye, son. I cried my good-byes, but good-bye lost its meaning, for words spoken would soon be forgotten. Wind would replace me in my child's memory. . . . I dived into the sea. The waves lifted me up and all was gone."

There was a lull.

"Long Live Sumi Wo, the people's writer!" the reader shouted. The crowd echoed her cry. The girl broke down in tears and had to be supported off the stage. A tenor followed with a rendition of the well-known "Internationale" in French. It was the old cliché of revolutionary fever, but its lyrics inflamed the crowd: *"Stand tall, hungry, cold, suppressed slaves of the world. Our chests fill with waves of hot blood. Be prepared to fight until the end."*

The people sang with him, and the echo of the march spiraled into the western mountain and reached for the cloudy sky. For a long spell, the revolutionaries were united, unsuppressed by dictators. Their blood boiled, in spite of the low temperature outside.

"We shall fight in peace," Lan-Gai shouted. "The nonviolence of Gandhi is our soul. Our words are our weapons, and our voices will not be muted until the sunshine of freedom paints our land."

There was chaos in the yard as the young factory workers joined the students in the "Internationale." The police blared their warning to the crowd: "Go home now or we will arrest you!" Policemen blew their whistles, marching in thick columns, rifles over their shoulders with bayonets pulled, but the singing roared thunderously, burying the police speakers. More whistles were blown and orders given. Lan-Gai stood helplessly on the stage, waving his arms, trying to calm the people, but the crowd ignored him. Bottles were thrown from a truck and policemen were hit. A squad of officers slipped their rifles off their shoulders and took aim. Students shouted to support the workers. More bottles sailed through the air.

My time had come. I pushed through the crowd and with one jump was on the stage. Hugging Lan-Gai, I thanked him and took over the mike, shouting, "Comrades, my name is Tan Long. You should all know me by now. After all, there are fugitive notices posted throughout this country for my arrest. But I fear nothing, least of all our corrupt government. I am with you, my fellow countrymen."

The crowd cheered.

"I am with you today to mourn for our fallen comrades. And to share an ugly truth that I hold in my hand—a hip bone of my dear old guard, Mr. Mei. A renowned forensic doctor has determined that the hole you see here is the result of a bullet penetration. I believe he was murdered." A wave of murmurs rippled through the crowd.

"And the murderer is no other than that colonel of the Garrison—Shento! The Shento who had Fei-Fei and Sumi arrested. The very colonel who burned down my plant so the truth would never be spoken . . ."

A flood of voices screamed "Down with the devil Shento!"

I held up my hands for silence. "My fellow countrymen, I am here to announce a new independent political party—the Democracy Party. Its goal is to relentlessly pursue the ideals of democracy until the day of free elections and constitutional guarantees! Only then will we forever weed this cursed nation of the recurring ghosts of Shento and his kind."

"Tan Long! Tan Long!" The shouts were deafening. Police surged in from all four directions while the police loudspeakers barked at top volume, "The fugitive Tan Long, step down immediately before we take action! Anyone who tries to assist him in escaping will be charged with treason! Felon Tan Long, surrender now!"

I paid no heed. "I challenge you to take to the streets and talk to your neighbors! Go back to your schools and spread the word of our future. This country belongs to us! Democracy is our only hope. Join the party! I shall carry the message to the rest of the country. I will wake up this land of giants and confront the evils of the past. Wake up, my countrymen, the future is now!"

"You should go now," Lan-Gai urged. "See the guns aimed at you? The police are closing in. Please run now!"

The audience rushed onto the stage, surrounding me, pushing me high into the air and carrying me on their shoulders, chanting, "Tan Long! Tan Long!"

Police sirens screamed. Near the stage, plainclothes officers formed a dragnet around us, their circle tightening.

I jumped down from the students' and workers' shoulders, huddled low among the mob, and slipped out the back of the stage, where Lan-Gai stood waiting.

"Good-bye, Lan-Gai," I whispered.

"Good-bye, Mr. Long. You are our new leader now. These people worship you." Lan-Gai slipped out of his white mourning robe and draped it over me. In the chaos, I disappeared into the woods, running a distance before finding a small path leading to the other side of Xishan Mountain. At the fork of the road, a woman with a yellow scarf fluttering in the cold wind sat in a car with its engine running.

"Lena," I said, jumping in.

"Fasten your seat belt. It'll be a rough ride down the hill." Lena stepped on the gas pedal and the car skidded down the icy road, jerked around sharp mountain turns, and headed onto the congested highway toward Tianjin. Stopping at a small storefront, Lena slipped out of her seat, hugged me, and kissed my cheek. "Good-bye, young man."

"Good-bye, Lena. The summer sun will shine soon," I promised.

As she jumped into another car, I took the driver's seat and floored the gas, speeding eastward, my heart heavy with what lay ahead—a life on the run and a mission the size of the ocean.

Shento

山头

CHAPTER 56

On the day of their departure, I hid in the shadows, behind my window that overlooked the deep courtyard, watching Sumi button Tai Ping's overcoat for the long journey ahead. Today, the comfort of house arrest; tomorrow, the chilly cells of Xinjiang. The wind chased dead leaves around the ancient courtyard, moaning: *My son, my son.*

I told myself again that it was Sumi who had betrayed me. And that betrayal of our past was tantamount to murder—murder of our past and of our future, causing the death of an old Shento and the birth of another, a lone wolf loved by none and forsaken by all. My life now was like the maple leaf I had once picked and placed between the pages of my diary to symbolize my love for her—dried, dissolving, falling apart. A Tang dynasty poem came to mind: "Before a sick tree, an entire forest greens in the spring. In front of a sunken ship, a thousand boats sail by."

A man with a weaker resolve would have accepted the fate of the sick tree or the sunken boat, dissolving in silence, letting the cycle of the season turn and the tide of the ocean wash, but such was not my character.

I had considered slicing Sumi's throat, which had leaked out all our forbidden secrets, or taking her heart from her chest, examining the dark and rotten contents that had been tainted with betrayal. But in my path stood two minor hindrances. The first came one sleepless night when I was sharpening my sword to kill Sumi. I pushed the weapon along the whetstone, each jarring sound stabbing my own heart, as if I were preparing to end my very own life, until I could not continue. I even imagined my own blood dripping down, in place of the water used to wet the stone, and realized then that no matter how loveless Sumi had turned, she was part of my flesh and blood. In a burst of anger, I sliced my own forearm and was stunned by the painlessness of the act and by the realization that her living meant more to me than my own life. Consequently, I broke the sword into pieces, striking it against the ancient palace sundial, and threw myself onto the stone-paved ground, heaving with dry tears until dawn, when the sentry guard found me and helped me into my den.

But the hate and the love continued to torture me, and once again I pondered ending Sumi's life, pain or no pain to myself. I could not stand seeing her stare at me with daggers of contempt in her eyes. I made three special silver bullets to use on her, but as I was polishing them, I heard the cries of my son, Tai Ping, the boy of my flesh and blood, his voice so similar to mine as a child. They were cries of hopelessness, an orphan's cry. I looked around the courtyard and saw no one, yet those phantom cries deafened my ears, impossible to block out, no matter how hard I tried to muffle them.

For two days, I had lurked behind the window, watching mother and son. I saw not the boy, Tai Ping, but myself, the scrawny village boy of Balan, barefoot, dressed in rough woven linen, docilely sitting by the mother I had never known, listening to sweet tales from the book in her hand. I cried, wetting my starchy uniform, moved by a mysterious joy of being loved vicariously by the shadow of my own mother.

Soon after, I settled on leniency. I decided to exile Sumi to the farthest prison in China's northwestern tip and to leave Tai Ping in her care with proper accommodation, so that the boy would be educated and groomed according to his station in life. Like ancient emperors before me, I banished Sumi like a disloyal concubine to the silence of the west, where she would live forever in regret, in a wilderness devoid of joy.

"Mama, I don't want to go away," Tai Ping said as he heard the news.

Sumi bent over and kissed him on the forehead. "It will be all right," she promised.

"Where are we going?"

"To a faraway place where you will see the mountains and deserts of the central kingdom."

Mother and son were pushed by a soldier into the back of a green military van. As if aware of my watching eyes, Sumi did not turn her head back once. She was composed and silent, her head held high. With Tai Ping on her lap, she leaned toward him and whispered something into his ear. The van started to move and my heart quickened. Was I making a mistake of eternal proportion? Was I committing the sin of my father?

The boy looked back, searching, smiling a little smile rippled with dimples. I shut my eyes to block out the unbearable image. Then I pushed the heavy curtain aside, pressing my nose to the windowpane for a last glimpse of the two itinerants well on their way. Weakly, I leaned against the dark wall. Only after a long moment was I able to compose myself and return to my outer self. Helped by one of Heng Tu's famous quotes—"To make revolution, sacrifice is necessary"—I walked back into the dark hallway of power. Hito Ling was waiting for me.

"Is it wrong of me to have them sent away?" I asked him.

"No, Colonel. During the Cultural Revolution, I turned in my father for sleeping with a classmate of mine. He was arrested, and I was promoted to first secretary of the Red Guard in my high school."

"And you were proud of yourself?"

"I was," Hito replied rather uncertainly.

I changed the subject. "Where is our fugitive, the Long boy, now?"

"Two days ago, he was seen in Shandong Province, at Nankai University, another liberal school. Then he made a speech on the campus of Tianjin University, where he drew three thousand Poison Tree Club members."

"Why didn't your men catch him?"

"He got away before we arrived."

"What happened to your national dragnet? We have the nation's police force at your disposal, and all you see is his shadow?"

"It is like looking for a needle in the ocean."

"Don't you see his pattern?"

"Yes, colleges. But we have thousands of colleges in this country."

"Get the local police to stake out all our major universities. And make that a top priority."

"Right away, Colonel."

"And release a public announcement about Sumi Wo's life sentence and Fei-Fei Chen's execution immediately."

"Execution?"

"Yes, to be carried out in three months."

"I haven't heard of this before."

"Of course you haven't. The ruling has just been issued by me."

"But doesn't our criminal procedure require that it go through the Supreme Court of People's Justice first?"

"The court works for the president."

"I shall draft the sentencing immediately, to be seconded by the justices," Hito said, jotting it down. "One question, Colonel. Why wait three months? Usually, we execute immediately."

"I want the effect to linger in people's minds."

Tan

CHAPTER 57

I was wrapped up thick and tight like a northern farmer facing the curse of a bitter winter. My beard was long and itchy, my hair greasy with dirt, and my face scratchy from the wind that blasted me day and night in my fugitive existence. My waist had shrunk and I had to notch out two new holes in my belt to keep my six layers of pants suspended around my waist. My coat carried the odors of my daily abodes—train stations, street corners, abandoned farmhouses, horse barns, and pigsties.

I walked with the gait of a drunk, dragging my heavy feet, conversing in unintelligible gibberish when spoken to and yawning smelly yawns. I smoked thick tobacco rolls made from torn newspaper wrapping and drifted among crowds of other dirty souls that belonged nowhere.

But that was the daytime me, the one I invented to dodge the many eyes of the police. My picture preceded me everywhere I roamed. Sure that everyone could tell who I was without disguise, I kept to the wrong part of the town, the place children were urged to avoid and where men, dark, hungry, unknown strangers of sin and penury, gathered like the garbage blown into gutters.

At night, I would sneak into an inn or restaurant bathroom. Usually, I would be stopped and allowed entry only after promising to depart immediately after my visit. Inside, I would open my suitcase, clean myself, and change into a neat shirt and jacket, always amused by how differently I was treated on the way out, leaving the manager to wonder where the pauper had disappeared to.

In Tianjin, I visited ten universities, met the leaders of the Poison Tree Clubs, made my speeches condemning the dark secrets of Shento and his tyrannical leader, Heng Tu. I spread the virtue of my new political party and called for the first free election this summer, when the fiftieth Party congress would meet in Beijing for their rubber-stamping session.

On every campus, I was the most whispered secret. Those young minds were like dry hay awaiting me to ignite them. One strike and their hearts were inflamed. They wanted to meet the forbidden hero on the run, and cheered my bravery in spreading the word of democracy and condemning the suppressing government. Students kept guard for me outside the halls where my appearance was expected. At one campus, a student was arrested for leading the police on an empty chase.

At the end of each meeting, the membership of the Democracy Party grew. I would leave each school feeling more and more sure of my mission and the desire to fight. But the road ahead became more treacherous at each town I visited farther south along the Pacific coast. In Yangzhou, an ancient town, I was forewarned by the club leaders that the campus meeting was a trap. Police and militiamen in plain clothes swarmed the campus. To thwart them, the club members instead planned a secret boat ride at twilight on the scenic Tai Lake, where long-legged crabs and fat prawns crawled the muddy bottom and budding peach trees swayed in the warm spring breeze. In the past, the lake had hidden many revolutionaries in their secret coves and shady bays. *I am a revolutionary,* I thought.

In the eyes of those young people, I had become a symbol of something bigger than myself. That belief was confirmed by two young men who swam up alongside the boat and begged to follow me as I took my crusade farther south.

"You are our hero. Everyone in the country wants to be like you. We'd like to join you, please," they begged.

"The road is dangerous ahead. I can't assure your safety."

"We want to protect you. We will die for you."

"Our party will need you later," I assured them. "Your life is precious. Cherish it."

As the two boys quieted with disappointment, we all heard a humming motor approaching. "Jump and swim to the shore!" the boys said. "The police are coming!"

When I dived into the warm water, the two boys followed, swimming behind until we reached the shore. "Thank you for the company," I said, peeling off my wet shirt and wringing it dry.

"I shall write this in my diary," one boy said.

"And I will someday write a book about this adventure," said the other.

I smiled and disappeared into the woods.

I bought my way onto a southbound freight boat loaded with sacks of cement. As I journeyed down the Pacific coast, I could see the change of climate. The sea was bluer, trees greener, flowers brighter, and the people prettier. In May, when I reached Shanghai, my hair was shoulder length and I threw my last sweater away, watching it float in the canal that used to cradle the emperor's southbound ships. The leader of Shanghai University's huge Poison Tree Club, a girl of twenty, waited for me at the small port with a shy smile around her sensuous mouth, clutching a bundle of wildflowers in her hands. She asked me if she could be the branch secretary of my Democracy Party in Shanghai.

Her name was Li-Ping, and she had the unusual knack of mixing politics with art and pleasure. She scheduled my appearances in venues ranging from cafés, where students sipped imported Colombian coffee with heavy cream and inhaled Marlboros, to noisy nightclubs, where half-naked girls slithered around barely clad male singers. When I appeared with Li-Ping, no introduction was needed. These people, the coolest bunch in Shanghai's new culture, stopped and cheered my message. Many times, like a rock star, I had to be shoved out the back door into a waiting car as female fans screamed and scratched, fighting to get near me.

Demonstrations would follow my visits, to the annoyance of the local authorities. Branches of the Democracy Party popped up at every campus I visited. Leaders of each small branch along the coastal cities began to communicate with one another. They composed songs and wrote poetry in praise of the birth of a secret revolution. Dozens of leaders left their schools in the middle of semesters to travel to other campuses that I had not been able to visit on my journey's path. They claimed to be my disciples. Some were arrested, and others were returned home to parental supervision.

As the summer sun scorched, the country burned like a land on fire—a fire of souls, a fire of hearts. Everyone talked about me as if I were a living ghost who lived only on the lips of those who worshipped me. Some went so far as to say that I did not exist. I was a mirage conjured up by the police as an excuse to tighten its grip on the people's throats. Yet my fresh audio recordings and the people who saw me with their naked eyes proved again and again that I did live among them and that the revolution had indeed taken root.

When I arrived at Fujian on the back of a thin mule and saw its lush mountains heaving in the bubbling heat, I clasped my hands and said a small prayer for this most unforgettable journey of my life. Kneeling by a brook, I splashed my face with the coolest mountain water and gulped the sweet water—tasting heaven on earth, quenching a hellish thirst in paradise.

Shento

山头

CHAPTER 58

Every day that passed with Tan Long at large pricked me like a venomous arrow. I flew like a mad mosquito at every sniff of Tan's blood, only to be told that his ghost had fled again. I flew as far as Xinjiang in search of my prey, only to be greeted, as expected, with more disappointment.

On that trip, I stopped by to see Sumi, who refused to speak to me and threatened to kill herself for the cause. But the worst was the slap across the face I received from my son. When I arrived, Tai Ping was chasing a butterfly; he lived within the confinement of the prison yard.

Son, forgive me. One day you will see who I really am. One day I will give you the world. I saw *one day* as an abstract deadline, somewhere in the future. When I assumed absolute power, I would take back my son. I felt justified leaving Tai Ping in this seclusion. I took solace in seeing the boy grown half a foot taller and enjoying the special treats that I sent to him every month—a bicycle, tins of candies, books—little luxuries that I couldn't even dream of as a child.

Not a day went by without some reported civil disturbance caused directly or indirectly by Tan Long. There were factory strikes spreading across the south and campus sit-ins in the northwest. At last count, the Democracy Party membership numbered an alarming half a million, not counting the other three thousand minor parties that had cropped into existence within the last several months.

"We have a real headache here," the president told me one day with a sigh. "The Communists overthrew the Nationalists in 1949 precisely the same way it is happening now."

"We have guns, armies, and a military base," I replied. "The people have nothing, just the ghost of Tan."

"What are you doing with the guns? What are you doing with the army? Why haven't you been able to catch that man after six months?"

"We have tried everything, sir."

"Send the army, navy, and air force. I care not what you do, but do something quickly. Shento, my son, I have never received so many complaints from the old ministers before. They want you fired. But I trust you and want you to have my seat someday. You must demonstrate your conviction and strength. I could use some stability here."

"You shall have it."

CHAPTER 59

June 18, 1986

BEIJING

Fei-Fei, now just a slight frame of a man, was pushed into a jail van, then transported to an unknown destination near West Mountain. When the van's door opened again, he was dragged out and tossed on the ground. A soldier read the sentence: "Fei-Fei Chen, you are hereby notified by the Supreme Court of People's Justice that you are to receive the death penalty on this day for your conviction on your anti-government charges."

"But I have never been to court."

"This is the final judgment. No appeal permitted."

"I want to live! I will confess anything!"

"Confession will not change anything."

"Please let me see my family and friends once more. I am entitled to a few days, at least."

Black crows cried nearby, hidden in the thick trees of the mountainous spot chosen for the secret execution. But the stone-faced government reporters showed little emotion. They were only there to witness and capture this brutal moment so that they could rush the bloody photos to the national newspapers.

"Please, reporters, do something! I am innocent!" Fei-Fei begged, on his knees.

Another soldier kicked him in the back, and he went down on his face, dust flying in a sudden puff around him. With one heavy boot stepping on Fei-Fei's back, the soldier pulled his trigger twice.

Fei-Fei's head exploded, his brain flying in all directions, his body jerked by the impact. He died instantly.

Cameras clicked, recording his final moment.

Sumi

CHAPTER 60

June 18, 1986

XINJIANG PRISON

At dawn, my cell door was kicked open and I was taken away, with Tai Ping crying from his cot. The guards rushed me to a torture tower and tied me to a metal table. An officer paced back and forth, hands behind him, then he motioned to a tape recorder nearby. "Say that you never knew Shento, that you made the whole story up," he instructed.

"My tongue is only to speak the truth, never a lie," I replied firmly.

"One last time."

"You are wasting your time." I spat at him.

"If you do not confess, you will never speak again," he warned, wiping my spittle from his face.

"I have nothing to confess!" I tried to spit again, but my mouth had gone dry.

"Surgeon!" The officer summoned in a man wearing a white coat and gloves. "Make her mute. I want to see this beauty lose her poisonous tongue."

Lose my tongue? Horror struck me. "Get away from me!" I screamed.

A syringe plunged into my arm without warning.

My mind lost its clarity and my vision blurred. In my receding awareness, I saw the surgeon reach out his hand and open my jaw, pulling out my tongue.

I tried to bite but felt no strength. I tried to shout but heard no sound. Then I saw his other hand holding a gleaming scalpel quickly coming down on me. I felt no pain, only a slight sensation across my tongue, like having been scraped by a young sea reed. My throat was suddenly flooded with my own blood, making me gurgle and choke.

I felt nothing after that.

Tan

CHAPTER 61

When photographs of Fei-Fei's execution and Sumi's severed tongue were splashed in all the major newspapers, the nation was shrouded in sadness, gloom, and anger. The Pacific coast blurred with clouds, thick and dark. Raindrops beat the windblown treetops relentlessly and waves roared like angry tigers, threatening to swallow towns and villages along the Pacific coast. Children whispered in small voices, questioning the frowns on their parents' faces. They only needed to be shown the pictures of brutal punishment.

"You could lose a tongue for speaking the truth?" children asked, perplexed.

"And your heads." Parents did not know what the truth was anymore.

LYING ON THE FLOOR of a small boardinghouse in Fujian, I cried until my tears dried. The devils! The time had come for revolution.

In my bold calligraphy, I composed a fiery communiqué to all the branch leaders of the Democracy Party and all other brother and sister parties formed during the last year. "It is time!" I wrote, calling for all the patriots of this land to march into the streets. The government could put down one or two, but when millions of people marched, then rulers should tremble. I urged all to gather in Tiananmen Square the following

Sunday, where I would lead a hunger strike against the government till such a time as the rulers were ready to sit down and negotiate with us.

My writing was immediately copied and tossed into crowds, market-places, school cafeterias, train stations, and bus stops in every city and town. My words were hope and fire. People, saddened by the atrocities, dared speak angry words. Fear was shed and courage born. Antigovernment slogans were pasted conspicuously along the walls of government buildings and along the streets. Students walked out of classes, and teachers followed in protest.

Cities, shimmering in the summer heat, were covered with black and white in mourning for Fei-Fei. The unspeakable cruelty of the severed tongue of the most eloquent author of this generation brought the angry crowd to a new level of indignation. They wanted blood. They wanted the criminals to pay. They wanted the death of Colonel Shento.

Within two days there were thousands of reported clashes with the police. On the third day, roaming armed guards stared at any gathering crowds with suspicion. On the fourth day, Saturday, more reinforcements were brought in from various regional commands, and with them came the onslaught of media from faraway lands. On Sunday, people from all walks of the city filled the ancient Tiananmen Square to its brim. The flags of universities and factories flew in the lazy breeze. By noon, half a million people sat, shouted, and sang, taking over the square.

Lan-Gai, the Beijing University leader, stood on top of a school desk in the center of the square, a loudspeaker in his hand, among ten thousand of his own classmates. Everyone wore white shirts, with black bands on their right arms and around their heads. Lan-Gai led one song after another.

At the western corner of the spacious square, students from the Art College set up a stage by putting some cafeteria tables together. Student leaders made rousing speeches that started with the logical criticism of the government and ended with shouts for blood and battle. In the east, the Iron and Steel University molded together an iron frame of the Statue of Liberty, draped with a red flag to symbolize the aspirations of this demonstration. To the north, the Agricultural University made a twelve-foot-tall effigy of Colonel Shento holding a miniature President

Heng Tu in his arms. All day long they shouted the same slogans: Down with Shento! Down with Heng Tu! Return Sumi's tongue! Remember Fei-Fei Chen!

The songs and shouts surged like relentless waves. Tens of thousands of Beijing's citizens pedaled their bicycles to the square to witness in silence this rare sight of defiance against their much-feared, corrupt leaders.

An old man with a birdcage dangling from his bicycle's handlebar shouted to the students, "Go home and have some meals. You're never going to win. Nothing's going to change because you go hungry for a few days."

No one paid any heed to the old man. He pedaled away to complete his daily ride.

Lan-Gai walked around, visiting other camps and chatting with comrades. They shook hands firmly like revolutionaries and hugged tightly like comrades in battle. They toasted and drank cups of water as if they were wine. They sang old Long March songs. Each face was a burning sun, each heart a churning sea. Thousands of flags flapped in the weak afternoon breeze.

Police stood on the outer rim, some of them chatting with the students, others sharing water with them. But it was not the soldiers who walked the beat that mattered; it was those pulling the strings behind their backs.

Where was their leader?

Spirits were waning, but then youthful factory workers, hundreds of them still in uniform, drove a dozen big and loud trucks into the square, carrying loads of bottled water and barrels of brewed tea. They poured drinks, hugging and shaking hands, cheering for the students.

A policeman stood on top of an army truck, loudspeaker in hand, and yelled: "Young people, please disperse peacefully! Go back to your schools, homes, and factories. We, the government, have heard your voices. You have made your point. It is time this illegal antigovernment demonstration came to an end. You will not be held responsible for your actions today if you follow instructions now!"

The crowd, temporarily quiet, burst into a deafening storm of shouts.

"Down with the murderer Shento!"

"Return Sumi's tongue!"

"Return Fei-Fei's life!"

Their chants buried the flimsy drone of the loudspeaker.

At nightfall, I emerged from the crowd and stood up on the stage of rickety tables against the background portrait of Chairman Mao. In a silent rush, three major American networks, the BBC, CNN, Tokyo NEWS, Britain's Sky Cable, and United Germany TV all pointed their long-necked video cameras at me.

Waves of students rushed up to me and lifted me high with their hands.

"Quiet! Quiet!" Lan-Gai shouted through a loudspeaker. "Speech, speech!"

The hands of the crowd returned me to the stage. I called out, "My dear friends, patriots, comrades of freedom, I am here with you! I have not eaten since yesterday, and I will not eat until the devils of this land succumb to us . . ."

Applause buried my words for a moment.

". . . We want answers! Not pity! We want power for the people, not tyranny. Fei-Fei's life has to be redeemed, and Sumi's tongue must not have been severed for nothing! We will not surrender until our questions are answered and our demands fulfilled."

Shouts surged, hope was regained, and a night of rejoicing ensued.

A NEW DAY BROKE. Hand in hand, young comrades sat on the cool stone ground, slumbering in yesterday's garbage. They dreamed of food they didn't have. Their bodies were small, curled up and reluctant, their eyes hollowed from the jarring hunger that occupied all their thoughts. They were not a generation accustomed, as their parents were, to the rubbing of empty stomachs. They had always had more to eat and less to worry about. They were the one-baby-a-family generation—masters of their princedom. And now they were hungry. All they consumed was water and more water, to keep alert and alive.

I evaded capture the first night by adopting Mao's guerrilla war tactics: always moving from crowd to crowd, calling on each group leader, spreading words of encouragement.

Early the next morning, there was a skirmish at the northern end of the square. The small crowd from the Diplomacy University blocked the Garrison guards who were trying to raise the flag. A solider slammed his rifle into the head of a protester, causing him to bleed profusely.

"Is there a doctor here?" Lan-Gai asked through the speaker.

Four medical students rushed over and bandaged the injured student as the strikers barricaded the guards away from the crowd. For the first time, the red flag of the People's Republic of China was not raised in Tiananmen Square since its establishment in 1949. The students cheered and the changing guards fled in defeat.

Midmorning, medical doctors from the People's Hospital arrived with IV equipment, a fleet of ambulances, and a team of efficient nurses. I shook hands with the chief medical doctor and thanked him for his thoughtfulness.

In the early afternoon, more trucks carrying factory workers and government employees arrived.

"We are here to say to the students that we are behind them," a steel-union leader declared. "We brought plenty of hammers and sickles for you youngsters to fight back with, if the soldiers dare touch you again."

At three in the afternoon, people from all walks of the city mingled and chatted with the strikers, passing cups of water and calling loudly for help for those fainting in the heat. They helped carry those too weak to walk to ambulances, and made the crowd part to let the emergency vehicles out and water trucks in. The mothers and fathers of Beijing knelt by youngsters' sides, wiping sweat, feeding liquids, begging the brave children to give up and go home. But somehow that support and advice caused the opposite effect. The strikers shook their weak heads.

At four, government speakers crackled. "It has come to our attention that there are bad elements behind young innocent students, stirring up civil unrest. We advise again for all students to quit the hunger strike and leave the square. You are being ill advised by counterrevolutionaries so that they, the real enemies of the country, can achieve illegal goals. Young people, your future is bright and the road ahead of you is long. Act carefully and cautiously. We are here to help you out of a bad situation. Go home. Otherwise we will declare a martial-law curfew by nightfall. If you stay here, you will be in violation of martial law!"

"We have to build barricades. Tell everybody," I said to Lan-Gai.

I stood up on the stage again and spoke through the loudspeaker. "Hungry we may be. But afraid we are not. We will remain here! We have the right to demonstrate! Martial law does not scare us."

The crowd cheered.

"But we are facing a feudal government as brutal as the Nazis," I warned the young students. "They will open fire and they will kill. It is inevitable. They will show no sympathy. They are deaf to the voice of the people. They choose not to listen to us. They are hiding because they are afraid of us. We are in the light; they, the darkness. The longer we survive, the more scared they become. They are counting their days in power. They will face death as murderers. Their hands—stained with the blood of the people—will be severed. They will be the rubbish of history and we, the gems of the future. Comrades, my dear comrades in arms, I salute you!"

That evening, though hungry and tired myself, I roamed around serving those younger than I with pitchers of water or cups of warm tea. Some refused even that in a quietly determined manner; others lay weakly, their eyes empty, their lips parched, taking sips from me only that they might stay on in this show of will, not wanting to be taken off the square to the hospital.

Night fell and the temperature dropped as a sea breeze blew and thinned the thick stench that now stood like a wall around the square. To my alarm, more armored troops carrying guns and rifles were streaming into the square. More tanks ground down the streets, leaving behind furrowed tracks. Powerful spotlights shot long beams of whiteness, piercing the dark night. Young people clung to each other, covering their weak bodies with dirty blankets. But the soldiers themselves, brought in from the country, were starry-eyed and youthful in spirit. Some even shared their water with the strikers.

On the third day, a soldier came carrying a white flag, asking to see the leader.

I stood up and asked, "What do you want?"

"The prime minister requests your representative for negotiation."

"How many are expected?"

"Two."

By a vote of raised hands, Lan-Gai and I were chosen.

The crowd parted and closed again behind us.

The negotiation was a farce. Prime Minister Tang preached for five minutes before I stood up to walk out.

"Stop! Who do you think you are talking to?" the fat prime minister asked.

I stopped and answered, "I am not quite certain. You are two people combined in one—a blind and a deaf. Your only imperfection is that you are not a mute."

"You are insulting me."

"You have been insulting our people ever since you took over your uncle's job."

"What are your conditions then?" the prime minister demanded angrily.

"The resignation of Shento, the young colonel of the Garrison."

The prime minister smirked.

"Does that amuse you? Let's go," Lan-Gai said.

The smirk disappeared. "What are your other demands?"

"Release Sumi Wo immediately," I said. "Capital punishment for Shento for his crimes and an immediate agenda for a free election."

"Colonel Shento is a trusted member of Heng Tu's administration," the prime minister sputtered. "He has served our country and revolution well."

"He is a fugitive of the law with blood on his hands," I returned.

"Be careful there, young man. Don't let your personal feelings affect your judgment. Are you leading innocent students on this hunger strike in order to avenge your own grievances?" Prime Minister Tang asked slyly.

"Let's go, Lan-Gai," I said. "The people out there will fight until the end."

"We cannot accept any of your conditions. Go tell your people to leave this square immediately or you will all be put under arrest."

Silently, we walked out.

Shento

山头

CHAPTER 62

I watched the negotiation with the student leaders via a closed-circuit broadcast, together with key cabinet ministers. We were gathered in a pavilion-shaped chamber deep inside the Forbidden City. Conspicuously absent was President Heng Tu, whose whereabouts were known only to one man—me.

Sitting in the president's seat, I shifted uncomfortably, eyeing my half brother on the grainy screen, hating every syllable of the conversation. I had vehemently opposed any negotiation, but the prime minister had requested it nonetheless. And what had he achieved? Nothing besides showing weakness, monumental weakness. I was incensed and had little to say. What needed to be said had been said—they had heard it all. The people out there wanted me gone. So did the people inside here. I stood up, declaring the meeting adjourned, only to be opposed by the head of the Central Committee, Mr. Fong, who cleared his throat and asked, "What should we do?"

"Nothing," I responded, proceeding to the door.

"But the people are asking and demanding things."

I stopped at the door. "They are demanding chaos. Are you suggesting we give them chaos?"

"It is not your call to make, young colonel. We do not think you have the right to be here," the white-haired committee secretary said in a belligerent voice. "You are not a member of this decision-making organ."

"I represent the president. Does he have a seat here?"

"We demand to have our president here!"

"You demand?" I chuckled.

"Yes, we demand. Right?" The old man looked around the thirty-member committee. Everyone raised their hands in support of his motion.

"I have been entrusted with the proxy of the president's full power and authority, as you all well know." I pulled out a piece of paper from my leather briefcase and waved it in the air. "Our president's wishes are all written here. He is utterly against any compromise or concessions."

"We should consider their requests carefully before any action is taken," urged another minister.

"Any defiance is an act of betrayal against the presidency," I said.

"We demand your resignation!" the finance minister said abruptly.

"We want you impeached, Colonel," demanded another.

"For what? I do what I have to do for the country, never for myself. You want to get rid of me for that? I fought for all of you so that you can sit here and enjoy the power that you have." I speared each of them with a look. "I shall report your sentiment to the president," I said, storming out. Instead of heading for the president's chamber, I headed to my own office, angered by the turn of the tide from within, but not shocked. I had always been a sore in their eyes, and I had long prepared for this day of betrayal. Calmly, after I had collected myself, I marched into the telegraph room and ordered a coded message dispatched to all my Young Generals: "The time has come. Act now."

AT MIDNIGHT IN FUJIAN, Ding Long, the retired general, was dragged out of his bed and brought to a navy ship docked near the port of Fuzhou. Blindfolded, with his hands tied behind his back, he was brought to the ship's dining hall, where the eight district command chiefs also sat, restrained in the same manner, each with a Young General standing behind him. When their blindfolds were lifted, they looked at one another in puzzlement and fear.

I surveyed the room, filled with the most dangerous men of this land—men controlling guns and foot soldiers. The fate of this nation rose and sank with them. This was the moment I had long dreamed about, the moment of revenge, a moment to savor. I strode to the center of the room.

Ding Long's hair was white, and there were wrinkles where the glow of youth used to be.

"You all look surprised that I have acted before you did," I said. "Your coup against me and President Heng Tu has officially failed, but that is not to say that you will be free from facing the consequences of your pitiful attempt." I turned to Ding Long and grabbed his lapel. "Do you know who I am, General?"

Ding Long squinted, gazing at me for a long moment before a light of recognition came into his eyes. "Shento?"

"Yes, your abandoned son. The bastard of the world."

"Son . . ." There was a pained expression on his face.

"Not even an apology." How I wanted to rip him apart. I remembered that slap I had received from his father-in-law many years ago. An eye for an eye. I slapped Ding Long's face so hard that blood trickled down from the corner of his mouth. "Hang him up."

"Around the neck?" my Young General asked.

"No, I want him to suffer, not to die yet. Hang him by his thumbs."

A rope was thrown over a beam and Ding Long was pulled up, a cry of pain spilling from his mouth.

I smiled and turned to the military chiefs. "I have in my hand a piece of writing that needs to be signed by all of you."

A soldier held the paper before the first chief.

"You do not need to know the contents before signing it, Chief," I mocked. "You will sign it because I want you to. That is the only way that you will leave this place alive."

"I can do it!" the Fujian chief cried. "But my hands are tied!"

"Free his hands," I ordered.

Fu-Ren took a long breath, rubbed his wrists, and signed dutifully. Then the Jiangxi chief, the Nanking chief, and the Lanzhou chief followed. When all had signed, I ordered, "Now bite your middle finger and smear your blood next to your signature for authenticity."

The chiefs looked at one another fearfully.

"I refuse to do this. You are a traitor to the people," the Lanzhou chief protested.

I pulled out my revolver and shot the man in the right arm. The man screamed as his blood splattered all over.

Obediently, the other chiefs bit their fingers and smeared their blood next to their signatures.

I took the paper, precious prosecutable evidence, and asked, "Do you know what you have signed?"

They shook their heads.

"Of course you don't. This is an accord for a planned coup d'état, masterminded by him." I pointed at Ding Long, hanging limply by his bloody thumbs, his toes barely touching the floor.

There were urgent shouts of protests among the chiefs.

"Now that you have outlived your use to the people and to me, it is time to say good-bye." I smiled. "Shoot them all and dump them into the ocean."

"What about Ding Long?" a Young General asked

"Don't shoot him, stab him. Spare him for the sharks."

"Son, I have always loved you," Ding Long whispered, weakened from pain.

"Sure you have; that's why I'm giving you a chance to live. You just have to survive the sea with all your comrades' blood swirling around you. Hey, I survived it. So should you. You are my father."

As I stepped out on deck, I heard eight shots fired, followed by a desperate scream of pain, then a thud—Ding Long had been loosened and dropped to the floor.

Tan

CHAPTER 63

At the stroke of midnight, Shento's army open fired on the crowd, first randomly, then at targeted locations. There were shouts of pain and confusion. The dead lay in pools of blood. The living cried, trying to save the dying. Youthful hearts sank with the burden of death as their worst fears were realized.

I ducked behind a table as a sparkle of bullets spit through the night air. The bullets came from everywhere. The youngsters didn't know where to dodge as I shouted instructions to run.

From the north, I heard the rattle of tanks. Grenades were being thrown from the tanks, exploding in the crowd. I cried to the soldiers and ran toward them but they kept shooting. "Stop!" I shouted. "Don't shoot the people! Take me! Take me!"

Bullets rained down like an angry storm—over my head and shoulders, past my ears. More dead fell. More comrades wounded.

I jumped over a barricade, grabbed a gun away from a frightened soldier, and started shooting, fighting my way out until I reached the corner of the square. I threw away the empty gun and looked back at the deadly square, now filling up with ghosts. Blood pooled in the drains, ambulances howled, police sirens rang, tanks groaned. People screamed and sobbed. Fear. Death. Youthful bodies cut down by the force of bullets.

I crouched near a wall, heaving. A soldier came by, aiming at me. I dodged and the bullet hit another. I ran to the injured boy as the soldier took aim at me again. I swung the young student over my shoulder and ran, the soldier charging after me as the student moaned, calling for his mother. He couldn't have been more than seventeen. "Shhh," I hushed him as I leaned him back against a brick wall, waiting for the obstinate soldier. When the soldier turned the corner, I charged him and struck the soldier's head against the stony ground until he passed out. I took his gun, stripped off his uniform, and kicked the man aside.

"You killed him!" the wounded student said, alarmed.

"To save us."

"Are you Tan Long, our leader?"

"Shhh."

"Where are you taking me?"

"The hospital."

"No, please leave me here and run as quickly as possible! They will kill you!"

Ignoring him, I put on the green uniform and carried the wounded student to the nearest ambulance. The sight there shocked me. There were hundreds of young people lying on the ground around the vehicle. Only a handful of medical workers hustled among the mounting patients. Some of the wounded had passed out, some were rocking in shock, others were crying and trying to stop the bleeding with their own hands or whatever cloth they could find.

How I wished I were a doctor, a god, or Buddha, and my hands could heal their wounds. But I was not. I was the reason for all this bloodshed. I knelt down to comfort one and ten others reached out bloodied hands for help.

A nurse came by and said, "Thank you. You're the first soldier to help."

Around the corner, machine guns still sprayed, hitting the crowd. Tanks lumbered, their wheels clawing like ugly teeth toward more innocent souls trapped in a bottleneck in the maddening rush to escape gunfire. Unarmed strikers screamed, terrified, but the soldiers did not stop. Loudspeakers continued to shout, "Get out! Get out! We will not cease firing until you are all out of here!"

We had long surrendered. Why were the soldiers still shooting? Whirling helicopters had also started shooting at those running away, a dozen aircraft hovering overhead, cornering every angle of the square. It was a death trap.

A group of soldiers came by, waving to me. "Come on, let's finish the job!" one said to me, spraying his semiautomatic around him.

"Let's shut these spoiled brats up for good!" another shouted.

"You didn't carry any wounded in, did you, soldier?" an officer in the group asked.

"Look at him fondling their hands. What a model people-loving soldier," another sneered.

I kept silent. The moment I opened my mouth, I would be exposed; all the soldiers seemed to have come from the south and had distinct accents. The loose platoon surrounded me, scrutinizing me carefully.

The nurse suddenly spoke up. "You are mistaken. This soldier was chasing after a big tall man, and merely stopped to question this student as to where the man had gone."

"Good soldier!" The officer slapped my shoulder and moved on, his men following him.

"Thank you, nurse," I said.

"No, thank you." The nurse made a V with her fingers. "Fight on," she whispered.

I bowed to her and disappeared in the darkness.

STILL DRESSED IN the army uniform, I sat limply against the metal wall of a train. A load of silent passengers throbbed with the movement of the ancient iron horse. The loudspeakers on the train crackled the serious announcement that had been repeated hundreds of times through radios, televisions, and newspapers: "Comrades, the people of the People's Republic of China, we are pleased to report to you that the June Fourth Tiananmen Square Incident has been squashed with success. Most of the antigovernment elements have been wiped out. We are equally pleased to inform you that a team of Communist leaders, led by General Shento, has put to rest a military coup d'état against our dear president, Heng Tu, coinciding with the evil activities in Tiananmen Square. To reward his effort and loyalty, our glorious president has installed General Shento as the new military chief of all three branches of our military establishment.

"The coup, led by the retired Ding Long and the other eight regional military chiefs, has been completely put to rest, but not the remnants of the Tiananmen Square Incident. The Central Government has thus issued a temporary martial law so that our soldiers can apprehend those student leaders who ran away and are still at large."

Father! I let out a little cry, startling my napping seatmates. Was my father dead? The ominous words of the announcement echoed in my head—"put to rest."

It had been two days since I scaled the wall and made it to the train station, which was bursting with people fleeing the massacre. I had walked up to the conductor on the train, without a ticket, rifle in hand. He asked me if I had any money. I gave him a hard stare. "All right, then, a regular seat," the conductor said. "All the soft bed compartments are taken."

When I boarded the train, people looked at me like I was a disease, a plague, a murderer. A child shrieked upon seeing me. The blood, the shots, the dead corpses piling up like mountains in the square, carted away by garbage trucks—how could you expect a child to love my uniform and what it stood for?

When the coast of the Pacific appeared like a little snake on my right, I knew it was the last stop. Fujian! I remembered the words spoken to me by my grandfather: "You know where home is." I knew. People here would help me. They would hide me in the big mountains or in the sea, where sea serpents swam. But I could not call on my family. There were a thousand traps awaiting me there, and my appearance would only worsen their plight. Instead, I called my old principal.

Looking not a day older, Mr. Koon met me at the dock of a small fishing town in Fu Ching.

"I am honored you called me," the monk said.

"You are the only one with the heart of Buddha. Is everything all right?"

"No," the monk cried. "Your father is still missing."

"Since when?"

"Two nights ago."

"Do you think he's dead?"

"Never. We are searching for him, a whole fleet of fishermen. We will find him. Don't you worry, son."

"How about my mother and grandfather?"

"They have been under house arrest since this purge came on. It is just like the Cultural Revolution with the Red Guards and worse. You Longs are targeted by someone very powerful. But we are here to help, the whole of Lu Ching Bay."

I bowed deeply. "I can't thank you enough."

"We the people thank you. You are our national leader, a freedom fighter. We are praying every day for you and all the souls who lost their lives—thousands of them. How could they?" He sighed wearily. "Now let's get you out there."

"Where?" I asked.

"To America."

"America!"

"I've got friends on the high sea. Amazing what a monk can do with prayer, huh?" Koon grinned.

DARKNESS PREVAILED over the choppy sea of Fujian as I stood at the head of the small steamboat that bobbed doggedly over waves, passing dark islands. The monk's bald head was the only shiny spot between the sea and the sky. I felt a thousand threads connecting me to the land and people I loved unspooling behind me. I couldn't bear to look back.

"Where are we going?" I asked.

"Taiwan Strait."

Lights gleamed ahead in the distance.

"Is that our contact?" I asked.

"No, that's the National Guard's High Sea Patrol Unit. Don't worry."

Koon gently pulled the boat next to the throbbing army steamer. A soldier in the National Guard's red uniform gripped the railing and shouted downward, "Who've you got there?"

"A rookie runner," the monk shouted back.

"So what is it gonna be?"

"No girls today. The martial law on land has complicated things, as you know. But I do have some fine French brandy, and this." The monk threw a small package up to him. The guard caught it and opened it.

"Monk! You're the best."

They parted like two ships that had never met.

"What did you give him?'

"Five hundred US dollars."

"Where did you get that?"

"I dabble in things that are unholy, Buddha forgive me." He clasped his hands and prayed, letting go of the steering wheel for a moment.

"I will pay you back ten times," I said.

"It is a gift from my heart and my redemption for things I should not have done and words I should not have spoken."

We spotted another boat. This time it was our contact. A light blinked five times.

"Everything is as planned. They have to wait there. They cannot cross the sea borderline," Koon said.

When we reached the fishing boat, I was pulled onto the other boat by three men.

"Come back when the sun shines again," Koon said, standing on the bobbing boat.

"I will," I promised.

"This is your land, the land of your father, and your father's father . . ." Koon circled the fishing boat once again in good-bye, then sailed off as I waved to him blindly.

"I am Tan Long," I said to the men.

"We know. And we are soldiers of the night." They saluted me.

I saluted them back. "Nameless soldiers, take me to a free land."

Tan

CHAPTER 64

1986

NEW YORK CITY

New York shouted at me. The skyline of the energetic city was the most beautiful sight I had ever seen. The shock of the buildings shooting to the sky, reaching for infinity, made my head light. New York! New York! The beautiful land. The plentiful land. The free land. I could not contain my joyful tears as I set foot in the city.

People—white, brown, yellow, black—rubbed shoulders while fighting for taxis, selling hot dogs, hawking cold pretzels, getting caught in half-open bus doors. The Plaza Hotel, the Pierre around the corner, Rockefeller Center in the distance, facing the gilded Saks Fifth Avenue. What a wonder. What a dream.

I walked along Broadway, cutting aimlessly across the gridded scheme of long streets and broad avenues. On the sidewalk, a young violinist was lost in his own melody. A painter dozed in the afternoon sun, his paint dripping on his sandaled toes. A Peruvian band wailed with the pungent flavor of their mountain tunes. The sassiness of Midtown. The ease of Greenwich Village—a sigh, a break before the streets slithered into Wall Street, which was darkened by business suits and choked by business cigars. Suddenly, the city came to an end and the land was no more. And there was the harbor, guarded by the angelic Statue of Liberty.

The first thing I did was look in the *Xing Dao Daily* and rent a small upstairs room in Chinatown.

"Where do you come from, with that odd accent?" my olive-shaped landlady asked me.

"China."

"I can find you a job as a dishwasher downstairs. You look like someone in need of money, and the food is free."

I became a dishwasher the next day, in a restaurant called Wei Bao. There were mountains of dishes, but I wasn't unhappy about it. I needed money, as the lady had pointed out, and I needed to lay low while waiting for my contacts to find me. The secret agents of China were all over the city. But Manhattan was still the best place to be a nobody. It was an ideal island on which to rest one's tired feet before treading to the next port of call on the distant horizon.

"You've got to stop this," I told the manager one night shortly after starting.

"What?" the manager barked back.

"The waste. Do you see? I am throwing away lobsters, half chickens, whole fish heads, and precious rice. Do you know how many children are starving in the world?"

The manager rolled his eyes. "This is America. People throw things away. They don't repair them. Don't fix them. Same way with their marriages; they divorce. No leftovers, you see."

"But that's wrong!"

"What planet are you from? What are you doing here if you care so much about starving children of the world?"

"We should all care."

"I leave it to you to care. My care is for the customers waiting in line. You go wash your dishes."

"It's all done."

"You got nothing to do?"

"Nothing. But I have been observing you. You make a point of being rude to people who want to eat here, as if you're doing them a favor."

The manager was silent, trying to find the right words to scold me with. In true New York style, he shouted back, "Who the fuck you think you are to talk to me like that? You manage anything before?"

"Yes, sir. I almost built China's Rockefeller Center."

"You did, huh? And I almost married Frank Sinatra."

I was surprised to find there were more than a dozen different newspapers in town. This *is* a free country, I thought. I read the *New York Times* and the *Wall Street Journal.* That left me with only enough change to buy either the *New York Post* or the *Daily News.* I opted for the *Post* because it was cheaper and had snappier headlines. So much to read, so little time.

The *Times* did a good job detailing the flight of my fellow student leaders. I read that Lan-Gai had been shot in the leg and taken into custody. Thousands of the students and workers—nameless, faceless—were dead. Hundreds had been arrested and were awaiting immediate execution. There were still numerous others, tied, shackled, with shaven heads, thrown into secret labor camps and prisons that no one in this world knew existed.

I prayed for them.

The next day, a handsome white man came to the restaurant and introduced himself as an operative from Human Rights Fighters.

"I am David Goldberg, president of HRF. I was referred to you through your contact in Taiwan. Welcome to America." He looked around the steamy, smelly kitchen and suggested, "Let's get out of here."

"But I have a job to do."

"Oh, no. You have a much more important job to do, believe me."

"But dishes have to be washed or they will stack up. Not only that, I need to deliver these leftovers to some homeless shelters near here."

"Leftovers for the homeless." Goldberg frowned.

"Yes, they taste great. I tried them."

"I know, but I don't think they would like knowing they were half-eaten. There is a difference between half-eaten and never-touched leftovers."

"But it is perfectly good food."

"I know, but this is America."

"Food is still food, no matter where you are."

"You are a fighter, Tan. I will show you how to be helpful. Come with me."

I gave up, washed my hands, and took off my apron.

Goldberg walked up to the manager and whispered into his ear.

"But who is going to do my dishes today?" the manager demanded.

"Here, take this." Goldberg took out a hundred-dollar bill and gave it to the manager, who took it and examined it against the fluorescent light.

"Give me that." I snatched the bill from the manager and returned it to Goldberg. "Since you haven't paid me, keep all my salary, and thank you for your help."

We left.

My first stop with Goldberg was the department store Macy's, where he bought me three suits.

"What for?" I asked.

"Media frenzy. We're going to crucify your government."

He arranged to have me appear on *The Today Show,* CNN, and some local news programs. They said I was a natural—charismatic, eloquent—and my lilting accent did not hurt, either. One local female anchor quipped that I could easily be a romantic Asian lead in Hollywood.

The most heartfelt reception was from the Chinese-American community. Wealthy patrons threw a lavish dinner party for me—red lobsters, live fish, crawling shrimps, half-dead frogs, liquor, and beer.

"What for? All this extravagance?" I asked the hostess, a Chinese society lady with an aged husband who owned countless take-out restaurants in the city and its boroughs.

"To celebrate your freedom."

"Why don't you save all the money instead and put it in a bank for the many comrades whom I have to help?"

"Don't worry about that. America is full of money. It will come. You are so handsome, convincing, and heroic that you make hearts melt and purses open. Why don't you write a book? That will bring you some money for yourself. All this hoopla will go away eventually and soon will be forgotten—people in America have a very short attention span. So make your mark now. Dollars. In order to do that, I suggest you lose your off-the-rack suits and have some tailored. Presentation is everything. They want to see a hero in custom-made suits. You are the image of patriotism, love, and bravery. Package it well."

"But I am not here to look for love or adulation. I am here to organize support so that I can return to China to run for president and have China liberated from tyranny."

"Point well taken. But you still need custom-tailored suits. I'm taking you to my husband's tailor tomorrow."

Just weeks later, in my newly tailored suit, I became the first Chinese Democracy leader to testify before the full Congress on Capitol Hill. When I walked onto the podium, before the true people's representatives, I received a standing ovation.

My speech was brief, but my message was powerful and alarming—China had returned to the dark ages, and the leader there was a threat to world peace.

My photographs appeared in all the newspapers of the world, and it was indeed a media frenzy as Goldberg had predicted. But it was all hype and no action. I began to wonder what I should do next. I had raised some money, but not enough for any substantial salvage program to get my friends out of China. Very soon, as the Chinatown society lady warned me, the sizzle went away.

Not long after I was confronted by my landlady, who stuck out her chubby hands and asked, "Where is my rent for the month, democracy fighter?"

"I will pay you soon."

"Where you going to find money? These streets aren't paved with gold, no matter what you've been told."

"You will not be shortchanged. I can always wash dishes downstairs if I come up short."

"Three days or I rent to someone else."

The next day, I took a lonely walk down Canal Street and ended up near Wall Street. The heart of capitalism, I thought, and I am penniless. I shook my head. But even in my state, I admired the relics of early capitalism stacked along this narrow street. The old Trinity Church had witnessed hundreds of years of the ups and downs of capitalism. J. P. Morgan, the financier with the bulbous, pockmarked nose, had walked this very surface. The Carnegies, the Vanderbilts, the Rockefellers, Salomon Brothers, Lehman Brothers—the list went on, long and thick. Legends and heroes, villains and foes, fairy tales.

I walked home with the slanting sun on my back and the heavy shadows of office buildings over my shoulders. I returned to my block, feeling sad and alone in a strange land, and wandered into the local liquor store to spend the last of my money on a bottle of Johnnie Walker. In my apartment, I drank the whiskey down, gulp by gulp, until I forgot where I was, and why. I threw the bottle on the floor, the noise causing the renter downstairs to poke the thin floor with a broom handle. Then I cried, sobbing like a regular drunk, doubling whatever sadness I had with the pulsating alcohol. All my friends had become ghosts. All their lives lost on that tragic midnight. Yesterday's dream became today's nightmare. My lost friends, my poor Sumi! Tears cradled me to sleep, until I was almost breathless except for the tiny puttering of my resilient heart.

I was awoken the next morning by a thunderous knocking that shook the door. "Not so loud," I groaned, staggering to open it. A smiling man with a mustache entered, wearing a custom-tailored suit, wingtip shoes, and French cuffs with gold abacus links.

"Mr. Long," the man said.

I wondered why in heaven's name a man so well dressed would be standing here in my meager apartment, smiling. But I wasn't dreaming.

"What can I do for you?" I asked.

"I am Peter Davidson, from J. P. Morgan and Company. Mr. Goldberg from Human Rights Fighters gave me your address, if you don't mind my intruding." He cleared his throat and surveyed my meager room. "Your grandfather, a venerable and highly respected central banker himself, deposited a certain sum at our Bermuda Island branch in his prime years."

"My grandfather? Do you know him?"

"We were classmates at Oxford. He picked Communist China. I dived into the bosom of capitalism. I am now the CEO Emeritus of J. P. Morgan Worldwide. And I am here to inform you of your grandfather's wishes and to hand over to you this sum."

"How much is this sum?"

"His initial deposit was twenty million US dollars."

The announcement almost jolted me out of my bed. The hangover was officially over. "And how much have you got there now?"

"A wise man your grandfather is. He advised us to put it all in stocks, and, as you know, we have just had a ten-year bull market."

"The number?"

"We have . . ."

"Doubled?" I guessed.

The man rolled his eyes at my impatience. "No."

"Twenty percent growth?"

"No."

"You're killing me."

"We gambled with some Wall Street arbs."

"Arbitrage bankers? Betting on hostile mergers and acquisition deals?"

Mr. Davidson's mustache twitched in surprise and satisfaction at my knowledge. "We quadrupled. The account is now worth in the neighborhood of eighty million dollars. But per your grandfather's request, I can only give you sixty million, which is the dividend. The twenty million in seed money shall remain under the care of our bank's trust department, in perpetuity."

I jumped up and hugged the man. Then I thought of a question. "Did Grandfather ever tell you where the seed money came from?"

"We never ask questions of that nature. We are bankers."

"I see."

"However, I do feel that it is a suitable compensation for a brilliant life wasted behind that bamboo curtain. Imagine your grandfather having made the choice I made. He could have been the titan of a banking empire in Hong Kong or Taiwan."

After the man retreated down the squeaky stairs, I let out an animal cry that shocked a few pedestrians down the street. "I am rich! Filthy rich!"

When I calmed down, I smiled. Grandfather, you old rascal! You did embezzle those millions like they said. You really did!

I leaned out the small window and shouted, "I love you, Grandfather!" hoping the old man could hear me on the other side of the Pacific Ocean.

"I love you, too!" shouted back a befuddled homeless man sitting at the street corner.

Shento

CHAPTER 65

1998

BEIJING

In mid-November, Beijing lay silently under its first snow. Heng Tu, in his late eighties now, heaved weakly, half asleep in his chaise like a crocodile in shallow water. His eyes teared up with every hacking cough, and his legs were swollen despite their supine position. Life, now consisting of warm piss, cold diapers, yellow mucus, and a smelly spit cloth, was narrowed down to a tunnel of labored breaths and wobbling stumbles. A piss without a burning tail was a prayer answered, and making it to the urinal, his monumental ambition.

Heng Tu used to love snow the same way he used to love a lot of things. He had, in a youthful literary outburst, authored a little revolutionary limerick in praise of the cottony flakes. The first three verses deserved no repetition, but the last one, an awkward attempt to steal a rhyme, was a real heartbreaker. "Snow that set my heart aglow is the true foe to a white soul." Red being the hue of Communism.

But old age had dampened his youth. Dreams dropped and lust sagged. Now the wintry chill, puffing its breath at fogged windowpanes, made his night seem long and his old body ache. The moon looked like a lone orphan. Seasons, the rhythm of life, now became ladders of escalating curses—late autumn was guaranteed bronchitis; early winter, assurance of lingering pneumonia; December, a bone breaker; and January, February, March, and April, a den of merciless thieves.

Summer was his foe with all its heat, noise, plump water, and bladed grasses belonging to the flowers, mosquitoes, frogs, and twittering cicadas—little lives and little bugs. All he deserved was the silence of a chilling night, the detachment of cold winter. He saw himself as a dwindling man of winter.

In the dimness of Heng Tu's soul, he felt the world turning around him, but his dead-fruit eyes saw little. He heard voices soaring and hovering over him, magnified by the silence within him, but his wax-filled ears understood nothing. On a good day, he lived what was left of his life with humor, and poked his doctors—the best, they said—begging them to give him their famous reverse count of his life.

"How many days do I have left?" Heng Tu would mumble.

"You'll live forever."

"Who wants to?"

"We want you to."

So he started his own countdown. Ten, nine, eight . . . Then he forgot his count and restarted the next day. All the while he was dying, he would nudge me to prepare for that final tally of a man—the funeral.

"Too early for that," I would say gently, sitting by his side in his private chamber.

"Never too early to prepare for your death. I want a simple funeral. I'm a revolutionary, you see." He paused to heave some labored breaths. "Not the dump-you-in-the-ditch revolutionary, but a simple, elegant revolutionary."

Bei Bao Mountain, the site of many dead Communist martyrs, would be a natural choice. But Heng Tu thought it a lair for a bunch of dead thieves, many of whom, at one point or another, had made his life a living hell. It should be plowed into a boneless field and turned into vistas of sweet corn and crawling potatoes, with vines afoot. But I would hear nothing of it. I sat by his side every day to chat and cry. Heng Tu cherished those tears, not that he thought he needed them, but he was still comforted by seeing them. Wiping the tears off my cheeks, Heng Tu felt loved, and that made his heart heave with sweet joy. He vaguely recalled a saying he had read somewhere, sometime in his past: *To be loved, even if by one person, is proof that one has lived.* He used to laugh at that trivialization of the abundance of life. A revolutionary wouldn't be caught dead with such a tender thought. But now a revolutionary was dying, and only now did he understand the wisdom of those words. How ironic that some knowledge only came when near death, that some truth was illuminated only in the darkening of life. He thought of another proverb: *Only in death did one know how he should live.* He smiled at the truth—the truth of the folly of life. Always too late. And never enough.

Along with the love he felt from me, he felt the angst of having to leave me alone in this world. Heng would die with a sigh in his heart like the rest of the tortured mortals. He, too, would leave an earthly trace of his lingering soul because he would breathe his last breath still loving me, and with that, he would never be in complete oblivion.

"You'll inherit nothing good from me," he whispered one day to me during my daily visit.

"You have given me everything," I said sincerely.

"In fact, it'll be worse than nothing."

"My own father could not have given me better things," I said.

"Is that so?"

I nodded. "You've given me love."

We cried, consoling each other.

"And for that, my boy, my legacy to you can only be one thing, one thing only—loneliness."

There was a long and agonizing lull. Then Heng Tu heard me say, "Because no one has loved me so."

"And no one has cared for me more. Whatever power you will inherit from me will only magnify your loneliness. No wonder old emperors used to call themselves the Lonesome One."

"I'll never be alone with you in my heart," I swore, dropping heavily to my knees.

Day and night, asleep or awake, Heng Tu prayed—not to any particular god, but to that invisible power that infiltrated his being—for enlightenment that would unlock the knob of his guilt and dissolve my suffering, assuring me a joy-filled earthly life without him.

It came in bits and pieces until the tapestry of his final words were stitched together in his mind. Finally, in the thick of winter, the tide of death quickened its feet. Heng Tu was that feathery bird, chased by the rolling waves, thrust forward into his destiny. He suddenly choked on a peck of blood-laced mucus that lodged near his lolling Adam's apple. His face reddened, bursting with beady sweats, while his body paled with limpness from the neck down.

Nurse Tang bent down to give him mouth-to-mouth after sucking out the mucus with her powerful lungs, trying to save him from the kiss of death. In a breathless duel, Heng Tu was resurrected, but only briefly. In a trembling voice, he begged, "Please write this down."

"What is it, Mr. President?"

"My last words for Shento."

All three doctors attending him pulled out their pens, awaiting the weighty words of power to be spelled out.

Slowly, with labored breath, Heng Tu huffed and puffed along. "Shento . . . remember . . . Sumi . . ."

Pens flew urgently.

". . . who is . . . your heart."

Heads nodded.

"Remember Balan . . . your soul." Hacking coughs ensued. "You should know . . . I was not . . . the one . . . who saved you . . . on . . ." Another mucus attack. Heng Tu trembled, his eyes bulging.

"On what?" a sweating doctor asked.

"Mr. President, please don't die."

". . . the . . . boat."

The three looked at one another.

Heng Tu fell docilely dead, like an infant who had never opened his eyes to see the world.

AT MY INAUGURATION, ten thousand people gathered to march before me in Tiananmen Square, carrying my large portrait and shouting, "Long live President Shento! Long live the Communist Party!" Fireworks went wild in the night sky, and songs and music rang out all over the city. Standing on the review podium, watching the antlike creatures shouting their meaningless slogans, I did not feel an ounce of raging joy, a morsel of head-numbing elation, or a tinkling of a soaring soul. I felt fatherless, and the extravaganza only felt like a continuation of Heng Tu's funeral, the boisterous music like a eulogy sweeping an endless empty space.

On this golden night of Napoleonic triumph, all I could think of was Heng Tu's last words and the irony of it all. Heng Tu had not been my savior. I had risked my life more than once for the old man. But I felt no regret. My love for the old man, though misplaced, had redeemed me, and such conviction had borne fruit, as was evident so abundantly before my eyes.

Looking into the masses beneath me in the bustling square, I wondered who had saved me, and for what unfathomable reason. Who was it? A man of pity or a man of kindness, allowing me to continue living so I could redeem myself? Or was he vicious, willing that I only leap from one sinking ship of fate to another, and continue my suffering, fatherless, motherless, with the world gazing on? The last soul of Balan, the boy who was meant to die with his very first breath. Who had saved me?

Heng Tu had known all along who I was, and still held me in his trust and faith. The blood, the son, ill gotten or well bred, of his sworn enemy. Or maybe that was the wickedness of Heng Tu, the mastery of the ultimate hatchet man, using the knife of a son to kill the heart of a father. Blood for blood, except it was Long blood all along. In the end, it was the son, I, the forsaken bastard, who had his own father stabbed and thrown into the sea, spilling the same blood that flowed within me, chasing out my own brother.

I put my hands in my coat pockets. I could almost see my hands dripping with invisible blood. But still no regret.

I wondered. Wondered about the powerful man who had believed the urgent tale of the necklace, told on the stern of that rocking navy boat where I was to be executed. Where are you? Why did you do it? Why aren't you up here beside me, claiming what is rightfully yours, the prize of saving the life of a *guiren,* a noble man? Had you come to me now, without asking, I would give you the stars and the moon within my galaxy, the delicacy and rarity within my kingdom. I would redeem my debt, lightening not your burden, but mine.

I sighed. For the rest of the inaugural evening, I felt like a weak old man, sagging with wrinkled thoughts. Oh, that cursed legacy—a destiny of loneliness. In my mind, I searched for things tangible, palpable. The only foothold was from the distant past. The echoes of Sumi's voice in the orphanage, shouting, her dainty feet, bare and bony in flight over the tender grass and morning dew.

I thirsted that night for those who could not return my love. Sumi gone, Balan burned. And yet in loving them—the unattainable—in the dead silence of my mind, I felt peace. I closed my eyes, letting my mind fly off to the land of my birth, to those rugged mountains. How I wished I were there. But I was surrounded, thick and tight, by my Young Generals, all dangling with medals of ranks that meant the world to them. Beyond them rings of security pushed away the well-wishers and the lesser officers of the court. I saw only masks of ingratiating faces. I found no friends, not even those who called themselves so.

Another round of congratulations woke me up. It was Hito, who pushed a flute of champagne into my hand while pointing out that the finest marching band in my army had arrived to play a song especially commissioned for my ascendance to the presidency.

The music was powerful and the rhythm strong. It reminded me of the mountains and the sea. I nodded and waved my hand, like Chairman Mao used to, and the masses beneath me roared with grateful shouts and excited shrieks.

I left early with my entourage, much to the dismay of my jumping Young Generals, and returned to my mansion behind the red walls, only to lie awake all night. My mind kept replaying images of my childhood. Then all the magnificent colors that filled those vivid years vanished into a blank. In that blankness, I was stripped of all my power, and returned to being the naked bastard that I was. My heart was hungry and my feet cold. And the outside world, shut out completely from my presidential mansion, was a muddy, pitted road in Balan during the wettest of monsoon seasons, lined by a myriad of rotten corpses. Hundreds of demonic soldiers were shouting, pursuing me like weak prey scratching a slippery cliff until I fell and kept falling into a gleeful current of a tumbling sea.

In this sadness I found comfort. In reliving this misery I found happiness. How very strange. I remained in this split state of mind the whole night, all the while thinking that fatigue would finally conquer me, and that I would sleep. When I woke up the next day, the world would be fine again. But I was wrong. My fractured mind forced me to stay in a dreamlike state for the next few days, during which I refused to eat or talk to anyone. I lingered in the memory of my childhood, trembling cold, though it was warm in my mansion. I felt nauseous and threw up several times. It worried those around me. They thought that their newly minted president was going out of his mind.

One day, when my instinct of preservation fluttered, I grudgingly agreed to an examination by both a traditional Chinese doctor and a white-coated Western-trained physician. The former felt my pulse, looked at my tongue, drummed my chest, and listened to the hollow but compact sound of my intestines. The latter drew a voluminous amount of my red blood, took skeletal pictures of my bony scalp and the ribbed ladder of my chest, ground my virile balls, and finally stuck one unapologetic middle finger up my anus, to my mighty indignation.

"There is nothing the matter with you, physically," said the physician who had studied Western medicine. "Your heart is strong and lungs clear. All your other organs appear to be normal and functioning well. Barring the unforeseeable, you should live to be a hundred." The good doc knew it was the head that was sick, but he dared not say so because the truth and its twin, honesty, had more than once landed him in jail, and he did not wish to relive that nightmare.

"Mr. President, you are as healthy as Wu Soon," the traditionalist told me, referring to an ancient legend of a man who killed a tiger with his bare hands and downed eighteen jugs of strong liquor without a burp. "Your life will be as long the Yangtze River." He should have warned me that my worry should not be my health, but my mind, a mind of darkness, a mind that had long gone awry, but he didn't. Such talk would cause the doctor to lose his Communist Party membership and push him down to the bottom of the hospital hierarchy.

DEPRESSION DEEPENED, and in those most vulnerable moments of my life, Sumi became my only hope. I longed for her, desperately. Every day was a slow torture, every night a simmering burn. Weeks became longer and the months darker each day she wasn't with me.

One autumn day, I jetted over the Gobi Desert to the Xinjiang prison where Sumi was detained, and peeped at her from a half-shut dark window, secretly and nervously watching her roam the pitted courtyard.

She was still beautiful, with her slender waist and the poetry of her motion as she picked her way among the pebbled path. I cursed the touch of silver streaking her flowing hair. It made me sad. Damn age. She should have eternal youth. If not for herself, then for me. But the snowflakes of winter had fallen and whitened her. I broke down and wept silently. How had I lost her, the most precious thing in this world?

I wanted to hold her tightly from behind, to soothe her, to make love to her, comfort and devour her, inch by inch, tasting her love and her soul, that sweetness of life. Suddenly, Sumi seemed to sense my presence; she turned to look toward the darkness of the window and stiffened. Sumi locked her stare on me and slowly backed away. Not wanting her to slip away, I leaped into the courtyard and ran to her. My long arms encircled her and lifted her up. She drummed my head, shoulders, and chest with her fists, but I did not mind at all. I was intoxicated by the fragrance of her body. I kissed her face, her neck, her bosom, moaning dreamily, "Oh, my heart, my soul, do forgive me . . ."

The stiff muzzle of the gun holstered at my waist jabbed Sumi's ribs. Without hesitation, she reached for the cold handle, yanked the gun free, wrapped her finger around the trigger, and pulled it three times.

My face contorted into a knob of puzzlement, but not yet of pain. My mouth let out little jerky and staccato cries. My hands loosened, my arms dropped, and I fell limply at Sumi's feet. "I deserve this . . . Forgive me . . ."

Red blood poured down my leg, but I didn't seem to notice or care. "Can you . . . forgive me now?" I gasped as a team of garrison soldiers rushed in.

THOUGH THE SHOTS didn't kill me, they did fracture my right kneecap, rendering me a cripple with a dragging limp. Bullets from another hand would have been unimaginable. But from her, it was a punishment I took gladly. As days went by and my pain lessened, I felt lightened by a thousand times. The dark thing inside me had died with the pain. Fragments from the precious past, my long-forgotten youth, seemed to have returned, some sweet, some bitter, but all good. When alone, in the quiet of the night, I replayed that encounter before the shooting—every little detail. It fanned my desire for Sumi, and the desire only flamed stronger desire, which caused me to think of nothing else in life, in work, in anything—only Sumi. Thoughts of her occupied me totally and completely. The siege was seamless. There was no escaping her.

My appetite returned and my zest for life was reborn. I would have my dinner table set for two in my elegant private dining room, decorated in a leafy Ming dynasty motif, and pretend to have animated conversation with an imagined Sumi sitting across from me. With dim candlelight and soft music in the background, I would laugh and drink as if my miraged dinner mate was enjoying the meal as much as I was.

In my heart, I thanked Sumi every day for the gift of her life, and I swore to do everything in my power to win her forgiveness, and ultimately her love.

What should I do? What could I ever do to make it all right again? I had done so much wrong and wrought so much wrath. My heart sank at the thought. The goal of redemption seemed beyond me. How I wished that the world was simple and innocent again.

ON MY FORTIETH BIRTHDAY, I locked myself deep in my spacious Zhong Nan Hai mansion, to the utter puzzlement of my closest Young Generals, who wanted to mark this memorable occasion. I wanted to be alone. In a dark mood, I found tremendous solace in a foreign poem I accidentally came across in my library, where I spent most of my time now. It was written by some wise and hopeless poet from another land, but the words seemed to be coming from my own head.

Whatever gods may be
No life is forever
Dead men rise up never
Even the weariest river
Winds somewhere safe to the sea

I took a long drink from a bottle of liquor and smiled at the wisdom. Death is the golden key. I was grateful that all lives are rivers that end in the sea. What a beautiful solution. When the camel got weary, the sun deadly, with no oasis in sight, death descended to relieve one like an angel. The cycle of life, so perfect. The best of life is death, for only then did the living find their rest.

I slammed the liquor bottle on the floor, thinking to use the jagged edges on myself, but the fluffy carpet saved the bottle. I laughed hysterically. I was the commander in chief of the army, navy, and air force, and I couldn't find a weapon suitable for my own demise. There was still liquor left in the bottle, so I tilted my head and drank until I swallowed the last drop. I was now ready to try again. I strove to raise my right arm to throw the bottle down, but it refused to follow my desire. The liquor was far too powerful. I tried once more, but the bottle slipped and fell with a dull thud on the carpet a second time.

No matter how hard I struck the bottle, it would not break. The more I tried, the dizzier I got, until a drunken stupor overtook me. I surrendered to the looming darkness. The peace that I had so craved would follow for as long as the potency of the brew lasted.

When I woke the next day, I was surrounded by nurses, doctors, and guards. Hito hovered over me as I lay limply in my bed.

"What do you want from me?" I rasped.

Hito smiled. "I'm here to give you two birthday presents."

"I don't need presents. I need . . . death. Give me death."

"This gift might promise that," Hito said, handing me a small package.

I knocked it away and it fell onto the floor. The rough wrapping broke and a pair of old wooden sandals, a size suitable for a child, fell out.

I sat up, staring at them. "My sandals." I carefully picked them up and shakily pressed them to my chest, tears rolling down my cheeks. "Where did you find these?" I asked urgently.

"A mad old man gave them to me."

"Where is he?"

"He is finally gone."

"Gone where? Tell me!"

"He called himself a doctor from Balan and came to our outer gate, begging to see you, his southern accent almost unintelligible. We drove him off. But he kept coming back. Three days later he was still there, refusing to eat and threatening to kill himself if we did not pass his gift to you, cutting off three fingers in protest. He would only leave when I promised I would give it to you."

I cried out. "Go find him!" I ordered.

"He's gone. He said he was returning to the mountains."

"What else did he say?"

"He gave me this note. For your eyes only."

I took the roll of silk, written with Balanese script. Through the blurry curtain of my tears, I read urgently.

My dearest boy,

Buddha saved me from the village fire, for reasons beyond my knowing. When I awoke, you were gone, and I had thought for so long that you were dead, my precious son. Oh, those years of solitude, those years of sadness without you and your mama.

I have cut off three fingers for your sake, one for each decade that I have missed you. Forgive me for having given you up in my thoughts. But you were always in my prayers. All the decades of sorrow must end. And the decades of blood must be cleansed. I'm here to claim you back to the purity of our land, away from the sins of this dusty world. I'm here to save again the boy that I once saved from the cliff.

I have another blessing awaiting you at our home in Balan. Please don't make me wait any longer. I am an old man. Death is with me every day now.

Your baba, by faith and by grace,
in life and in death

I cried bitterly like a child. I closed my eyes and prayed silently, for the first time in many long years, to the invisible tall mountains of Balan. Peace and love returned to my heart. I was happy. Grateful. I could feel hope again. I closed my eyes and let my mind travel like an ethereal spirit across the red soil of the northern plain, past gleaming rivers to hover over lush mountaintops. And there, in the ever dreamy greenness of a summer valley, I saw the face of my adoptive father, his wrinkles thick like the veins of mountain rocks weaving slowly into a smile of kindness, of love and Buddha. My baba opened his arms, embracing me. I felt loved again.

A powerful thought came to me. I quickly pulled out a pen from my desk, lest it fly away. I composed a letter that I could never have imagined myself writing only minutes before. I wrote till my hands shook.

Dear Sumi,

I'm setting you free, free to fly the earth again. And I'm giving up the seal of power that has condemned me thus far to never-ending servitude. The old Shento has died. A new one stands. I've reached the bottom of the abyss. Only darkness I see, save for one gleam of light that is you.

Forgive me that I have sinned. Spare me a chance so that I can redeem, act by act, the wrongs, the sins, countless that they might be. I am ripe for a new beginning; it can only be granted by your grace.

Join me. Come cleanse me in the pristine air of Balan, the pure stream of my homeland. Come remake Balan with me, dig up the ruins, rebuild upon what is left and what has endured. Come mend my broken wings, lighten my darkened soul. Come, so I can repay you what cannot be repaid in many lives to come.

With trembling hand,
Your soiled one

I kissed and sealed the envelope. Tomorrow, my words of love would go far away, to the only girl I had ever loved. Tomorrow, I would risk it all.

Tan

CHAPTER 66

1998
NEW YORK CITY

I dressed in my favorite Savile Row tailored suit, wingtip shoes, Hermès tie, and a pair of cuff links in the shape of an abacus, a gift from the J. P. Morgan banker. All this was merely my uniform, the cost of doing business in the midst of Manhattan skyscrapers. And what a business I had accumulated with my grandfather's seed money—shipping, stocks, construction, oil, and real estate. I owned a few buildings on Wall Street, my favorite being 40 Wall Street, a classic monster of capitalism, sitting solidly amid other titans on the street. But I favored Midtown in general, and Park Avenue in particular. That was where I chose to situate my headquarters, surrounded by other stylish and smart members of the capitalist elite, modern law firms and latter-day investment banks. I never regretted the price I paid for the pitch-black high-rise with a marbled floor atrium and a grand rooftop, which allowed me to arrive by helicopter. The helipad was circled by a jogging track, and had the most magnificent panoramic view of the ritziest section of Manhattan. Within only a year, the value of the building had already doubled. Crazy Manhattan real estate. You had to live here to understand its beauty.

There was a construction boom going on in the Far East, and shipping was better than ever. Goods had to be shipped out from manufacturing hotbeds in Asia, and oil and gas reserves that my company had helped to drill and distill from Russian Siberia were gold mines that only called for a bigger fleet of ocean liners. The list could go on and on. But business was not all that occupied my mind.

Not a day went by when I did not think about my movement, about democracy in China, and that tyrant of a half brother, Shento. The former I would die for; the latter, fight against to the death. I had gotten hundreds of dissidents out of China and sent millions of dollars in aid to the people there actively fighting Shento's reign. Tens of millions more would be on their way, as soon as I could get my banks in Hong Kong to convert them into renminbi, the currency in China.

The best news, the knowledge I had been longing for, was that not only were Grandfather and Mother safe and sound, but Father had been saved by a fisherman and was residing quietly under a disguised identity in a fishing village, under the care of Mr. Koon.

But all these wonders in life and gifts from Buddha only deepened my grief over the absence of Sumi in my life. I often found myself standing in my lonely apartment on the fortieth floor of Trump Tower, looking into the sea of lights blinking at my feet, thinking and dreaming about Sumi.

I could see the red and desolate Gobi Desert surrounding Sumi, burning and withering her youth and beauty. The tranquil moonlight, the goddess of love, stretched from the Atlantic to the Pacific, linking me beyond the oceans, the plains, and the valleys to Sumi. I laughed with her, talked with her, and dreamed with her. To hear the echo of her thoughts and of her soul, I would read a passage from her book and then close my eyes, remembering how she'd soften in my embrace.

As time went by, Sumi ceased to exist in the world of concrete things and thrived only in the creeked echoes, brooked shadows, and willowed valleys of my soul. I feared the day when she would be no more. Every day that thought tortured and punished me, an ever-enlarging emptiness that bled into the core of my existence. At times I was consumed by burning guilt. Why did I get to live free while she suffered a dark dungeon existence? And I was not just living free, but living well, Park Avenue well, Trump Tower well. Too damned well.

When will I see you again? The thought flooded me every day, wherever I was—in my opulent office, in my limousine, during heated business meetings with my ambitious employees, and throughout rosy reports of my company's staggering success.

When?

One day I received a phone call from my old friend David Goldberg, who invited me to lunch. The man usually called for two reasons, one of them being money. I had transformed from a dissident needing help to one able to offer ample assistance. When the call was about money, Goldberg was a charming and patient man. But today, he sounded much too breathy and urgent for the call to be of a financial nature. The call must be about the other reason—Sumi. Hurriedly, I had my secretary shove aside all my appointments and make a reservation at a Japanese restaurant near my office.

"I hate this restaurant," Goldberg said, loosening his tie upon arrival.

"I do, too," I said.

"Why are we eating here then?"

"The prices drive everyone away so we can talk comfortably."

"In that case, sake, please," Goldberg said.

"Only if you let me pay."

"Have I ever said no?" Goldberg studied his menu. "And you ought to be treating, for what I have to tell you."

"Do tell me, then," I said impatiently.

Goldberg looked around the nearly empty restaurant and whispered, "Our mole inside the Xinjiang prison system informed me this morning that the devil went to see Sumi."

"What did he want from her?" I asked, my chest heaving.

"You won't like hearing this."

"Another round of sake, please," I shouted to the waiter.

"Love."

"Love? The man cut out her tongue!"

"Our man reported that Shento was all over her, hugging and kissing her, until she shot him . . ."

"She shot him? Is he dead?"

"No, unfortunately, he survived."

I downed the shot of sake and slammed it on the table so loud that even the sushi chef stopped what he was doing and came out to apologize for the tardiness of the service.

"There is only one thing left to do," I said.

"Can I help in any way?"

"Find me the specific location of Sumi's whereabouts—the exact position of the prison in the desert. And get me the security routine of the prison."

"I don't think that's a good idea . . ." Goldberg put down his chopsticks.

"One more thing. Please let her know in advance so she is prepared."

"I'm not going to help. You'll die trying to save her. She will . . ."

"Get me what I need. In case of my death, a million dollars will be willed to your discretion."

"I don't know what to say."

"Say nothing. Just do what I asked of you."

"Tan, don't do it," Goldberg begged quietly as I got up to leave the restaurant.

THE SKY WAS BLUE, dreamy blue, the mountains menacing, and the earth scrappy and hilly, lying vulnerable and naked below me. I felt small and insignificant, sandwiched between a giant heaven and a mammoth earth, in the dusty flight across this golden desert.

I only had one thought in mind—Sumi. Every second that clicked by brought me closer to her. I had been nervous when we started out from the border of Afghanistan with the help of Ali Mossabi, Goldberg's Arab friend and a fellow human rights activist. But when the helicopter crossed the sparse yellow China border, I calmed. All the nervous energy condensed into an urgency to save Sumi. I played and replayed the images of seeing her again—embraces, kisses, words of love, checking every inch of her, every cell of her to make sure she was whole, total, and complete. A feeling of elation swept across me. Atop it all, I was acutely aware of the danger and, yes, insanity, as Goldberg said, of being involved in such a covert mission.

The fact that I was surrounded by former navy SEALs was only a small consolation. For I was facing one crazy devil. If the mission had been leaked, Shento would have deployed the meanest, biggest weapons to bring us down.

Endless sand dunes cut across my vision, and a dried riverbed swept by. In a few minutes, we would be changing aircraft. From that point on, there would be no turning back.

"The flag," the pilot, a Vietnam veteran, said, looking ahead.

On the horizon, a dot of a flag burned in the drabness of the sand, enlarging as we inched closer and closer. A few men were waving, standing near a helicopter painted with a red flag, the insignia of the People's Liberation Army.

Thank you, Father, I whispered. Father had helped me concoct this operation. Father had contacted men from the old army whom he would still trust with his life. And these men were here, ready and willing to take me to where my love lay.

Our helicopter circled around the red flag and landed, causing a sandstorm. For minutes, dust swirled and whirled as if cursed by heaven. Then it settled.

My six men and I, all dressed in green Chinese army uniforms, jumped down onto the ridges and furrows of the sand. The touch of the ancient desert was soft, forbidding. No man had been here before.

Though time was life, and every ticking second its heartbeat, I felt an undeniable urge to kiss the land. This was the land of my father, and my father's father. A land that forever resided in my dreams. In the minute grains of sand, I could feel the love of my parents, and taste their tears and anguish.

I knelt and bent my head deeply, kowtowing five times, one for each of my loved ones. Then I stood up and gazed into the distance.

"Are you good to go, Mr. Long?" Captain Gibson shouted. He was the squad commander. The Chinese army helicopter's propellers had started up again, and the turbulence threw the earth into another sandy whirlwind.

I hopped in the open door, and with a push, I was on board. As I looked around the crowded helicopter, I was stunned.

"Father? Mother? Grandfather?" Seated inside, Father was dressed in a green uniform, with guns, a grenade, and ammunition strapped all over him. Grandfather cradled a nasty Uzi in his arms. And Mother, ever the delicate dresser, had wrapped her head with a silk shawl and was carefully holding a small silver revolver. They reached over and hugged me in a stifling embrace.

"Oh, my dear son. You look so wonderful," Mother said.

"Tan, boy, you've grown a beard," Father said.

We peeled away to size up one another. Years of separation seemed to disappear like vapor in a hot desert. Mother kept squeezing my hand. Father just looked at me, smiling proudly. Grandfather was the first to speak again. "So I hear you are doing really well."

"Thank you, Grandfather. I did not know how farsighted you were. I wish only to have a third of your wisdom."

"That might be in question, considering what we about to do today."

"Why did you all come to risk your lives?" I asked.

There was a moment of silence as the helicopter flew over the sea of waving sand.

"We thought to catch a ride out of China with you," Mother said pragmatically.

"And I can help," Father said.

"So can I," Grandfather said. "What good is an old man like me, anyway? Let's kick some butt."

I nodded silently, my eyes tearing up. I hugged the three of them again and again, as if it was the first time and the last.

"Now," said Father, "We'll be there in a matter of minutes. I have my ground people guarding the position for our retreat. As soon as we snatch her, we will cross the border into Outer Mongolia. From there I have friends waiting to take us up and across Russia."

"Russia?" I asked.

Father nodded. "Where money can buy anything."

"From there, I'll show you the world," I promised.

"Preparing for landing," the pilot announced. In the swirling horizon, a speck of buildings appeared, sprawled on the desert like a coiled snake. A red flag limped weakly from its pole, and guards were visible with automatic rifles slung over their sloping shoulders.

My heart was thumping at my throat, my head hot and throbbing with an urgent rush of blood. An intense feeling of hate mingled with the softening emotion of love. My breathing was labored and my hands shook slightly.

The noise stirred the sleepy compound. A few dogs were barking mutely, running in circles beneath the aerial shadow. There was a general confusion of guards running and pulling their guns ready from their shoulders.

"Act quickly, men," Captain Gibson shouted.

"Yes, sir," his men replied.

"Our operation will end in two minutes," Gibson said.

"Yes, sir."

"Are you ready, Mr. Long?" Gibson asked.

"Yes, Captain."

"We'll cover you as you go in. When Sumi is in our hands, leave her to us. You return immediately to our helicopter."

"What if we can't find her?" I asked.

"We abort our operation in two minutes, no matter what. Or we'll be risking all our lives."

The helicopter almost kissed the ground now. It flew over Sumi's courtyard. I saw a little man flying a red flag there. The contact.

"Bye for now, Mother, Father, Grandfather."

"We'll cover you," Father promised.

"I have a feeling she's not going to be there," Mother suddenly said.

"Mother, this is not the time."

"Just that you know," she said.

The guards down below were shouting and running frantically. Father shouted through the helicopter's speaker, "Xinjiang Army Division is conducting a surprise military maneuver. There is no need for alarm. Please stay calm."

The guards calmed a bit. The helicopter door slid open and four of the men jumped down into the courtyard with Gibson in the lead.

I dashed to window 307, marked by the contact. From there, I glimpsed Sumi's tiny cell. It was all darkness. "Sumi!" I shouted.

No response.

I ran to the cell. It was empty.

The contact shouted weakly, his voice swallowed up by the helicopter's roar, gesturing violently.

"Where is Sumi?" I asked.

"She is gone!"

"Killed?"

"No, just gone."

"Where?"

"Don't know."

"You mean I've come here for nothing?"

"She left this for you." The contact handed over a small folded note. "Read it on the helicopter. Go now, before they grow suspicious and start using the machine guns."

"But I can't . . ."

"You must go now."

"Please, what else can you tell me about her?"

"Nothing else. She left in a hurry."

"One minute and ten seconds," Gibson shouted. "I see a machine gun at eleven."

I was lost. I could not believe this was my fate. I knelt, pounding the ground with my fists. Gibson shouted again. "Let's move out, Mr. Long. Mission is aborted."

"I can't go without Sumi!"

From the bullets hitting the roof, I could tell there was more than one machine gun at work. They sounded like pelting raindrops. I kissed the cell bar through which Sumi must have looked every day for these last few years.

As I turned away from the empty cell, a bullet struck me in the right thigh. Instantly, I was brought down. Blood wet my trousers. I did not feel any pain. On the contrary, I felt proud that my blood was shed here for her. I smiled and stood up, leaning on Captain Gibson, and let the man carry me. I came for love and left with love in my heart.

The captain and two of his men threw me into the chopper, and off we flew into the yellowness of an endless desert.

It was long time before I could think again. I barely noticed my mother, who had been crying, or my father, who was cursing. Grandfather just quietly prayed. I opened up the fist that still clutched the bloodied note from Sumi. In pain, I read words from the one whom I would love forever and who had once again eluded me.

My dearest Tan,

By the time you read this letter, I will have journeyed to the south, where our love began. In my solitude, I often dwelled on those golden days of youth. Oh, how I longed to relive those times gone by. A timely invitation from Mr. Koon to be principal of the Lu Ching Bay High School made my wish possible. The peace of Lu Ching Bay matches the silence within me; lonesome I will never ever be again. I will be surrounded by the sounds and fury of the youthful and vibrant. Life will be reclaimed vicariously and prolonged as such.

Good-bye, love.
Sumi

P.S. Tai Ping is with me. He told me he loves you. And he should.

Shento

山头

CHAPTER 67

1998

BALAN

Had I to paint the portrait of my death coming, I would have brushed my blank canvas with the following scenery—a Balanese mountain peak in the fog, a soaring eagle vying for the deep blue sky, the undying spirit of the young mother who bore me. The hillsides are dotted with rampant, dreamy flowers growing in clusters, breaking away from the crush of boulders and rocks, amid cracks of earth. The first glow of a rising sun floods the earth with a soothing touch. In the air floats the thin sweet echoes of young shepherds calling to their flocks of sheep and yaks. Amid all the things painted are the shadows of my loved ones, those faces who frequent my dreams.

But reality is often the antithesis of one's dream.

On the slope of Mount Balan, I limped along, trailed only by my own shadow. Coming to meet me was my baba, the old doctor who was now half-blind and nearly deaf. His shaking hands—three fingers missing—felt the space before him, anticipating and waiting. "Shento. Shento, my child." Tears rolled down the old doctor's twitching cheeks.

I threw myself forward on the dusty path and knelt before him in silence. "I failed you, Baba," I said.

"You didn't. Your fate did." Baba held my face. He kissed my forehead, then hung a silver medallion over my neck.

"My medallion," I burst out in surprise. The fateful gift from Ding Long, snatched away from me on that cursed navy boat. "Where did it come from?"

"The man who saved you from your execution."

"Who?"

"The same man who entrusted me with this," Baba said, handing me a sealed envelope. "An elderly man who found me after reading about my hunger strike outside your palace in Beijing."

Quickly, I ripped it open. I was shocked to see a certified check in the glaring amount of $20 million made out to my name. The payer bank was none other than the fabled J. P. Morgan and Company of New York, United States of America.

There was only one man who could have done both deeds—the banker. My face paled and my cheeks burned. My hands trembled as if the check were a sheet of flame, jabbing the tenderest part of my soul. "No. No, it can't be."

"This medallion is a symbol of your past. This money stands for your future," Baba comforted me. "In the custom of Balan, that tradition of piety and blood, you have done nothing to deserve either. But they are tokens of love. The grace lies with the giver, in the act of giving. The taker must not shame them with refusal. Both gifts should reside in your possession forever, or the grace will be defiled and love lost."

"Is there anyone else waiting for me?" I asked, barely having composed myself.

"No," Baba said. "Just me and this letter for you, posted from Fujian."

Desperately, I opened it. My heart sank, though words of love blurred my vision.

Shento,

It soothes me to know of your intentions. One is never beyond redemption. God smiles on those who wake up to see the light of virtue again. Love is never to be forgotten. Hate will be washed away. Balan is your cradle, where it all began. Its earthly spirit will nurse and nourish you from your bruises and broken-

ness, and lift you up, restore you anew. Don't look for me. No need to look for me. I am where peace lies and silence is.

Sumi

Only after a long silence did I look up into the distance . . . the blue, blue distance of the sky.

This land of mountains.

Land of yellow dust.

Land of beginning.

Land that knows no ending.

Author's Note

Brothers, my debut novel, is an homage to my late father, who endured much and suffered even more during the Cultural Revolution in China. He lost his youth, his hopes, and nearly his life during those dark years, but he never lost his dream—a dream not for himself but for his sons and daughters. He has since passed on, used up by the Revolution, broken by many a trial of life. All he left behind were words he'd spoken that resonated with my young mind. These words would eventually map the novel that I embarked upon nearly a decade ago.

My father often said, while smoking his water pipe, that no matter the intention and endeavor, one is given to the whimsy of fate. That we humans are the petty pawns of a mammoth cosmic game unseen to living earthly mortals. That the path of one's life, though seemingly random and curvy as a river, is a chosen one, predestined not by you, but by some unknowable divinity. Each day a mere step in a beguiling game of chess, rendered on a befuddling chessboard, at the mercy of a knowing deity, who guides us along and pushes us forward. Each event an unpredictable move, an unforetelling of what lies beyond, though stealthily connected to other events in ways that elude our eyes and escape our senses. He would add that the gist of life is living—living fiercely and with rigor, unbending to the exertion of fate, unyielding to the scourge of destiny.

This sadly fatalistic and doggedly defiant view embodied the pattern of my father's life and befitted the rhythm of his struggles.

He and his only brother were the sons of a wealthy landowner in the southern province of Fujian, China. They set out in their youth to build high schools on the island of Taiwan, across the Taiwan Straits. At their parents' request, they returned to the mainland to get married on the same fortunate day in a ceremony called Double Happiness. My uncle returned to Taiwan soon after the wedding, but my father was asked by my grandfather to stay a week longer, so he could help take care of some family farming business. It was during that fateful week in 1949 that the Communist Red Army arrived in our village, took away all of our land, and forbade us from returning to Taiwan. The Revolution ensued, thrusting my father from one political purge into another. He had no job and no land, and was forced to farm on a meager plot from the commune that hardly yielded enough to feed nine mouths. Oh, how changed his life was. My father had grown up quite pampered, with three nannies to care for him. Now he endured hardships and political torture—but he did so like a giant. Never did he complain of his ill fate, caring for his ailing parents and feeding five growing children while facing endless political persecutions year in and year out. He seemed resigned to the cosmic scheme put upon his head.

In the fall of 1985, I, my father's youngest child, arrived in Lincoln, Nebraska, to attend Union College on a scholarship. As soon as I arrived in the States, my uncle flew from Taiwan to see me—it was his first contact with family lost behind the closed curtain of Red China in more than four decades. He rushed to the gate at the Omaha International Airport and walked right up to me, hugging me tightly, his tears wetting my shoulder. When I asked my uncle how he could recognize me among hundreds of other Chinese passengers arriving at the gate, he said it was easy because I looked exactly like my father had forty years earlier, when my uncle said good-bye to him for the last time.

Some books are inspired by certain images; others by words. *Brothers* comes from the essence of my father's belief. It is not only an exploration of the vagaries of fate, but an ode to that sacred and rare human spirit that endured the unforeseeable and overcame the unforetold.

Brothers

a novel

DA CHEN

Reader's Group Guide

The questions below are intended to help guide your reading group's discussion of this epic, dynamic historical novel by bestselling memoirist Da Chen.

1. Tan's family and Shento's adoptive family differ greatly in economic situation and social status. How do the upbringings of the two boys affect who they become, what they believe, and what they eventually accomplish as men?

2. Does Shento's birth under tragic circumstances determine his fate, as his mama and baba speculate?

3. What do Tan's two grandfathers represent for him throughout his youth? Does the incident on his first birthday with the abacus, the toy tank, and the globe foreshadow any of his actions later in life? How?

4. What does Sumi represent for Shento and, later, Tan? Why does each man fall so passionately in love with her? And, in turn, what does each man represent for Sumi, and what does she get from his love?

5. What does New York City represent for Tan? Why do you think he so glorifies early capitalism in America? Why are J. P. Morgan, the Carnegies, the Rockefellers, and the Lehman brothers such important historical figures to him?

6. Which characters act as saviors, both literally and figuratively, throughout the book? Whom do they save? How? Why?

7. What is Shento's reaction when his hero, President Heng Tu, tells him on his deathbed that he was not the one who saved Shento's life all those years ago? Why do you think Heng Tu took Shento under his wing, knowing he was the son of his sworn enemy, Ding Long?

8. In what ways can Shento and Tan each be considered a revolutionary, both in a political sense and in a philosophical sense?

9. Tan and Shento are worshipped as heroes by different people and groups throughout their lives. Who are these people/groups, and what do Tan and Shento represent for them?

10. Discuss the theme of betrayal in the book. How is Shento betrayed at different points throughout his life, and by whom? How about Tan? Sumi? How does being betrayed drive each of them to pursue his or her goals?

11. Near the end of the book, both Shento and Tan get shot while trying to get Sumi back. How does each shooting happen? How does each man react, and why do you think he reacts the way he does?

12. Do Shento and Tan find peace and personal redemption at the book's conclusion? How? Do you think they begin to forgive those who have betrayed them?

13. Could this story have taken place at a time in history other than during the tumultuous period after China's Cultural Revolution? What

about these two contrasting protagonists—one representing communism, the other democracy—makes this particular time and place such an ideal backdrop for the tale?

14. With whom do you identify more strongly as a character, Shento or Tan? Why?

About the Author

Da Chen is the acclaimed bestselling author of *Colors of the Mountain,* which was a New England Booksellers Association Discovery selection, a Book Sense 76 selection, a Borders Original Voices selection, and a Barnes & Noble Discover Great New Writers selection. His young adult autobiography, *China's Son,* was a Borders Original Voices Award finalist, an American Library Association Best Books for Young Adults final nominee, a New York Public Library Book for the Teen Age, and a PBS Teacher-Source recommended book.

A graduate of Columbia University Law School, he lives in New York's Hudson Valley with his wife and two children.

For more information, please visit his Web site, www.dachen.org.

About the Type

Bembo is an old style serif font based on typeface cut by Francesco Griffo for Aldus Manutius' printing of *De Aetna* in 1495. Today's version of Bembo was designed by Stanley Morison for the Monotype Corporation in 1929. Bembo is noted for its classic, well-proportioned letterforms and is widely used because of its readabilty.